QUINN

ALSO BY IRIS JOHANSEN

QUINN

IRIS JOHANSEN

ST. MARTIN'S GRIFFIN
NEW YORK

QUINN. Copyright © 2011 by Johansen Publishing LLLP. All rights reserved. Printed in the United States of America. For information, address St. Martin's Press, 175 Fifth Avenue, New York, N.Y. 10010.

www.stmartins.com

The Library of Congress has cataloged the hardcover edition as follows:

Johansen, Iris.
Quinn / Iris Johansen.—1st ed.
p. cm.
ISBN 978-0-312-65121-3
1. Police—Fiction. 2. Duncan, Eve (Fictitious character)
—Fiction. 3. Women intelligence officers—Fiction.
4. Missing persons—Fiction. I. Title.
PS3560.O275Q56 2011
813'.54—dc22

2011005978

ISBN 978-1-250-01157-2 (trade paperback)

First St. Martin's Griffin Edition: November 2011

10 9 8 7 6 5 4 3 2 1

QUINN

CHAPTER
1

STOP ME. FIND ME. KILL ME.

Agony tore through him as John Gallo pushed through the brush, the branches scratching his face as he ran.

How long had he been on the run?

Hours? Days?

And why couldn't he stop?

Why couldn't he let the sheriff's men find him, shoot him? He knew these woods so well that it was easy to avoid capture. Whenever they had come near, instinct and self-preservation had kicked into high gear, and he had fled.

And those instincts were so good, he thought bitterly. They had been honed by all the battles, all the killings, all the ugliness of his life. Save yourself so that you can kill again.

But at least he had not stayed to kill his hunters. That was part of the reason why he had not exposed himself. He couldn't trust himself not to kill them. He was too well trained, too expert in the ways of destruction.

And then there was the madness.

There was no telling where that sickness would take him.

He was climbing, he realized. He was climbing the high hill where he'd done his last kill.

Paul Black. He'd broken his neck.

And Joe Quinn. If he was dead, that, too, could be laid at his door.

He broke free of the shrubs and trees and was standing on the edge of the cliff over the lake.

What was he doing there?

One step, and he would plunge over the precipice.

Why not?

Maybe that damnable instinct would not kick in when he hit the lake below.

"It will, you know."

He stiffened, afraid to turn around to see who had spoken.

Madness. It was back, taunting him, torturing him.

"Look at me."

He slowly looked over his shoulder.

A little seven-year-old girl, with curly red-brown hair wearing a Bugs Bunny T-shirt.

The same T-shirt she had worn the day she had died.

The day he might have killed her.

The agony was overwhelming, searing through him, blocking everything but the sight of her and his own guilt.

His daughter, Bonnie . . .

Milwaukee Airport

Milwaukee, Wisconsin

"YOU'RE JANE MACGUIRE?"

Jane turned away from the baggage claim carousel to see the woman who had spoken walking toward her. It had to be Catherine Ling, she thought. Her adoptive mother, Eve, had described the CIA agent in detail, but the reality was even more stunning. Catherine Ling was part Asian, part Caucasian, and more exotic and magnetic than any woman Jane had seen except on the movie screen. She appeared be in her late twenties, tall, graceful, with high cheekbones, huge dark eyes slightly tilted at the corners, olive-gold skin, long dark hair pulled back in a chignon. But it was the aura of power and vitality that surrounded her that was the most impressive. As an artist, Jane's first impulse was to ask her to pose for her. The second was to squeeze every bit of information she could from her. "I'm Jane. You're Catherine Ling? How is Joe?"

"Is that your bag?" Catherine lifted Jane's suitcase off the carousel with easy strength. "Joe was no better when I left the hospital. But as far as I know, he's no worse. Eve doesn't want to leave him, so she asked me to pick you up. I've made reservations for you at a Hyatt near the hospital. We'll check you in, then I'll take you to the hospital."

Jane shook her head. "To hell with that. I'm going to the hospital to be with Eve. I should have been with her ever since Joe was admitted. It's been almost two days. Why the hell didn't she call me before this?"

"You were in London, and there wasn't much you could do. Joe was in surgery for a long time. Eve said she didn't want to talk to you until she could give you good news." She headed toward the exit. "That didn't happen, so she called you anyway. She thought you should be here."

Jane nodded jerkily. "That's what she said. She was so upset that she didn't realize how that sounded. I felt like I was flying to a deathbed." She took her suitcase from Catherine. "She didn't even tell me what happened with Joe, only about his wound. A knife thrust to the back that did serious organ damage." Her lips tightened. "A knife. Whose knife? I don't want to stress Eve out by asking questions. That means you're on the hot seat, Catherine. I want to know everything before I walk into that hospital."

Catherine nodded. "I thought that would be my job." She stopped before a silver Toyota. "Get in. I'll fill you in while I drive you to the hospital." She slipped into the driver's seat. "But I'm going to go through a drive-through McDonald's and get you a cup of coffee."

"You think I'll need the caffeine to get through this?"

Catherine gave her an appraising glance as she started the car. "I think you're probably a cool customer. But you love Eve and Joe. They raised you from the time you were ten. You have a right to be upset and need a little bolstering." She pulled out of the airport parking lot. "And if you don't, I do. You're going to be pissed at me."

"Am I?" Jane stiffened. "Why?"

"I'm partly the reason Joe was hurt."

"Then yes, I'll be pissed at you. I'll want to break your neck. Is Eve angry with you?"

"No, she says no one could have stopped Joe."

Jane slowly nodded. "She's right. No one could ever stop Joe from doing what he wanted to do. I knew that the first time I saw him. But it relieved me. I knew if Joe ever became my friend, it wouldn't be because Eve wanted him to do it. It would be because he wanted it himself. That was important to me. I was a ten-year-old Eve had picked up from the streets because we'd known the moment we'd come together that it was right we stay together. But Joe was a big part of her life even then. I didn't want to have to walk away."

"And you didn't have to do it," Catherine said. "You became a family." She smiled faintly. "A very strange family. Eve Duncan, a famous forensic sculptor, Joe Quinn, a police detective, and you, a kid from the streets."

"We learned to mesh," Jane said. "Eve was no problem. Joe was slower. But we both loved Eve, so we worked at it." She smiled. "And then as we got to know each other, it wasn't work any longer. Funny how love makes everything easier."

"Yeah, funny." Catherine pulled into the McDonald's drive-through. "Do you want anything besides coffee?"

"No."

"Black?"

"Yes."

She studied Catherine as she gave the coffee order. How much love had Catherine had in her life, she wondered. Eve had told her she'd been a street kid like Jane but had grown up in Hong Kong. She'd married a much older man, then been widowed. She had come into Eve's life when she'd asked Eve to help her find her son, who had been kidnapped by a Russian criminal wanting revenge on Catherine. Eve had helped her rescue him, and they had become close friends. There was no doubt in Eve's mind that Catherine adored her son, Luke. But Jane had gotten the impression that, other than Luke, Catherine's life had been her job as a CIA agent.

"You're looking at me as if you're trying to take me apart." Catherine's look was quizzical as she handed Jane her coffee. "Is it your artist's eye, or are you taking aim?"

"Maybe a little of both." Jane met her gaze. "I admit the first thing I thought when I saw you was that I'd like to paint you. But you'll definitely be on my list for extermination if you had anything to do with Joe lying in that hospital. Tell me what happened to him." She looked away, and added, "Let me start you on the path. It was about Bonnie, wasn't it?"

Catherine nodded. "It's not surprising that was your first guess. I imagine you've lived with Eve's obsession for finding Bonnie since you came to her."

"Guess?" Jane took a drink of her coffee. "Finding her daughter's murderer and her daughter's body has guided her life. It's guided all our lives. She's tried for many, many years to bring her Bonnie home." She looked out the window at the passing scene. "And Joe's been with her, trying desperately to understand, to help, to find Bonnie, so that Eve could be at peace. I can't tell you how many times she's come to what she thought was that final resolution and been disappointed. But she never gives up."

Catherine added quietly, "And Joe was getting tired, weary of worrying about her, wanting her to come to terms."

Jane looked back at her. "Yes, how do you know? Joe wouldn't complain."

"Joe and I are a lot alike," Catherine said. "And I had to examine all facets of Eve's problem before I made a move to ask her to help me find my son, Luke. I didn't want to make a mistake."

"Mistake?"

"I promised her I'd pay her back for helping return my son to me," Catherine said. "She wouldn't accept anything, but I couldn't let it go. I knew the only gift she would think worthwhile would be for me to find her daughter's killer." Her lips twisted. "So that was what I had to give her. Whether or not it might destroy the life she had with Joe."

"You found him?" Jane's eyes widened. "You actually found Bonnie's killer?"

"I found two possibilities. Paul Black, who was already on Eve's search list."

"She told me about him."

"But I was betting on a new stallion in the race. One that would be much more troublesome. Naturally, I had to pull him front and center."

"Who?"

Catherine's eyes were fixed on the towers of St. Joseph's Hospital, which had come into view. "John Gallo. He was Bonnie's father."

Jane stiffened. "What? But Eve told me he was dead."

Catherine shook her head. "A cover-up by the military. Eve will explain everything later. I'm just giving you the bare bones. But there was evidence Gallo was in Atlanta the month Bonnie was kidnapped. So I gave Eve all my information and threw in my opinion."

"And she went after John Gallo," Jane whispered.

"And Paul Black," Catherine said. "But she felt terribly guilty about risking Joe again. So she tried to leave him out of it."

"She should have known that wouldn't work," Jane said. She knew how guilty Eve felt about involving Joe, but she could no more stop hunting for Bonnie's killer than Joe could abandon Eve and stop protecting her. Both were facts of life. "Gallo hurt Joe?"

Catherine shook her head. "Paul Black. And Gallo killed Black."

"Good."

"Not so good. Before he died, Black told Eve that Gallo had killed Bonnie."

"And she actually believed the bastard?"

"She told me that she would swear Black was telling the truth. And Gallo took off and disappeared. Neither the police nor I have been able to find him."

"But what would make him kill his own little girl?"

"He was suffering from bouts of schizophrenia and violent delusions caused by years of mistreatment in a prison in North Korea."

"My God." Jane shook her head. "That must have been a terrible nightmare for Eve. How can you imagine a man who gave you a child could kill it?"

Catherine's lips tightened. "Well, I handed Gallo to her and made her imagine it." She pulled into a parking spot in the lot of St. Joseph's Hospital. "And then I helped Joe try to find him whether Eve wanted him along or not." She turned off the ignition. "Are you still blaming Joe and not me?"

Jane gazed at her a moment. "You're blaming yourself enough. You don't need any help." She got out of the car. "Where can I find her?"

"ICU. The visiting hours are very short, but Eve can watch him through the glass. If she's not in the waiting room, she'll probably be in the hall at ICU."

"Are you coming with me?"

Catherine shook her head. "Eve needs family. I'll check you in at the Hyatt and take your suitcase up to your room. Give me a call when you're ready to leave the hospital."

"Thanks." Jane turned to walk away.

"How did you feel about Bonnie?" Catherine asked suddenly. "I know it's none of my business, but I'm curious. You said that the search for her killer ruled your lives. That must have been difficult for an adopted kid to accept."

Jane shook her head. "I knew what was important to Eve when I came to her. I wasn't her child, I was her friend. That was enough for me. How could I ask for more?"

"Some kids would have been more demanding."

Jane lifted her brows. "You?"

Catherine shook her head. "But then I probably wouldn't have accepted any relationship when I was your age. I was an independent young demon. I suppose I still am."

"Eve is always the exception," Jane said. "You obviously have a close relationship with her now."

Catherine smiled as she started to back out of the parking place. "You're right. You and I are more alike than I would have believed. Eve is the sun we all revolve around."

Jane watched her drive out of the parking lot before she started to walk across the parking lot toward the front entrance. She could feel the tension increase with every step. She was going to Joe, who might well be dying. She was going to Eve, who could lose the man who made her life worth living.

How did she feel about the search for Bonnie? Jane had said all the right things, and they had all been true. What she hadn't told Catherine was the agony she felt when Eve and Joe were put in danger by that search. She could accept it. But she couldn't stop wishing that the search would end.

And she couldn't stop wishing that Eve would release Bonnie.

Or, dear God, that Bonnie would release Eve.

EVE WALKED SLOWLY DOWN the corridor toward the ICU.

Soon she would be able to see Joe again. He'd be pale and drawn, his features appearing as cleanly carved and beautiful as the visage on a tomb. It would scare her to death as it always did.

But it scared her more not to see him and to imagine him slipping away with her not by his side.

That was where she should always be. Next to Joe.

If God would let him stay with her. And if Joe still wanted her if he did come back. The memory of that last day at the lake house was suddenly before her. His eyes looking down at her as she sat in the swing.

"I can't be easy. It's not my nature. But it's my nature to love you."

And it was her nature to love Joe.

Please be better, Joe. Be awake. At least, have more color.

"Good afternoon, Ms. Duncan." The ICU nurse was coming out of the unit. "May I get you anything?"

"Yes, permission to go sit with him."

She shook her head. "Not yet." She hesitated. "But the doctor said that maybe we should let you go to him soon."

She stiffened, her heart leaping. "He's better."

The nurse shook her head. "I shouldn't have said anything," she said quickly. "Dr. Jarlin will talk to you."

Fear surged through her. "You talk to me, dammit. He's worse?"

The nurse was looking at Eve with that same sympathy and kindness that had struck terror in her heart since she'd brought Joe to the hospital. "Dr. Jarlin will talk to you. I'll call him and tell him that you're concerned." She hurried back toward the nurses' station.

Concerned? She was sick with fear.

Joe was dying, and they weren't going to be able to save him. That was why they were going to let Eve go to him. To say good-bye.

She couldn't say good-bye. He had to stay with her.

She leaned her head on the plate-glass window and closed her eyes. She felt the tears running down her cheeks as the agony flowed through her.

Look at him. Surely she'd be able to know, to sense some change. Maybe they were wrong. Doctors didn't know everything.

She took a deep breath and opened her eyes. She stiffened in shock.

Bonnie.

Through the years she had often had visions and dreams of her daughter. Then she had come to believe they weren't visions at all. It didn't matter. Real or not, having Bonnie come to her had made life worth living and let her come alive in so many ways.

But now something was different.

Bonnie, in her Bugs Bunny T-shirt, her red-brown hair shining in the lights of the ICU, as she stood by Joe's bed, looking down at him.

Her expression . . . Love. Perfect love.

Why was she here?

The fear became terror.

To take him away, to ease the transition from this life to the next?

"No, Bonnie!"

Her daughter looked across the room at Eve standing behind the glass.

She smiled luminously. But then turned back again to gaze down at Joe with that same expression of love.

What did that smile mean? Could she help him to live?

Or could she only help him to die?

Eve's palms pressed against the cold glass as tension and sorrow tore through her.

"Joe!"

SWIRLING darkness.

Someone calling.

"Joe!"

Calling him . . .

But he didn't want to leave the darkness. There was comfort here and yet also a strange excitement and anticipation.

Was this death?

He had never been afraid of it. He wasn't now.

But that voice calling . . .

Eve.

She was hurting, needing him. He should go back.

And there was someone else . . .

Bonnie.

She was there in the darkness. Always before she had been the stranger, the one apart; but now she was close, as familiar to him as Eve, and much of the comfort was coming from her. Did she want him to stay in the darkness?

But he could feel Eve's terror and sadness.

He had to stop them both and try to make Eve happy.

As she made him happy . . .

He had known from the first moment he had seen her all those years ago that he could not be happy if he was not with her.

Strange . . . He had not believed that love could come out of nowhere and stay forever. He had been such a cynical son of a bitch. Smart, young FBI agent, sure of himself and everything around him, ready to take on the world.

He'd been certain the Bonnie Duncan kidnapping wasn't going to be a problem. The local Atlanta police were sure that she was the victim of a serial killer, and the little girl would never show up alive. Sad story, but Joe had worked on other serial killings and had experience in profiling as well. He was well qualified to take on the case. He'd go down to Atlanta and dive in and show the locals how the FBI could handle a case like Bonnie's.

But he wouldn't get involved with the family of the victim no matter how sympathetic he was toward them. That was always a mistake. It was better to stand apart so that he could work without emotion. That would be far more efficient.

Yes, after all, it was just one more case. A few months in Atlanta, and he'd be coming back to start another job. There was nothing about this Duncan case in Atlanta to interfere with his career, certainly nothing to interfere with his life . . .

CHAPTER
2

"I HEAR PACKER GAVE you the Duncan case." Jenny Rudler smiled as she stopped by Joe's desk. "I was hoping to get it. There's been a lot of media attention since the kid was taken. I could use a high-profile case. It would help me break through the glass ceiling. But, no, the fair-haired boy was the chosen one."

"Does the FBI have a glass ceiling?"

"You're damn right it does." She perched on the corner of his desk. "Why not tell Packer you need a partner?"

And Jenny would be stepping all over him trying to break that ceiling. He didn't need that. "Maybe next time."

Her smile faded. "Bastard. Damn, you're cocky. You have it all, don't you? Rich kid, Harvard grad, hero in the SEALs. Then you decide you want to be an FBI agent. So everyone is supposed to bow down and give you anything you want."

He held on to his temper. "That's right. But I'll make an exception in your case. I'll settle for you just staying out of my way. I worked for everything I've gotten here at the Bureau. Back off, Jenny."

She hesitated, and suddenly the belligerence was gone. "I'm sorry. You're right." Her smile was dazzling. "I was really upset. It seems as if I'm not getting anywhere, and I'm frustrated as hell. Forgive me?"

He shrugged.

"No, I mean it. Let me make it up to you. When do you leave for Atlanta?"

"Tomorrow."

"Then come over tonight, and we'll have a few drinks."

Which meant that they'd end up in bed as they had a few times before. For a moment, he was tempted. She wasn't bad in bed, and he required sex often and varied.

"You were real good," Jenny murmured. "Maybe the best. We had a good time, didn't we?"

But he didn't need the strings that Jenny would attach to any relationship, even the most casual. He didn't mind paying for sex, but not in the workplace. That could be a big-time headache.

"I'm busy. Sorry."

Her smile disappeared. "I'm not. Who needs you?" She turned on her heel. "There are a lot of people here who resent you and are just waiting to stab you in the back. You'd be smart to keep the friends you have. Have a good time in Atlanta."

Translated that meant go to hell, Joe thought, as he watched her walk away. She had a nice ass. Should he change his mind and go after her? He was always more attracted when there was a challenge involved. That was why he had come to work at the FBI. Life had been too flat after his service in the SEALs.

No, curb that recklessness for once. He'd find enough of a challenge in Atlanta. Probably not physical, but definitely mental.

He turned back to the folder on his desk and flipped it open.

Bonnie Duncan.

230 Morningside Drive
Atlanta, Georgia

IT WAS A NICE LITTLE HOUSE in a nice little neighborhood, Joe thought as he got out of the rental car. Inexpensive, but clean and freshly painted. It had a wide front porch, and red-orange geraniums were overflowing from a hanging straw basket.

A car was in the driveway, a gray Ford at least seven or eight years old. It appeared as clean and well taken care of as the house. Every detail of the house and automobile spoke of meager funds but a determination by the occupants to make the best of what they had.

But in Joe's experience, the obvious didn't always end up to be the truth.

He rang the doorbell.

No answer.

He waited and rang it again.

No answer.

There were reasons why Eve Duncan would not answer the bell, but he still felt a little annoyed. How the hell could he help her if she shut herself away from him like this? Overcome it. Do your job, he told himself. He had to do the interview before he could dismiss Eve Duncan from his mind and get down to the business of finding her daughter's killer.

He went around the house to the steps leading to the kitchen screen door. Through the screen, he could see a woman at the stove with her back to him. He wanted to pound impatiently but instead knocked discreetly.

"Ms. Duncan. FBI. I rang the front doorbell, but no one answered. May I come in?"

She looked at him and turned back to the stove. "Yes, I suppose you may."

He opened the door and entered the kitchen. "I can understand why you wouldn't want to answer the door. I hear the media has been harassing you. I'm Special Agent Joe Quinn. FBI. I wonder if I could have a few words with you."

She glanced over her shoulder at him. "Questions? I've answered millions of questions. It's all in the ATLPD records. Go ask them."

He stiffened as he gazed at her. She wasn't what he had expected. Eve Duncan was tall and slim, with shoulder-length red-brown hair and hazel eyes. The high cheekbones of her face made it more fascinating than pretty. His report said she was only twenty-three, but she could have been any age. She was . . . extraordinary.

Usually when meeting a woman, his first impression was of beauty or ugliness, not intelligence and personality. That came later, along with an evaluation of whether he wanted to go to bed with her. But gazing at Eve Duncan, he couldn't think of single aspects but the woman as a whole being. He was only aware of the tension, the painful restraint, the burning vitality of her. Why couldn't he look away from her?

Get a grip. What had she said? ATLPD. "I have to make my own report."

"Red tape. Procedures." She scooped up the omelet and put it on a plate. "Why didn't they send someone right after it happened?"

It had only been two weeks, but it had probably seemed a lifetime to her. "We had to wait for a request from the local police."

"You should have been here. Everyone should have come right away." Her hand was shaking as she picked up the plate and put it on a tray. "I suppose I'll have to talk to you. But I have to take this omelet to my mother. She hasn't gotten out of bed since Bonnie disappeared. I can't get her to eat."

"I'll take it," he said impulsively as he reached out and took the tray. "Which room?"

"First door at the top of the stairs."

What was he doing? Joe wondered as he started up the stairs. So much for his philosophy of noninvolvement. He had practically jerked that tray out of her hands. Why?

To help her, ease her, make all that pain go away.

Crazy. He had seen Eve Duncan for only a few minutes. Sympathy, yes. That was natural and right. Not this urgent need to banish the torture she was experiencing in any way possible.

Okay, deliver the omelet to her mother and go back down

and interrogate Eve Duncan. No doubt that temporary aberration concerning the woman would have vanished by that time.

He stopped short as he saw a framed sketch on the wall. It had to be a sketch of Bonnie Duncan, but it was extraordinary. The photograph he had in his file was good, but the little girl in this sketch was drawn with such love and skill that it made her come alive.

Who had drawn it? Eve Duncan?

Stop wondering about her and stick to his job.

He knocked, then opened the door. "Mrs. Duncan? I'm Agent Joe Quinn. Your daughter sent you breakfast. May I come in?"

"I suppose . . ." Sandra Duncan was lying propped up in bed, and her Southern accent was much heavier than her daughter's. "But I'm not hungry, you know. I haven't been hungry since Bonnie . . ." Her eyes filled with tears. "I miss her. Why can't you find her?"

Eve Duncan's mother was in her late thirties and prettier than her daughter, but she had none of her strength or that riveting vitality.

"That's why I'm here." He carried the tray over to her and put it on her lap. "That's my job. But you have a job, too. You have to keep up your strength and help your daughter."

"Eve's so strong," she whispered. "I've never been strong. Except for Bonnie. I took care of her when Eve worked, and I did a fine job. Eve told me that all the time. But then somebody took her away."

"But your daughter is still here. She needs you."

She frowned. "Does she?"

"Yes. I want you to eat that omelet and take a shower, then go downstairs and help her. Will you do that?"

"I'd rather go to sleep."

"It doesn't matter. She needs you." He handed her the fork. "We all have our jobs." He turned and headed for the door. "It's time that you did yours, Mrs. Duncan."

"Sandra. Everyone calls me Sandra."

He smiled at her over his shoulder. "Pretty name for a pretty lady. My name is Joe. I hope to see you downstairs next time I visit here."

Sandra smiled tentatively. "You're strong. I like a strong man. But are you strong enough to help Eve to find our Bonnie?"

"If you'll all help me." He closed the door and paused a moment before he went downstairs. Involvement. He should have let Eve Duncan handle her own personal problems. His only duty was to find her daughter's killer. Yet he hadn't been able to resist pushing Sandra Duncan to help her. According to his report, Eve Duncan's mother was a former drug addict who had been rehabilitated at the time of her grandchild's birth. It wouldn't take much for Sandra Duncan to slip back into addiction at a traumatic period like this, and that burden would be all Eve Duncan would need on her shoulders.

Protecting Eve Duncan again. What the hell? The woman hadn't even said a kind word to him.

It didn't matter.

And that was more disturbing than anything about this encounter.

Go down and face her, talk to her, and that weird fascination would probably disappear.

He paused in the kitchen doorway. She was standing at the sink, washing the pan. He inhaled sharply. Impact. Strong. Stronger than before.

Ignore it. It will go away.

"She started to eat," he said as he came back into the room. "Maybe it was the shock of seeing a stranger."

"Maybe."

"And how are you eating, Ms. Duncan?"

"I eat enough. I know I can't afford to lose strength." She started drying the pan. "What do you want to know, Agent Quinn?"

Yes, she was strong. He could see it, feel it. Like a fragile tree that would bend but never break. It hurt him, somehow. He quickly looked down at his notes. "Your daughter, Bonnie, disappeared at the park over two weeks ago. She went to the refreshment stand to get an ice cream and didn't return. She was wearing a Bugs Bunny T-shirt, jeans, and tennis shoes."

"Yes."

"And you didn't see anyone suspicious loitering anywhere nearby?"

"No one. It was crowded. I wasn't expecting anyone to be—" She drew a deep breath. "No one suspicious. I told the police that I wondered if maybe someone had seen what a sweet kid my Bonnie was and taken her away." She stared at his face. "And they only looked at me the way you're doing and made soothing noises. It could have happened that way."

"Yes, it could." He paused. "But the odds are against it. I'm not going to lie to you."

"I knew that. I'm not a fool. I grew up on the streets, and I know all about the scum who are out there." She looked won-deringly up at him. "But I have to hope. She's my baby. I have to bring her home. How can I live if I don't hope?"

He felt as if he were breaking apart inside. He could feel her pain, and it was becoming his pain. "Then hope." His voice was hoarse. "And I'll hope with you. We'll explore every way we can to find her safe and alive. There's nothing I won't do. Just stick with me and give me a little help."

She hesitated, gazing up at him.

Believe me, he urged her silently. Put your hand in mine, trust me, let me guide you. Something strange is happening here, but it's not anything bad. I won't let it hurt you.

She moistened her lips. "Of course I'll help." She stood star-ing at him for a moment. She could feel it, sense what he couldn't say, he realized. In her pain, she couldn't define the nature of what she was sensing, but perhaps it would become clear to her later.

As, God help him, it was becoming clear to him.

She glanced away from him as she put the pan in the cup-board. "I'm afraid, you know," she said unevenly. "I'm afraid all the time. My mother gave up and just went to bed, but I can't do that. I have to keep fighting. As long as I'm fighting, I have a chance to find Bonnie."

Tentative trust. It was the first step. Come closer. Let me hold you safe from the storm.

But he could only nod, and say, "Then we'll fight together. I'll stay with you until we get through this." He paused. "If you'll let me."

Together. The concept was strange on his lips. He had always been a loner, totally self-ruled, shunning the dependence implied in the word. But he offered it to her.

And Eve didn't even realize how much it meant.

Or maybe she did. There was something in her expression . . .

She slowly nodded. "I think that would be very kind." Her words were oddly formal. "Thank you, Agent Quinn."

AFTER HE'D LEFT THE HOUSE, Joe sat in the driver's seat of his car, staring at the sunny front porch of Eve Duncan's home. There was nothing sunny about anything inside that house, he thought. There was pain and trouble and a woman who was battling just to stay alive after her reason for living had been taken from her. The short time he'd spent with Eve had been full of disturbing images and emotions. Emotions he hadn't expected and had wanted to reject. His responses had been completely foreign to who he thought himself to be.

What the hell had happened to him?

He had felt like Sir Galahad wanting to fight dragons and lay them at her feet. She had moved him, possessed him, and made him see himself in a different light.

It was insane. She was only a woman and one who would bring him only trouble. Dammit, he couldn't even think of sex in connection with her. She was wounded and might remain that way for a long time. Sir Galahad? There was nothing pure about Joe. He was earthy and sexual, and he had always leaned toward being more like wicked Mordred, or maybe Lancelot, who enjoyed toying with a married Guinevere.

Okay, it was temporary insanity. If he couldn't have her,

then what he was feeling would surely pass. That was his nature where women were concerned.

But sex hadn't been the force that drove him toward Eve Duncan. It might have been a light shimmering in the background, but he hadn't been aware of wanting her sexually. And that was a first for him. Maybe it had been there, and he hadn't wanted to admit it.

No, it was something else, powerful, protective, completely without precedent in his experience.

And he wouldn't put a name to it.

If he didn't recognize it, then it might go away. Much better for him. Much better for her. Because he wasn't a man who could let go. Even now he was thinking, planning, how he would keep his promise to her. Yeah, try to walk away from her. Find her kid's killer. Help her to come to terms with reality when she learned her little girl was never coming back.

But don't put a name to this strange feeling that was beginning to disturb him.

Time to stop thinking about Eve Duncan on this level and begin working constructively on her daughter's case.

He drove to the nearest drugstore and placed a call to his contact with the ATLPD, Detective Ralph Slindak. He was glad they'd given him Slindak. He was a good man, and he and Joe had a history. They'd been in the SEALs together though Slindak had left the service two years earlier than Joe. "Joe Quinn. I'm in Atlanta."

"I heard they were sending a hotshot down to shape us up," Slindak said. "The other detectives in the squad were a little pissed. But I told them they had nothing to worry about.

Nothing hot about Joe Quinn I told them. He's cold as ice unless he gets annoyed. They didn't like that either."

"I can always count on your support," he said dryly. "I've just interviewed Eve Duncan. You've been handling the case?"

"Or it's been handling us," Slindak said sourly. "The media thinks that we're blowing it. That's why the captain asked for help. We need to share the blame."

"Great attitude," Joe said. "Suppose we forget the media and just try to find the kid's killer?" He paused. "If there is a killer. You're sure that she won't be found alive?"

"I wish I didn't think that Bonnie Duncan was a victim. Sweet kid. Did you see her photo?"

"Yes." It was in the file, and he could see why the photo was one of the reasons the media were being so tenacious. The child's smile seemed to light up the world, and it had completely touched and captivated the public. "I know that cases like this almost always end with a corpse. But do you have anything concrete?"

"No. Except that there have been several similar disappearances over the last few years in this area. We found one child's body six months ago, a little boy. Butchered."

"Oh, shit."

"Yeah. That's what we thought. And the killings have gotten enough media attention so that Eve Duncan must know about them. She has to be trying to close her eyes and block them out."

"Wouldn't you?"

"No question. I have a four-year-old boy myself, and I nearly threw up when we found that murdered kid."

"You have a boy? Are you married?"

"No, you know me and commitment. But it may end up

that way. She's a nice woman, and we all get lonely." He added, "Except you, Joe. You never needed anyone, did you?"

Not until now. Not until I walked into that house and saw her.

He didn't answer the question. "No clues? No info? He didn't leave any evidence?"

"Oh, we have evidence. He was pretty careless with the disposal of the body, or we wouldn't have found it. But we can't connect it to anyone to make it work for us. We think he's a local since he's been working exclusively in the Atlanta area. We've checked nearby cities, and they have no similar cases during the time span of the Atlanta kidnappings."

"But a big city is better hunting grounds for predators. If he lived in a small town, he wouldn't necessarily do his killing there. Not if he was smart."

"You think he commuted to do his kills?"

"I'm just not ruling it out. I'm not ruling anything out. What about a killer close to the family? Bonnie's father?"

"She was illegitimate, and Eve Duncan never put his name on the birth certificate. She said the father was a John Gallo, who was killed while he was in the Army. It all checked out. Her mother was a possibility since she was into drugs for years, but she was with Bonnie's mother when the little girl was taken."

Think like a professional. Stop trying to protect her. "That doesn't mean anything. Maybe they were in it together and protecting each other. Neither one of them has to be a monster. It could have happened in a moment of anger, when the child was struck, and it ended in death. Then they had to scurry to make up a story to keep themselves from being charged."

Slindak was silent. "You think that's likely?"

Hell, no, everything within him was rejecting the scenario he had put forward. "I'm just saying nothing should be ruled out."

"I think you'd have ruled it out if you'd seen Eve Duncan after the kid was taken. I was one of the detectives who came to the park where the kid disappeared that day. Eve Duncan was terrified. And angry. And ready to take on the world to get her daughter back."

"Then maybe we'll be able to erase her name from the suspect list after we investigate a little further. You've made inquiries of neighbors and teachers?"

"The kid was bright and friendly and loved the whole damn world. Everyone said that Eve Duncan was totally dedicated to Bonnie. She was respected, even admired, by everyone we questioned. She worked two jobs, was finishing college with a 4.0 average, and still managed to be a great mother." He paused. "I like her, Joe. Though she's given our department nothing but grief since her daughter was kidnapped. Who could blame her? I'd do the same. Don't give her a hard time."

"I'm not trying to hurt her. I generally don't like to become involved with the families of victims." That was the truth. "And I can see why you'd admire her and want to protect her." And God knows that was the truth. "If everything checks out, we'll assume that we have a serial killer. I'll check into a hotel, then come down to the precinct and go over the case files on the missing children."

"I'll be here," Slindak said. "We're all working extra hours on this case." He hung up.

Joe stood there for an instant longer after he'd replaced the receiver, thinking about what Slindak had said. Everything that Slindak had recounted about Eve had been exactly what his own senses had told him. She was a victim who refused to be a victim. How could you help but want to come to her rescue? Slindak had obviously had that same response to her.

No, it hadn't been the same for him. No one but Joe could have had this crazy, wild reaction when he'd seen Eve Duncan. It was too bizarre. He remembered what Slindak had said about him.

Cold as ice?

Never in this world. Not where Eve Duncan was concerned.

Two Weeks Later

"YOU SAID YOU'D HELP me," Eve said, when Joe picked up the phone. "All those fine words, and you're not doing a damn thing. Why haven't I heard from you?"

Because he'd been trying to forget that first interview, divorce himself from his reaction to Eve herself, and concentrate on the case. He wasn't about to tell her that concentration had been centered on going through all the files of known child molesters in the Southeast. "I haven't had anything to report to you."

"Well, I have something to report to you. Come and see me."

He stared at the phone after she'd hung up. He could send Slindak.

But he knew he wasn't going to do it.

He pushed back from the desk and stood up. He was feeling alive, eagerness mixed with a low, simmering excitement. This was what he had been waiting for no matter what he had been telling himself.

It was starting . . .

EVE THREW OPEN THE DOOR before he could ring the bell. "You took your time. Come in." She turned her back and strode toward the kitchen. "I have something to show you."

She was the same and yet not the same, he thought as he followed her. She was dressed in khaki slacks and a loose white shirt. The fragile restraint that was so difficult to watch was still there, but she was more forceful. The vitality that had so drawn him was burning high. She was not even quite as pale.

"What are you looking at?" She had turned at the kitchen table.

"You," he said quietly. "You look better. You're still too thin, but you appear to have been eating. That's good."

"I told you that I wouldn't neglect myself. And I'm always thin." She raised her brows. "You probably don't like skinny women. Most men don't. They like boobs and ass."

He was surprised at her bluntness. "I find that thin women usually have a grace and elegance that's appealing."

"Very tactful. Very polite. But I understand that your tastes are definitely on the voluptuous side. So don't be tactful. All I want is the truth from you."

"About boobs and ass?" His brows rose. "And just how do you understand anything that intimate about me?"

"I called your office at Quantico. I told them I wanted to know everything there was to know about you. They tried to put me off and sidetrack me, but I kept at them. I called five times and got different agents. I finally found one who gave me what I wanted."

"And why did you do that?"

"Because you made me believe you." She stared him in the eye. "And I had to be sure there was something to believe in."

"I see. And what did they tell you?"

"More than I thought they would. The person I talked to didn't give me much of an argument. He seemed to be taking a kind of malicious enjoyment from telling me about you. I don't think he was your friend."

"That doesn't surprise me. Who was it?"

"An Agent Rick Donald." She saw his expression. "He doesn't like you?"

"We've been in competition a few times." And Donald had not come out on top. "No one can please everyone. What did he tell you?"

"Part of it was okay. That you've only been with the Bureau for a few years and have already solved three difficult cases. That you were a SEAL and decorated twice. Harvard graduate. Rich boy. Parents dead. You inherited a potload of money and don't need to work." She paused. "I didn't like that. I have no use for a dabbler. But they said when you were on a case that you were totally dedicated. So I guess that's all right."

"I'm glad I don't have to divest myself of all worldly goods," he said mockingly.

"This isn't funny," she said. "I have to have someone who

will take Bonnie seriously. You talk the talk, but I have to know."

"And you evidently had to know about my private life as well. I'm not surprised he told you everything you wanted to know about me. He was probably as amused as hell. I'm just surprised you thought it important."

"It's important. You're good-looking, you're tough, you have a sort of virile magnetism that would be appealing to women. If you liked them too much, then they'd distract you." Her lips tightened. "I grew up in the projects, and I know all about vices. Sex can be as addictive and distracting as any drug. I don't want you screwing around when I need you. When Bonnie needs you."

He looked at her in disbelief. "My God, I feel as if I'm applying for a Secret Service job."

"And you're probably pissed. I can't help that. I have to do whatever needs doing. If you don't like it, go back to Quantico and have them send me someone else."

"I don't like it," he said coolly. "But I'm not pissed. I'm considering the source. But stay out of my private business, or I'll start delving into yours."

She looked surprised. "Really?" Then she shrugged. "But my private business couldn't be more boring. Delve away."

"I'll do that. So I assume I've passed muster if you called me here to chew me out."

"That's not why I wanted you here. I just had to be honest with you." She moistened her lips. "And I had to be sure you'll be honest with me. The police won't tell me the truth. They just make soothing noises and look away. And you said you'd help, but then you disappeared and pretended I wasn't there."

"Oh, I knew you were there." Every minute. Though he'd tried his best to block her out. Now he realized there would be no blocking her out, and they would just have to learn to deal with each other. But this bolder, blunter Eve Duncan was easier to accept than the woman who had touched him so deeply that he'd wanted to scoop her up and heal every wound. He could handle this woman, and it was better for him to keep this aspect of her in the forefront. "I was busy." He added with deliberate rudeness, "I didn't know I was supposed to be here to hold your hand."

She instantly flared. "I never asked you to—I don't want pity. I want help."

"Then tell me how you want me to start. Isn't that why I'm here?"

She nodded. "Yes." She drew a deep breath, obviously struggling to control herself. She looked down at the box of papers and envelopes on the table. "I need you to look at these. I want every one of them to be investigated."

"What are they?"

"Letters. I've received a lot of letters since Bonnie was taken." She tapped one pile. "These are the ones that are from people who say they've seen her alive and well in different locations." She tapped the next pile. "These are the sick ones. Some of them say I'm to blame and should go to hell for letting Bonnie be taken." She moistened her lips. "Some of them are from people who say they took Bonnie and describe what they did to her before they killed her. There are only three of those. Two of them I got the first week, and I turned them over to the police. They checked them out and said that they were nutcases and actually had alibis for the day that Bonnie was kidnapped. The last one I received yesterday. I held it to give to you. I was careful about fingerprints." She gestured to the box. "Take them all."

"You said that you'd told the police about them? The ones where Bonnie had been sighted?"

"Of course, I did," she said harshly. "They said that they'd checked those out, too. I don't trust them. I want you to do it again."

He carefully opened the last letter she had received yesterday and was scanning it. Incredibly ugly. Sickeningly explicit. It must have been pure torture for Eve to read it. "Didn't Detective Slindak tell you to just give the unopened letters to him?"

"Yes. I couldn't do it. They were addressed to me. She's my daughter. I had to be part of what happened to her."

"These aren't part of what happened to her. These are just a bunch of hyenas crawling out of the woodwork and trying to tear you apart. I've seen it before in these cases."

"Have you? Well, I haven't. It's all new to me. So I have to treat everything that comes my way as if it had never happened to anyone else before. Maybe you and the police are taking it too much for granted because you don't have the same perspective as I do. Maybe you're not careful enough."

"I'm careful." He carefully put the letter back in the box. "I'll check these out again for you."

"Particularly the ones where Bonnie was seen alive."

"Particularly those," he said gently.

"I want to go with you."

"That's not procedure."

"To hell with procedure. You said we'd search for Bonnie together. Was that bullshit?"

"No, but I didn't think you'd be this proactive."

"I was supposed to sit here and wait for you all to do everything according to 'procedure'?" Her eyes were glittering fiercely, her hands clenched. "I can't do that. I've waited for her to come home. I've waited for you to tell me you've found her." Her voice was uneven. "I've waited for you to tell me my baby is . . . dead. I can't wait any longer. I have to find out for myself." She took a step closer to him. "Can't you see that? I won't behave like some hysterical female. I won't get in the way. But I have to help bring her home."

She was tearing him apart. What she was asking was strictly against the rules and procedures. He'd be handed a reprimand and could even be taken off the case.

To hell with it. He couldn't deny her the chance she wanted.

He turned away. "I'll drop this last letter off at ATLPD for processing. Then I'll come back and pick you up, and we'll go interview those four people who say they've actually seen your Bonnie."

"I could go with you now," she said eagerly. "I'll just get my—" She slowly nodded. "You don't want to be seen with me while you're investigating. You'll get in trouble. I don't want you to lose your job."

"I won't lose my job. I just want to avoid difficulties." He smiled faintly. "But what would you do if you thought that I would?"

"You've got plenty of money. It wouldn't hurt you like it would some people. Still, it wouldn't be good." She hesitated. "But it wouldn't change what I had to do. I'd just call your boss and tell him that I'd go to the media and tell them how uncooperative the FBI was being with a bereaved mother. I don't think they'd like that."

He chuckled. "Lord, you're tough."

"I told you, I grew up in the projects. I had to fight every day of my life in one battle or another." She turned away. "Go to the precinct and see if they can start the process of finding out anything from that poison-pen letter. I can wait." She sat down at the table and opened one of the envelopes. "I've gone over these letters dozens of times to see if I could find anything in them that would offer me any hope or insight as to where Bonnie might be." Her hands were shaking as she spread out the first letter. "It won't hurt me to go over them again. Maybe I'll notice something more this time. Then I'll phone the people who wrote the letters and ask them for permission to come to see them."

She was sitting very straight, her lips tight, and her gaze fixed on the letter. Her concentration reminded Joe of a painting he'd once seen of Anne Boleyn in a London museum, staring at the sword that was going to take her head. The same fascination, the same resolution, the same tortured bewilderment. It was incredibly painful for him to stand there and watch her. He wanted to reach out and touch her, ease that terrible tension.

She glanced up at him. "What are you waiting for? Go on. We need to get started checking these right away."

And the chances that they'd come up with anything new were poor at best. The sad thing about that knowledge was that in her heart, Eve knew it as well. But he'd be damned if he'd voice it. He turned away. "I'll be back as soon as I can. I'll call you if I get delayed."

CHAPTER
3

"MRS. NEDRA TILDEN. IT'S THE last name on your list," Joe said quietly. "Are you sure you want to talk to her?"

"You mean because the other so-called witnesses were such disasters? I can see why the police didn't want me involved," Eve said. "Facing the mother of a victim must be difficult for anyone. Two of them were embarrassed about their mistake when I pinned them down to a description of her. The other man was belligerent and just wanted me to go away and leave him alone." Eve was gazing at the cedar-shingled gray house at the end of the block. "At least you haven't said I told you so."

"I'll never say that to you."

"I'll hold you to that." She opened the passenger door. "Let's go see, Mrs. Tilden."

"Eve," he said hesitantly. "According to the police report, she's not quite rational."

"You mean she's nuts?" She shrugged. "That doesn't mean

that I should ignore the chance that she may have seen something. Maybe the police didn't question her thoroughly because she seemed unbalanced." She glanced at him before she stopped at the front door. "I'll go in alone if you think you're wasting your time."

"I didn't mean that," he said. "I just don't want you to be punished unnecessarily." He punched the doorbell. "By all means let's talk to the lady."

It was opened immediately by a small, plump woman somewhere in her seventies or eighties whose eyes were bright as an inquisitive squirrel's. "You're Eve Duncan." Her dark eyes were fixed eagerly on Eve's face. "Come in. Come in. I've been waiting for you. It's about time you came to see me. If I'd wanted the police to come knocking, I would have called them." She glanced at Joe. "You police?"

"FBI." He put his hand on Eve's elbow. "Thank you for seeing us, Mrs. Tilden. We'll try not to take too much of your time."

"I'm seeing her, not you." She gazed back at Eve. "You'd think you didn't want that little girl back. You should have come sooner."

"I'm here now," Eve said. "You said you saw my daughter the night after she was taken? Where?"

"Right in front of my house," the woman said. "It was a full moon, and I saw her walking down the street beside a man. She was wearing that Bugs Bunny T-shirt that the newspapers said she was last seen in."

"What did the man look like?" Joe asked.

"I couldn't make him out. Sort of dark. Tall. The little girl was skipping to keep up with him. She looked like she was trying to tell him something."

"She didn't seem frightened?" Eve asked.

"No. She seemed kind of . . . worried. But not scared." Nedra Tilden nodded. "Why should she?"

Eve gazed at her in disbelief. "She was kidnapped, Mrs. Tilden. Of course, she would be frightened. Perhaps it was another little girl you saw."

Her lips tightened. "Don't you tell me who I saw. It was that Bonnie Duncan. I may be getting a little up there in years, but that only makes me see things clearer. I'm closer to the other side."

"Other side?" Eve repeated.

"Do you think your daughter is still alive?" She shook her head. "It was a spirit I saw. You might as well stop looking for her. It was her ghost that I saw running beside that man and trying to get his attention."

Eve inhaled sharply as if the breath had been taken out of her. "A spirit?"

"I see them all the time. The first one was my first cousin, Edgar, about ten years ago. Then there was my neighbor, Josh Billiak, who was killed in an automobile accident in the next block. After that they just seemed to keep coming. It made me nervous at first, but then I got used to it." She lifted her chin proudly. "I decided that I must be special or something. That's why it didn't surprise me to look out my window and see your Bonnie. No sirree, you're not going to find her alive. She's dead as a doornail."

Joe wanted to strangle the woman. "Thanks for your time." He nudged Eve toward the door. "We have to go now."

"No thanks?" Nedra Tilden stepped forward and grabbed Eve's arm, her dark eyes greedily searching Eve's face. "You didn't want to hear what I had to say, did you? But I did you a favor. You have to come to terms with the grim reaper."

"You come to terms." Joe opened the door. "We'll wait until we have more evidence."

"Wait." Eve pulled away from him and looked at the woman. "You hurt me. Why did you want to hurt me?"

"I only did my duty," Nedra Tilden said righteously. "You have all these cops and FBI people running around and spending taxpayers' money. I barely manage to get by on Social Security, and they're pouring out cash trying to find a lost kid. You should accept that your Bonnie has been butchered and let everybody go about their business."

Eve turned pale. "But I can't accept that." She turned away and walked out of the house. "Any more than I can believe that if she was dead, she'd make an appearance to someone who is as vicious as you."

Joe followed, but stopped to bite out to the woman who was starting to scurry after Eve out on the porch, "Say one more word and I'll have you taken in for a psychiatric evaluation." He slammed the door in her face and ran down the steps after Eve. "Vicious is right." He opened the car door for her. "I told you she wasn't stable."

"That's very close to saying I told you so, Joe," she said dully.

"No, it isn't. I'm just reminding you that you shouldn't pay any attention to anything the bitch said." He ran around and got in the driver's seat. "None of that bullshit was in the police report. Evidently she was saving it for you."

"How kind." She was rigid, staring straight ahead. "I wanted to hit her." Her hands were clenching on her lap. "No, I wanted to kill her. I've seen cruelty before, but not like that. I couldn't understand why she'd do it. I'd never done anything to her, and yet she was drinking in my pain . . . she liked it."

Joe nodded. "That's why I wanted to get you out of there."

"Thank you." She looked back at the porch, and Joe could see her start to shake. She was sitting so straight, struggling desperately for control, but her body was betraying her. "I couldn't understand . . ."

And Joe couldn't take it any longer. He reached over and pulled her into his arms.

She stiffened. "No."

"Shut up," he said hoarsely. "You're hurting, and I'm offering comfort. That's all this is about." It was a lie. But God, he hoped she believed him. He had to find some way to help her, or it would kill him.

She was still, frozen. Then she slowly, tentatively, relaxed against him. "She said 'butchered.'" Her words were muffled against him. "She said my Bonnie was butchered."

"Because she's a crazy woman." His hand was in her hair. He loved the feel of her, the textures of her. Ignore them, help her. "And you handled her; you told her the way it is. I was proud of you."

"I couldn't let her words hurt me, hurt my Bonnie." She gave a long, shaky sigh. "I wouldn't believe the police or you. I had to talk to them myself. And now look at me. I'm acting like a child." She started to push him away.

Not yet. Another minute. Another hour.

Another lifetime.

His arms tightened, then he slowly released her. "You're no child. You're very brave. And I feel honored you let me be here to help you. That's what friends are for."

She met his gaze. "Are you my friend, Joe?"

"I think we're on our way." He pushed back a strand of red-brown hair that had fallen across her forehead. "Don't you?"

She didn't answer for a moment, then nodded. "I believe we may be. It feels very strange for me. I haven't had time for friends. First, I was fighting my way out of the slums, then there was Bonnie."

"I was fighting, too, but not in the same arena." He started the car. "Come on, let's find a restaurant and get some dinner. You haven't eaten all day."

"You don't have to do this," she said quickly. "I've taken enough of your day. You can take me home."

"Yes, I could," he said. "But I'm not. You're going to eat and we'll talk, and by the time you go home, you'll have forgotten that bitch." He grimaced. "Well, not forgotten, but you'll have a different perspective on her. Now, where do you want to go to eat?"

"I don't care."

"I'll pick someplace close to your place so that you can dump me and walk home if I bore you."

She smiled slightly. "That's a good idea."

One step at a time. Just don't let her close herself away from you, he thought.

She was looking out the window. "What if that woman was right? Bonnie could be dead. We both know it, Joe."

"Yes, but we knew it before we went to see that witch. It was no revelation."

"She said Bonnie wasn't frightened. That was a revelation. I pray every night that Bonnie will be safe and not frightened."

"Eve, back away from what happened tonight. She's crazy. And you're crazy to let anything she said linger with you."

"Am I?" She glanced back at his face. "Is it a sign of our budding friendship to call me insane?"

"Damned right. I'm being honest. You said that was important to you. It's important to me, too. Only the best of friends have the guts to tell you the truth."

"I can see that," she said quietly. "But no pity, Joe."

"I wouldn't be honest if I didn't tell you there will be moments that I won't be able to help myself from pitying you. You can only feel what the situation dictates, and this situation pretty much sucks." He smiled. "But I'm a callous bastard. I'll have no trouble keeping it to a minimum."

"Are you callous, Joe Quinn?" She tilted her head. "You don't impress me as being . . . but we don't know each other. All I know is that you've been kind to me."

"Plus all the stuff you managed to squeeze out of the Quantico office," he said. "I'll let you judge for yourself after I tell you the story of my wicked life over dinner."

She smiled. "That will be interesting. It will be good for both of us to think of something besides me and my problems. Are you promising to be honest about that wicked past, too, Joe?"

He nodded. "Every detail."

Being honest about the past would be no problem.

It was the present that would have giant lapses of truth.

One step at a time. Protect her. Help her. Never let her see anything beyond what she wanted from him.

Damn, it was going to be hard.

"I LIKE THIS PLACE." Eve gazed out the window at the Chattahoochee River flowing lazily only yards from the restaurant. "It's peaceful."

"Slindak recommended it." Joe handed the menus back to the white-jacketed waiter. "You've never been here before? He said it was popular, and you're a native."

"I've heard of it." Her gaze shifted back to him. "But it's not cheap, and I'm a single mom with a daughter to support. A night out for me is a visit to McDonald's."

"Then you should have ordered something besides salad and a sandwich. No wonder you're thin."

"I'm not hungry." She looked out the window at the river again. "Atlanta has so many creeks and rivers. I worried about them after Bonnie was taken. I thought what if she wandered away and slipped off a bank and— But then I worried about everything. You never realize how many dangers there are in the world until you have a child." She leaned back as the waiter came and set their salads in front of them. "Growing up, I was totally fearless about anything happening to me. I thought I was immortal—like all kids. Then I had Bonnie, and I found out a pinprick could cause tetanus, a tiny germ could give her pneumonia. So many things to fear . . ."

"Stop looking at your salad and eat it." Joe picked up his

own fork. "And I don't believe you were the kind of mother to hover over her child. You probably made sure that she enjoyed life."

She smiled and nodded. "That was easy. She loved every single minute of the day." Her smile faded. "Past tense. I keep falling into that trap. I mustn't do that."

No, ease her away from it. "You were sixteen when you had her?"

"Yes." She picked up her fork and began to eat. "You know all that from the reports. She's illegitimate, but I made sure she didn't miss having a father."

"I'm sure you did. But you must have missed the emotional support yourself."

"Why? I had Bonnie, I didn't need anyone else." She shrugged. "Stop thinking of me as some heartbroken victim. Sex was the only thing that bound me to Bonnie's father. I made a mistake. Our time together happened like a lightning flash, then it was gone. But I had my daughter and that was all that mattered." A luminous smile suddenly lit her face. "Anyone who has never had a child like Bonnie is the victim, not me."

"I can see that." He had been watching with fascination the play of expressions that flitted across her face. Every now and then he could capture the Eve she had been before she had been forced to face the horror that now dominated her life. "It just surprised me that it happened when you were so young."

"It surprised me, too. I assure you I wasn't prepared to be a mother. All I wanted to do was get out of the projects and build a decent life for myself."

"But you decided to keep her."

"She was mine," she said simply. "I couldn't give her up. You'd understand if you had a child." She tilted her head. "Or do you?"

He chuckled. "You mean you don't know? Rick Donald must have slipped up."

"He said you weren't married, but that doesn't mean you don't have a child." She finished her salad and put down her fork. "I can't tell you how many unwed mothers lived in the projects where I grew up. Men don't have a great sense of responsibility where their children are concerned."

"I'd take care of my own." He smiled faintly. "And, no, I don't have any kids. I've been too busy to make that kind of commitment. And for me, it would be a commitment. I know what it's like to feel like an orphan."

"Oh, yes, your parents are dead. Were you very young?"

"No, it was after I went into the service. A yachting accident. Just the way they would have liked it."

"Weren't you a little old to feel like an orphan? I was feeling sorry for you. I don't know why. You have as much money as Richie Rich."

"Richie Rich? He was a comic book character, wasn't he? Lord, I admit I haven't had anyone compare me to him."

"Bonnie liked those comic books. She thought all the gadgets and toys Richie owned sounded fun."

"I'm surprised you encouraged such blatant materialism."

"Why not? It was a world full of fun and adventure. Bonnie never wanted to own any of the toys. She just liked to learn about them." She smiled. "And they were so outrageous that I doubt even you owned anything like them. Did you?"

"I received a few fairly 'outrageous' gifts from my parents from time to time. Usually, they were sent as a substitute for some trip they'd promised me. Or when I'd been unusually good for a time and not gotten tossed out of the current school of choice where they'd sent me." He grimaced. "That didn't happen often."

"You weren't a good boy?"

"I was a bastard," he said flatly. "My parents didn't care as long as I didn't get in their way. I did that a lot. I was willful and reckless and willing to fight to get what I wanted. It was no wonder that I wasn't welcome in their orderly lives. My father was a stockbroker and my mother was a socialite who did nothing but look pretty and act as my father's hostess, companion, and mistress. They lived smooth, pleasant lives, parties and trips to the Hamptons, journeys on my father's yacht. That's all they wanted, and I disturbed the flow." He lifted his shoulders in a half shrug. "So most of the time, when I wasn't being a son of a bitch, I just stayed away from them. It was better for both of us."

"I can see that it might be. Poor little rich boy."

He chuckled. "Are you mocking me?"

"Yes." She met his gaze. "Because whatever hurt you, you've managed to put it behind you. You can take a little mockery now, can't you? I feel sorry for the boy whose parents didn't want him, but I'm familiar with a lot of those kinds of stories. Most of them didn't include the soothing clink of coins to ease the pain. Sorry if you think that I'm not suitably sympathetic."

"But you're trying to be honest."

She nodded. "I think you were as tough a person then as

you are now. We're alike in that. We've both learned to look ahead, not behind us."

"And you're not impressed by my wicked past?"

"Not as a kid. You'll have to do better than that." She frowned. "If you were kicked out of all those schools, how did you get into Harvard?"

"I cheated?" He shook his head. "No, I'm too damn smart. Things are easy for me. That's why I was so frustrating for everyone. My parents swore I'd never get into Harvard, so I set out to do it. And I made it through."

"Brilliantly?"

"Of course, it wouldn't have given me any satisfaction if I hadn't done it well." He waited for the waiter to change out their salads for the sandwich plates. "My parents wanted me to go into politics. They thought a senator would be a nice addition to their circle. I took a look at Congress and decided that I'd probably be a zombie by the time I was thirty. So I joined the SEALs instead."

"From what I've heard, they definitely don't develop zombies."

"No, I've never felt more alive in my life. They made me into the quintessential warrior, with all the skills and opportunities for battle. I'd found my niche in life."

"Then why did you get out?"

"I liked it too much," he said simply. "And I was too good at it. At first, I considered myself a patriot, and that was okay. Then there comes a point when you know you're coming too close to the line between fighting for a reason and doing battle for the sheer heady love it. If you don't stop before you cross that line, then you become what you're fighting. I was tottering on the brink because I knew I was good enough to let loose all that violence and skill and probably never have to account to anyone. It was a hard decision for me to make."

She studied him. "I can understand how it would be."

Yes, she could sense that streak of wildness and violence in him, and he wouldn't try to hide it from her. She wasn't afraid of those qualities in him. If she was, then he'd have to handle that as it came to the forefront. He wasn't going to lie to her about that side of his character. He hated deceit, and he was having to practice too much of it with her.

"Why the FBI?" she asked.

"It offered a certain amount of action, the technology interested me. I'd always been good at search and destroy. I'm insatiably curious, and I liked puzzles." He nodded at the waiter, who was filling their coffee cups. "And it forced me to be the good guy." He smiled. "You wanted frankness. Did I give you too much?"

She shook her head. "Because you're no saint? I admire the fact that you know yourself and are setting up barricades to be the person you want to be. I don't believe I've ever met anyone who had the discipline to do that."

"Necessity. Everyone has a choice to make about the path they take." He lifted his cup to his lips. "And I noticed that you have a great deal of discipline."

"I thought I did." She took a sip of her coffee. "I'm a mother and a daughter, and I worked two jobs and went to college. That kind of responsibility forces you to develop discipline, or you end up a basket case." She looked down. "Particularly in this situation."

He acted quickly to distract her. "You're a student. What are you studying?"

"Electrical engineering."

"I wouldn't have thought that would be your forte."

"Why not? I'll be good at it."

"I don't doubt it. No offense. But you don't impress me as . . ." He half shrugged. "I saw that sketch of your daughter in the upper hall of your house. It was very good. I can see you as an artist or a designer. But, then, I could be wrong. Am I?"

"You're very perceptive. I've dabbled at drawing in my spare time. When I'm not waiting tables at Mac's Diner, I work for a photographer part-time doing sketches of kids and dogs. Some parents prefer sketches to the realism of the camera. I like it, but I've never been tempted to try to earn a living at it. Engineering is more practical and secure. I have to support my Bonnie." She looked him in the eyes. "If I still have my daughter. That woman tonight . . ."

"Has nothing to do with reality."

"I keep telling myself that. But the reality is that hope might not be enough. Sometimes I wake in the middle of the night screaming." Her hand tightened on her cup. "I don't have to tell you what I'm dreaming. There are monsters out there."

"Yes, there are."

"And you know about them, you've dealt with them. These last two weeks, you've been looking for the monster that might have killed my little girl." She moistened her lips. "I knew that, but I didn't want to admit it. I wanted to close my eyes."

"That's understandable."

"Stop being so damn understanding. I can't close my eyes

after today. I can't rely on hope." She was beginning to tremble. "I have to accept that she might have been taken by one of those monsters. But maybe he didn't kill her. Maybe she's a prisoner somewhere. That could happen." She shook her head and said through her teeth. "Stop *looking* at me like that. I know what the odds are that if she was taken by someone like that she's probably dead. I made Slindak tell me, and he said that almost all children who were kidnapped by those kinds of monsters are killed within the first twenty-four hours. But there's a chance you're wrong." She whispered, "There's a chance I'm wrong."

"Not a very good chance, Eve," he said gently.

"It doesn't have to be a good chance. I'll take what I can get." She drew a shaky breath. "But I didn't bring this up because I wanted you to tell me it was likely that I'd get Bonnie back. I'll follow every clue, every path that could lead me to my daughter alive and well. But I have go down that other ugly path, too. The one you and the police are almost sure that she's taken. Maybe I'll find her there." She smiled with an effort. "But maybe I won't, and then I'll still be able to hope."

"What are you saying, Eve?" he asked quietly.

"You've been searching for the man they think killed those other missing children, haven't you?"

He nodded. "Among other leads. I'm not closing the door on anyone or anything."

"What does that mean?"

He didn't answer for a moment. "I'm looking through records on child molesters." She flinched, and he swore softly. "It's just routine."

"Because the routine has proved valid."

"Yes."

"I want to help you." She held up her hand. "No, not doing that. I'd do it if I had to, but I'll skip that punishment if I can be useful somewhere else. And, I *can* be useful. I want you to give me copies of the cases of those children who have disappeared. I want to study them and see if I can see similarities or anything that might pop up in the way of a lead."

"That's my job, Eve."

"No, it's my job, too. My daughter may have been taken by the same man who killed that little boy who was found by the freeway. If I find him, I may find her." Her jaw squared. "I have to try. If you don't give me a copy, then I'll go to the morgue or the newspaper and ask them to let me study past issues. It will be slower, but I'll still be able to do it. But the police report would give me a head start. Will you do it?"

"I'll think about it."

"I'm putting you on the spot again, aren't I?" She added wearily, "I don't want to do that, Joe. I like you. Maybe I should go check out the newspapers."

"Screw that. I'm not worried about being put on the spot. I'll do what I want to do." He said roughly, "I've gotten to know you. You're going to get attached to those kids in the reports. You're going to identify with the parents. It's going to hurt you big-time."

She just looked at him.

Yeah, what's a snowball going to matter when it's thrown at an avalanche, he thought.

"I can help, Joe," she whispered. "No one would work

harder or concentrate more on doing this than I would. Let me help find my daughter."

"I'll think about it," he repeated. He signaled the waiter for the bill. "No promises."

"And if I don't find Bonnie by doing this, I may discover something that will help those other parents," she said urgently.

"You don't have enough on your plate? See, you're already beginning to worry, and you haven't even started." He reached into his wallet and drew out some bills and threw them on the tray. "Finished?"

"I'd better be," she said dryly. "I have an idea you're about to scoop me up and throw me into the car."

"It's a possibility." He stood up. "You're backing me into a corner, and I have to get some space between us. You're not going to stop. You'll keep coming at me, won't you?"

She nodded as she got to her feet. "I don't give up easily." She preceded him out of the restaurant and paused beside the car, gazing at the river. "You've been very kind to me tonight, Joe. You're right, I'll never forget what that woman said to me. But you made some of the sting go away. I'm very grateful to you." She glanced at him as she got into the car. "And I'm sorry that I'm going to keep on giving you headaches. You don't deserve it."

He smiled. "I can take it. It's nice of you to apologize in advance." He ran around and slipped into the driver's seat. "And this place is only fifteen minutes from your house. I can ward you off for that long."

"I'm done for the night." She added, "I'll call you tomorrow."

And she would, he realized, and keep on calling until she had the answer she wanted. He was only beginning to realize the ruthless determination that existed behind that fragile exterior. "I'll make my own decision, Eve," he said. "I won't let you push me."

"I won't push. I'll just remind you that there's a decision to be made. And I have to keep you on track in case I have to take that other route." She leaned back on the seat and wearily closed her eyes. "I'm so tired. But I learned a lot about you tonight. I know how strong you are. I know you have a balance of values that few people possess. I know there's bitterness and independence and recklessness. You've told me that you could be violent, but you're very protective of me. I feel as if I'm coming close to understanding you."

"That doesn't mean you can control me, Eve."

"No, but it means I can argue and try to persuade." She opened her eyes to look at him. "As friend to friend."

But not as lover to lover.

Get used to it. Accept it. There was no telling how long it would be before she could even contemplate a relationship that held anything beyond the comfort of friendship. But he had made strides in understanding himself tonight. And he was beginning to know Eve as well. Eve, the person, not the object of this crazy fixation that had struck him the first time he had seen her. It was a relief that he actually liked Eve. He appreciated her courage, her discipline, her honesty, her lack of vanity.

What the hell would he have done if he'd found her a complete bitch? Would it have negated that instant powerful attraction? Or had he somehow sensed who and what she was, and that was the reason she had drawn him to her? Who knows? Love at first sight was all very well, but it was confusing as hell and out of his realm of comprehension.

"Love." It was the first time that he had used that word even to himself. It was too sentimental and too much of a commitment. He didn't know anything about it. But what other word could he use for an emotion that made him feel like a cross between a knight in shining armor and a kid with his first crush. Perhaps he'd get lucky and it would go away as fast as it had come.

"Friend to friend?" Eve repeated.

He smiled and nodded slowly. "As long as you realize that it's always a friend's privilege to say no."

"Of course." She closed her eyes again. "It would be unfair to think anything else."

But it would be hard to say no to Eve. Even if he thought that to refuse her might be the best thing for her. "I'm glad that you have such a keen appreciation for justice."

"I do. But I'll still phone you tomorrow . . ."

"YOU'VE HAD THREE CALLS." Sergeant Castro looked up as Joe came into the squad room the next afternoon. "Two from Washington, one from Eve Duncan. They all want you to call them back." He made a face as he handed Joe a slip with numbers on it. "I have other things to do than act as your secretary, Quinn. Where have you been?"

"I was at that park where Bonnie Duncan disappeared. Sorry."

The calls from the Washington office were from Jenny Rudler and Rick Donald. He had no need to return them. It would be Jenny making contact and trying to inveigle her way into the investigation. Rick Donald would have been sly and a little gloating to discuss what he'd told Eve about Joe.

The call from Eve?

He knew what that was about, too.

And he'd been weighing his decision for the greater part of the day.

He stared at the message for a long moment.

Then he turned on his heel and strode out of the squad room.

CHAPTER
4

"CASTRO SAID YOU WANTED to see me." Slindak gazed curiously at the huge pile of reports on the table beside the copy machine. "What are you photocopying? I could have had someone do it for you."

"I wanted to do it myself." Joe turned to face him. "I'm glad you're here. I wanted to talk to you."

"Yeah?" Slindak had picked up one of the sheets. "Kenny Lemwick's missing person's report."

Joe nodded. "And I have the other reports on the other children. I'm making copies of all of them." He paused. "I'm going to give them to Eve Duncan to do a comparison check."

Slindak stiffened. "What the hell?"

"You heard me. I'm going to have her assist in the investigation."

"Are you crazy?"

It was no more than Joe expected. "She's smart, dedicated. I believe she could give valuable input."

"Her kid could be one of those victims. You're asking for trouble. I don't know how your superiors at the FBI feel about family involvement in an investigation, but I could get fired for it if I got caught doing anything that nutty."

"They wouldn't like it either. That's why I'm being up-front with you." He stared him in the eye. "If you want to report me to protect your ass, do it now."

"I'd rather talk you out of it." Slindak scowled. "But I'm not going to be able to do that, am I?"

"No way."

"Dammit, *why?*"

"Eve Duncan has the best reason in the world to find the man who caused those kids to disappear. She'll do a good job."

"But that's not the real reason, is it?" Slindak's eyes were narrowed on Joe's face. "You're not the man I knew in the service. You've always been a loner. There's no way you'd have taken on a partner, not even me. And breaking the rules and involving the mother of a victim? Not in a thousand years."

"People change."

"I can see how she'd arouse your sympathy, but there's a reason for those rules against fraternizing with family members. There are not only the legal ramifications, but their emotional state leads them to act irrationally, and the department might—" He stopped and gave a low whistle. "But you're not just sorry for her, are you? You've got a thing for her. You're doing this to get her into bed."

Joe wished it was that simple. "No." He ran another report

through the copier. "I'd be very stupid to think that she'd hop into bed with me because I'm letting her help with the investigation. You've met her. You know what kind of person she is."

"I know she's desperate. I think she'd do anything to find that kid."

So did Joe. He was trying not to think about it. "I may be a son of a bitch, but I wouldn't try to make that kind of deal with her."

"But she'd be grateful," Slindak said softly. "One thing could lead to another. You like women too much to go the platonic route. Are you fooling yourself, Joe?"

Maybe. He didn't know where this path was taking him. He just knew that he had to follow it. "I'm going to work Eve Duncan and myself to the bone to solve those disappearances. I promise I'll find who is responsible and hand him over to you." He added curtly, "Now are you going to file a report on my making these copies? I'd like to know so that I can be prepared."

Slindak hesitated. Then he slowly shook his head. "I may be sorry, but I'll trust you not to make an ass of yourself and me. Keep her under control." He turned on his heel. "Hell, keep yourself under control."

Joe watched him walk out of the copy room.

Keep yourself under control.

He was trying. It was getting harder by the hour.

EVE THREW OPEN THE DOOR to his ring. "You didn't return my call. Why—"

"I was busy." He pushed past her and strode into the kitchen. He opened his briefcase and pulled out the pile of files and loose papers and dumped them on the table. "The missing children. You wanted them. They're yours." He met her gaze. "And mine. We work on them together."

She stood looking at him, then slowly moved across the room. "I wasn't sure you'd do it." She touched one of the files with a tentative finger. "You didn't want to let me help. Why did you decide to do it?"

"Impulse?" He smiled recklessly. "How the hell do I know? Neither would anyone else at the precinct. My old buddy, Ralph Slindak, had an interesting thought. He said that he believed you were desperate enough to go to bed with anyone who'd give you a chance to find your daughter."

She looked up at him. "He's right," she said quietly. "I wouldn't think twice. Not with Bonnie in the balance. It wouldn't matter at all." She met his eyes. "Is that what you want? I wouldn't think that I'd be your type, but all you have to do is ask."

Oh, shit.

Not his type? If he was going to feel this overwhelming emotional response for her, why couldn't it have been confined to compassion? But even while he felt that pity, he wanted to touch her, put his hands on her, take her to bed, and make her forget everything but him. He couldn't separate the mental from the physical. And the physical was burning hot and trying to submerge everything else.

It didn't help that now when he looked at her that he'd remember what she'd said, that he could have her if that was the price he demanded to help her. Another thought to block, another image to try to forget.

Look away from her. Don't let her see what you're thinking.

"I didn't want to hurt your feelings, but I'm afraid you're right. You're not my type. You look so fragile that I'd be afraid I'd break you." He snapped his briefcase shut. "Besides, I can get a lay anytime." He smiled at her. "I have a lot more trouble keeping friends." He could see relief lessen the tension in her face. "So, if you don't mind, we'll skip the roll in the hay."

"I just wanted to make my position clear. I know I'm asking you to do things that are a little outside the boundaries."

"You're being very clear." Too damn clear.

"I just want you to know that I value you. I felt very much alone before you came. It's better now."

"Then suppose you give me a cup of coffee. Then we'll get down to going over those reports."

"I'll give you the coffee." She went to the cabinet and got down a tin of coffee. "But I'm going to ask another favor. Would you leave me and let me look through these reports by myself tonight?"

"Why?"

"Because I can concentrate better if—" She shook her head as she put on the coffee. "No, I won't lie and protect myself. You were right when you said that I'd be upset when I read about these kids. I can be tough about some things, but not about children. After I get through the reports once, I think that I'll be okay." She smiled with an effort. "I guess I don't want you to see how weak I can be."

"Then by all means read them by yourself. I'm just a guy, and I have trouble coping with tears. I'll come back in the morning, and we'll talk."

"That would be good." She glanced at the files. "There seem to be quite a few. I didn't realize that there were that many cases." She frowned. "I thought I read . . . six? And that included the little boy they found in the grave by the freeway."

"That was all the ATLPD and the media had on their list. But they were all local and within the last five years. They checked nearby cities and came up with nothing. But I found cases in more distant cities in Georgia and Tennessee that I thought were worth looking at. And I dug down another ten years. I ran across a story about the body of a child found in a swamp near the Florida border twelve years ago."

"Fifteen years. You think he's been killing that long?"

"Or longer. It might not be the same man, but it could be. Serial killers like what they do. They tend to make it a life's vocation." He took the coffee she handed him. "You'll find enough there to keep you busy tonight. There are eight or nine that I thought close enough to run a comparison."

"And only two bodies found?" She shivered. "Those poor parents. In agony all these years, not knowing . . ."

"After a certain amount of time passes, just the lack of knowledge is a sort of proof that the child is never coming home. That must be a kind of comfort."

"The hell it is. There's nothing worse than a child who's lost or thrown away like some piece of garbage. A child has value, she should be cared for and brought in from every storm." Her voice shook with passion. "Dead or alive, I'd have to bring my child home."

"Then maybe we can help some of those parents in the reports." He poured her a cup of coffee. "But you need to calm down and get a breath of air before you start. Walk me to the porch."

She took the cup and followed him out onto the porch. "I get too . . . upset. I didn't used to be like this. You're being very patient with me." She leaned against the porch rail and lifted her gaze to the night sky. "Everything reminds me of her. We'd sit here on the steps and look up at the stars and I'd tell her stories about all the constellations and we'd try to identify the Big Dipper and Orion and . . ." She took a sip of coffee. "Sorry. I'll shut up."

"Not for me. She's part of you. And memories can save, not destroy, if you accept them."

"Can they? I only know I wouldn't give up a single memory of her no matter how much it hurt." She added, "My mother doesn't feel that way. She loves Bonnie, but she's trying to block the thought of her. I guess everyone handles grief differently."

"I haven't seen your mother the last two times I've been here. Is she still staying in her room?"

Eve shook her head. "She's been going to church. She was never religious, but a local pastor came to visit and invited her to come to services. I think the congregation has taken her on as a project. They keep her busy. That's fine, Sandra needs people. It may keep her off the drugs. She quit when Bonnie was born, but this is a dangerous time for her."

"What about you? She's the only family you have. She should stay with you and give—"

"Stop being so protective." She smiled and finished her coffee. "The last thing I need is Sandra hovering over me. We're both surviving in the best way we can. She has her congregation, and I have Joe Quinn." She took Joe's empty cup and turned toward the door. "I'll see you tomorrow, Joe. It's time I got to work."

"Good night. Lock your door."

"Why? I'm not worried about being in any kind of danger."

"I know. But I'm worried for you. It's a violent world. Lock your door."

"Whatever."

He watched her as she entered the house and waited until he heard the click of the lock.

No, she wasn't worried. She couldn't care less about her own physical safety. It had no meaning for her in comparison to her loss of her child. He realized that he was the one who was going to have to care for her.

Another duty for him to assume in the emotional storm that had come to him.

Protecting Eve.

Watching over Eve.

Loving Eve.

That word was coming easier to him now. He was beginning to understand the elements that comprised it. Perhaps the fact that he had to block sexual desire made him more aware of what else he was feeling.

But it also made him aware that the storm of feeling was

growing stronger. He was no longer rejecting it. He wanted to go back inside the house and stay with her, be with her . . .

Tomorrow.

He turned and went down the porch steps and strode toward his car.

"COME IN," EVE CALLED, when Joe rang the bell the next afternoon. She looked up impatiently from the papers she was working on as he opened the door. "For heaven's sake, why are you still acting like a visitor? Just walk in."

"I'll keep that in mind. Have you gone to bed yet?"

"For a couple hours. I had to get away from them." She grimaced. "But they followed me. I decided I'd rather deal with them than dream about them. There's coffee on the stove."

"Have you had any?"

"Too much." She nodded at the two piles of files that were in front of her. "I've divided the children into two categories. Male and female. Whoever took these children obviously preferred girls. There are nine cases here, and six of them were girls. But evidently he doesn't entirely rule out little boys." She leaned back in the straight chair. "I had questions. I wanted you here."

"I wanted to be here." He poured a glass of orange juice and brought it to her. "What questions?"

"You know about profiling and all that stuff. You were studying records of sexual molesters." She moistened her lips. "Are these killings all about sex? Is that why he likes little girls? Does he rape them?"

"Probably." He looked away as she flinched. "But it's not about the sexual act as much as it is about power. Most serial killers are addicted to power. Sexual domination is a form of power. Perhaps little boys don't give him the same rush as little girls." He sat down across from her. Look at her. Ignore the fact that every word was hurting her. "Perhaps that's why he butchered that little boy so terribly. He was angry with him for not being what he wanted him to be. But we can't be sure because we've never found any of the little girls' bodies." He stared her in the eyes. "Any more questions?"

"Not for the moment." She swallowed hard. "But thank you for not trying to sugarcoat your answer. I had to know. Then it's all about power?"

"And ego. If a killer has murdered successfully for a long time, then he begins to think he's impervious to capture. He usually develops a pattern according to how often he needs his fix."

"Fix," she repeated. "It's truly an addiction?"

He nodded. "And he'll be as reckless as a heroin addict to get what he needs. More, because he believes no one can touch him."

"A pattern." She looked down at the sheet of paper in front of her. "The dates of the disappearances of the first three girls are approximately five months apart. Janey Bristol, six years, disappeared from Dunwoody three years ago on August 10. Linda Cantrell, eight years, was reported missing on January 30 from her home in Marietta. Natalie Kirk got off the bus but never made it home on June 5." She glanced up. "But the other disappearances were less predictable. The next disappearance didn't happen for another eighteen months. And the next two followed almost immediately. Within a few weeks of each other." She tapped the third pile of files. "And none of these out-of-town disappearances took place during those eighteen months. They were all before the local Atlanta killings started. And there was over a year between those kidnappings. If he's what you say he is, I don't think he was taking a vacation. Where was he? What was he doing?" She added unsteadily, "Who was he killing?"

"That's what we're going to find out. He could have been away from the area. Or he might have been in jail." His gaze narrowed thoughtfully. "First a year, then five months. He's getting hungrier."

"Bonnie would have been three months. So maybe she wasn't one of— I'm trying not to think of Bonnie." She took another sip of orange juice. "That was one of the nightmares I was having last night."

"And my nightmare is your having a nervous breakdown and leaving me without someone to help me find this bastard." He took a pile of files from her. "So we'll both go over these files and make notes and talk about them for another two hours. Then I'll keep on, and you'll take a nap on the couch."

"I won't be able to sleep."

"Then I'll call a doctor and get him to give you a shot. Take your choice."

"We'll talk about it later." She went back to the file in front of her. "What are we looking for?"

"Circumstances surrounding the disappearance. Similarities, indications of any common traits in the victims or family members."

"Family members?"

"It's possible revenge was taken against the child for a perceived slight by the parents."

"Why wouldn't he just kill the parents?"

"It could still be on his agenda. He might want them to suffer first."

"Yes, that would do it." She opened the first file. "That's a lot of things to look for, Joe."

"And better done with a clear head."

She ignored the jab. "How can you continue to work on cases like this? Doesn't it make you sick?"

"Sometimes. But it makes me sicker to know that some arrogant son of a bitch is out there killing whoever he pleases and thinking no one is going to catch him." He was scanning the files in front of him. "Seasons don't seem to make any difference to him. In some instances, killers only murder in certain seasons or time of the month. Here we have victims in summer, fall, winter . . ."

"Maybe they're not all dead," Eve said. "We keep talking about killings. Maybe some of them were runaways or taken by relatives. Maybe they're not— But I have to think of them as victims, don't I? I have to look at these damn reports and think that a monster grabbed them and how and why he did it."

"You don't have to do it. Let me bundle up all these reports and take them away. No one is forcing you but yourself."

"I know that." She focused her gaze on the report in front of her. "Linda Cantrell." The picture of the girl showed a child with dark hair and eyes and a wide white smile. "She was Hispanic, but that didn't seem to have anything to do with her being chosen. The other children were black, white . . . no Asian . . ."

* * *

"I DON'T WANT TO DO THIS." Eve glared up at him even as she lay down on the couch three hours later. "I can keep on going. I don't want to sleep. You have no right to threaten me with your damn doctor."

"No, I don't. But might is always right, and I have the advantage." The sun had gone down an hour ago, and he turned off the lights in the living room. "So go to sleep." He sat down in a chair across the room. "Four hours at least. Then I'll let you work a little longer before I leave and go back to my place."

"Go now. I don't want you sitting there in the dark like a guard at an asylum."

"Asylum. Strange choice of words. Why not a guard at a jail?"

She didn't answer.

"Unless you're worried because you might have a nervous breakdown. Do you think about it?"

"No, I don't think about myself at all. I don't matter. That just came out. Now stop trying to dig into my psyche."

"Naturally, you're distraught, and all kinds of crazy ideas are going through your mind. You're walking a fine line, but we'll get through it."

"We? I'm the one who is walking that line. You're strong and sane, and everything is in control in your world."

"I'll walk the line with you. If you think you're going to fall, reach out, and I'll be there."

She was silent. "Why are you being so kind to me? You're tough and cynical and . . . I don't think that you're one of those do-gooders who want to save the world."

"The world is too big a project. You're damn right I'm not a do-gooder. I usually run the other way. But every now and then, I run across someone who it bothers me to see struggling. I want to see you come out on top of this. It will make me feel good. It's purely selfish."

"Well, that relieves me," she said dryly. "I'd hate being someone's project."

He chuckled. "No chance. You'd toss me out on my ear."

"Maybe not," she said. "I told you that I didn't feel as alone when I was with you."

"Then I may be safe for a while. Until the situation turns around, and you don't need me any longer. Now why don't you stop talking and try to nap."

"I don't want to sleep. You can force me to lie here, but you can't make me sleep."

"Are you paraphrasing that proverb about leading a horse to water?"

"I guess so." She was silent again, and the next words came haltingly in the darkness. "Three months. The pattern is wrong for Bonnie. She has a chance that it wasn't that monster, doesn't she?"

"She has a chance."

"You're so damn encouraging. Give me a break."

"I'd like to give you anything that you want from me. But I won't give you lies . . . or false hope."

"Damn you." She said a moment later, "No, bless you."

"Go to sleep, Eve."

"If I do, the nightmares will come."

"No, they won't. I'm here for you. After you go to sleep, I'll turn on that little stained-glass lamp by the door. If you show any signs of distress, I'll wake you."

"You'll keep them away?"

"I'll guard you through the night."

"I shouldn't be this weak. I hate it. I should be able to handle . . . I *hate* it."

"I know you do. But it's my turn now. When I'm walking my fine line someday, I'll expect you to guard me from the night monsters."

"I'll do it. I promise . . ."

She was still, but Joe didn't hear her breathing even and steady for another five minutes. Then he got to his feet and turned on the stained-glass lamp. He tucked a worn red cotton throw over Eve before he went back to his chair across the room.

He leaned back and watched the play of the soft, colored light on her face. Her cheekbones were more prominent than he had noticed before. She had lost weight in the short time since he had first met her. She couldn't afford to lose it. He had to get her to eat more, dammit.

Eat and sleep so that she could survive.

So that he could survive.

HE DIDN'T HAVE TO WAKE Eve until almost three hours later.

She jerked upright when he put his hand on her shoulder. "No!"

"It's okay," Joe said. "You were starting to breathe hard. I figured that you were being ambushed."

"I was." She pushed the hair back from her forehead. "But you showed up with the cavalry just in time." She swung her feet to the floor. "I need to get a glass of water and wash my face." She glanced at the clock. "I assume I'm being permitted to get back to work?"

"For a little while." He headed for the kitchen. "I'll put on a fresh pot of coffee while you—"

Eve's phone rang, and she picked up the receiver on the chest by the door and answered it. "Just a minute." She frowned as she handed the receiver to Joe. "Detective Slindak. He said you told him you'd be here."

He nodded. "I had to give him a contact number. I was planning on calling him anyway." He spoke into the phone, "Quinn."

"I tried to get you at your hotel first," Slindak said sourly. "You must be burning the midnight oil."

"You might say that. Problems, Slindak?"

"Big-time. Some hunters found a child's remains in a cave in Gwinnett County."

"Girl or boy?"

He could see Eve tense.

"Girl. There wasn't much left of the kid, but the scraps of clothing that remained coincided with the description of what Janey Bristol was wearing when she disappeared. I'm heading out to the crime scene. I thought you'd want to go, too."

"I'll meet you there." He pulled out his notebook and pen. "Give me the directions." He scrawled rapidly. "Is forensics already there?"

"Yes. And the officers who were called secured the area as best they could. There were three hunters who made the discovery, and they ducked into the cave to shelter from the rain. It's still raining cats and dogs up there. They pretty well messed up the crime scene."

"Great," Joe said sarcastically. "Not that it would probably have done much good anyway. The kid has to have been subjected to animal and environmental exposure for all these months. But there might have been something. I'm on my way." He hung up.

"Who?" Eve asked.

"Not Bonnie. We can't be sure. The body is in poor condition, but the clothing would point toward Janey Bristol."

Eve crossed her arms across her chest as if to keep them from shaking. "Six years old . . ."

He turned toward the door. "I'll call you when I know more."

"I'm going with you."

He had been half-expecting it. "This is going way beyond just looking at records, Eve."

"Yes, it's looking at the remains of that poor kid. It makes me sick to think of it. But I have to be there." Her hands clenched into fists at her sides. "I know nonprofessionals aren't welcome at crime scenes. But you've stuck your neck out for me before. Do it now. I won't get in your way. Look, I won't even go to the crime scene itself. I'll stay in the car."

"And you'll still see things you don't want to see."

"So I'm supposed to bury my head in the sand? No, I don't want to see it. But that little girl didn't want to be killed, either. It could have been Bonnie." Her lips tightened in a mirthless smile. "Why not let me go? Slindak should be expecting it. You said he thought we might be sleeping together. He'll just think that I'm getting what I paid for."

"And what if I don't want him to think that?" Joe asked grimly.

She ignored the question. "Take me, Joe," she said urgently. "You knew I wouldn't be satisfied with studying those reports. You knew where this would lead."

Yes, he had known. Why was he even arguing? When he had copied the reports, he had made the ultimate commitment.

One more attempt.

"What would you do if I said no?"

"Follow you."

He turned back toward the door. "Grab a raincoat. It's raining up in Gwinnett County."

THE MEDICAL EXAMINER'S VAN was parked on the side of the road, and Joe drew in several yards behind it. "Stay here."

Eve nodded. "You don't have to remind me. I promised I wouldn't get in your way. I just want to be here in case you find out anything."

"Which will probably be nothing until we get the forensic reports." He jumped out of the car and was immediately soaked by the pouring rain. He followed the glow of lanterns carried by shadowy figures that turned out to be officers moving behind the yellow tape several yards from the road.

"Quinn."

He turned to see Slindak coming toward him. He was

wearing a yellow slicker, but his head was bare, and his hair was as wet as Joe's. "Where's the cave, Slindak?"

Slindak nodded to the left. "Around that bend. It's only a football field's distance from the road. And it's only two miles from a ritzy subdivision. The son of a bitch who killed her has balls of steel."

"He thinks that he's too smart to be caught. Not unusual." But the degree of boldness was not common, Joe thought. "And he buried that other kid beside the freeway. How the hell could he be sure not to be seen by a driver while he was disposing of the body?"

Slindak shrugged. "Nuts." He was sloshing through the mud toward the cave. "But he'd have to be crazy to do what he did to that little girl. She doesn't have a head. At first, we thought an animal had taken it, but we found it on a shelf of the cave. He cut it off and put it on display."

Joe felt the anger tear through him. "Bastard."

"Did you and your lady find anything in those reports?"

Joe gave him an icy glance. "Ms. Duncan worked very hard, but didn't come up with anything yet. And you will speak of her with respect, or you'll find yourself facedown in this mud while I wash out your mouth."

"Hold it," Slindak said quickly. "No offense. I do respect her. I just called it the way I saw it."

And Slindak hadn't been really insulting. It had been Joe's anger at the killing that had become mixed with his annoyance with Slindak. Joe couldn't blame him for reading sexual overtones into his connection with Eve. On Joe's part, those overtones were definitely there, and it wouldn't take a psychic to see them. He just hoped they weren't as clear to Eve. "You saw wrong," he said curtly. "There's no payoff. No matter what I'm feeling, I'm not that much of an asshole."

Slindak shook his head. "You poor bastard," he murmured. "I'll be damned. I never thought I'd live to see it."

"You may not if you keep on talking," Joe said grimly.

"My lips are sealed." They had come close to the cave, and Slindak gestured to the opening. "I think they're ready to bring out the body. Do you want to go inside?"

Joe nodded and moved carefully to enter the cave. Two techs were carefully transferring the body parts to the tarp on the stretcher. The parts were mostly skeleton. The little girl was hardly recognizable as a human being. The anger was searing again, and he took a moment to overcome it before he glanced around the cave. It was a small area, and evidently the child hadn't been buried or hidden in any way. It was a wonder that the body hadn't been discovered sooner.

Again, the killer's boundless arrogance was staring Joe in the face.

"We're ready to go." A young forensic tech kneeling beside the body was looking up at Joe. "Do you need anything else, sir?"

"The skull was on that ledge?" he asked.

"Yep, it nearly scared those hunters shitless," Slindak said. "The field rats had gotten to it."

"Can we zip her up?" the tech asked again.

"Yeah, go ahead." Joe turned away as they zipped up the body bag. "Did we get any footprints besides those of the hunters?"

"A possible near the ledge, but it's badly eroded," Slindak said. "He didn't even try to erase his footprint. It's like the other case. If we could catch the bastard, we could nail him in court."

"He doesn't think we're going to catch him. That couldn't be more obvious." Joe watched the techs pick up the stretcher and carry it out into the rain. They were going to take it to the M.E. van.

And Eve was going to see them put that pitiful sack of bones into the van.

"Is there anything else I should see?" he asked Slindak.

Slindak shook his head. "I just thought you'd want to be here."

"You were right." He turned toward the cave entrance. "Let me know when we get a definite ID."

"That may not be easy. I can't bring in the parents to ID that skeleton. No prints. I can only try to get dental records."

"Damn," Joe said in frustration. "We just had a lecture at the Bureau about the potential for using DNA in identifying victims. But that's still down the road a bit. I want it *now*."

"I'm satisfied with the old tried-and-true methods," Slindak said. "We get along just fine without your fancy scientific bullshit."

"Except when all you have to work with is a skeleton." Joe walked out of the cave. The rain felt good on his face after the stench and closeness of death inside the cave. He moved quickly through the stand of trees toward the road.

The techs were closing the back doors of the M.E. van as he came out of the woods.

And Eve was standing beside the car, watching them.

"Shit." His pace quickened. He reached her in seconds.

"Dammit, why did you get out of the car?" He opened the passenger door and gently pushed her onto the seat. "You're wet as a drowned rat."

"I had to see her," she whispered. "But there was nothing to see, was there? It looked like a bag full of . . . nothing."

Joe ran around the car and got into the driver's seat. "It wasn't nothing. It was a skeleton, but the bones were . . . not together." He started the car and drove past the M.E. van as quickly as he could.

"Animals?"

"Partly."

Her hands clenched together on her lap. "And what's the other part? Tell me."

"So you can hurt more?"

"So I can know what he is."

She wasn't going to give up. He said curtly, "He cut off her head and put it on a ledge over her body."

She inhaled as if he'd struck her.

"And now you know what the bastard is. Does it make you any happier?"

"No. Poor little girl . . . It's Janey Bristol?"

"We're not sure. There's not much to ID."

"It's going to kill her parents. I want to help them."

"You can't do anything."

"I guess not. I'll think about it. Is there any evidence?"

"A possible footprint. He didn't try to hide what he'd done. He's bold as brass."

"You said that before. Then we should be able to find him."

"We'll find him. Stop thinking about him for a while."

"We may find other bodies. He's being careless."

"That's a possibility."

She was silent for a long time, watching the rain hit the windshield. "I'm glad she was found. She was alone so long in that cave. When we find out who she is, she'll be able to go home to people who love her."

She was identifying the child with her Bonnie, Joe knew. His heart was aching for her, but there was nothing he could do. "I'm glad she was found, too."

"I keep thinking that . . . it might have been Bonnie. I have a chance that she's still alive. But if he did take her, then I have to find him to be sure either way."

And she was beginning to accept that her daughter could be dead, a victim of the monster who had killed the little girl in the cave.

He pulled the car to a stop in front of her house. "Come on. Let's get you inside. You need a hot shower and some rest."

"Go home, Joe." She got out of the car. "I wouldn't put it past you to strip me down and throw me in the shower."

"It's an interesting idea."

"Not really. I'm too skinny for you, remember?" She shook her head. "I have some thinking to do. I don't want you here."

He didn't want her to be alone, dammit. Should he push it?

She started up the steps. "I'll be fine. Stop worrying. I got along before you dropped into my life."

"But not as well."

She turned as she unlocked the door. "No, not as well." She smiled slightly. "Though I hate to cater to your ego. I'll see you tomorrow, Joe."

"I'll call you first thing in the morning. I want you to tell me that you slept a little."

"I'll work on it."

"But you're going back to those reports."

"He's a monster, Joe," she said quietly. "He might be *my* monster. We have to stop him." She disappeared into the house.

Joe waited until the lights went on inside before he pulled away from the curb. He couldn't force her to let him help her. He'd already invaded her space and compromised her independence. It was a wonder that she hadn't rebelled against him before. He'd go back to the precinct and see if any of the forensic reports were completed yet.

Whether the man who killed that little girl in the cave was Eve's monster or not, he was definitely a monster. Joe could feel the anger tear through him as he remembered the hideously macabre scene in the cave.

Get to work. Show the bastard he wasn't as invulnerable as he thought he was. Joe felt a familiar exhilaration mix with the rage. The warrior instinct that had been a part of his life for years was starting to simmer.

Yes, he was in the mood for hunting monsters.

CHAPTER
5

JOE THREW A FOLDED NEWSPAPER on the table in front of Eve the next morning. "The media got hold of the story. Interviews with the hunters. Descriptions of what they saw in the cave. *Damn* them. We hadn't yet notified the Bristols that it might be their daughter. We were waiting to check with her dentist. The phones have been ringing off the hook from parents of those kidnapped kids, and we can't even tell them yes or no."

Eve opened the newspaper and shook her head. "Why didn't they wait? This is cruel."

"It's a scoop. The reporter wanted to get ahead of the competition. The bastard will do anything for a story."

"Brian McVey," Eve read the byline. "I hope he's happy about this ugliness." She looked up at him. "How long before you get a confirmation on the dental records?"

"This afternoon." His lips tightened grimly. "And the information will not go to Brian McVey. We'll leave him so far out in the cold, he'll freeze to death." He looked at the files in front of her. "Did you find anything?"

"All the children were in the age brackets from four to eight, all of them were from middle- to high-income families, all of them lived in homes in nice subdivisions." She looked up. "Except Bonnie. I'm poor as dirt, and this is a rental property. It's nicer than anywhere I've lived before, but it doesn't compare with one of those houses in Towne Lake or Chestnut Hill subdivisions. I was very happy when I saw that she didn't make the A-list. That's two things that are different: three months between the kidnappings, and the kind of place where she lived. It may not seem a lot to you, but to me it's gigantic."

"It's gigantic to me, too," he said gently. "Anything else?"

"Not yet." She leaned back in the chair. "What about the footprint in the cave?"

"We're working on it. It's not the usual shoe. It's rubberized . . ."

"A tennis shoe?"

"Not exactly. The pattern is different . . . We're working on it. We'll get there. I'm going to go to a shoe manufacturer downtown when I leave here and see if he can identify it." He was glancing through the reports. "But first, why don't we go and take a look at these houses."

"Why?"

"These are the kids' home bases. Children stay close to their home at this age. It's where they may have been kidnapped."

"But according to the reports, only two of the parents think their child was taken from the neighborhood."

"We'll still take a look." He turned. "If you want to go with me."

"Of course, I do." She was beside him in a moment. "And to the shoe factory, too."

He shrugged. "Just routine investigation. I could just as well phone you after I finish."

"Nothing is routine." She got into the car. "I've forgotten what the word means."

So had Joe. Since the moment he had met her, nothing had been routine or commonplace in his life. "Where, first?"

"Chestnut Hills. Linda Cantrell. It's in Kennesaw."

His brows lifted. "You rattled that off. I'm surprised you haven't memorized the address."

"I have. I've memorized all of them. I'll tell you when we're closer."

"THE HOUSES ARE ALL DIFFERENT styles," Eve said. "Tudors, modern, cottage . . ." Her gaze wandered over the neat lush lawn and clipped bushes that surrounded Nita Teller's home. "Small, medium, large . . . As home bases, they have very little in common. They're just pleasant houses in suburban neighborhoods. I think we struck out."

"Maybe. Maybe not." Joe was staring thoughtfully at the house. "I can't put my finger on it right now, but something may strike me later. What's next?"

"Janey Bristol. She's the last one in Atlanta. The others are from your list of outside the city. She's about five miles from here, in Roswell. Do we have time before we go downtown to that shoe company?"

Joe nodded. "We got through these neighborhoods quickly. You had them organized very efficiently."

She handed him the address. "I put her last. I guess I wasn't very eager to imagine Janey where she was happiest. It hurts after last night." She tilted her head. "You're very thoughtful. You do think this was helpful?"

"As I said, sometime something sticks in your mind, then it comes together later."

"You're very good at this, aren't you?"

He smiled. "Hell, yes."

"And so modest."

"I've never lacked an appreciation for my own worth. I see nothing wrong in confidence as long as it's not misplaced."

"Neither do I. It was the first thing I noticed about you," she said quietly. "I wanted the FBI to send an older agent. Someone who had worlds of experience and could use it to find Bonnie. I was angry that instead they sent me a young man who acted as if he knew how to shape the world to suit himself. You were good-looking, tough, smart, and oozed assurance. I wanted to kick you."

"I appreciate your restraint."

"And then I saw something in you. And I thought that maybe it would be okay between us."

"And it is." He glanced at the address again. "The Bristol subdivision should be just ahead."

She tensed. "Last night I kept thinking of that skeleton and the skull. I couldn't get it out of my mind. I kept thinking how I'd feel if that was all I had left of Bonnie."

"And it tore you to pieces."

"Yes, that goes without saying. But I wanted to help the Bristols. And there was nothing that I could do." Her smile was bittersweet. "I almost feel as if we're all a family who have been visited by some catastrophic disease and have to nurse each other through it."

Joe turned into the subdivision. "I think you have enough on your plate without trying to cure all those other victims."

"There is no cure except catching that monster. I believe we have to— What on earth!"

Joe muttered a curse as he stomped on the brakes. The street before the Bristol house was full of cars and media vans. Three ATLPD squad cars were in the driveway. "Son of a bitch, some-one must have leaked the information about Janey Bristol to the media. We weren't even supposed to have a dental confir-mation until later today."

"It looks like those reporters are on the family like locusts," Eve said. "Can't you keep them away from them? It nearly killed me to have to deal with them after I first lost Bonnie."

"I can knock a couple of heads together and end up in court. I may do it. But you can't interfere with the freedom of the press." He stiffened as he saw someone get out of one of the squad cars. "There's Slindak. What the hell is he doing here?" He rolled down the window. "Slindak!"

Slindak turned at his call and strode over to the car. "How did you hear about this mess, Quinn?"

"What are you talking about? Did someone leak the results on the Bristol dental records?"

Slindak shook his head. "We haven't heard anything yet." He glanced at Eve. "She shouldn't be here. Those reporters are going to recognize her, and they'll surround her like sharks. I'll get someone to take her home. I need you inside, Quinn."

He nodded as he jumped out of the car. "Why? What's going on?"

"Ellen Bristol answered the phone this morning. It was a phone call from a man who claimed he was the one who killed her daughter. He told her that Janey was the victim that they found in the cave." His lips tightened grimly. "And then he gave her details about exactly what he did to her child."

"Oh, my God," Eve whispered.

"She collapsed, and her husband grabbed the phone. But the man had hung up. Ellen Bristol is hysterical, and her husband isn't much better." Slindak muttered a curse as he heard an outcry from the reporters, who were running across the lawn toward them. "Get her out of that car and inside the house! They've recognized me."

Joe was already around the car and jerking open Eve's door. "Come on, move."

Eve was out of the car and running toward the front door.

But she was too late. They'd recognized Eve as well. She was surrounded by reporters and photographers. Bulbs were flashing in her face. Questions were being hammered at her.

"What are you doing here, Ms. Duncan?"

"Did you receive a similar call?"

"Has your daughter's body been found?"

"No comment." Joe muscled his way through the mob and took her wrist and pulled her toward the front door. "She's just here as a gesture of sympathy toward the Bristols. Now give her space, dammit."

"Inside." Slindak was throwing open the front door.

Joe pushed Eve over the threshold, then followed her and turned to the reporters. "You'll get a story when we have one to give." He slammed the door.

Eve was pressed against the wall of the foyer. She shuddered. "I felt as if they were going to devour me."

"No wonder you were so wary of the media when I first came down here." He turned to a tall, dark-haired officer who was standing attention just inside the living room. "Where is Mrs. Bristol?"

"Upstairs with the doctor and her husband, Agent Quinn." The officer shook his head. "She's in a bad way."

"What a surprise." Eve drew a ragged breath. "I'm surprised she's not in the hospital. But what I want to know is how all those reporters knew about that call. Surely the Bristols didn't phone them."

"You'll have to ask Detective Slindak."

"I intend to do that," Joe said. "Do you know when the Bristols received the call?"

"About nine forty this morning. We were called in about ten. The media started arriving about ten fifty-five. It was all happening pretty—"

"Shit." Slindak barreled through the door and slammed it behind him. "I feel like a damned rock star. They were practically tearing me apart." He looked at Eve. "Are you all right?"

She nodded. "I should be used to it. But I'm not."

"I'll have an officer drive you home as soon as I can."

"No, you won't," Joe said. "They'll follow and camp out. I'll find someplace else for her."

"That doesn't matter," Eve said impatiently. "What happened here? How did those reporters know that Ellen Bristol got that call?"

"They got calls themselves. At least CNN and the *Atlanta Constitution* received calls from the killer. The other stations were tipped off when they started moving."

"What kind of calls?" Joe asked.

"Similar to the one Ellen Bristol received." Slindak paused. "And they were told that Ellen Bristol had been phoned. I suppose just to make sure that she was roasted over the flames a little more."

"How vindictive can you be?" Eve asked.

"Evidently there aren't any bounds," Joe said. "What was the content of the call? Are we sure it wasn't just some weirdo wanting to take credit for the murder? He could have read the newspaper account the hunters had given."

Slindak shook his head. "He knew other details. The placement of the body. The fact that one of her tennis shoes was thrown in the far corner." He paused. "I think that he killed her, Joe."

"Then why don't you catch him?" The man who had spoken was coming down the stairs. George Bristol was a man in his early forties, with a high forehead and blue eyes that were glittering with moisture. "Why did you let him do this to us? Why did you let him do this to Janey?"

"I'm sorry, Mr. Bristol," Slindak said quietly. "I don't wish to intrude on your grief, but I wonder if I could speak to you regarding the call? It would help us to track him."

"I didn't talk to him. Ellen was the only one—and she can't talk to anyone right now. It nearly drove her into hysterics telling me what he said. You'll have to make do with my report." He had reached the bottom of the stairs, and his glance fell on Eve leaning against the wall. "You're Eve Duncan."

"Yes."

"Last night, when I heard they'd found a little girl in that cave, I hoped it was your daughter. Terrible, isn't it? But I hoped it was anyone's daughter but mine. Anyone but Janey."

"I understand," Eve said unsteadily.

"Yes, you would understand." He closed his eyes for an instant, then opened them. "What are you doing here?"

"I wanted to help. I didn't know about—I wanted to help."

"Thank you. But you can't help us. No one can. You can't bring my baby back. You can't stop those foul things that monster did to her. Do you know what he said when Ellen asked for his name? He said to call him Zeus because he was as powerful as a god. He could reach out and take and destroy and no one could ever stop him. And then he started to tell my wife what he meant. Ellen said he sounded as if he liked it, that he was proud." He shook his head in wonder. "He'd have to be Satan to enjoy hurting a sweet little girl like Janey. Maybe he is Satan. Do you think that could be true?"

"I don't know," Eve said. "Whoever he is, I hope we can catch and punish him."

"I want him punished. I'd like to kill him myself. But it's

too late for Janey." He turned back to Slindak. "If you'll send someone, I'll give a statement, but I can't leave my wife."

"That won't be necessary," Slindak said gently. "I'll have someone here later today if you think you won't be too tired to do it."

"I can do it." He started back up the stairs. "It doesn't matter if I'm tired. It has to be done."

"One question, Mr. Bristol," Joe said. "Was there any accent, any indication of where the caller might be from? Southern accent? Midwest? New York? Did he sound like anyone to whom she might previously have spoken?"

"I think Ellen would have told me if she'd recognized the voice. And she wasn't concerned with accents. She was listening to what he was saying." He was going slowly up the stairs. "I believe that's all she'll ever remember."

"If you get the opportunity, would you ask her?" Joe asked.

"Don't expect anything anytime soon. The doctor is going to keep her unconscious for a while, then bring her back very slowly. He's hoping to keep her from having a complete breakdown." He looked back over his shoulder at Eve. "I'll pray for you. I can afford to do it now. But I don't think it will do any good."

"If I can help you . . ." Eve broke off as George Bristol turned the corner of the stairs and was lost to view. She turned to Joe, her eyes swimming with tears. "Why? Why would he call and taunt them?"

Joe didn't answer. He turned to Slindak. "Did the newspaper or TV station he called manage to tape or trace the call?"

"No, the calls were made one after the other with no advance notice. They weren't expecting it. He asked for the program director at CNN. At the newspaper he asked for Brian McVey, who wrote the article in this morning's paper. McVey tried to put him on hold and stall, but he hung up."

"Damn. But at least we can talk to them and ask the questions we can't ask Ellen Bristol."

"If they'll answer," Slindak said sourly. "They may want to protect their story."

"They'll answer," Joe said grimly. "They'll tell me everything I want to know." He turned back to Eve. "Come on. I'll check you into my hotel. Those reporters may be camped out in front of your house."

He took out his car keys and tossed them to Slindak. "Get one of your officers to drive my car outside the subdivision to the gas station on the corner and leave it there. Eve and I will go out the back door, cut across the yard, and try to lose ourselves in the subdivision."

Slindak nodded. "It's your best shot. You'll probably be seen, but we've ordered the media not to trespass on the Bristols' property." He made a face. "Not that they don't break the rules when the stakes seem high enough. But it will give you a little time." He gave the keys to the officer guarding the door. "You heard him, Dunigan. See if you can't lose them if they follow you. Then report back here." As the door closed behind him, he turned back to Joe. "This is nasty. But it may be a break for us. At least we're not dealing with a phantom any longer."

"No, I think that the Bristols would agree that it wasn't a phantom that savaged them today," Joe said.

"I'll go out in front and give a statement," Slindak said. "That should distract them until you get out of here."

"Thanks." He took Eve's arm. "Let's see if we can find that back door."

She nodded. "The kitchen." She was already moving down the hall. "There it is to the right."

A moment later, they were on the deck outside the kitchen door. A chain-link fence. No back gate.

"We go over the fence," he said. "Then cross the backyard next door and keep on moving. At the end of the block, we turn north one block and double back toward the subdivision entrance. Okay?"

She nodded and ran down the steps. "Stop planning and start moving."

He glanced around, but couldn't spot any media. That didn't mean they weren't under observation. But Slindak might have drawn them away. They might get lucky. He followed Eve, who was already across the yard and had entered the bed of daffodils bordering the fence.

She slipped and almost fell. "Be careful. Mud."

He nodded. "Irrigation. There's a price for these nice lawns and landscapes." He helped her across the fence and climbed after her. "Run!"

JOE GLANCED OVER HIS shoulder as he opened the car door for Eve at the gas station. "I think we made it. I'll drive around for five or ten minutes to make sure that we're not being followed."

"I feel as if I'm in some Alfred Hitchcock movie. Jumping over fences, dodging from yard to yard," she said as she got into the car. "This isn't right. It's not the media that we should be afraid of."

"We're not afraid." He drove out of the gas station onto the street. "We're just avoiding an unnecessary annoyance. And getting you to a place where you'll not be hurt by their questions. You looked like a butterfly being stabbed by a dozen pins when they surrounded you."

"You got me away from them." She was gazing out the window. "I'm used to the reporters now. I was more shocked by what had happened to the Bristols than I was about being attacked by them. I was just too stunned to react. It was the last thing I expected." She looked at him. "You didn't answer me. He called those poor people and the media. He hadn't done anything like that before. Do you have any idea why he would do it now?"

"Maybe. Ellen Bristol said that he sounded proud when he told her about killing Janey."

Eve shuddered. "Horrible."

"Yes, but it may be the key to why he made the call. He's proud of his cleverness, he's proud that he's managed to kill and never been close to being caught."

"Then why would he be this reckless and risk everything?"

"But you see, no one knows how clever he is. No one knows what power he has. It may have been enough for him to have this delicious secret for all these years. But now that his confidence has grown, and he thinks that no one can touch him, he's ready to be admired by one and all. He even gave himself a name, Zeus, so that there's no question of anonymity."

"Power," she murmured. "Who has more power than a god?"

"And Zeus was far from virtuous and completely absorbed in his power. The choice was logical."

"Is that hunger for fame common in serial killers?"

"It's not uncommon. Some are satisfied to stay beneath the radar for their entire career. Others get restless and want to thumb their noses at authority and show their power. My guess is that maybe when they found the remains of that little boy by the freeway, he got a taste of notoriety and liked it. Then when the news story appeared in the paper this morning, he was primed to exploit it and show everyone what a truly superior fiend he was. That call to the media wasn't only to twist the knife in the Bristol family. He was hungry for more attention, more fame." He shrugged. "But often that need for public attention only lasts for a limited amount of time, and they go underground again."

"So he may not make any other calls?"

"As I said, it's not predictable."

"But if he did call again, you'd have a chance of catching him. The newspapers wouldn't be caught off guard again, they'd be prepared. You could set up ways to trace him."

"If."

"But Slindak said this may be a break in the case. Dammit, stop being negative."

"I told you I'd never lie to you. Any change in the status quo offers opportunities, but it's not a sure thing. I've briefed you on all the theories and my experience with them, and that's all I can do."

"So what are you going to do? Are we still going to that shoe factory downtown?"

"No, I'll give that job to one of Slindak's men. I have to go and question Brian McVey and that program director from CNN." He added emphatically, "And you are not going with me. I want answers, and all I'd get would be questions from them if you were within viewing distance."

"I'm not arguing. I realize I'd be a distraction."

Since the moment he'd seen her. "As I said, you can check into the Hyatt. The media may still track you down, but we won't make it easy for them."

She shook her head. "Too expensive. I'll be fine at the house."

"I'll put you on my expense account."

"You wouldn't do that. You're too honest. Which means you'd probably be paying for it out of your own pocket."

"One night. Just enough time to take the heat off," he coaxed. "Otherwise, I'd feel obligated to camp out in front of the house. It's worth paying for your room just to make sure I get a good night's sleep."

"It's not worth it to me." She paused. "There's a cheap motel about two miles from the house. I'll check in there with my mother for tonight. I don't need the Hyatt." She made a face. "I'm no fancy Easterner who has to have room service and a concierge."

"Yeah, guys like me need a lot of care and nurturing. Otherwise, we just wither away. Where is this motel? I'll take you there, then go to your house and pick up your mother and have her choose some clothes to pack for you."

"I can call her."

"Where is the hotel?" he repeated.

"It's the Rainbow Inn on Piedmont."

"Sounds very whimsical."

"Not very. You'll turn up your nose at it." She leaned wearily back in the seat. "Ask me if I care."

"After my stint in the Middle East, it takes a lot to make me turn up my nose. If it has a shower, I'm good with it."

"It has a shower." She was silent for a moment. "Mr. Bristol said he'd pray for me. I'd rather he prayed for Bonnie. But he doesn't think she's alive. When he was talking, I was having trouble . . . I still have a chance. Things were different in her pattern from the other children who— I have a chance."

"George Bristol is a man in pain. He probably doesn't realize what he's saying."

"He knows." She was silent again. "We've got to find that monster, Joe. For all those children, their parents. For Bonnie. He mustn't be allowed to be proud of killing any more children. He's got to be stopped."

For Bonnie.

She was getting closer and closer to accepting that her daughter could be dead.

"That's what we're trying to do."

"Not 'trying.' We've got to do it."

She didn't speak again until they arrived at the Rainbow Inn.

He gazed at the small one-story economy motel skeptically. It appeared in fair repair but had probably been built at least thirty years before. "Definitely no whimsy. You're sure it has a shower?"

"I'm sure." She got out of the car. "And telephones. Will you call me after you talk to CNN and Brian McVey?"

He nodded. "Or I'll tell you in person after I've finished with them, and I bring your mother here."

"I'll call her and tell her to come in my car. I might need it."

"No, she might be followed, and all this would be for nothing. I'll make sure we're not tailed. Do you need anything besides a change of clothes?"

"Tell her to bring my notebook and that box of missing person's reports. I have to go over everything again. There has to be something there that we missed." She moved toward the office, and there was a touch of despair mixed with the frustration in her voice. "He's being so damn reckless. He has to have done something that will give us a lead."

Joe backed the car out of the lot after the door shut behind her.

He couldn't blame Eve for the exasperation that been founded on fear. Today had been a bad day for her, a complete roller-coaster ride. She had identified with the Bristols, and George Bristol's certainty that Bonnie was dead had come as a shock. No matter how often she told herself that was a possibility, she couldn't accept that it might be true.

How the hell would he handle it when she could no longer deny that the distant horror was a reality? And he could see that nightmare hovering on the horizon. Eve was taking comfort in the exceptions, the differences. He was seeing the similarities, and his experience and instincts were scaring him. He could try to prepare her, but at some point she would block him out and stop listening. It would be a purely self-defensive device.

Stop worrying about something he couldn't change. He'd

face that problem when he had to. He checked the address and phone for the *Atlanta Constitution*.

Now his problem was Brian McVey.

"I DON'T HAVE TO ANSWER your questions, you know." McVey leaned back in his chair. "I gave Detective Slindak a statement, so I'm not impeding the progress of the investigation. I could send you back to him."

"You could," Joe said. "But you're a young reporter on your way up. You don't want to antagonize anyone if you don't have to. You're going to have enough enemies."

"You think so?" McVey chuckled. "That's what journalism is all about. A lot of people don't like the truth."

"Particularly in stories like the one you wrote about the hunters finding Janey Bristol's body. It was pretty grisly."

"But all true." His smile was cocky. "I was the first one to get the story, and I ran with it. And the public loves a little blood with their morning coffee."

"You'd know that better than I."

McVey's smile faded. "Don't be so patronizing. I've done my research on you. I may write about it, but I don't kill. While I understand you were absolutely terrific at it. Who stinks the most, Quinn?"

"I suppose it's a matter of perception."

McVey nodded. "And I'll win a Pulitzer before I'm thirty, and you'll still be hunting crazies for the next twenty years."

"Entirely possible. But you'll not win a Pulitzer by publishing crime-scene details just to appeal to the masses."

"Why not? I gave everyone what they wanted, and I didn't hurt anyone." He met Joe's eyes. "I could have described the bits of clothing that would have tipped the ID in Janey Bristol's direction. I didn't go that far. I decided to let the police get a firm ID before I laid that on the Bristols."

It was a restraint Joe hadn't expected. "It was still a shock to every one of the parents of those missing children."

"Give me a break. I'm no angel. But I do have a few scruples."

"As long as they don't get in the way of your Pulitzer."

"You're laughing, but I meant it. You have to have a goal, and I'm aiming at the big prize." He sat forward, his eyes sparkling with enthusiasm. "And I'm on my way. How would I know that first story on the hunters would get me an interview with the killer himself? It was fate."

"No, it was your byline on a story that stroked the monster's ego," Joe said dryly.

"Whatever. It happened, and next time he calls, I'll have a tape recorder and—"

"You think he'll call you again?"

"Why not? I listened. I figure he wanted an audience, and I gave him what he wanted." He grimaced. "Though it made me want to puke."

"But anything for the Pulitzer."

"Well, I did try to ask him questions, but he ran right over me. But that could be good. I didn't make him mad, and that could mean he'll call me again. Lots of reporters have formed relationships, even friendships, with killers."

"I wouldn't count on it. He called CNN, too. I don't think you're that special to him."

McVey's face fell with disappointment. "I can hope. In the meantime, I can milk the story for all it's worth. Would you like to comment? I don't have an FBI quote."

"I'd like a few comments from you."

"Exchange?"

It would be easier than using force or threats. Joe nodded. "Did he say anything different to you than what he told Ellen Bristol?"

McVey shook his head. "Not from what I can tell from what Slindak told me. He made a big thing about calling himself Zeus. I think he wanted to make sure I had that for the story. Maybe like the Zodiac Killer or something. All the rest of the details were vague except about the murder itself. He was very explicit about that."

"Would you recognize the voice if you heard it again? Was it distinctive?"

"I'd recognize it. It was deep and smooth."

"No accents?"

He shook his head. "Hard to tell. Not Southern. Just . . . American."

"Well, that helps," Joe said sarcastically.

"Sorry, I'm no elocution expert. I even tried to concentrate while he was talking because I knew it would be important, but I couldn't tell anything." He stopped. "There was one thing. House."

"What?"

"He mentioned watching the Bristol house. He said the word a couple times. House. Only it didn't sound quite the same as we say it."

"What was the difference?"

He shook his head. "It's hard . . . It was almost the same."

"You're sure he was American?"

He nodded. "Everything was the same except for that one word."

"What kind of emotion? What was he feeling?"

McVey thought about it. "Excitement. Eagerness. Pride. He was speaking quickly, with energy."

"Did he mention any other children?"

"No, not specifically." His eyes suddenly narrowed. "You were with Eve Duncan at the Bristol place. Has she been contacted?"

"No."

"Pity. She's interesting. All the other parents are steady, ordinary couples. Boring. A young woman who has an illegitimate child sparks the imagination. Why was she at the Bristols'?"

"You'll have to ask her."

"I can't. I tried, but she wasn't at her house. Did you hide her away?"

"Now why would I do that? Surely you and your colleagues wouldn't bother a grieving woman. You do have some scruples."

"I'll find her," McVey said softly. "It's the story of a lifetime, and she's part of it. I don't know what chapter she's in, but I'll find out."

"Leave her alone, McVey. You don't want to deal with me."

McVey studied him. "No, but I'll do it. It would be worth it." He paused and picked up his pencil. "Now, what's my quote?"

"The FBI is aiding the investigation of the ATLPD and offering the full services of the Bureau. We're making progress and hope to have a break in the case soon."

"Got it." McVey looked up. "Anything else?"

"Yes." Joe turned and started down the aisle toward the door. "Go screw yourself."

"THAT'S ALL?" Eve asked, disappointed.

"It's more than we had before," he said. "We'll have to work with it. But I think you'd better stay away from your house for a few days more. McVey is going to be persistent. He's a very ambitious man, and he's got his teeth into this story."

"I'm not going into hiding. I can't afford it, and it makes me angry. I'm going home tomorrow."

He shrugged. "I tried. I didn't think I'd succeed." He nodded at the box he'd brought into the motel room and set on the coffee table. "There are the reports. I suppose you're going to tackle them again?"

"Yes, I'm going to look at Janey Bristol. Did you receive the dental-record confirmation?"

"Yes, it came in right before I stopped to pick up your mother. I'm afraid I failed in my mission. She wouldn't come with me."

"I know. She said if she couldn't spend the night at home that she'd go to stay with Pastor Nambrey and his wife. They are always inviting her," she said. "It was definitely Janey Bristol?"

"Yes."

"Poor little girl." She shook her head. "Do you know I just felt a rush of relief? I'm like George Bristol. I wanted it to be anyone but Bonnie. He said he was terrible. I guess we're all ruthless when it comes to protecting our children." She paused. "If I still have a daughter to protect." She went on haltingly, "But I was thinking about what you said about that skull being hard to ID unless you knew where to find the dental records. What if you didn't have any idea who that victim was? She might be lost forever, maybe buried by the county in a nameless grave with her parents never knowing. It breaks my heart to think about it. There are a lot of victims like that, aren't there, Joe?"

He nodded. "Too many."

"It breaks my heart," she repeated. "What if it were—" She drew a deep breath and gestured to the boxes. "Thank you for bringing these."

"That sounds like a dismissal."

"You don't want to go over these records again. Things are moving for you. You have things to do."

"And you don't want me to be here."

She met his gaze. "No, I don't. I have some thinking to do, and I want to be alone to do it. I don't want to be soothed or protected. I've been leaning on you too much."

"I haven't noticed."

"And I don't want to look at you and know that you're wondering how I'll survive when I find out my Bonnie is dead." She added jerkily, "You've been very kind, but I need a break from you, Joe. Get out of my life for a while."

He hadn't realized he was that transparent to her. But Eve was intelligent and more savvy about people than anyone he had run across. Even upset as she had been today, she had managed to pick up on all the signals he had not wanted her to see. Damage control was clearly necessary. "What about throwing me out after dinner? You have to eat, and I'd bet this place doesn't have room service."

She smiled faintly. "I've been rude as hell, and you still try to take care of me."

"It's beginning to be a habit. I like it. I never had a cat or a puppy when I was kid. I was always envious of the kids on TV who had animals. You're supplying a need."

Her smile widened. "You're nuts. I refuse to be a substitute for Lassie."

"Dinner?"

Her smile faded. "No, I meant it. I need to be alone and think. What happened today may . . . it could open a door."

"What door?"

"I don't know. That's why I have to think about it." She added pointedly, "Without you to question me while I'm doing it."

She was determined. Okay, back off before she tossed him out on a permanent basis. "No problem." He turned away. "If I hear anything that might interest you, I'll be in touch. Call me if you need me."

"Thanks, Joe."

"You're welcome." He smiled at her over his shoulder. "But I'll stop at that pizza restaurant across the street and ask them to deliver a pizza and a drink to you in about an hour."

"Joe . . ."

"I'd do the same for Lassie."

His smile vanished as he shut the door and strode toward his car. It was going to be hard as hell to give her space. He wanted to hover, build a wall, keep all the ugliness away from her.

And he didn't like the fact that she was distancing herself from him. She had gone through a tremendously painful experience at the Bristols'. Instead of it drawing her closer to him,

she had become quieter, more independent. He had been almost able to see her strengthen as each blow had struck her.

If he hadn't cared before, that courage would have made
him love her.

He stopped at the pizza restaurant and sat in the car for a
moment. No, he couldn't go back. He would do what he'd told
her he'd do.

Be patient. Keep in contact, but give her a moderate amount
of space. Do his job and find the bastard who had killed her
Bonnie.

And be ready to catch Eve when she was downed by that
final horrible blow.

CHAPTER
6

"**WE GOT THE REPORT** on the print on the shoe." Slindak stopped by Joe's desk the next afternoon and handed him a sheet of paper. "He's big. Size thirteen. It's a work shoe, but it's not the usual model built for construction workers. The pattern on the soul is different and deeper. It's not a product of any of the major U.S. companies. Schweitzer, the owner of the shoe company, is going through his catalogs and seeing if he can locate where it was purchased."

"Different and deeper," Joe repeated. "What the hell is that supposed to mean?"

"I suppose we'll know when Schweitzer gets back to us."

"That's not good enough. I'm calling the Bureau and getting them on it." Joe reached for the phone. "I'll make a copy of this before I give it back to you."

"Suit yourself. My feelings won't be hurt. That's why we

called you into the case." Slindak strolled across the room toward his desk.

Joe finished his call and leaned back in his chair. Call Eve and tell her what they'd learned? Which was virtually nothing as yet.

Hell, yes. It was a reason to make contact. She had only been going to spend the one night at the motel. She should be home now. He was about to dial again when the phone rang.

"Mr. Quinn?" It was Sandra Duncan's soft, Southern voice. "I do hope you'll excuse me for phoning you. It's really nothing, but you've been so nice to me I just knew you wouldn't mind me bothering you."

"You're right. I'll be glad to help you. Are you still at Pastor Nambrey's? Do you need a ride home?"

"No, Eve doesn't want me to come home yet. She said I was to stay at the pastor's until she called me."

Joe's hand stiffened on the receiver. "That's . . . strange."

"That's what I thought, but Eve didn't want to talk about it." She hesitated. "Eve's been real upset. You know that. I just wanted to make sure that she wasn't— It was such an odd call."

"You believe she might try to hurt herself?"

"I don't think so. Not when she's so set on finding Bonnie. But she was firing all kinds of orders at me and wouldn't answer questions. Then she just hung up."

"What orders?"

"Not to come home. Not to pay any attention to the afternoon papers or anything else. To stay with the pastor and not go with anyone I don't know. Don't you think that's peculiar?"

"Yes, very peculiar." His heart was pounding, and all he

wanted to do was to get off this damn phone. "But I'm sure she has a reason for everything she said. She'll be fine." God, he hoped he was telling the truth. "And it's probably best to do exactly what she told you."

"Well, I did promise her. But I thought that maybe you knew more, and I could find out what Eve was talking about. I know how much Eve trusts you."

That was more than he knew, Joe thought grimly. "No, she didn't confide in me. I have go now, Mrs. Duncan. I'm sure Eve will be fine. If you have any other concerns, just call me."

"I knew you wouldn't mind me phoning you. I do feel better after talking to you. Sharing always helps, doesn't it?" She didn't wait for an answer but hung up.

Sandra's sharing didn't make him feel better, Joe thought as he jumped to his feet. It was scaring him to death.

He had to get his hands on the afternoon paper. There was a machine downstairs.

Suicide? Yesterday had been a nightmare for her, and he'd known she was coming closer to accepting that her daughter was dead.

But she had been stronger than he had ever seen her last night before he had left her.

Yet she had pushed him away, and he hadn't been able to persuade her otherwise. She would know that he wouldn't let her harm herself.

He didn't wait for the elevator, but ran down the stairs. The newsboy was cutting the cord on the pile of newspapers that had just been delivered. Joe snatched up the top newspaper.

Son of a bitch.

"What the hell is she doing?" Slindak had come up behind him. His expression was tense as he grabbed another newspaper. "The captain just called me from a meeting at the mayor's office. He wants to know if we had anything to do with this. Did we?"

"Hell, no."

There was a photo of Eve on the front page. She looked sober, but her chin was lifted defiantly. That gesture was the theme for the entire story below the photo.

The story was written by Brian McVey.

"I'm going to murder him," Joe muttered as his gaze scanned the interview.

It led off with an emotional introduction to Eve Duncan, who had lost her child. Then it went to the Q&A directly following.

Q. "You've heard about the death of Janey Bristol. Do you believe that your daughter was taken by the same killer?"

A. "It's possible. The man who killed Janey Bristol was obviously a coward who only has the nerve to prey on children. Adult interaction obviously terrifies him. He was so stupid he didn't even hide the child's body but left it in that cave to be discovered."

Q. "Stupid? He's allegedly killed at least nine children without being apprehended."

A. "Children. He's a moron who is only capable of attacking and overcoming little children like Janey. That's why he concentrates only on them. It takes logic and intelligence to attack adults. Someone told me that killers like him are into power. Since he'd be defeated by anyone other than a five-year-old, he'll probably continue to kill help-less children. He won't attempt to attack anyone who might challenge him."

The article continued for another two columns, but it was all in the same insulting vein.

Slindak gave a low whistle. "Ugly. She couldn't be more insulting. Is she trying to get herself killed?"

"Don't ask me," he said through his teeth. "She didn't consult me about this insanity."

"And I thought you were so close," Slindak murmured.

"Not now," Joe said curtly. "I'm very near to blowing, Slindak."

"I can see that." He added, "But I told you that there was the danger of not being able to control her. Now she's going to cause us a hell of—"

"I know what she's doing." He strode over to the lobby telephone booth. "And she would have done this if I'd never shown up here in Atlanta. She'd have found a way to reach out to the bastard."

"Reach out? She bludgeoned him. Are you calling her?"

He was trying. But she wasn't picking up on her home phone. She could be there, but not answering. He hung up. "I'm going to her place and talk to her."

"You may have to stand in line. She could have made Zeus mad enough to want to have his own discussion with her." Slindak added, "The captain isn't going to be happy if Eve Duncan ends up in a cave with her skull on a shelf. We're getting enough heat without that maniac expanding his chosen field."

"Dammit, it won't happen. She *won't* be killed." He tore out of the precinct and down the steps.

Thirty minutes later, he was at the house on Morningside. No answer when he rang. The front door was locked. He went around to the back porch. No answer there.

What the hell? He jimmied the window and climbed into the kitchen.

Five minutes later, he'd searched every room in the house, and Eve was not to be found.

But there was an envelope on the kitchen table.

Joe

He tore it open.

You'll be angry, but I had to do this. It's my chance. You told me that this monster is all ego, and I thought this way I could draw him closer to me.

You wouldn't let me do that, but McVey has no qualms about it. As you said, he's hungry. He doesn't care about anything but getting his story.

Isn't that lucky for me?

Thank you, Joe.

Eve

His hand clenched on the paper.

Lucky.

Yeah, lucky enough to have that bastard zero in on her and slice her to pieces.

QUINN   115

Cool down. Panic wouldn't get him anywhere. He had to find her, talk to her, persuade her to step back and away from acting as bait for McVey.

Find her.

She wasn't in the house. Her mother didn't know where she'd gone. But she was working with Brian McVey. He might have thought he was using her, but he'd soon find out differently. Eve would be in control.

He called the *Atlanta Constitution*.

Brian McVey had taken an indefinite leave of absence and could not be contacted.

Strike one.

The hell he couldn't be contacted. He called the ATLPD and had a clerk pull out all the profile information they could gather on McVey.

"What are you doing?" Slindak came on the line. "What does Duncan say?"

"I'd know if I could get hold of her," Joe said. "She's not home. I think that McVey has her stashed somewhere while he runs these stories. Get off the line and let me get the info I need."

"I've got it here. McVey has an apartment in Dunwoody—1321 Ashford."

"That would be too easy. Anything else?"

"Let me see . . . He inherited a house from his mother two years ago. It doesn't say whether he sold it or still has possession."

"Address."

"It's 4961 Rosecreek Drive. It's near Lake Allatoona." He paused. "McVey's story has caused a buzz with the rest of the media. There was lot of talk on the local TV news this evening. Including Eve Duncan's quotes."

"That doesn't surprise me. McVey might have even given them a call."

"And shared his story? Not likely."

"To stir the pot. To add the final irritant that would make an explosion certain. Anything else you can tell me about McVey?"

"I can tell you he's a member of the press, and you should be careful what you do to him. I know you're pissed at the hot spot he's put Eve Duncan on, but he can cause us big-time trouble."

"Ask me if I care." He hung up.

The apartment in Dunwoody or the house near Lake Allatoona?

The Dunwoody apartment was closer, and he didn't know whether McVey still owned the house he'd inherited.

But his instincts were leaning toward Lake Allatoona. He called the telephone company, identified himself, and asked if there was still a telephone connection at 4961 Rosecreek Drive.

Yes.

Private number.

Joe waited for the operator to call Washington on another line and check his authority. Five minutes later he had the number.

Name of party holding the service?

Edna McVey.

Brian McVey had never changed the name and evidently occasionally still used the house.

Okay, phone the number he'd been given?

If Eve was there, then she'd be given time to leave before he could get there.

He strode out of the house and jumped in his car.

THE MCVEY PLACE ON ROSECREEK Drive was a pleasant two-story cottage only a few hundred yards from the edge of Lake Allatoona. Its gray sideboard needed painting, but there was a cane rocking chair on the wide porch that gave the place a comfortable ambience.

There was light gleaming from windows on the first floor.

Joe cursed softly. Nothing like leaving a welcoming beacon.

He parked his car a good distance away from the house and moved silently into the woods.

He was a hundred yards to the rear of the cottage when he knew someone was following him.

He paused, listening.

To the left, in the brush.

He faded into the stand of trees to the right.

A sudden crashing of shrubs to the left.

Definitely following him.

He circled swiftly, silently, to the left to get behind the pursuer.

A male figure in a black Windbreaker was now moving ahead of him.

Now.

He covered the distance between them in seconds and brought him down.

The man started to struggle frantically.

Joe's hand tangled in his hair and jerked back hard as the edge of his knife was pressed to the man's throat. "Don't move, or I'll cut your throat."

The man froze. "For God's sake, Quinn. What are you doing? Let me go."

McVey.

"Why should I, you son of a bitch?" He deliberately pressed the edge of the knife a little harder so that it broke the skin. "I'm a little angry with you. Maybe you can tell."

McVey went rigid. "I can tell. But I don't think you're pissed enough to commit murder."

"But you told me that I was so good at it."

"Let me up, Quinn. You know you're just toying with me."

Joe drew a deep breath. "Toying"? McVey didn't know how close he'd come. All of Joe's training, his instincts, the savagery that had been both his friend and his enemy had come racing back in that moment.

"Let him go. What are you doing, Joe?"

He looked over his shoulder to see Eve standing with a gun pointed at him.

"A gun, Eve? Did McVey give you that gun? He probably thought you'd need it if you were going to have to rely on him."

"I asked him for a weapon," Eve said as she lowered the gun. "But I don't need to use it against you, Joe. Dammit, you scared me. I thought you were going to— Let him go."

Joe shrugged and took the knife from McVey's throat. "It

was a close call for him. I was mad as hell, and the bastard decided to follow me. I thought he was a threat." He got off McVey and stood up. "As much threat as a day-old Chihuahua."

"You cut me." McVey's fingers were on his throat and came away with blood on them. "You knew who I was, and you still cut me."

"I cut you *because* of who you are, you son of a bitch. Maybe I should tie you up on the front porch and see how you like being bait. You've got our killer all primed. He's probably almost as angry with you as with Eve. What do you think he'd do to you if he found you helpless?"

"None of this was McVey's idea," Eve said. "It was all mine, Joe. I called him and sketched it out to him."

"And he jumped at it."

"Of course, I did," McVey said as he got to his feet. "Do you think I'd turn my back on a chance like this? I told you that I'd do whatever I had to do." He glared defiantly at Joe. "I didn't go out of my way to cause a killer to go after her. That wasn't my fault. But I wasn't going to say no if she wanted to run the risk. Hell, if we catch Zeus, it might mean that we'd save some other kids. What's wrong with that?"

"You sound almost noble, McVey."

"Stop this, Joe." Eve turned to McVey. "Come back to the house and I'll try to find something to put on that cut." She glanced at Joe. "You're not going away, are you? I can't convince you."

"You can't convince me."

"Then I suppose you'll have to come with us, and we'll

talk." She turned and strode toward the house, with McVey at her heels.

Joe watched them until they reached the porch, then faded back into the brush.

"**WHERE HAVE YOU BEEN?**" Eve was standing waiting on the porch when Joe came toward her twenty minutes later. "I didn't know what had happened to you."

"Were you worried? Good. I was worried about you, too. And with a hell of a lot more reason."

"Where have you been?" she repeated.

"You decided to declare war on Zeus. This evidently was going to be your first battle site. I know about war. First, you familiarize yourself with the terrain and the places that lend themselves to ambush. While you're doing it, you make sure the enemy isn't already within the gates."

"That's what McVey was trying to do."

"Not well. He'd have had his throat cut, and the way to you would have been open. Where is he?"

"Inside. He's calling in tomorrow's story."

Joe muttered a curse.

"Do you want to go in and cut him again?" she asked sarcastically.

"It's tempting."

She shook her head in exasperation. "For God's sake, be civilized. This isn't his fault."

"But there's a wide streak in me that isn't at all civilized. I think you've always sensed that. If you'll be honest, you'll admit that's one of the reasons that you thought that I could help you find Bonnie. You didn't want some slick, dutiful cop who would make all the right moves. You wanted *me*. Because you knew I'd break any rule I had to break to get what I wanted. Isn't that the truth? Well, you can't have it both ways. You wanted me. You've got me. And there's no way I'll let you turn your back on me."

She stared at him, her expression a mixture of frustration, anger, and something else that he couldn't define. "Damn you, Joe. Okay, come in and talk. But don't you dare hurt McVey." She turned on her heel and opened the front door.

"I'll try to resist." He followed her and glanced around the living room. Nothing fancy. The furniture was contemporary, but there were doilies on the arms of the blue denim couch. Probably another legacy from McVey's mother. It surprised him that McVey hadn't stored them away. He wouldn't have thought the reporter would be that sentimental. "McVey must not use this house much."

"Only an occasional weekend. He told me he has a boat that's stored at the marina a few miles away." Eve led him down the hall to the kitchen. "But it was convenient for our purpose. Private. Out of the way. And he still had the phone service connected. Since he's a reporter, he has to be reachable even on his time off."

"Yeah, very convenient. It wouldn't do to invite a killer to a place that wasn't isolated. He might not accept the invitation."

"That's right." She poured him a cup of coffee. "You might as well sit down. Though you can cut the sarcasm. I got the point. You don't have to belabor it."

"I'll try." He dropped down in a white chair at the kitchen table. "I'm having trouble with control at the moment."

"That couldn't be clearer." She poured herself a cup of coffee. "I think you scared McVey."

"He should have been scared."

She sat down opposite him. "I never saw you like that before."

"But you always knew it was there, didn't you?" He stared directly into her eyes. "You said you grew up with violence all around you. Well, violence isn't confined to the housing projects. It can exist anywhere. It may be a breeding ground, but you have to have someone to throw out the seeds."

"And you're a regular Johnny Appleseed," she said dryly. "I didn't expect you to get so angry. And I didn't think you'd track me down so quickly. I thought I'd have time."

"It wasn't that difficult. I just had to stretch a little. Time for what? It's obvious to anyone that you're trying to set yourself up as bait. Would you like to tell me how you expect to do it without getting yourself killed?"

She glanced away from him. "I expect him to call me. McVey has set up a tracer on the phone. If I can keep him on the phone long enough, I can find out where he is."

"And you don't think he won't suspect that's what you're doing? If he has any brains at all, he'll know why you were so insulting in that interview."

"He'll suspect it. But if he's as egotistical as you think, then he'll still come after me. It would be a feather in his cap to be able to get to me in spite of a trap." She moistened her lips. "And I'm counting on rage. He has to be full of rage if he could do what he did to those children. That's why I was so insulting during the interview. I wanted to trigger that rage."

"I don't believe you'll be disappointed."

"I hope not," she said quietly.

His hand clenched on his cup. "Look, he's crazy. Nothing could be more evident. Crazy people don't react as normal people do. Even when they know that there's danger, they just keep on coming."

"Maybe he won't come after me. We may be able to trace his call and have the police pick him up before it gets that far."

"Eve . . . Dammit."

"Joe . . . Dammit." She smiled unsteadily. "I had to do this. He can't be allowed to go on. I know that the chances aren't wonderful of everything coming out the way I want them. That's why I didn't want you involved. I knew you would try to stop me."

"Damn right, I am."

"Too late, Joe. If he's as crazy as you think, he'll already have his sights on me."

"I could knock you out and have Slindak stuff you in a cell as a material witness."

"And when he let me out, the problem would still be out here waiting for me."

"Not if I find Zeus first."

"What are the chances of that?" She shook her head. "My way is better."

"Your way is as crazy as he is." But he could see that he wasn't budging her. "So what are you doing? Just camping out here and waiting for him to call you?"

"Yes."

"And what if he comes instead of call? That's what I did."

"That's why I had McVey get me a gun. But if I made him angry enough, he won't want to just kill me. He'll want to connect with me, tell me how wrong I am and what he's going to do to me."

"Maybe."

"Am I supposed to argue with you? None of this is written in stone. I'm guessing, based on what you told me about the mind-set of serial killers."

"I should have kept my mouth shut."

She shook her head. "You were trying to help me. You did help me."

"Enough to put you squarely behind the eight ball with the help of Brian McVey."

"Am I hearing my name taken in vain?" McVey strolled into the kitchen, his gaze fixed warily on Joe. "Has Eve convinced you that you shouldn't take my scalp?"

"We hadn't gotten around to discussing you yet," Joe said coolly. "But I doubt if she'd be able to tell me anything about you that would tip the scales."

"I went to him," Eve said. "He only agreed to what I wanted from him. It's entirely my doing."

"I'm insulted," McVey said. "I contributed. I wrote a damn good article. Maybe not Pulitzer quality, but it's the quantity of work that counts in this case. And I furnished the house and the telephone, not to speak of the equipment and technician who's going to trace the dreaded call." He grimaced. "Though it's not really dreaded. It's much anticipated. I admit I want to get this over with as soon as possible. I wasn't expecting you to appear and offer me bodily harm."

"I only offered. If you'd been following the one you'd set this bullshit trap for, you'd be missing a larynx." He paused. "And you've convinced me that you're just as much to blame as I thought. So maybe we should take it outside and start over."

"You will not," Eve said. "Since you won't go away, you'll stop trying to vent your temper on McVey."

"Eve to the rescue," McVey murmured. "I know it's supposed to be the other way around, but I've always believed in women's liberation. It's much more comfortable."

Joe ignored him and stared at Eve. "This is sloppy as hell. It would be a miracle if it worked."

"But our killer isn't neat or tidy. He's sloppy, too. Or should I use the word 'reckless'? Either way, he might take a chance if it suited him."

"I can see that happening and that's why I'm going to call Slindak and have him surround this place," Joe said.

"No, Joe."

"Why the hell not?"

"We may not get the trace. If we don't, then he'll come after me. A police presence would scare him off."

"Exactly."

She shook her head. "He's a monster. He's killed all those children. He may have killed Bonnie. I can't let him get away."

Joe's hands clenched into fists at his sides. It was the one argument for which he had no response. There would be no persuading her because Bonnie and those other children were the only thing that mattered to Eve. She did not care about the possible danger. It didn't matter to her.

"What would you do if I said I was going to do it anyway?"

"I'd go away somewhere you couldn't find me and set up the trap all over again," she said quietly. "I'd have no choice. I don't know how long I can stand feeling this helpless before I break. It has to end."

How could he argue when he was aware of the terrible strain that she was enduring? He had watched her fight it with every bit of her strength and been unable to help her with anything but silent support. Now she had taken the only path she thought she could and still survive. Hell, maybe she was right. Perhaps they were just down to a question of survival.

"Lock the doors and windows." He turned to McVey. "Show me where you've set up the equipment for the trace. I want to check it out. If we're going to do this, we might as well do it right."

"It's in the dining room," McVey said. "But it should be okay. I had a geek who's done stuff like this for me before to set it up. I was going to use it in the newsroom, but then Eve called."

"I'll still look at it." He glanced at Eve. "He may not call tonight. It may take some time for him to search out where you are. And this is a private number. They wouldn't have given it to me if I hadn't been FBI."

"He won't have that much trouble."

"Why not?"

"I figured that he'd try my house and McVey's apartment first. He won't find anything at my house, but I asked McVey to leave a scrawl on a notepad in the office with my name on it and the word 'Allatoona.'"

"And?"

"There's a Rolodex on the other side of the desk. It would

be natural for him to scan through it. This is the only address and phone number in the Rolodex in Allatoona."

"You had it all planned."

"But it all depends on whether he taps McVey's apartment." She smiled faintly. "I tried not to be too 'sloppy.'" She got to her feet. "I'll go lock those doors."

They watched her leave the kitchen.

"Smart lady." McVey looked at Joe. "I expected her to be different. I tried to get an interview with her right after her kid was kidnapped. She was a basket case. She's changed. She took over from the minute she called me on the phone. She trumped me every time."

"And you didn't harass or try to manipulate her? What a surprise."

"Knock it off, Quinn." McVey gave him a sour glance. "Look, I'm still pissed about what you did with that damn knife. Sure I'd have tried to manipulate her. But she wasn't having it. If anyone was manipulated, it was me. And that was fine. I couldn't be happier. All I want is my story. I'm not going to get in your way as long as you know my priorities. You're better at this than I am. Take over."

"I intend to do that."

McVey's brows lifted. "Then you'd better watch out for Eve. She may cause you problems."

He'd had nothing but trouble from Eve since the moment he'd walked into that house on Morningside. Those problems had been escalating lately from hills to mountains. He started down the hall. "I'll worry about that when I have to. Just show me that equipment."

* * *

HE PHONED SLINDAK TWO HOURS later. "Just thought I'd check in. I've located Eve and McVey and I've been trying to persuade them to call off this craziness. No luck so far."

"Do you know McVey has another story running tomorrow? I talked to his editor, and it's almost as inflammatory as the one today. Is the bastard trying to get her killed?"

"It's all Eve. I can't blame McVey this time. Though I'm doing my damnedest. Anything else new?"

"The shoes may have been manufactured either in Buffalo, New York, or Toronto, Canada."

"You said they were different. Did you find out what was different about them?"

"Heavy rubber content in the soles . . . and maybe the uppers. I'll call you back when I contact the manufacturer and find out who would buy a shoe like that."

"Toronto . . ." He remembered something McVey had said. "Check the Canadian connection first. McVey said he thought the man on the phone was American, but that he pronounced the word 'house' a little oddly. I knew several Canadians when I was in the service, and you'd swear they were raised in the U.S. except for tiny differences in pronunciation."

"Toronto, first," Slindak said. "I'll get back to you as soon as I can. Are you at your hotel?"

"No, I'll check back in with you."

A silence. "And you're not going to tell me where you are?"

"I'm with Eve Duncan. You can make what you like of that. You did before."

"I'm not about to make any insinuations. I don't give a damn if you're going to bed with her any longer. In fact, I hope that's what you are doing. It's safer than anything else she might draw you into." He paused. "You're putting a lot on the line for her. Is it worth it?"

Strength, exquisite fragility, intelligence, a smile that was a luminous rainbow in the darkness, the feeling that he was complete only when he was with her.

"She's worth it." He hung up.

He glanced at the clock on kitchen wall.

Eleven forty.

It's close to midnight. Do you believe in the witching hour? Many murderers stage their kills based on superstition or the time of day.

He left the kitchen and strode down the hall to the living room. Eve was sitting in an easy chair beside the fireplace. Her back was straight, and her muscles appeared as tight as her expression.

She smiled with an effort. "Well, is everything satisfactory? I haven't seen you for a couple hours."

"It's as good as it can be." He turned out the overhead lights and dropped down on the couch. "Let's keep this one off. Now it's dim but not dark. There's still light streaming in from the foyer."

She was silent. "You don't want us to be targeted from outside."

"A precaution. I don't think it would happen. He's angry, and he'll prefer a knife to a bullet. If he comes tonight at all. Where's McVey?"

"In the dining room playing with that equipment again. He appears besotted with gadgets."

"They can be interesting." He leaned back in his chair. "I like them, too."

"You spent enough time with McVey examining it. Will we be able to get a trace?"

"Good chance. It's hooked up correctly, and it's fairly sophisticated. Why don't you lean back and try to relax? You look as if you're so stiff you'd break if I touched you."

"I can't relax." She made a face. "But you look as if you're having no problem. This kind of situation doesn't bother you?"

"It bothers me." But only because of the danger to Eve. "But I like it. This is why I joined the Bureau. Moments like this are as close to what I felt as a SEAL as I can get."

"Living on the edge?" She was studying his face. "Yes, I can see that you like it. I've never seen you more alive. You're relaxed, but you look as if you're ready to jump up and go for the kill." She smiled faintly. "Aren't you lucky that I furnished you with a reason to resurrect old times?"

"I'm lucky as long as you stay out of it and let me—"

The phone on the table beside her rang.

McVey was in the room in a heartbeat. "I switched on the machine. Let me take the call." He picked up the receiver. "McVey." He listened, then shook his head at Eve. "Thanks, Pauley." He hung up. "Pauley Williams. He's in the next apartment and has a key to my place. I asked him to listen for any disturbance and check if he heard anything." He added quickly as Eve made an exclamation, "I told him to be careful. Don't worry, Pauley isn't that self-sacrificing. He wouldn't go in if he didn't think it was safe."

"And did he hear anything?"

McVey nodded. "And he found the lock was broken. I left the desk neat as a pin, and the pad was on the floor and the Rolodex had cards missing from it." He grinned jubilantly. "I think we've got him, Eve."

"It seems you're right." Her hands were clenching the arms of the chair. "When did this Pauley first hear an intruder?"

"About fifty minutes ago. Like I said, he wouldn't take a risk. He waited to go into the apartment until after he thought he heard the front door close."

"Less than fifty minutes," Joe said. "And he has this phone number and address." He looked at Eve. "Now he only has to choose which one to use."

"He'll phone." She moistened her lips. "I think."

"Fifty minutes. If you guess wrong, he could be here from that apartment in Dunwoody in another ten minutes."

"He'd want to be sure."

"Maybe. Or maybe he's furious enough to kill anyone here he can get his hands on."

"Why are you trying to scare me?"

"I want you to get the hell out of here and leave this to me."

"After all the preparations we've made?" McVey interceded. "It's not going to hurt her to take a phone call, then I could—"

"Be quiet, McVey," Joe said. "Eve?"

She shook her head.

Joe had known that she'd refuse, but he'd had to make one

last attempt. He turned on his heel. "Then get back to the dining room and make sure that we can trace any call, McVey. I'm going to scout around outside and make sure the area is secure." He unlocked and opened the door. "In case you're wrong, and he wants immediate and lethal contact."

CHAPTER
7

JOE RETURNED THIRTY MINUTES later. "No bogeyman is lurking at the moment," he told Eve. "That doesn't mean the situation might not change in another five minutes." He headed toward the room. "I'm going to go to the kitchen and listen on the extension if there's a call."

"Okay."

It was only a breath of sound, and he glanced over his shoulder at her. Then he muttered a curse and turned and strode over to her. He took her face in his two hands and stared fiercely down into her face. "Don't be afraid. It's going to be fine. Whatever happens, I'll make sure you're safe. I won't let that son of a bitch touch you. Do you hear me?"

"I hear you," she whispered. "But there's no way this can turn out fine. Unless there's a miracle, and Bonnie is alive and not been thrown into some hole by this monster. I'm not afraid for myself, Joe. I'm afraid of what I'll find out if we do catch him. That's terrifying me so much I'm sick to my stomach."

And there was no way he could take away that fear. All he could do was share her pain and let her know she wasn't alone. "We'll get through it together." He brushed his lips gently across her forehead. "We've not done so badly so far."

She laughed shakily. "When you're not yelling at me and trying to cut McVey's throat."

"That's only a sign of closeness. I only abuse the people I care about." He kissed her forehead again and let her go. "If he does call, he'll try to hurt you. Don't let him. Assume he's lying until we find out otherwise." He turned and walked away from her. "If you want me, just call."

"Joe."

He looked over his shoulder.

"I'm not afraid for myself, but I'm afraid for you. Take care of yourself. I don't have that many friends. I can't afford to lose you."

"You don't have to have that many friends if you have me. I fulfill all needs." He smiled and walked out of the room.

THE PHONE RANG FORTY MINUTES later.

Joe stiffened, then picked up the phone at the same time as Eve did in the living room.

"Have you been expecting me, Eve?" A deep voice, but it wasn't smooth, as McVey had described; it was rough with ugliness and fury. "I think you have. I know what you're doing. I'm not the moron you called me. I suppose the cops are right there recording everything I say. I don't care what they do. They're not going to catch me, so it doesn't matter."

"They'll catch you," Eve said. "You've already left so many clues around the crime scenes that the detectives are stumbling over them, Zeus." She stopped. "And that ridiculous name you've given yourself. That's as stupid as everything else you've done. Pretensions of grandeur. You probably picked it because Zeus was supposed to be all-powerful. There's nothing godlike about a child killer. You're just a vicious, ludicrous comic-book character, and you don't even know it."

"Ask the Bristols if I belong in the comic books," he hissed. "Ask Linda Cantrell's mother if she thinks what I did to her little girl is funny."

"You pick on children because you're afraid to face anyone else. You're a coward."

"And you're a bitch who doesn't even know that she's a dead woman." He paused. "I'm going to send you to join that red-haired brat that I took from you. But I'm going to make it go even slower with you."

Silence.

"That got you, didn't it?" he asked. "Not so brave now. Do you know why I take the kids? Because there's no greater power to be had than when you kill a man's child. It's like throwing a stone into the pond and seeing all the circles that spread and never stop. The death of a kid touches everyone around her."

"You're saying that you killed . . . my Bonnie?"

"She was dead six hours after I took her. I'd tell you how and when, but I'm going to cut this call short. I'll do that before I cut your heart out. I know you're probably tracing this call. I've got to be gone before the cops get here." His voice lowered to malignant softness. "I just wanted to tell you that you're the stupid one to think that you could bring me down, bitch. Look over your shoulder, and I'll be there. Go to bed, and I may be in the closet waiting for you to sleep. Get in a car, and you'll never know if I've rigged a bomb to blow you to hell and back. If you feel as if someone is watching you, then you'll be right. I'll be right behind you until the day I decide to send you to hell." He hung up.

Joe crashed down the receiver and ran into the dining room, where McVey was looking up from the machine. "Where?"

"2030 Cobb Parkway. It's a pay phone at a convenience store."

Joe grabbed a phone and called Slindak.

"You woke me up. Don't you ever—"

"Send a patrol car to a convenience store at 2030 Cobb Parkway. He's probably already taken off, but we might be able to get a description."

"He?" He paused. "Zeus?"

"Yes. Get someone out there fast." He hung up and turned to McVey. "None of this gets into print. Do you understand?"

"Not unless we get lucky and catch the bastard," McVey said. "I can wait for the big story." His eyes were shining with excitement. "But we're close. I could hardly breathe while Eve was talking to him. She did a good job, didn't she?"

"He tore her apart," he said savagely. "Couldn't you tell?"

He didn't wait for an answer. He was striding down the hall to the living room.

Eve's was sitting frozen, her face paper white. "Did we . . . get a location?"

"Yes, a convenience store on Cobb Parkway."

"So he could jump in his car and get away. So it was all for nothing."

"We could get a description."

She reached up a shaking hand to her forehead. "And there's something else . . . I'm having trouble thinking. He hates me. I think he was telling the truth about shadowing me until he finds a way to kill me. We've got that advantage."

The desire to reach out, to comfort, was an ache inside him. But he couldn't touch her right now. He didn't have the control, and she would realize the truth.

And that realization would rob her of what little comfort he could give her.

"Some advantage," he said tersely. "Did it occur to you that your logic is a little twisted?"

She nodded. "I guess it is. It's all I've got." She looked up at him. "You heard what he said about Bonnie?"

"Yes."

"I'm trying to remember what you told me. That he'd probably say anything to hurt me. He could be lying."

"Yes, he could."

"But what if he's not?" she whispered. "What if she's . . . gone?" She swallowed. "What if he did the same things to her that he did to Janey Bristol? I can't stand the thought of . . ." She stopped to steady her voice. "But I don't know that, and I can't let him break me and keep me from going after him. I have to hold on, don't I?"

He nodded. "You have to hold on with all your strength."

She got to her feet. "Then I can't just sit here. I want to go to that convenience store and talk to the clerk. I want to know what a monster looks like."

"Slindak will be taking care of that. And don't expect Zeus to look like a monster. Most of the serial killers I've seen have looked like your next-door neighbor."

"I still want to go. I need to go."

He hesitated. "Why not? Stay here a minute and let me look around outside." He grabbed his flashlight, left the house, made a quick tour of the perimeter, then came back. "Let's go."

"I told McVey what we were doing. He wants to stay here and transcribe his notes from the phone call."

"Good. He's not invited. I can take only small doses of McVey." He held the door for her, and his hand cupped her elbow as they walked down the driveway to the car. "And he probably couldn't resist getting in the way while we're questioning the clerk."

"You're too hard on him. McVey is just doing his job."

"It surprises me that you defend him considering what a beating you took from the media. He'd probably be after you like a vulture if he—"

"What's that?" Eve was standing next to the car, staring at the windshield wipers.

Joe froze, his gaze following hers. A piece of paper was folded beneath one windshield wiper. "I don't know. I didn't notice it when I came by the car when I was out checking the perimeter. But then I wasn't looking for it. I was hunting bigger—" Eve was reaching for the piece of paper. "No, let me get it."

She already had it and was cautiously unfolding it. "Give me some light, Joe."

He reached into his pocket and pulled out his flashlight.

She inhaled sharply as the beam illuminated the message on the paper. It was printed in large letters with a black pencil.

Stupid Bitch.
Do you think anyone can keep you safe?

"He was here," she said. "He was outside all the time."

"He was here. But not all the time. He wasn't here the last time I checked the perimeter before you got the phone call. I don't make mistakes like that. But he came very soon after, checked out the house, and decided that he didn't want to chance an attack on you with me and McVey on the premises. Then he took off for the convenience store to make his call." He carefully took the paper from her. "I'll put this in the glove box and give it to Slindak to check for prints and analyze the handwriting." He shrugged. "If there are any prints. He may be arrogant, but he was very savvy about the trace. He was probably wearing gloves. But he may have screwed up on the note."

"Yet he was so reckless about leaving evidence at those crime sites."

"Maybe he's recognizing that it's not the same ball game. He's willing to play, but he knows the rules may be different." He opened the passenger door and put the note in the glove box. "You've taught him that, Eve."

"Have I?" Eve got into the car. "That supersize ego was one of our best weapons against him. I just hope that he won't become cautious and take off. That would ruin everything."

"I don't think you have to worry about that," Joe said grimly as he started the car. "You've seen to it that Zeus is wholeheartedly committed to do at least one more kill before he goes to a different hunting ground."

TWO PATROL CARS AND SLINDAK'S gray Honda were parked in the lot of the convenience store when Joe arrived.

Slindak strolled over to the car as Joe opened the door. "Pretty much a waste of time. The store manager said someone used the outside phone booth to make a call, but he was busy and only got a quick glimpse of him."

"Model of his car?"

"He was parked down the street, and the manager didn't notice the model. You're sure it was Zeus?"

"I'm sure. Did you dust the phone booth for fingerprints?"

"We've taped off the booth, and the forensic team will be here soon." He glanced at Eve. "Hello, Ms. Duncan. You don't look too well. Could I have someone see you home?"

"I'm fine." She got out of the car. "It's . . . been a difficult night."

"I can imagine," Slindak said dryly. "I'm sorry, but you brought it on yourself."

"I know that." She watched another patrol car pull into the parking lot. "Forensics?"

"Yes, and I had them roust a sketch artist we use occasionally out of his bed. Kim isn't going to be pleased."

"Artist?" Eve nodded. "I've heard that you can sometimes get an accurate facsimile from a description."

"Sometimes. In this case it's important that we try to do it right away since the manager said he only got a fleeting glimpse. Memory tends to fade quickly, and we need him fresh."

"May I go and watch him?"

Slindak shrugged. "Why not?"

"And I sketch a little myself. Could I have a pad and see what I can do?"

"I'll ask Kim Chen." He gestured to the small, spare man of Asian descent who had gotten out of the patrol car. "As long as you don't get in his way, I don't think he'd object."

"Thank you. I'll ask him myself."

Joe and Slindak watched her walk over to the artist.

"I thought she was close to fainting when you pulled in," Slindak said. "She bounced back pretty quickly. Is she always like that?"

"When she has a purpose. I'm glad she found one right now." He was watching the play of intense emotion across Eve's face as she spoke to Kim Chen. "And I'll be interested to see what she does with that sketch. I saw a sketch she'd done of her daughter in her house. It was remarkable."

"It's not the same thing."

Joe knew that, but Eve had a talent that he'd never seen in a police artist. "Her sketch came alive. It was as if Bonnie's personality was leaping from the page. Let's see if she can do the same thing with a description."

"Don't hold your breath."

As Eve and Kim entered the convenience store, Joe turned toward the phone booth. Three techs were already brushing it down for prints. "I have a note that may have Zeus's prints on it that you may be able to match. He left a calling card on my windshield at the cottage." He reached into his car and retrieved the note from the glove box. "Or maybe not. He guessed we were tracing the call and setting him up. He may have worn gloves."

Slindak carefully took the note and handed it to one of the forensic crew. "That close, huh? She must have really pissed him off."

An understatement. He was trying not to remember the bastard's words. He nodded curtly and started to cross the lot. "Let's go down the block where he left his car and see if we have any witnesses."

EVE WAS COMING OUT of the front entrance when Joe and Slindak came back to the convenience store over an hour later.

"Finished?"

She nodded as she came toward them. "I did the best I could. It was hard. The skill isn't really in the sketching. It's the questions that you have to ask the witness. Kim Chen is very good at what he does. And you have to be ready to change every feature as the witness changes their mind. That evidently happens a lot. It's definitely a work in progress all the way through."

"But she did very well for a beginner," Kim Chen said as he came out of the store. He smiled at Eve. "But you should have changed the eyes."

"Why? The manager said he didn't see the eyes from the front, so it's purely a matter of opinion what they looked like. I just went with instinct."

"But I told you that you're supposed to go with generic features in that case. You have a greater chance of coming close to a resemblance."

She shook her head. "It just felt right."

"'Felt'?" Kim Chen frowned. "You don't rely on feelings. You're not creating, you're duplicating."

"You're probably right. Detective Slindak is lucky he has your sketch to use."

"It was nice meeting you, Ms. Duncan." Kim handed the pad to Slindak. "Here's the best I could do. Not bad. The manager remembered more than he thought."

"Thanks, Kim. Sorry I had to get you out here in the middle of the night."

"So am I." Chen grimaced. "But it's better than trying to pry a description out of someone after they've had a day or two to let it blur." He waved and strolled toward the patrol car.

Slindak glanced at the sketch. "He's not a handsome specimen and looks pretty ordinary." He handed the sketch to Joe. "What do you think? Those cheekbones a little Slavic?"

"Maybe." Joe studied the sketch. High, broad cheekbones, a wide, full mouth. Dark curly hair, cut close to the head. Ordinary-shaped dark eyes and brows. "Let me see your sketch, Eve."

"You heard Kim. I injected too much into the eyes in the sketch." She handed him her pad. "I did okay with the rest, though. I came pretty close."

Joe gave a low whistle. "I can see what Kim meant."

The dark eyes looking up at him almost jumped off the sketch. They were large, close-set, and seemed to glitter with ferocity. The brows above them were straight slashes as dark as the eyes they framed.

Slindak was glancing over his shoulder. "Nothing ordinary about that face."

"He's not ordinary," Eve said. "He's a monster. I don't care if you tell me monsters seldom look like what they are. I think the soul must reveal itself in some way. This felt right to me." She turned to Joe. "Use it or not. I don't care. But I think that I have an idea now what he looks like. I may need it."

"We'll use it," Slindak said. "We'll use both of them. It may be the only thing useful to come out of this. Joe and I found two witnesses who saw Zeus, but not close enough for a description other than he appeared big and muscular. Neither of them agreed with the other about the car. One said it was a brown Ford, the other a dark blue Honda."

"Maybe you should get Kim back to draw the car for them," Eve said dryly.

"Maybe I should. But I don't think it would do much good." He turned and walked over to the forensic crew, who had just finished with the phone booth.

"Are you ready to leave?" Joe asked Eve. "I don't think there's much more we can learn here."

She nodded wearily and got into the car. "I guess you're right. I just wanted to do something that would get us closer. Something concrete."

"The sketch will help."

"If that store manager gave us the right information." Her lips firmed. "But I have to think positive, don't I? I can't think we're just going down a blind alley, or I'll go crazy."

"I'm taking you back to my hotel, okay? No Rainbow Inn."

"No Rainbow Inn." She leaned her head back against the rest. "Take me home, Joe."

His hands tightened on the steering wheel. "No way."

"Take me home." She looked at him. "You heard him. He's coming after me. He has to be able to find me."

"So you're making it easy for him."

"No, I'm sure that you'll make it a challenge," she said. "You're not going to let me be there alone."

"And you're not arguing with me about it?"

"I tried that, and it didn't work." She smiled with an effort. "You just keep on coming."

"You're damn right I do." He paused. "That second newspaper article McVey wrote will be coming out in a few hours from now. It's going to cause Zeus to blow sky-high again."

"Then maybe he'll make his move sooner. Or he'll get so angry, he'll make a mistake. Either way, it won't be bad for us. Nothing will be bad as long as he doesn't get discouraged and disappear. I figure we can hold him here if he knows I'm there in that house, and all he has to do is worry about how to get to me."

"We probably can," Joe said. "But I'm not going to be your only protection, Eve. That's bullshit after we saw how close he came. I'd like to surround you with an army, but I'll limit it to pulling in one of Slindak's men to watch the house." He held up his hand as she started to speak. "Don't worry; Zeus will be expecting it. One man will be a challenge, not a deterrent. I just want the extra insurance."

"You may be right." She was silent, thinking about it. Then

she slowly nodded. "If you promise he won't interfere. I don't want him in the way."

"It would take a lot to discourage Zeus. Having you within his sights will be like putting a steak just outside the cage of a hungry wolf. It will only be a question of time before he finds a way to break out and get it."

"You're calling me a piece of meat? Not at all flattering, Joe."

"I'm not in the mood to be flattering. The only thing I can see good about this is that I'll be with you in that house."

She was silent a moment. "That's the only good thing I can see good about it, too, Joe. You help keep away the darkness."

Forever. Let me hold the darkness at bay for you. Let me help you find the dawn.

Don't say it. Keep it on an even keel.

"I'm glad we're in agreement on something at last. It's about time. But I've decided that it's your house that's dark. I think that we'll paint a couple rooms while I'm staying there."

She stared at him in bewilderment. "What?"

"It will make the time pass. I thought the living room could use brightening. What color do you think?"

She said blankly, "I have no idea."

"Maybe a gold-beige?" he suggested. "Think about it while I stop at my hotel and pick up a bag. It shouldn't take long . . ."

Two Days Later

"WHAT IS THIS STUFF?" Eve asked as she tentatively tasted the salad. "Exotic. You know I'm just a simple Southern woman with down-home tastes, Joe. Are you trying to educate my palate?"

"It's not 'stuff.'" Joe sat down across from her. "I got the recipe from an Indian woman in Bombay. And you're about as simple as an Einstein equation. Try it. You'll like it."

She took another bite. "It's good. Where did you learn to cook?"

"When I was in the service. I was young, with a tremendous hunger, and food was only part of it. I was all over the world tasting and experiencing everything. The good things I wanted to take home with me."

"And the bad things?"

He shrugged. "I learned from them, too, then tried to let them go."

"Not easy."

"No, but that's life." He smiled. "I'm glad you let me loose in your kitchen. Cooking relaxes me."

"And it bores me. I had to put wholesome meals on the table for Bonnie, but I assure you that they lacked inspiration. And definitely nothing exotic." She finished the last bite. "I doubt that I would have picked up any exotic recipes even if I'd gone to India. Which I most certainly didn't. I've never been out of Georgia."

"You've missed a lot. I'd like to show you some of the parts of the world I've visited. It would be great seeing them through your eyes."

"I don't feel as if I've missed much. I had everything I wanted or needed here. It would have been nice to take Bonnie to those places when I could afford it, but it wasn't important to me." Her face clouded. "But maybe it would have been important to Bonnie. She enjoyed every minute, every new experience."

He quickly changed the subject. "I'm glad you like the salad. The main course is much more ordinary." He got to his feet. "Steak and mushrooms. I'll let you take the dishes into the kitchen while I serve it up. Get to work."

"Right." She picked up the salad plates and followed him into the kitchen. She put the dishes in the sink and stood watching him as he served up the steak and mushrooms on a plate. She said quietly, "Thank you, Joe."

"Wait until you're sure I'm not going to give you indigestion before you thank me."

"No, thank you for making these days bearable for me. I would have gone crazy without you," she added with frustration, "Where *is* he? I thought that he'd contact me long before this. Not one word after that second news interview came out."

"He's biding his time. He's probably enjoying the hell out of thinking about you on pins and needles, waiting for him to strike."

"But you don't think he's given up and gone away?" she asked anxiously.

"No." He looked up and met her eyes. "I think that he's close, waiting for his chance."

She breathed a sigh of relief. "That's good."

"Do you know how sick that sounds?"

She nodded, then asked immediately, "And that policeman outside hasn't seen anything?"

He shook his head. "Bramwell says that there's been no suspicious activity since he took over the duty day before yesterday."

He handed her a plate. "Now go sit down and try my steak. I made it medium well-done. Okay?"

"Fine." She didn't move. "I meant it, Joe. You kept me so busy painting that damn room that I had no time to think."

"Oh, you were thinking. I just tried to keep everything troubling on the edge of your consciousness." He headed for the dining room. "Now let's finish dinner, and we'll have coffee on the front porch. I made Turkish coffee with a few interesting spices."

"Coffee with spices?" she repeated warily. "I'm not so sure about that. Coffee should be black, strong, and hot, and not subject to all your fancy exotic tinkering."

"I realize that I'm taking a chance in fooling with your holy of holies." He smiled as he glanced over his shoulder. "But trust me one more time. Try it, you'll like it."

"HERE YOU GO." HE HANDED Eve the small demitasse cup and sat down in the cane chair next to her. "I guarantee it's black and strong and a small enough quantity that you won't have to sample much. I heard the phone ring when I was in the kitchen. I gather it wasn't Zeus."

She shook her head. "My mother. She wants to know when she can come home. Evidently, she's bored. I thought it might be McVey again."

"He called you this morning, didn't he?"

She nodded. "He won't give up. He wants to come here and become part of the action." She made a face. "When and if there is any action. I told him that he can't do it."

"I'm sure he didn't like that."

"He's being very persistent. I said we'd give him an exclusive as soon as the story broke."

"That's more than he deserves."

"You're still angry with him."

"He took you to that house on the lake and let you stake yourself out for that nutcase."

"It was my call."

"And he grabbed at the chance to help you to do it. No trying to talk you out of it. Just set up a house in an isolated area and let the bad times roll. Anything to get his story." He took a sip of his coffee. "Yes, I'm still angry."

"Then I'll try to keep you away from him. He was scared of you, but he's so ambitious that he'll keep pushing." She took a sip of the coffee. "I don't want him to—" She gasped. "Good Lord, what are you doing to me? It's *nasty*." She made a face as she thrust the cup and saucer at him. "It's like cinnamon-flavored tar."

"Maybe it's an acquired taste."

"If you ever give me anything but the real thing when I ask for coffee, I'll murder you."

He chuckled. "I knew it was taking a chance."

"You knew I'd hate it. It's some kind of sick joke."

"You malign me. Would I do that to you?"

"I'm beginning to think that you have a wicked sense of humor. You just haven't let me see it before."

"I had to wait to show that side of my personality. You weren't ready for it." He got to his feet. "I'll take your cup inside." He stood from a moment, looking out into the darkness of the quiet street, the well-kept yards, the lamplight streaming out of the windows. "So peaceful. It's a nice neighborhood. Bramwell said that it was a hell of a lot easier watching your house than the usual neighborhoods he's been accustomed to monitoring." He moved toward the door. "Stay here. I'll get you a real cup of coffee."

"Don't bother." She got to her feet. "All that painting has worn me out. I think I'll shower, then go to bed." She moved toward the door. "I'll do better without coffee."

"You're sure?" He held the door open for her. "My duty is to please."

"Tell that to McVey."

"There's always an exception to prove a rule." He turned on the light in the living room and watched her walk up the steps. She did look tired, but it had been a fair day. He had worked her at painting, making sure the physical exertion would be enough to block out the mental torment that was always with her. He checked his watch. It was near ten in the evening. He'd check in with Slindak and go to bed himself.

He hoped he could sleep. Eve wasn't the only one who was on edge from all this waiting.

Where are you, bastard?

THE PHONE RANG IN THE middle of the night.

He reached over to the pick up the receiver of the phone on the end table beside the couch on which he was sleeping.

Eve was already on the line.

And so was Zeus.

"You have such a pretty house there, bitch. Does it make

you feel safe to be with the FBI man? Are you sleeping with him?"

"No. And, yes, I do feel safe. All your threats, and you weren't able to touch me. You're a coward. I was right in all things I told the world about you."

Oh, shit, Joe thought. That's right, wave the red flag at the bull.

But Zeus didn't seem angry. When he spoke again, his voice was calm and honey-smooth. "You're trying to make me mad. Are you trying to trace the call again? You'll be disappointed. I have only one thing to say to you and then I'm gone . . . for a little while."

"What?"

"You didn't say 'thank you' when I complimented you on your house. That was rude, but I'll forgive you. Do you know what I like about your house? It's that lovely porch, with the hanging basket of flowers. I like plants and flowers far better than I like people. They have no ugliness about them unless I choose to make them ugly. Flowers make a statement, don't they? You should pay attention to that statement." He hung up.

He heard Eve's exclamation before he crashed down the phone.

He threw on his clothes and ran out to the hall to see Eve at the top of the stairs.

"The porch," she said as she ran down the stairs. She flipped on the light in the foyer. "He was talking about the porch. Why would he—"

"Don't go out there." He passed her and drew his gun as he carefully opened the front door. "Let me take a look. I just hope

Bramwell doesn't mistake me for Zeus and decide to take a shot at me."

"Be careful, dammit."

"Always." His gaze was darting over the porch, street, and neighboring houses. It was still and dark except for the street-light on the corner. "I don't see anything."

"That doesn't mean he's not there." Eve pushed closer to him, following his gaze. "And where's Bramwell? Shouldn't he have come running when the lights went on?"

"Yes, he must be in back doing his hourly tour." His gaze again wandered over the same area. "I don't see anything. Maybe it was a bluff." He took a step out onto the porch. "He might have wanted to keep you—" He broke off, stiffening.

She was right behind him. "What is it?"

"Go back inside."

"The hell I will. What's—" She inhaled sharply as she saw where he was looking.

A group of dark liquid drops was spattered on the floor of the porch.

As he watched, another drop fell from the hanging basket to the floor.

"Blood?" she whispered.

"Go back inside," he repeated. He was remembering the de-tails of Janey Bristol's crime scene. He took a step closer and took out his flashlight. "You may not want to see this." He shined the beam up to the bottom of the basket.

The earth at the bottom of the basket was soaked with blood that dripped steadily downward.

His beam traveled upward.

"Hair!" Eve's eyes were focused on the patches of blood-soaked hair clinging to the head that had been shoved into the basket. "Oh, my God."

"Easy."

"Who is it? Another child?"

"I can't tell. It could be Bramwell. I'll have to move around to the other side to see the face." He said through his teeth, "Have you had enough? Or do you want to see that, too?"

"No, but I'm not going to leave you out here to do it alone." She braced herself, and said unevenly, "And it could be Bonnie. He told me he killed her right after he took her."

"There wouldn't be all this blood." He moved around to get another view of the skull. "This is a fresh kill."

"You said it might be Bramwell?"

"Maybe." He was now shining the beam directly into the face. "No, it's not Bramwell."

She was suddenly beside him. "Then who is—" Her back arched as if struck. "McVey!"

Sandy hair soaked in blood, blue eyes staring at them, lips open in a silent scream.

"Dear God . . ." Eve ran to the rail of the porch, bent over, and threw up. "Brian . . ."

"I told you to go inside." Joe was beside her, his hands on her shoulders. "Will you do it now? Lock the door. I need you to call Slindak and get him out here. I have to find Bramwell."

"Yes . . ." She staggered toward the door, then, clinging to the jam, she turned to face him. "No. You can't go without me. What if it's some kind of trap? What if he kills you like he did Brian? I can't—"

"What's going on?" Bramwell was running up the porch steps. "Why are the lights—" He stopped short as he saw the bloody head. "What the hell?"

"That's what I want to know," Joe said grimly. "I have a lot of questions to ask you, Bramwell." He turned back to Eve. "I evidently don't have to go hunting him down. Now will you call Slindak?"

She nodded jerkily and disappeared into the house.

"Who is it?" Bramwell was looking up at the basket. "Pretty gory, huh?"

"Brian McVey."

"The reporter? He doesn't look much like the photo that runs with his byline." He grimaced. "That was stupid. Of course he doesn't. Poor guy."

"How did he get here without you seeing it?"

"It wasn't here before I made my rounds thirty minutes ago."

"And why did it take you thirty minutes to make those rounds?"

"I saw something funny. The flowers in the border were all crushed, and the back gate was open. I was looking around to see if I could find the reason."

A red herring, Joe thought, to give Zeus enough time to deposit McVey's head in the hanging basket, get away, and make his phone call to Eve.

"And you saw nothing suspicious before you started your rounds. A car? A pedestrian?"

"The Simmonses, that young couple who live in that duplex down the street, drove in and went into their house, but that's all. I was on the job and watching close, Agent Quinn."

He looked again at McVey's head. "But evidently not close enough. Slindak is going to kick my ass."

"Probably. I may help him." He turned and went down the porch stairs. "Stay here and guard Eve Duncan. If you screw up, I'll put your head in that basket with McVey's."

Five minutes later, Joe was looking down at the broken lock on the trunk of the Simmonses' Saturn. It would have had to be held shut from inside so that it wouldn't fly open as the car was driven. He carefully lifted the lid of the trunk.

Drops of dark blood on the black plastic interior.

He tensed as the smell wafted up to him.

And something else . . .

CHAPTER
8

"SLINDAK SHOULD BE HERE ANYTIME," Eve said, when Joe walked into the house. "He said to tell you that he can't wait until you go back to Washington, so that he can sleep through the night." Her lips were trembling, as she added, "Of course, he had a few words for me as well. He holds me to blame for all of this."

"Did he say that?"

"No, don't go on the attack. He didn't have to say it. It couldn't be clearer, could it?"

"He's lucky to have your help. At least, we have a chance of bringing Zeus down now. They were running around in circles a few weeks ago. He can stuff his damn blame where the sun doesn't shine."

"Lucky?" Her lips tightened. "And was McVey lucky to have my help, too?" She shuddered. "I must go out on the porch and tell him how lucky he is."

"I knew this was coming." He pulled her to her feet. "We're going into the kitchen. I'll make you a cup of coffee, and we'll talk." He pushed her down at the kitchen table. "Sit there and block out everything." He turned to the cabinet and got down the coffeepot. "That shouldn't be hard. You have plenty of practice."

"I do, don't I?" Her smile was bitter. "Only I think that the blocks are beginning to crumble. What do I do when the flood rushes in and overwhelms me?"

"No problem. I'll be there to pull you out." He heard the sirens. "You'll have to finish making this. I have to go out and report in to Slindak. It's probably better for you to be busy anyway."

"Yes." She got to her feet and reached for the tin of coffee. "Go on. I don't need you to coddle me."

The coffee was ready, and Eve was sitting at the table with a cup cradled in her hands when he came into the kitchen thirty minutes later. "Is he . . . gone?"

He knew she didn't mean Slindak. "Yes, they took him a few minutes ago." He poured a cup of coffee. "But forensics is still working on the porch and the backyard and the Simmonses' car."

"The car?"

He nodded. "Zeus hid in the trunk of the car of the young couple down the block. He couldn't just walk down the street carrying a bloody head under his arm. He was watching and knew that you were guarded. He waited in the trunk until he saw Bramwell go toward the backyard, then got out and placed the head in the basket. He'd already gone around back and arranged a suspicious scenario for Bramwell to investigate to keep him from coming back too soon."

"And then he made the call to me." She shook her head. "Zeus had it all planned." Her lips twisted. "I thought he'd go after me. But I should have known that I wouldn't be enough. He couldn't get to me easily, so he went after Brian." She shook her head. "And I called him stupid."

"He's cunning." Joe sat down across from her. "But he took a big chance. It's clear he's still as arrogant as he ever was. McVey was no fool. He wouldn't have been an easy mark."

"But Brian wasn't expecting to be targeted. Maybe if I hadn't set myself up in the aggressive role, he might have suspected. But we both thought that the setup would lead Zeus straight to me."

"It did."

"And I dragged Brian along with me."

"Bullshit. He wouldn't have had it any other way." He held up his hand as she opened her lips. "Yes, I know that you think that I'm biased. You're right. I wouldn't have wanted McVey killed, but I did blame him for letting you set up that scenario at the lake house. I can't deny it. But I'm not letting you think that anyone but Zeus is to blame for McVey's head being in that basket."

Eve was silent. "He was only twenty-six, Joe. He told me he was going to have a Pulitzer by the time he was thirty."

"He told me the same thing. Too bad. He was smart and had enough drive to make it. But you have to remember, he was nagging you to let him come here and make another try at Zeus as late as yesterday morning. If you want to blame something besides Zeus for McVey's death, then hang it on McVey's ambition."

"It was horrible." She closed her eyes. "Brian's eyes . . . I'll never forget his face."

"Then you'll be giving Zeus exactly what he wants. Don't do it, Eve."

"I'll do my best." Her lids opened to reveal eyes shining with tears. "Because you're right. You're pretty damn smart, Joe. How did you get that way?"

"I'm a natural. Me and Solomon and a few other gifted guys out there. We could run the world if you gave us a chance."

"I believe Solomon tried." Her voice was steady, but her hand was shaking as she lifted her cup to her lips. "Okay, I'll stop blaming myself because of McVey and see if I can help find that bastard who murdered him. Zeus must be feeling very triumphant right now."

"Yes, smug and self-satisfied as a Cheshire cat. But he may have tripped up."

She went still, her eyes locking with his. "What are you talking about?"

"Ego. He's always been careless because he thought no one could touch him. I thought I'd seen signs that he was changing but maybe not. Maybe that arrogance is just too ingrained to overcome."

"And why do you think he may have tripped up? How was he careless?"

He shook his head. "I'm not discussing it with you yet. I have to check on some things, then think about it. I know you, Eve. You'll grab hold and try to run with it. I'm not ready to do that."

"Tell me."

He shook his head. "When I'm sure." He finished his coffee

and stood up. "Now get to bed and try to sleep. I'm going out on the porch and see what I can help wrap up. And I want to make sure that they clean it, so that it's not going to hurt you every time you go out there."

She was glaring at him. "You're not being fair."

"No, but I'm making it easier on myself. It won't hurt you to wait. I'm not having you disappointed if my theory doesn't pan out." He headed for the door. "And thinking about how angry you are at me will keep you from dwelling on what happened to-night."

"Your decision, your opinion. Tell me, dammit."

He paused at the door to look back at her. Her eyes were glittering, and her cheeks flushed with color. Much better than when he'd walked into the house earlier. Good.

He turned and went out onto the porch. "When I'm ready."

THE LAB TECH HANDED JOE the report the next morning. "Here it is. No wonder you didn't send it up to the Bureau for analysis. A first-year intern could have done this one."

"Thanks." Joe scanned the report before turning away. It was what he'd expected, but he still felt a flare of excitement at the confirmation. "I appreciate your making it a priority."

The tech shrugged. "No problem. Literally."

Joe moved quickly down the hall toward the elevator.

One down.

A moment later, he was at Slindak's desk in the squad room. "Did you check out that shoe factory in Toronto?"

"Yes, we haven't got the report yet."

"Give me the name and phone number. I'll follow up."

"Sure." Slindak studied Joe's face as he searched the papers on his desk for the information. "You're wired. What's happening?"

"Nothing yet." He took the report Slindak handed him. "But maybe soon." He turned and went to his desk across the room.

A moment later, he was dialing the number in Toronto.

Fifteen minutes later, he leaned back in his chair and looked down at his scrawled notes. It was all coming together.

But there were still a few pieces to fit into the puzzle. Get to work and make it happen.

He reached for the telephone again.

EVE MET HIM AT THE FRONT DOOR when he came back to the house that afternoon. "Well?"

"You're barring the door. Does that mean you're not going to let me in the house unless I divulge everything I know?"

"You've got it." She grimaced and stepped aside. "I'd do it if I thought I could get away with it. I'm frustrated as hell, Joe. I didn't think you'd—" She stopped, staring at his expression. "You look . . . Joe?"

"How do I look?" He passed her and went into the living room. "Slindak said 'wired.' Yeah, that's what I feel." More than that, he thought, as he turned to face her. He had the bastard in his sights and was aching to pull the trigger. "I think I've got him."

She inhaled sharply. "What?"

"Or at least I know how to get him."

She dropped down on the couch. "Talk to me. Who is he?"

"Zeus could be either Donald Novak or Ralph Fraser."

"You don't know which one?"

"I will by the end of the day." He paused. "I'm going to go pay him a visit."

"You know where he is?"

He nodded. "It was easy to trace him. He's not trying to hide. He doesn't think it's necessary."

She shook her head. "My mind is spinning. Start at the beginning."

"The beginning." He pulled her up and toward the back door. "We'll start here." He threw open the door. "What do you see?"

She looked at him in confusion. "Fence, flowers, lawn."

"A nice lawn. Pretty flowers. Did you put in the landscaping after you moved in?"

"No, I wouldn't have been able to afford it. It was already established. I just took over the care of it."

"But you were offered a maintenance contract by the landscape company who does most of the rest of the neighborhood."

She nodded. "The price wasn't too bad, but I'm a student and work two jobs. I can cut my own lawn." She frowned. "Where is this leading?"

"It's leading to the fact that there was a landscape-maintenance crew in your neighborhood several times a month. Including five of the homes on this block. That's why all the lawns and gardens look so well kept."

Her eyes widened. "Yes . . ."

"And all the houses of the victims' parents that we visited

had the same nice lawns. They all had that in common if nothing else. Such a little thing . . ."

"The landscape company?" Eve repeated. "Is that what you're saying? He works for the landscape company?"

"It would be the perfect opportunity for him to observe possible victims playing in the neighborhoods where he was working. He could take his pick of the children."

"Are you guessing?"

"Yes, but I'm betting I'm right. In the trunk of the car where he was hiding last night, there was blood, but there was also a scraping of something that looked like dirt. It wasn't dirt; under testing, it proved to be fertilizer. It was a common brand used by most landscapers in the area. I contacted the company in Toronto that manufactured the shoes from which we got that print in the cave. Heavy rubber content. The company said that it sold those shoes almost exclusively to professional gardeners and irrigation specialists."

"And last night on the phone Zeus said something about liking plants and flowers better than he liked people," Eve said. "I didn't think anything about it." She moistened her lips. "But you did."

"Only because it was all coming together for me."

"This landscaping company . . ." She lifted her hand to her cheek. "I know I've seen their truck in the neighborhood, but I can't even remember the name."

"Johnston and Son. They service every one of the subdivisions of the kidnapped children. It's a big company, and they have branches all over the Northeast as well as the South. The operations are extensive in Georgia. It wouldn't have been a stretch for Zeus to have killed those children who disappeared outside Atlanta." He paused. "But the company is based in Toronto, Canada. I checked with Johnston and Son personnel in Toronto, and the only workers they have in Georgia who were hired in Canada are Novak and Fraser."

"What difference does that make? Zeus is Canadian?"

"I couldn't tell on that first phone call, but on the second he was talking about your house. McVey was right, the pronunciation is different. Novak is Canadian. Fraser is a U.S. citizen, but raised in Toronto."

Her hands clenched as she looked out at yard. "It makes . . . sense."

"Yes."

"And this man could have been working on one of the yards on the block and watching Bonnie. I could have passed him when I went to the bus stop to meet her."

"It's possible," he said gently.

"If he killed her. I can't be certain. I won't be certain."

But it was coming close to the time when the truth would be thrust upon her, Joe thought. "The only thing I have to be certain about right now is catching the son of a bitch."

"You said you were going to pay him a visit. Where is he?"

"The crew Novak and Fraser are on is working at Nottingham Subdivision in Towne Lake today." He turned. "I'm on my way there now. I've changed cars so that Zeus won't recognize it. I just wanted to stop and let you know what was happening."

"You didn't send the police to pick them up?"

"They'll be there outside the subdivision. First, I have to make sure I locate him before he gets spooked by the squad cars pulling into the subdivision. The crew doesn't all work on the same house. He could be anywhere in the area."

"But you'd recognize him. You saw the sketch I drew of him." She paused. "And I'd recognize him."

"Yes, you would," he said quietly. "But he'd also recognize you. I know where this is going, Eve."

"Of course he'd recognize me. But that's no argument. We both know while he was doing surveillance on this house that he saw you. If he spots you, he'll take off."

"You want to go with me."

She met his gaze. "And you want me to go. Why else did you stop here before going after him? You may have told yourself you just wanted to keep me informed, but that's bullshit. You knew I had to go. You know I deserve to go."

"I don't want you hurt," he said roughly. "I don't want him to touch you."

"And that makes it hard to do the right thing. That's why you're lying to yourself. You promised we'd do this together." She threw back her head and stared him in the eye. "Do you want me to make it easier? If you walk out that door without me, I'll be at Nottingham Subdivision before you get there. If you take me, I'll stay in the car. But I have to be there. I have to see him captured. I want to see his face when he knows that he's not Zeus any longer."

She was right. He had known that it would come down to this when he had come here. They had taken this journey together, and he couldn't leave her behind now. He just couldn't admit it to himself because it caused him to break out in a cold sweat at the idea of letting her come that close to Zeus. Yet he had to admit it and drown that fear because he could not cheat her.

"Joe?"

His hand closed on hers. It was a soft, graceful hand belying the strength that lay beneath that fragile surface. His grasp tightened. "You stay in the car," he said hoarsely as he led her toward the door. "Unless you want to drive me crazy, you stay in the car."

NOTTINGHAM SUBDIVISION WAS an upper-middle-class neighborhood that had been built within the last ten years and had all the amenities. Including a homeowners' association that demanded the homeowners pay to keep the verdant lawns and shrubs meticulously maintained.

And Johnston and Son had a truck that was parked close to the clubhouse and swimming pool.

Joe parked across the road from the clubhouse, his gaze raking the surrounding area. "There's a man in the truck, but I don't see any workers." He got out of the car. "I'll go ask questions. Lock the door."

"You think the man in the truck is a supervisor?"

"He's not doing hard labor. That's a good sign."

She frowned. "Aren't you going to call the police waiting outside the gate to assist?"

"As soon as I can point the way to Zeus." He crossed the road and drew out the photos of the sketches of Zeus as he approached the truck.

"May I help you?" The man in the truck smiled politely at

Joe. "Les Cavanaugh. I run this crew. I know we're a little late coming to do the maintenance this week, but we got behind because of the rain. We'll get to your yard as soon as we can."

Joe showed his ID. "FBI. You can help me with an identification. You have an employee working for you who we have an interest in questioning."

Cavanaugh stiffened warily. "What for? Look, we got rid of that joker who was planting marijuana in some of the flower beds. We don't stand for anything like that."

"I'm glad to hear it. But the FBI doesn't deal with drugs." He handed him Kim Chen's sketch. "Do you know him?"

Cavanaugh frowned. "He's . . . familiar."

He handed him Eve's sketch. "Is this clearer?"

Cavanaugh's eyes widened. "Hell, yes. Ralph Fraser." He looked at Joe. "But Fraser is a good guy. Been working for us for years and never caused any trouble."

"Where is he working now?"

"In the flower bed behind the clubhouse, next to the pool. But he's not the guy you're looking for. He's real quiet, works hard and—"

"Stay in the truck." Joe started for the clubhouse.

And saw Ralph Fraser come around the corner toward him. Shit!

Fraser stopped, then whirled and ran into the clubhouse.

Joe tore after him, but instead of going through the front entrance, he ran around back and entered from the pool area.

A bullet splintered the jamb of the door as he dove down and to the left.

"Put down your weapon. You're under arrest."

"The hell I am." Another bullet, closer.

But Joe had the direction now. Fraser was behind the bar across the room. He aimed and got off a shot. "Give it up, Fraser. Last chance. I'll kill you. It's what I want to do anyway. Why waste the taxpayers' money on shit like you?"

"You're not going to kill me. All these years, and you assholes haven't been able to touch me. I'll get out of here and kill you and that whore, too." Another shot. "Just like I did that newspaper reporter."

"But it's really me you want to kill, isn't it, Fraser?"

Oh, my God, Eve.

She was standing in the front doorway. But only for an instant, then she dove to the right behind the couch in front of the huge fireplace.

A bullet embedded itself in the soft cushions.

"You missed," Eve called. "Stupid, Fraser. Incompetent and stupid and—"

Take advantage of Eve's distracting him.

Another bullet struck the coffee table. "Bitch." It was a scream of rage. "I'll blow your—"

The scream was cut off as Joe dove across the bar on top of Fraser, jerking the gun from his hand and tossing it aside.

"No!" Fraser struggled wildly.

God, he was strong. Joe would have to put him out quickly.

But Fraser had rolled over, taking Joe with him. His face was contorted with rage as he looked down at him. There was fierce malice imprinted on every line of his heavy face. "You helped her. You helped the bitch. I'm going to cut your—"

Joe's knee jerked up into Fraser's groin.

Fraser groaned with pain.

Joe bucked him off his body. He moved swiftly to give him a karate chop to the neck.

Fraser went limp as he lost consciousness.

Joe was breathing hard as leaned back against the bar.

Eve was beside him, looking down at Fraser. "It's him. It's Zeus?"

"Ralph Fraser." He reached in his jacket pocket and pulled out handcuffs. "And you were supposed to stay in the car."

"And you were supposed to call in the police when you knew where Fraser was." She was still looking down at him. "And then I saw you run after him. What could I do?"

He cuffed Fraser and sat back on his heels. "And you wouldn't have come running to the rescue anyway? I could have handled it, Eve."

"I had to be sure." Her glance shifted to Joe. "And I had to make certain that you didn't kill him."

"I gave him the usual warning."

"But I think you wanted him dead. Didn't you?"

"He's a son of a bitch. I didn't want some slick lawyer to find a way of getting him off."

"That's not all. You're my friend. I think you wanted it over for me."

"Maybe. And now we have to wait for a jury to pull the plug on him." His lips twisted. "And I have to watch what that does to you. Is that what you want?"

"I have to talk to him. I have to make him tell me if he lied about killing Bonnie."

It was coming as he'd known it would. Joe could almost see the dark shadow looming over her.

"Maybe he lied," she added shakily. "Maybe he'll tell the truth if he thinks it will get him off."

"And maybe he'll lie again." He got to his feet. "Come on, let's get you in the car and away from him."

She didn't move. "I have to ask him, Joe."

"You're not going to get anything from him but curses if he regains consciousness anytime soon." He took her elbow. "We need to call Slindak and get those squad cars up here."

"They should be here any minute. I told that man in the truck to go down to the gates and get them as I ran past him toward the clubhouse."

"Good." He glanced once again at Fraser. He still wasn't stirring. "I don't think he's playing possum, but perhaps I'll stay here until Slindak gets here."

"Because he might be strong enough to walk away from this? I never thought evil could be as strong as good. I hoped it couldn't be that powerful." She shuddered. "But that was before I lost Bonnie."

Joe heard the sirens and gently took her elbow again. "He won't walk away from this." He nudged her toward the door. "I promise you, Eve."

"When can I see him again?" she asked. "I have to see him. He has to tell me about Bonnie."

"We'll talk about that later." A long time later, he thought. When she was stronger, when he could find a way to cushion the blow. As if he could ever cushion that blow. "Let me take you home."

Two Weeks Later

PAPERWORK, JOE THOUGHT SOURLY as he finished the third page of the report. It was the bane of every law-enforcement officer's life, and that went double when you had to make reports to the local police department as well as the Bureau.

"You look pissed." Slindak had stopped by his desk. "You shouldn't mind doing a little bragging on paper. You're a rising star. The Bureau is probably going to give you a promotion."

"Knock it off."

Slindak hesitated. "How is Eve Duncan?"

"Fine."

"Did you see her today?"

"Last night."

"Did she mention Fraser?"

He raised his head. "Every day. She wants to see him. I've been making excuses."

"I think that she saw through them. I just got a call from the jail. She's talking to Fraser now."

"What?" He jerked upright in the chair. "How did she get in to see him?"

"She went to his lawyer, and he arranged it."

Joe was cursing as he jumped to his feet. "Damn him. Do you know what that's going to do to her?"

"I have an idea. I thought you'd want to know. She doesn't need any more . . ."

The last words were lost as Joe ran out of the squad room.

Fifteen minutes later, he was taking the stairs two at a time to the second-floor room where they'd brought Eve for her visit with Fraser.

She was coming out of the room when he reached the top of the stairs.

She was stark white and was moving slowly, like an old woman.

"Eve, dammit."

She looked at him as if she didn't recognize him. "Joe?"

"Why did you have to do it?" He put his arm around her waist to support her and pulled her down the stairs. "I knew he'd do this to you."

"Did you?" She almost fell as they started down the next flight. She was walking stiffly, as if her legs weren't be able to function. "I guess I knew he would do it, too. But I had to ask him. It's Bonnie. Do you know what he told me?"

"Shh. Not now. Let me get you home first."

"If that's what you want."

"That's what I want." They were walking out of the station, and he put her into the passenger seat of the car he'd parked at the front entrance.

She stared straight ahead as he drove the twenty minutes to her home, but he doubted if she was seeing anything. Her breathing was shallow and quick.

He brought the car to a screeching halt in front of the

house. The next moment, he was around the car and half lifting her out of the seat. "Come on. Only a little farther."

She was looking at the empty place where the hanging basket had been. "He's a beast," she whispered. "Why did God let him come into the world?"

"Maybe he didn't. I think he's a creation of Satan." He had the door open, and he pushed her over the threshold. "And Satan will take him back soon."

"Not yet. Not until he tells me where to find my Bonnie." She stood straight, frozen, looking straight ahead. "He did it, Joe. He really killed her. I was afraid it was true, but I didn't really believe it. I didn't see how anyone could kill my Bonnie. But he did it. He looked into my eyes, and he smiled. And then he started to tell me what he did to her." Her voice was uneven. "I sat there and I wanted to scream, but I couldn't do it. I wanted to cover my ears, but I was frozen in that chair. So I listened and listened and I—"

"Hush." He couldn't stand any more. It was tearing him apart. "Just give me a minute." He lifted her in his arms and carried her across the room and up the stairs to her bedroom. He placed her on her bed, then followed her down, holding her in his arms. Her skin was cold where he touched her. "I didn't want you to go to see him. God, I didn't want you to go."

"I know. You wouldn't help me. I had to do it myself."

"You should have told me. I would have tried to make it easier for you. I'd never want you to be alone."

"I am alone. I'll always be alone now. He killed her."

He could feel the moisture sting his eyes. "He'd lie anyway, Eve. Are you sure?"

"He gave me details. Details down to the flavor of the ice cream she got from that booth in the park. It was her favorite flavor. Details about how soft and curly her hair was to the touch . . ." Her voice broke. "It was so soft, Joe. I remember her sitting on my lap the night before he took her. I was singing a song to her, and her head was pressed against my cheek . . ."

He could feel the pain in every word, it reverberated within him. He desperately wanted to take it away, but there was no way to do it. All he could do was give her his warmth. His arms tightened around her. "Do you want to talk about her?"

"Not now. All I can think about is Fraser and what he said about her. It hurts, Joe. I can't tell you how it hurts. It keeps twisting inside me. I want it to go away."

He couldn't even tell her the pain would get less. The loss of a child was eternal. "I'll be here to share it with you. Always."

"No . . . not fair. No one should . . . Go away, Joe. Not fair."

"It's fair, if I say it's fair." He was stroking her hair. "What's a friend for?" And what's a lover, a guardian, a warrior to protect you, for? I have to be all things to you, Eve. Something crazy happened, and my whole world changed when you came into my life. "So be quiet and just let me hold you."

"I want it to go away. I don't think I can stand . . ."

That was one of the things he'd feared when he'd known what Eve was going to have to face. "You can stand anything. You're tough." His hand was gentle on her hair. "Give it time. The state's going to kill that bastard, then some of the—"

"They can't kill him. I have to know where he buried Bonnie. I can't let them do it."

"He didn't tell you?"

"He said to come back, and he might tell me."

"And put you through this torture again? No way."

"I can take it. I have to take it."

"I said you were tough. I didn't say you were invincible."

"I'll find a way to block it out. I have to make him tell me."

"Eve . . ."

"You've never had a child, Joe. You don't know how important it is for me to bring her home. I can't leave her out there alone. Every night of her life, I tucked her into her bed, sang to her and kissed her good night. She was safe, she was home, she knew she was surrounded by love. Now I have to tuck her in one final time. I have to surround her with my love. I think wherever she is that she'll know it." Her voice was hoarse. "I have to . . . bring her home."

Oh, God in heaven. What could he say? What could he do?

"We don't have a weapon to use against Fraser, Eve. He knows he's going to be convicted of one of those killings. It's just a choice which case the state is going to choose to prosecute. But the bastard has a weapon he can use to hurt you, and he'll do it."

"I have to try. It's not only Bonnie. It's all those other lost children, too. If I go there often enough, he may get cocky and let something slip. I have to try."

He couldn't make the attempt to talk her out of it. Not right now.

She lay there silent for a long time. "Your cheek is damp, Joe. I feel it." She reached up and touched his lashes. "Are you crying for my Bonnie?"

"Yes, and for you." He cleared his throat. "It wouldn't hurt you to do a little crying yourself. It might help."

"I can't cry. I can feel all the tears in a tight little ball deep inside me, but they won't come out. Maybe later . . . After I've brought Bonnie home."

"Then I'll cry for you."

"Will you do that?" She cuddled closer to him, her cheek in the hollow of his shoulder. "You're so good to me. Maybe Bonnie will know that, too. She was so special, so full of love. I wish she'd known you, Joe . . ."

For an instant, he could almost see how different their lives would have been if tragedy had not entered it. An Eve vital and smiling, the child, Bonnie, who would love Joe as well as her mother. The image was bittersweet, but he would not push it away. That was neither their life nor their future, but he would work with what he had. He'd drain every bit of joy and happiness around them that he could to make it a good life, create a shelter and a haven for them.

His lips gently brushed her forehead. "I wish I'd known your Bonnie, too, Eve."

Diagnostic Classification Facility

Jackson, Georgia

January 27

11:55 P.M.

IT WAS GOING TO HAPPEN.

Oh, God, don't let it happen.

"Lost. She'll be lost. They'll all be lost," Eve said.

"Come away, Eve. You don't want to be here." Joe tried to

hold the huge black umbrella over her. "There's nothing you can do. He's had two stays of execution already. The governor's not going to do it again. There was too much public outcry the last time."

"He's got to do it." Her face was white and strained, her expression frantic. "I want to talk to the warden."

Joe shook his head. "He won't see you."

"He saw me before. He called the governor. I've got to see him. He understood about—"

"Let me take you to your car. It's freezing out here, and you're getting soaked."

She shook her head, her gaze fixed desperately on the prison gate. "You talk to him. You're with the FBI. Maybe he'll listen to you."

"It's too late, Eve." He once more tried to draw her under the umbrella, but she stepped away from him. "You shouldn't have come."

"*You* came." She gestured to the horde of newspaper and media people gathered at the gate. "*They* came. Who has a better right to be here than me." Sobs were choking her, but there were no tears. She hadn't shed one tear all the time that Fraser had gone through his trials and appeals. Joe had prayed that she would cry and gain at least a little release from the terrible tension. But she had never broken down through all the agony. "I have to stop it. I have to make them see that they can't—"

"You crazy bitch." A man jerked Eve around to face him. He was in his early forties, and his features were twisted with pain and tears were running down his cheeks. Bill Verner, Joe realized. His son was one of the lost ones.

"Stay out of it." Verner's hands dug into her shoulders. He shook her. "Let them kill him. You've already caused us too much grief, and now you're trying to get him off again. Damn you, let them burn the son of a bitch."

"I can't do— Can't you see? They're lost. I have to—"

"You stay out of it, or so help me God, I'll make you sorry that you—"

"Leave her alone." Joe stepped forward and knocked Verner's hands away from Eve. "Don't you see she's hurting more than you are?" All those months of torture and torment Fraser had put her through had been enough to drive a less strong woman mad. And still, in the end, Fraser would not tell her where he'd buried Bonnie.

"The hell she is. He killed my boy. I won't let her try to get him off again."

"Do you think I don't want him to die?" she said fiercely. "He's a monster. I want to kill him myself, but I can't let him— There's no time for this argument." She was suddenly frantic again. "There's no time for anything. It must be almost midnight. They're going to kill him. And Bonnie will be lost forever."

She whirled away from Verner and ran toward the gate.

"Eve!" Joe ran after her.

She pounded on the gate with clenched fists. "Let me in! You've got to let me in. Please don't do this."

Flashbulbs.

The prison guards were coming toward them.

Joe was trying to pull her away from the gate.

The gate was opening.

The warden was coming out.

"Stop it," Eve gasped. "You've got to stop—"

The warden gave her a sympathetic glance. "Go home, Ms. Duncan. It's over." He walked past her toward the TV cameras.

"Over. It can't be over."

The warden was looking soberly into the cameras, and his words were brief and to the point. "There was no stay of execution. Ralph Andrew Fraser was executed four minutes ago and pronounced dead at 12:07 A.M."

"No!"

Eve's scream was full of agony and desolation, as broken and forsaken as the wail of a lost child.

Joe caught her as her knees buckled, and she slumped forward in a dead faint.

He turned and carried her quickly toward the parking lot, his eyes never leaving her face. Even unconscious, her features were frozen in agony.

But, as he watched, two tears brimmed and slowly rolled down her cheeks. The tears she had not been able to shed for her Bonnie. Was it the start of healing?

God, he hoped so.

"Sir." A guard had followed him. "Is there something I can do? May I help you?"

"No." He looked down at Eve, and suddenly the love was flowing over him in such a powerful tide that it was spiraling, cresting, filling him with hope. "We'll get along fine. You can't help." His arms tightened around Eve as he started across the dark parking lot. "She's *mine*."

CHAPTER
9

St. Joseph's Hospital

Milwaukee, Wisconsin

Present Day

MINE ...

All through the years. Always mine . . .

Even in the glowing soft darkness that was trying to take him away from her, Joe could remember what had been and was feeling a wrenching sadness.

Eve . . .

But Eve was far away, and he could barely feel her now.

"THEN GO BACK TO HER. She needs you."

It was Bonnie. He could not see her, but the vision of her was there before him. A child, curly red hair and a smile that lit the darkness. Bonnie who had dominated his life since he had first known he loved Eve. He was not surprised to see her. What could be more natural than to have Bonnie here with him as he slipped away? It was not the first time he had seen the spirit of Eve's daughter.

When she had first come to him, he had thought he was going crazy, that the constant search had affected his reasoning. It had taken a long time before he had accepted that what he perceived as reality had an exception in the form of the ghost of Bonnie. It had not really affected his life with Eve, which was based on trying to find Bonnie, keeping Eve alive while she searched for her daughter, making life a gift instead of a burden through the long hunt.

"And you did all of that," Bonnie said gently. "But it's not over yet. Mama still needs you. Can't you feel how she's hurting?"

He could feel it. "I don't think I can go back. You can stop it. She loves you."

"But she loves you, too. And I love you, Joe."

"Do you? There were times that I resented you. She wouldn't let you go no matter how much it hurt her."

"How could I not love you when you loved and cared for her? It didn't matter what you felt about me. I knew you only wanted what was best for her. But you can't leave her now, Joe. She's going to need you more than ever soon."

"Is she? Then I have to be there for her. But I don't know if I can make it back."

"You can make it. We're walking together now, and now we have a destination. Can't you see it?"

Eve.

And beyond her something else.

"The . . . end?"

"There's no end in a circle, but there's sometimes the loosening of a knot in the fabric. I guess you could call it the end. But she needs you to help her do it. We all need you, Joe."

"Then I'll be there. I'll find my way."

"No, take my hand. It will be easier for you."

Somehow, she was clasping his hand, and he suddenly felt as if light was streaming through him, around him. "Dear God."

"See, the darkness is going away. You can see her more clearly now. And you're growing stronger, aren't you?"

"Yes."

"We're almost there, Joe. Hold on. I won't let you go. Just as you've never let her go."

Brilliance. Radiance. Love.

His heart pounding with wild eagerness as he saw Eve at the window of the ICU.

I'm coming. Don't be afraid. I'm coming, Eve.

"I'm letting you go, Joe," Bonnie said. "For a little while. I'll be with you again, but you don't need me now, do you?"

"No." He couldn't look away from Eve's face. Why had he thought that he could ever leave her? "It's okay for you to go, Bonnie. I'll take care of her now. After all, she's mine."

"No." Bonnie smiled. "She's ours, Joe."

SHE WAS GONE BUT THE LINGERING golden radiance was still keeping the darkness at bay.

And he couldn't wait to dispel it entirely.

He opened his eyes.

And then he smiled at Eve.

JOE WAS SMILING at her!

Eve could feel the tears running down her cheeks.

Good-bye? Surely not good-bye.

Bonnie had vanished only seconds before, and Eve had feared the worst. But there was a flush of color in Joe's cheeks, and he was smiling.

"Oh, God, thank you." She tore open the ICU door. "And thank you, baby." She was at Joe's bed in seconds. She took a deep breath. "Hi . . . took you long enough," she said unsteadily. "No, don't say anything. I just want to touch you." She pressed the bell for the nurse. "I want to hold your hand."

"So—did—she," Joe whispered.

"Who?" She answered herself as she took his hand in both of hers. It wasn't as warm as it usually was, but she could feel a faint pressure. He was alive and it was a miracle. The only miracle she knew had a name. "Bonnie?"

He nodded. "Bonnie." His eyes closed. "I couldn't—find my way back. She knew . . ."

"Yes, she knew." Her clasp tightened. "Don't talk anymore. I'll let you go, but don't you get lost again. Do you hear me?"

He nodded. "I hear . . ."

He was asleep again.

But the flush was still on his cheeks, and his hand was holding hers.

He was going to live.

The nurse was running into the room, a frown on her face.

They would tell Eve to go, and she would do it. She would put him in their hands to heal.

As Bonnie had surrendered him to Eve's hands.

* * *

EVE SAW JANE GET OFF the elevator as she left the ICU.

"Eve?" Jane was hurrying toward her, her face concerned. "You're crying. You look . . . how's Joe?"

She smiled shakily. "He's going to be fine."

"That's what they told you? But Catherine said he could be dying."

"Could doesn't mean that's going to happen." She wiped the tears from her cheeks. "He's taken a turn for the better. I just talked to him."

"Thank God." She took Eve in her arms and held her. "I was nearly frantic when you told me."

"I thought it was the end." Eve hugged Jane tighter. "He came so close, Jane."

"But he's tough. We both know that." She released Eve and handed her a handkerchief. "You seem to be a little damp. I'm pretty close to a deluge myself. Dammit, you should have told me right away. Do you think I would have let you go through this alone?"

"It was enough for one of us to go through this." Eve dabbed at her cheeks. "I told you when I thought I should."

"Should you leave him? Can you go to the waiting room? I'll buy you a cup of coffee."

Eve looked back at Joe, who now had three nurses and an intern by his bed. "He won't need me. They're not going to let me near him until they figure out which of those brilliant doctors managed to save his life and turn him around."

"And which one did?"

"None of them. They'd written him off. Joe did it on his own." She paused. "With a little help."

Jane stiffened. "Help?"

"He said Bonnie held his hand." She glanced at Jane. "I think she did and showed him the way home."

Jane didn't answer for a moment. "I'm not going to argue with you. You know I have a few problems with the idea that Bonnie pays you visits, but if you tell me it's true, then I accept it." She glanced at her and smiled. "And if you tell me that she helped keep Joe alive, then I'll jump up and down and shout hallelujah."

"Don't jump up and down. This is a hospital." She smiled brilliantly. "But you can do it in the parking lot."

Jane nodded. "Later." She went to the coffee machine and pressed the button. She let her breath out in a long sigh. "I can't tell you how relieved I am. I was so scared riding up in that elevator."

"I've been scared for days. Since the moment Paul Black stabbed him, it's been a nightmare." She took the coffee that Jane handed her. "Catherine told you everything that happened?"

"In broad strokes." She got a cup of coffee for herself and came back and sat down by Eve. "I got the gist of it. I was too on edge to cross-examine her. Though I think she's probably not a good candidate for interrogation. She impressed me as being a very tough cookie."

"She would have let you ask her anything. She's a good friend to both Joe and me." She took out her phone. "Which reminds me; I have to call her and tell her about Joe."

"Even before you get the official news from the doctor?"

She made a face. "You're right. Catherine is very practical. She always wants everything crossed and dotted. She'd run down here and have the doctors backed against a wall demand-ing guarantees."

Jane's brow rose. "But you still like her very much."

"Very much. She's as close as I've ever had to a woman friend." She reached out and squeezed Jane's arm. "Except you. I'm glad you're here."

"Me, too." She lifted her cup to her lips. "Catherine's at the Hyatt getting me settled."

"You don't have to get settled. You can go back to London if you like. Everything is going to be okay here."

"Stop trying to get rid of me. Do you mind if I stay and be with you? I'll go when Joe is better."

Eve nodded. "I just wanted to give you the option."

"You're rushing me out of here, and you haven't even heard that he's definitely on the mend."

"I've heard." Eve took another sip of coffee. "Joe told me."

"And no one with more authority."

"Well, Bonnie told him, and who has more authority than that?"

"Impossible." Jane chuckled. "But I'm so glad that you're this happy and giddy that I don't give a damn. It was the last thing that I was expecting. You're absolutely certain, aren't you?"

"Yep." Eve leaned back in her chair and felt the happiness flowing through her. She did feel giddy. After the tension of the last days, the relief was overwhelming. "And you will be, too. We'll just sit here and give those doctors time to congratulate themselves, then come out and tell us how clever they are." She lifted her cup in a mock toast to Jane. "And then we'll call Catherine and tell her to come and celebrate with us."

* * *

"I CAN'T BELIEVE IT." Catherine's face was luminous as she came into the waiting room. "The doctors confirmed it? Joe's going to be okay?"

"Believe it," Eve said. "It's true."

"No danger of his slipping back?"

"Oh, they tried to tell me that we had to be cautious. That there was a possibility of a relapse." She shrugged. "That's what they always say when they're confused. But I'm not confused. It's not going to happen."

"She has it on the highest authority," Jane said with a grin.

"I'll take your word for it," Catherine said. "Next question. How long before Joe is on his feet again?"

"It depends on his progress. Joe usually heals quickly."

"Months?"

"Weeks," Eve said. "But I don't know how many weeks. It will take as long as it takes. I don't want him to hurry and injure himself."

"Once he starts to recover, it's going to be hard to keep him down." Catherine frowned. "You know that, Eve."

Eve's smile vanished. "I'll keep him down even if I have to tie him to the bed."

"That may have to be the solution," Catherine said grimly. "Once he finds out that you believed Paul Black when he said it was Gallo who killed Bonnie."

Eve's smile faded. "Black believed what he was saying. I could see it." She paused. "And so did John Gallo. That's why he ran away."

"And Joe will be right after him."

"No." Eve could feel the fear tighten her chest. "We can't let him do that."

"No, we can't," Catherine said. "Which means I have to find Gallo first."

"You've been trying. Everyone's been trying."

"Then I'll try harder. I haven't had a chance to concentrate yet. I've split my time between searching those woods and running back here and checking on Joe." Her lips tightened. "I'll find him."

"He may not even be in those woods," Eve said. "If he got clear of them, he could be anywhere in the world. He has plenty of money, and he worked for Army Intelligence for years as a troubleshooter and assassin. It's not as if he won't know how to slip in and out of the country."

"I know that," Catherine said. "But it wouldn't have been easy for him to escape the sheriff and deputies we called in when Joe was hurt. They had him on the run. He was sighted at least twice."

"And then they lost him, and he hasn't been seen since," Eve said. "You told me yourself that it was as if he dropped off the face of the Earth."

"I think he's still in those woods. He owns the property. He knows it better than anyone hunting him," Catherine said. "I have a feeling."

"Instinct," Jane murmured. "I believe in instinct."

"So do I," Catherine said. "And it's saved my ass too many times for me to ignore it." She met Jane's eyes. "I don't like leaving Eve here alone. Are you staying?"

"I'm staying," Jane said. "I wouldn't leave her."

"Good." She turned back to Eve. "Is there anything I should know about Gallo? Anything that could help me?"

Eve thought for a moment. "He's not . . . When he killed Bonnie, he may not have been aware of doing it. He claimed he loved her, and I believed him at the time. He had blackouts after those years of torture in that North Korean prison."

"And does that mean you think she should be easy on him?" Jane asked in surprise.

"Hell no; if he killed Bonnie, he deserves everything anyone could do to him," Eve said coldly. "I'm just telling Catherine that he's definitely unstable, particularly where Bonnie is concerned. She may be able to use it."

"It's a possibility." Catherine turned to Jane. "And no, I won't be easy on him. It's tough that he went through hell in that prison through no fault of his own. But if that turned him into a child killer, then he deserves to be exterminated."

"No, you can't do that," Eve said quickly. "Not until he talks to me. I have to know where my Bonnie is buried."

"If he remembers. He might not if he's as unstable as you say."

"I have to talk to him," Eve repeated.

Catherine didn't speak for a moment, then shrugged, and said, "Okay, I made you a promise, and I'll keep it." She smiled. "And now I think I'll go to the ICU and see Joe."

"They won't let you visit him," Eve said.

"Then if he's awake, I'll make faces at him through that glass window. He'll get the message." She gave Eve a hug. "Take care. I'll be in touch and tell you how it's going."

"See that you do."

Eve watched her leave the waiting room and walk quickly down the hall. There was purpose in Catherine's steps and determination in her demeanor. She looked like a warrior going into battle.

"I was right. She's tough," Jane said. "Is she as good as she thinks she is?"

"Better, probably." And Eve was feeling a rush of relief about having Catherine moving quickly to find Gallo. Having Gallo out there was a double-edged sword. He'd be both a threat and temptation to Joe once he was in his right senses. And she was still experiencing the pain of that moment when Black had told her that Gallo was guilty. The bond between them as Bonnie's mother and father had turned tight and bitter, but she found that it still existed. It was Eve's job to go after Gallo and bring him to justice, but for the moment, she had a more important job in helping get Joe well. She could rely on Catherine to search in Eve's place until she was able to turn her attention away from Joe.

"I'm going to call the Hyatt and get a room for you, too," Jane said. "We'll probably both be here at the hospital most of the time, but we don't have to live here as you've been doing. It seems the urgency is gone."

"Yes." She again felt that profound rush of thanksgiving she had felt when Joe had opened his eyes. "The urgency has definitely been downgraded. You make your call, and I'll go back to the ICU and try to get the nurses to let me go in and sit with him again."

Jane smiled. "You feeling lucky? You said the rules were pretty stern."

"Yeah." Eve threw her cup in the disposal. "I'm feeling very lucky, right now."

JOE WAS sleeping.

Catherine stood at the window and gazed at him and the nurse moving around the ICU.

His color was good, and the sleep appeared normal.

Catherine let out a sigh of relief. She had believed Eve when she'd told her Joe was on the mend, but she'd had to see for herself. It was too easy for love to paint a false picture.

And the love between Eve and Joe was very strong. Catherine had had moments of envy when she had seen them together. When Catherine had married, she was seventeen, and her husband was sixty-two. They had both been CIA, and it had been more a partnership than a love affair.

Not that she had not loved him. But it was a quiet affection rather than a passion. She would not have done anything any differently. If she had not married Terry, she would not have given birth to her son, Luke. Why would she change anything when she had been given that gift? Her son was everything.

But the love that Eve and Joe possessed appeared to have all the facets missing in Catherine's marriage. Yet she had not even realized that they were missing until she'd met Eve and Joe.

Joe was opening his eyes. Did he see her?

Yes, he was smiling at her.

She blew him a kiss.

He smiled again and closed his eyes.

Yes, rest, my friend. Get well. I'll stand guard over Eve. You can trust me.

She turned and moved down the hall toward the elevator. But first she had her own decks to clear before she went on the hunt.

She took out her phone as soon as she was in the car. She dialed her number at the house she rented in Louisville. It was after midnight, but her son, Luke, probably would still be awake. He read till all hours of the night and still managed to be up early in the morning. She'd tried to tell him it wasn't healthy, but Luke would only look at her and not say a word. It was hard trying to convince him such an act would affect him in any adverse way when it brought him pleasure. Luke had not had much pleasure in his life. He had been kidnapped at the age of two from her home in Boston by Rakovac, a Russian criminal, as an act of vengeance against Catherine for undermining his mafia operation. She tried not to think of the torture and deprivation he had suffered until she and Eve and Joe had managed to free him. Nine long years. He had been two when he'd been kidnapped and eleven when they'd managed to free him.

It was no wonder that, now that he was safe and free, he was gobbling up experiences as if they would be snatched away from him in a heartbeat. He still didn't totally trust her, but he was coming close. She had to handle Luke with the most delicate touch imaginable, so that he wouldn't walk away from her.

She tried to make her tone light when he picked up the phone. "Luke, what the heck are you doing? Didn't that tutor I hired give you a curfew?"

"Yes, Mr. O'Neill said that I had to get to bed before three. I'm in bed."

Thank heaven that Sam O'Neill didn't keep Luke to an ordinary child's schedule. But Sam was too savvy to do that. That was why Catherine had chosen Sam as Luke's tutor. He was not only ex-CIA and fully capable of protecting her son, but he was a wonderful teacher. After what Luke had gone through during his captivity, strictness would have been absurd. He had been stunted in many ways by his isolation, but his childhood had been stolen from him. His independence had to be respected. "But you're reading. What's the book tonight?"

"*Midsummer Night's Dream*. I'm trying to understand it. But it's very odd."

"Yes, it is. But don't give up on it. You might learn something."

"I never give up."

No, he had boundless stamina and determination, or he would never have survived those nine years. "What else are you and Sam doing?"

"Swimming. Tennis. Golf. I don't like golf. It's too slow," he said quickly. "You're going to tell me that golf is like *Midsummer's Night Dream*. I might learn something."

"You might. There are a lot of golf pros out there who don't think it's slow."

He was silent. "Why did you call me in the middle of the night? Are you in trouble?"

"No." She paused. "Can't I call you without being in trouble?"

"Maybe I said it wrong." He didn't speak again, and she

could almost hear the cogs turning. "I meant you think that I might worry about you being in trouble."

"And would you worry, Luke?"

"You're very strong and smart. It wouldn't be reasonable for me to worry. Everyone says that you're very good at what you do."

"I didn't ask if it was reasonable. I asked if you'd worry."

He was silent, then said slowly, "I'd worry."

She felt a warm rush of love and joy. Every admission from him of a growing affection between them was a triumph. When she had rescued him, she'd had to start at the beginning in earning his love. After his emotional deprivation, she could not push him, but slowly he was learning that there was a bond between them.

"I don't mean to insult you," Luke said. "But I'd be willing to come and help you if you need me. I've been taught very well."

Taught the skills of weapons and guerrilla fighting, taught violence and cruelty, taught to bear pain without flinching. All the things a child should never have to face. Lessons that Rakovac had known would torture Catherine when he told her about them. And it had been torture, it had nearly broken her heart. "I know you have. But I'd like you to forget that now."

"But how can I do that?" he asked in wonder.

She had responded instinctively. She wanted to block out all that ugliness, but she knew she had to deal with her own horror and accept what Luke had become through those experiences. "That was stupid of me. Of course, you can't forget it. And thank you for the offer. If I find I need you, I'll be sure to call." She added lightly, "But I'd rather think of you having a good time with Sam. You like him?"

"I think so," he said cautiously. "He knows a lot." Another silence. "He smiles quite a bit. But I don't think he's laughing at me."

"I'm sure he wouldn't dare. Maybe he's just enjoying his job. He always wanted to go back to teaching."

"I guess that could be why."

"Did I tell you that Kelly was coming to visit you this week?"

"No, but she called me," he said shortly. "She told me to get ahead in my studies so that we could have some time together. She's very bossy."

"But you like her." It was true that fourteen-year-old Kelly Winters could be very domineering with Luke and had been from the start of their relationship. But he seemed to accept it from her as he would not have taken it from an adult. They struck sparks from each other, but it didn't stop them from getting along. Kelly was as mature and scarred in her own way as Luke. She had come into Catherine's life because Catherine had been sent to rescue her and her father when they'd been prisoners in the camp of a drug lord in Colombia. Kelly had survived, but her father had been killed before her eyes. She was a genius on the scale of a young Einstein, and that had led her down another rocky path. Perhaps that was why she and Luke understood each other. "I hoped to have her with us before this, but she has to attend that think tank at that college in Virginia."

"I didn't miss her. Well, maybe a little. She's kind of . . . interesting."

"I'm sure she'd appreciate it if you'd tell her."

"No, she wouldn't. She doesn't need me to tell her stuff."

He paused. "She won't like it that you aren't here. She likes you better than anyone. She told me you saved her life."

"We're friends. But she likes you, too. So enjoy yourselves and don't argue too much. Okay?"

"Okay." He added haltingly, "You know, I think I'd like it better if you were here, too." Then he added quickly, "But I'm not like Kelly. I don't need— You go do what you have to do."

He would never say he missed her, but this was so close it brought tears to her eyes. "I want to be there with you, too. You know I wouldn't have left you right now if it hadn't been to help Eve. I can't ever repay her for helping me find you, but maybe this is a start. Do you understand?"

"I think I do. It's like the honor thing in all those Knights of the Round Table books. Sometimes it's hard to connect the ideas in books with real life."

And books were all Luke had had to go by in that barren world Rakovac had made for him. "Yeah, it's like the honor thing. I'll be back as soon as I can." She cleared her throat. "In the meantime get back to *Midsummer Night's Dream*. And talk to Kelly about it. Maybe she'll have an opinion that will make you see something worthwhile in it."

"Nah, she'll only tell me to look for the patterns in the story. That's all she thinks about."

Catherine chuckled. "Probably. Good night, Luke."

"Good night, Catherine." He hung up.

He never called her "Mother," and she would never insist on that intimacy. Perhaps it would never happen. It was enough that he looked upon her as a friend. They were just learning each other, taking small, halting steps.

But this step tonight had been bigger and might lead her closer to him. Lord, she hoped that it would. Sometimes she ached with the need to tell him how much she loved him, how desperately she had loved him all through the years they'd been separated.

Play it cool. Don't blow it. Let him come to you.

She shoved her phone in her jacket pocket and started the car.

But for now put him out of your thoughts and go do your job. One of the big reasons she had her Luke back was the risk Eve and Joe had taken to rescue him. Now, as she'd told Luke, it was payback time and Catherine had an agenda.

Give Eve what she wanted most in the world.

Keep Joe from injuring himself more by trying to get out of that hospital bed and going after Bonnie's killer.

Find Bonnie's body and the man who killed her.

Where are you, John Gallo?

CATHERINE HEADED NORTH TOWARD the vast woodland acreage Gallo owned about seventy miles north of Milwaukee. It wasn't an easy area to search: thick woods and shrubbery, hills to the north that plunged to a huge lake hundreds of feet below. She had told Eve she believed in instinct, and she would go with it until proved mistaken. Gallo knew those woods, they were familiar, almost home to him. He even had a cabin on the property.

Not that he would be at the cabin. With the sheriff and his deputies crawling all over the property, it would be stupid for him to stay anywhere but in the wild. Gallo wasn't stupid. She had only met him face-to-face once, when they'd been on the hunt for Paul Black. It had been a fleeting encounter and barbed with antagonism on her part, but she'd become accustomed to making quick judgments. It had often been necessary to save her neck. She had grown up on the streets of Hong Kong, and that ability had developed in those first years of childhood. Her first impression of John Gallo was of sharp, lethal capability.

Definitely not stupid.

But she had to know more than that about him, dredge her memory of every single inkling she'd had of Gallo in that moment. Not only in that moment, but what she knew of him in general from Eve and her own research. She would take time as soon as she reached the property to go over everything that she knew and felt about John Gallo.

You always had to know your target.

CHAPTER
10

TWO HOURS LATER, SHE DREW up before Gallo's cabin, where two sheriff's cars were already parked.

She was surprised. When she'd been there before, the sheriff had been doing twenty-four-hour searches, but she'd not expected them to set up a command center. She certainly hadn't expected them to be there at this hour of the morning. It was nearly 3:00 A.M.

A young man in a deputy's uniform came out of the cabin as she opened the car door. He was stocky and sandy-haired, and his boyish face was very wary. "Ma'am?"

"Catherine Ling. CIA." She showed him her ID. "Is Sheriff Rupert here?"

"Deputy Rand Johan." The concern in his expression vanished as he grinned. "No, ma'am. He only left a couple of us here overnight in case Gallo showed up. The sheriff will be back in the morning."

"He thought Gallo would show up at his cabin?" She shook her head. "Not likely."

"Well, the search is kind of winding down. Actually, Sheriff Rupert thinks maybe he's left the area. He says we'll continue the search for the next few days, but then we'll gradually start pulling back."

"I see." Evidently the sheriff was getting frustrated and had the same thought as Eve concerning the possibilities that Gallo would try to leave the woods. Catherine had thought he'd give it more than these few days before he'd abandon the hunt.

The deputy saw her expression, and said quickly, "It's not as if Gallo is any real threat. He's only wanted for questioning."

"He killed a man in these woods only a few days ago."

"Paul Black. But we've got the report back on Black as well as Ms. Duncan's statement." His lips tightened. "A serial killer who specialized in murdering kids? Anyone deserves a medal for killing a snake like that. I'd do it myself."

And so would Catherine, but she wouldn't admit it to this youngster. "Black made a statement to Eve Duncan that Gallo was guilty of the same crime, the killing of her daughter, Bonnie."

"Who's to say the scumbag wasn't lying? Like I said, Gallo's wanted for questioning. Don't get me wrong, we're doing our job. But it's not a case of life or death, and we've spent enough of the taxpayers' money." He smiled. "Would you like to come in and have a cup of coffee? The sheriff didn't tell me the CIA was interested in this case. Gallo isn't connected to terrorists or anything, is he?"

"No."

"I didn't think so." He turned toward the cabin.

But Catherine had been caught by that first response. "Why didn't you think Gallo was connected to terrorists?"

"Gallo's not the type. He seemed to be a real nice guy."

She stiffened. "Wait a minute. You've met Gallo?"

"Yeah, he invited us all up here for a barbecue when he took over the place. He said that you never could tell when you needed the law to protect you, and he wanted to make sure that we all knew each other and exactly where the place was located."

"What?"

"It was a real nice barbecue. My wife brought the potato salad."

"How . . . nice."

"He's a local. He was brought up in Wisconsin before he went into the service. He was an Army Ranger, you know."

"Yes, I did know."

"I always wanted to be a Ranger, but then I met Sarah. That put an end to that. I'll be right back." He ducked into the cabin.

She pursed her lips in a silent whistle. A barbecue? Just a local boy trying to protect himself by getting to know the local authorities. Clever and foresighted. Gallo was a man who was accustomed to trouble and trying to minimize the impact.

And he had done just that with the sheriff and his deputies. They would do their job, but they liked Gallo and would give him every benefit of the doubt.

And by tomorrow she would be almost alone in these woods with Gallo.

Under the circumstances, that would not be a bad thing. No one to get in her way. She'd always preferred to work alone. No one for her to worry about when she got on the hunt.

"Come on in." Deputy Johan stood in the doorway. "Andy is putting on the coffee. He's real eager to meet you. He said the sheriff told him about you." He grinned. "The sheriff said you were one of those Lara Croft types. You sure look the part."

"Thank you . . . I think." She moved toward him. "I actually came to take a look around the cabin and see if I could find anything that would be helpful. I don't really know what I'm looking for. Do you think the sheriff would object if I did that?"

"Nah, you're one of us. Though I think you're out of luck. Do you want us to help?"

"No, I know my way around. On the night that Gallo took it on the run, I brought a child here who Paul Black had kidnapped. I had to find a haven for her until we could get her out to safety."

"See, Black was a real scumbag. Not worth bothering about."

"Yes, I see your point." She took a last look at the dark woods before she entered the house.

You're out there. I feel it, Gallo. You felt safe here with all these good old boys looking for you, but that's going to change. I'm going to know you so well that you're not going to be able to breathe without me knowing how deep. Before long, we're going to be close as lovers.

Lovers. Where had that come from? Probably because Gallo had been Eve's lover all those years ago when she was only a sixteen-year-old kid.

"Agent Ling?"

Her smile was dazzling. "Coming. I need that coffee. Then you and Andy can tell me all about the barbecue and everything that you learned about Gallo. Probably a lot of details sank into your mind though you didn't realize it. It's automatic with a good law officer like you . . ."

CATHERINE WATCHED THE TAILLIGHTS of the three sheriff's cars fade in the distance before she turned and went back into the cabin. Sheriff Rupert had been pleasant and firm and as much as told her she was wasting her time, continuing to search for Gallo.

And she had been pleasant and firm and resisted telling him to go to hell. It had been a very satisfactory interchange because she was now rid of them and could run her own show.

Should she get some sleep before she took off into the woods?

Probably. She wouldn't get much rest once she was on the hunt. She'd had breakfast cooked by the accommodating deputies, so that she could dispense with food for a while. She'd have the field rations in her backpack when she needed them. She'd be living with that backpack for the next days or weeks. She'd leave her suitcase in the trunk of her car and take only the necessities of the hunt.

But first she'd go over the Gallo information as she'd meant to do when she'd first driven up to the cabin. She sat down at the kitchen table and opened the folder she'd taken from her knapsack.

She knew most of it by heart, but there might be something she'd missed. Some of the information she'd gathered from various intelligence agencies. Some were notes about details Eve had told her about Gallo during the period she'd known him as a young girl.

Those Eve notes were very short and to the point. She'd lived in a housing project in Atlanta. At sixteen, she'd met John Gallo, who had recently moved down to the neighborhood from Milwaukee so that his uncle could get medical treatment from the local veterans' hospital. She'd become impregnated during the four weeks they were together before he'd left to join the Army. After that time, she had not seen him again and had been told by his uncle, Ted Danner, that he'd been killed on a mission to North Korea. She'd given birth to her daughter, Bonnie, and her life had gone on without John Gallo or contact with his uncle.

All brief, cool, and cut-and-dried. Yet Catherine was sure that there was nothing cool or unemotional about that period between Gallo and Eve. Even as a sixteen-year-old, Eve would have been strong and in control, and for her to be careless and become pregnant would be unlikely. Eve had told her there had been no emotional bond between her and Gallo, and that it had been a purely sexual relationship. But that sexual affair had been enough for Eve to take a chance that would change her life forever.

And Gallo had been the catalyst.

She took out the picture of Gallo taken when he had gone into the Army.

Olive skin, dark eyes, a full sensual mouth, a faint indentation in his chin. Yes, stunning good looks. Mature for his nineteen years. Anyone could see why a woman would be drawn to him.

And the brief glimpse she'd had of the older John Gallo had been even more impressive. A streak of silver in that dark hair, wariness, confidence born of experience . . . and yet still that hint of recklessness. And a personality so strong that he had managed to persuade Eve that he was innocent when she'd found out he was still alive and a suspect in her daughter's murder.

Innocent and able to point the way to a suitable substitute, Paul Black.

"You're quite a spellbinder, John Gallo," she murmured. "Now what can I do to break that spell and bring you down?"

She switched to the intelligence reports on Gallo. He had been a Ranger who had been sent with two other soldiers into North Korea by Army Intelligence officers Nate Queen and Thomas Jacobs on a supposed mission to retrieve a ledger with information regarding North Korea's attempts to acquire nuclear materials. The mission had gone south and he had hidden the ledger before he was captured. He had been thrown into a prison and undergone deprivation and torture for seven years before he escaped. In the hospital in Tokyo he had been diagnosed as mentally unstable, a schizophrenic with frequent blackouts. Yet Queen and Jacobs had taken him out of the hospital and continued to use him in their intelligence missions abroad. Catherine had thought it bizarre the first time she'd learned about it. The action stank of a suicide mission. But Gallo had survived and learned that Queen was dirty, involved in drugs and smuggling. He had retrieved the ledger from Korea.

The ledger.

Catherine flipped back to the statement Eve had given her about the story Gallo had told her about the ledger. It had proved to be evidence of Queen's and Jacobs's involvement in the drug trade and had been held by a North Korean officer who had been their partner. Gallo had used it to blackmail Queen to make them release him from those missions that were becoming increasingly deadly in nature. He had demanded money for his years of incarceration as a prisoner of war and built the fund into a fortune by his ability at card counting, a skill he had taught himself in prison.

Her telephone rang.

Eve.

"How is he?" Catherine asked when she picked up the phone.

"Better. I wanted to let you know Joe asked for you. He wants to see you."

"Did he tell you why?"

"Yes, he said to wait for him."

Catherine chuckled. "Tell him to tend to his job of getting well, and I'll tend to mine. He's afraid he's going to be left out of the action."

"Is he? What are you doing?"

"Not much. I'm at Gallo's cabin." She glanced around the living room and kitchen. "It's nice. Rough, but all the basic comforts. I like it much better than those A-frame luxury cabins I've seen. That's not even like being in the woods. You were here when you were setting a trap for Black, weren't you?"

"Yes." Eve paused. "I can't imagine you lolling around doing nothing."

"I didn't say I'm doing nothing. I'm thinking and trying to get a mental fix on Gallo," she said. "But it's hard without having the most important piece to the puzzle." She paused. "I know that for years Queen had Black in his employ as an assassin who removed everyone who got in Queen's way. I know that Gallo supposedly thought that Paul Black had killed Bonnie as revenge against him and went after him. He searched for him for years."

"So what's the missing piece?"

"Bonnie. John Gallo never had any contact with Bonnie. He couldn't have even known about her until after he got out of that prison. Why did he care enough about her death that he would devote all that time to finding her murderer?"

Eve was silent.

She obviously didn't want to answer, but Catherine couldn't drop it. She had to know. "You told me once that he'd told you that he loved Bonnie, and I said that he couldn't. He never knew her. But he had to have told you something that convinced you. What was it?"

"What difference does it make? I was gullible. He spun me a tale, and I wanted to believe him."

"What tale?"

"It doesn't matter. You don't have to know that to be able to find him."

"You're wrong. I have to know *him*."

"Then heaven help you. He'll probably dazzle you as he did me."

Dazzle. Yes, it was a good word for the way Gallo was manipulating everyone around him. "You're not going to tell me."

Eve was silent again. "You wouldn't believe me."

"We're friends. I know you."

"You wouldn't believe me. If you catch up with John Gallo, ask him."

"I will. But by that time, the question may be moot."

"I'm going to hang up now and go back to Joe. I'll keep you informed of his progress. He's already making great strides."

"Then I'd better stop thinking and start moving." She chuckled. "I don't want you to have to keep that promise to tie Joe to the bed. How is Jane?"

"Protective, loving. She's with Joe now. Good-bye, Catherine. Take care." She hung up.

Catherine slowly put the phone back in her jacket. Eve had been of little help. Catherine wouldn't believe Eve? They were close friends. Eve should know that she'd trust anything she told her.

But the bond that was between Eve and Gallo was complicated, and Catherine had been aware of the emotion that still lay between them. No longer sex. Not love. Eve loved Joe with her entire being. But that clearly didn't stop her from feeling something for Gallo.

What? If Catherine was forced to kill him, would Eve feel a hidden sense of resentment? She said she'd kill him herself because of Bonnie's murder, and Catherine had believed her.

Eve was not going to talk to her about it, so she might just as well block it out and work it through on her own. That was her usual procedure anyway. Why was this any different?

Because Eve was her friend, and that was a treasure beyond price, and Catherine was trying to bend over backward to keep from hurting her.

Stop fretting about it. She got up from the table and went to the tiny bedroom and lay down. Four hours' sleep. Then she'd be up and leave the cabin.

She pulled up the coverlet and closed her eyes. She was lying in Gallo's bed. It felt . . . strange to have this strong sense of awareness of him. If anything, she should be aware of those deputies who had recently used this bed. Before they left, they had changed the linens and made up the bed in case she wanted to use it, but it wasn't of them that she was thinking.

Gallo.

He was dominating her thoughts, and it was natural she would imagine him lying in this bed in the cabin that belonged to him.

But it was closer to *feeling*. She could almost smell the scent of him. The mattress was hard against her body, and she wondered if that was the way he liked it.

She had promised herself that she was going to be as close to Gallo as a lover.

Was this the way it started . . . ?

St. Joseph's Hospital
Milwaukee, Wisconsin

"I JUST SPOKE TO CATHERINE," Eve said as she sat down beside Joe's bed in ICU. "She said to tend to your business of getting out of this hospital and not to nag her. Or words to that effect."

"She's on Gallo's property?"

Eve nodded. "She's at the cabin." She added quietly, "She'll find him, Joe. I know how you're feeling. I want to be out there hunting Gallo, too. It's my job, not Catherine's. But we have to wait until you're better."

"I am better. They're moving me out of ICU in a few hours," he said impatiently. "What would it hurt to give me a little more time?"

"It would be more than a little. You almost died, Joe."

"Yeah, I know." He was silent. "But I'm going to heal fast. She won't have to wait long."

"Tell that to the doctors. Their most optimistic prediction is four weeks."

"Then they'd better go back to the drawing board. I'm not going to be here that long."

"Joe . . ." Her lips tightened. "Dammit, stop this. Do you want to scare me? You can't jump out of bed just because you want to do it. Let yourself heal."

"You think I'm just being bullheaded." He didn't speak for a moment, looking down at their clasped hands. "And considering the fact that I'm usually the most stubborn ass on the planet, you have a right. But I'm not about to get out of this bed until I'm strong enough to function. I'm just telling you that time is coming very soon."

"That's not what—" There was something in his expression that caused her to stop the protest she was about to make. Her gaze searched his face. "How can you know that?"

"We're coming to the end," Joe said simply. "She says I have to be there for it."

She stiffened. "Catherine?"

He shook his head.

She whispered, "Bonnie?"

"She brought me back. She took my hand and told me it wasn't time for me to go." He looked up and met her gaze. "She said you were going to need me."

"I always need you."

"No, this is different." He paused. "We're coming to the end, Eve."

She laughed shakily. "Does that mean we're going to be called to the great beyond?"

"Maybe. I don't think so." His hand tightened. "But if it did, I wouldn't mind if you were there with me. That was my only regret when I was in that darkness. I didn't want to leave you. I wanted you to live, but I wanted to be there to make sure you were happy."

"Joe, you've spent most of our years together trying to make me happy."

"And that was my privilege." He lifted her hand to his lips. "I don't think that a love like this happens every day. I couldn't believe that it happened to me. And then I realized there had to be a reason that I had to nurture that love and the gifts it was bringing me."

"Yeah, some gifts." She stroked his cheek. "Dealing with my obsession for finding Bonnie, being put on the back burner whenever I was doing a reconstruction."

"And the gift of your honesty . . . and your love."

"Oh, I *do* love you, Joe," she said softly. "It's a wonder you were patient enough to put up with me until I saw it. Talk about gifts." She could feel the tears welling, but she had to get the words out. "When Bonnie was taken from me, I couldn't see any light at the end of the tunnel. Everything was dark. But then you were there, and I knew something was . . . different. I didn't know what it was, but I felt as if I might be able to make it through." She drew a deep shaky breath. "And then later, when I knew how much I loved you, I'm not even sure that you knew it, too. I said the words, I tried to show you, but my love for Bonnie was always there between us."

"I knew it." He smiled. "And how could I blame Bonnie? I wouldn't have known you if it hadn't been for her. As I've been lying here all these hours since I came around, I've been wondering if maybe it was Bonnie who purposely brought us together. You were alone. Did she know you needed someone to love you as much as I do?" He made a face. "Though I'm glad that she didn't make a ghostly appearance on that first day I met you. I was having enough trouble coping with the way I was feeling."

And Joe had begun seeing Bonnie only recently, and it had still shaken him, Eve thought. He had been on edge and uncertain and questioning his own sanity. It had taken him a long time to accept that the spirit Bonnie was no hallucination, and he had never been comfortable with the idea.

But there had been no hint of disturbance in his demeanor now when he was talking about Bonnie bringing him back to Eve. His expression was calm, thoughtful, and yet there was determination and strength in the set of his mouth and chin.

"It's possible, I suppose," she said. "I believe in the power of love, and Bonnie loved me. And she loves you, too, Joe."

He nodded. "I know she does. She told me." He was silent again, thinking. "I got to know her very well while we were traveling in that darkness. All through our years together, Eve,

I could never love her because I never knew her. She was gone before I came to you. But I know her now. She *touched* me. She took my hand, and I experienced everything about her. She's . . . beautiful."

"Yes, she is." The tears were falling now. "Like you, Joe."

"Don't say that too loud. It will destroy my macho image," he said. "But I can love her now. It's so easy . . ."

It had been a long time coming, but the joy Eve knew at those words would have been worth a much longer wait. It formed a bridge that spanned the emotional abyss that had been the only rift between them. "I'm glad that you got to know her," she said unsteadily. "I tried to tell you, but there weren't any words."

"There still aren't." He reached out and touched the tears on her cheeks. "Don't do this. It hurts me."

"It shouldn't. I'm happy." She wiped her eyes. "But next time you talk with Bonnie, tell her that she should bring me into the conversation. I can never count on when she's going to show up, and it's disconcerting when she tells you to disobey doctor's orders."

"She didn't exactly tell me that. I just knew."

"Knew what? That she wanted you to bail out of this hospital?"

"No, that she was going to help me to heal. It should be a cinch for her to offer a little mojo in that direction. After all, she managed to pull me back from the pearly gates." He chuckled. "If that was where I was heading. It felt pretty good, so maybe I might have gotten lucky."

"No, I was the one who got lucky."

"Keep thinking that way." His gaze went to the door, where a nurse and two orderlies were coming into the ICU. "And here's my escort to my new room. It's the first step, Eve. Tell Catherine I'm on my way."

One Week Later

SHE HAD found him!

Catherine wriggled snakelike down the incline that led to the cliff that fell off steeply to the lake below.

She had caught a glimpse of Gallo as he moved through the forest a half mile back. At first she hadn't been certain it was Gallo, but then he had come out of the shadows of the trees, and she had caught a glimpse of his face. Slight indentation at the chin, dark hair . . .

Yes.

She had been concentrating on this area of the property for the last three days, and she'd had a hunch she was getting near.

She propped herself against a boulder, and her gaze narrowed on the thicket of trees on the slope. He should be coming out of those trees any minute, and she'd have him.

Eve wanted him alive. Catherine silently took her dart gun from her backpack and inserted one of Hu Chang's special darts. Not as special as some others her old teacher had made for her. But the mamba venom and a few other lethal poisons weren't applicable in this case. This sedative would put Gallo out for a solid five minutes and give him another fifteen of lethargy.

"Come on, Gallo," she whispered. "Let me give you a little nap."

One minute.

Two.

He didn't come out of the trees.

Five minutes.

Dammit, where was he?

And then she felt the hair rise on the back of her neck in the most primitive of signals.

Someone was watching her.

He was watching her.

She instinctively dove behind the boulder and waited.

Where are you, Gallo?

Her heart was pounding.

She could feel him out there in the darkness.

Or was he behind her?

She wasn't sure. She listened.

She couldn't hear him. God, he was good.

But she couldn't stay there when he knew her location, and she didn't know his. Since she was trying to get him without a lethal commitment, she was at a disadvantage.

Fade away. Disappear. If she caught a glimpse of him, then try to line up the shot.

If not, give up the opportunity and come back another time.

She dove into the bushes that bordered the scraggly line of pines beside the boulders.

No sound.

Move swiftly.

She no longer felt his eyes on her.

But that might only mean he was close but could not see her.

And she couldn't see him, dammit.

Put distance between them.

Damn, she hated to run from Gallo.

She'd almost had the bastard.

She *would* have him.

Only an opening foray, Gallo.

The battle is yet to come . . .

Two Days Later

SHE WAS GETTING CLOSE again, Gallo realized.

He felt a rush of excitement as he caught a fleeting glimpse of Catherine before she disappeared into the pines.

She was probably going to circle and come at him from behind. He was still, listening for a sound.

There was no sound. But he'd bet that she was in motion.

Stay and confront her? Risky. She had almost gotten close enough to take him out twice in the last few days.

Why not stay? What did he care?

But he did care, or he would have plunged off the cliff into the lake in those first hours after he'd gone on the run.

Bonnie had made him care.

And he cared because Catherine Ling's pursuit had pierced the wall of despair and desperation that surrounded him and injected him with a shot of pure adrenaline. The hunt brought back memories of the missions that had been his life for so many years. Memories that enabled him to block out the more recent painful recollections.

The missions had been brutal, fast, deadly. Hunt, find, kill.

But Catherine Ling's pursuit had not been brutal. In the few glimpses he had caught of her, he had thought she was like a black panther, stalking, graceful, beautiful.

But, yes, definitely fast and deadly.

So did he run again?

He started moving. As silent as Catherine. As fast as Catherine. He could feel his heart start to pound, the excitement electrifying every muscle.

Follow me.

Let's play the game a little longer.

Who knows? I may let you win it.

CHAPTER
11

One Week Later

SHE NEEDED A BATH, Catherine thought as she woke in the cave where she'd sheltered for the day. She slept from dawn until late afternoon because the hunt was at night. She'd taken a chance and swum in the cold lake on the property the day before yesterday. She couldn't afford to do it again anytime soon. She had thought she sensed Gallo and had quickly returned to shore.

It could be imagination. It seemed she was always sensing Gallo these days. His presence was all around her, in the trees, the hills, the lake.

He was the last thing she thought of before she went to sleep and the first thing when she woke in the morning. Not that she slept much.

Not since she became aware that Gallo was also stalking her.

The realization had come to her about two weeks after she had found and begun to stalk him. This hunt had been like nothing in her experience. He was like no one she had ever targeted. A phantom, silent, swift, moving all around her and yet only permitting her brief glimpses, the slimmest of opportunities.

After that first encounter he could have chosen to leave the area, but he hadn't done it. He had stayed and let her stalk him. Then, as time passed, she was aware that it had become a duel. He was no longer content to be the prey.

Why?

She didn't care any longer. She had been swept up in the dance, and every minute was charged, every hour was electrified by the knowledge that any minute she might see him again.

And that minute might be her last.

Her phone vibrated, and she pulled it out of her jacket.

Eve.

"You haven't called me in the last two weeks," Eve said.

"I've been busy."

"And you sound funny."

"I just woke up." And she hadn't spoken to anyone for the last two days, when she'd called home and checked on Luke. "How is Joe?"

"Better all the time. He's out of bed and in therapy. He may get released soon." She paused. "I hoped I'd hear something positive from you before that."

"So did I. Nothing yet."

"You still think he's in those woods?"

"Oh, yes." She gazed at the shrubs several yards away. He could be as close to her as those trees. But she didn't think so. She would feel him. These days, every nerve, every muscle of her body seemed attuned to him. "He's here. I may be getting closer."

As close as a lover.

"Well, you may have company soon," Eve said. "I won't be able to keep Joe away from there for long. Then we'll both be up there to reinforce you."

"No!" The rejection was sharp and instinctive, and it had nothing to do with protecting Joe, she realized. This dance with Gallo belonged to her. She didn't want anyone else to cut in before the end. "Do your best to keep him away."

Silence. "Are you all right, Catherine?"

"I'm fine. I'm dirty, I stink of sweat and dirt, and I know this forest better than I ever wanted to know any place. But other than that, I'm doing well." She added, "I'll try to call you more often. Give my best to Joe." She hung up.

She took a protein bar out of the knapsack. Eat. Find a creek to wash her teeth and face, then start out again.

The eagerness was beginning to sing through her as she bit into the bar. It was going to end soon. She would find him and put him down.

Or Gallo would find her.

Either way, it would be the end of the dance.

Eight Days Later

CATHERINE'S BREATH WAS COMING hard and fast as she ran up the hill.

He was no more than a football field ahead of her. She had

caught a brief glimpse of him on the lower slopes, then another a few minutes ago.

He was getting careless. He could have stayed deeper in the brush, and she might not have seen him. Are you getting tired, Gallo? I'm not. I can go on forever.

As long as the adrenaline of the dance kept her moving.

But he'd reached the top of the hill and disappeared into the trees.

She slowed, and her hand closed on her dart gun.

Her catching sight of him could have been a deliberate ploy on his part to lead her into a trap.

She darted into the trees, her gaze searching the darkness.

No Gallo.

She moved carefully toward the opening in the trees near the top of the hill. Where was he?

She stopped short as she reached the edge of the trees.

Gallo. Out in the open. The moonlight revealing him with crystal clarity.

He was on the shale slope of the cliff.

Why the hell had he led her there?

It didn't make sense. He had to realize there was no cover for him until he reached the trees over forty yards away. He had been increasingly reckless for the last two days, and it had bewildered her. Dammit, did he want her to shoot him? For all he knew, it wouldn't be a dart but a bullet that would cut him down.

She was being ridiculous. What difference did it make how reckless he was being? It was her chance to take him down.

She lifted her dart gun.

But if she shot him while he was on that slippery shale slope, he would probably roll down off the cliff to the lake hundreds of feet below them. She would kill him.

He glanced behind him.

She knew he couldn't see her in the trees, but he was aware that she was there. Just as she knew when he was near her. It was part of the dance.

He smiled, and she knew it was at her. He was taunting her. Crazy. Dammit, he knew he was in range.

"Damn you, get off that slope," she whispered.

He moved slowly, deliberately, toward the trees on the other side of the slope.

She breathed a sigh of relief. Now to figure a way that she could cross that barren strip of shale and track him into the trees. Maybe go up toward the top of the hill and work her way—

The edge of the slope broke away from the hill and threw Gallo to the ground. He rolled toward the edge of the cliff!

"No!"

She was out of the trees and crossing the shale slope, her boots sliding on the slippery surface. The slope was still crumbling . . .

Where was Gallo?

Clinging to the edge of the cliff. His fingers white as he gripped the edge.

She stood over him. He was looking up at her, his gaze on the gun in her hand.

"Do it," he said hoarsely. "All it would take would be one shot. Even that dart gun would do the trick."

She hadn't even known she was still holding the gun.

"Do it." His dark eyes were glittering fiercely into hers. "Dammit, one shot."

"Screw you. I'll do what I please." She threw the gun aside and fell to her knees. "Give me your left hand and boost yourself on the edge with the right when I pull."

He didn't move.

"You *listen* to me. I won't have it. It's not going to end like this. Dammit, give me your hand."

"You're not strong enough to bear my weight."

"The hell I'm not." She gripped his left hand and wrist with both of her hands. "Now when I count to three let go. One. Two." She braced herself. "Three!" She pulled, jerking backward with all her strength. Then she lunged forward as the weight of his body unbalanced her. But his right hand was bracing on the ground, lifting his weight as she grabbed him under the arms.

She jerked backward, and he came down on top of her as he scrambled over the edge of the cliff!

The breath was knocked out of her. She struggled to breathe as she fought the darkness. Then Gallo was off her, and she was looking hazily up at him. Dark eyes glittering, lips tight and bitter . . .

There was something in his hand . . .

A gun.

"I told you to shoot me," he said. "I expected it. You should have done it."

He pulled the trigger.

Darkness.

* * *

SHE OPENED HER EYES TO SEE a fire only feet away from her. A campfire, shouldering low . . .

And the shadows of the flames playing on the face of the man sitting cross-legged on the ground across the fire.

Gallo . . .

"Good. You're awake. I didn't know how potent the drug in that little pop pistol was going to turn out to be. You could have set up the dose for me, and I'm a hell of a lot bigger than you. How do you feel?"

She felt fuzzy and lethargic. But that was how she should feel, she realized, as his words sank home. He had turned her own weapon against her. "I'll live . . ." Her tongue felt thick as she tried to speak. "Disappointed?"

"No." He stirred the fire with the stick he was holding. "Aftereffects? Paralysis?"

"I'll be back to normal after fifteen minutes."

"A very efficient drug. What is it?"

"You . . . wouldn't recognize it. Hu Chang made . . . it for me."

"Hu Chang?"

"An old friend." The thick lethargy was starting to clear, and she realized that her wrists were bound in front of her. "You have me tied up like a pig for market. Are you . . . afraid of me, Gallo?"

"Yes. You're formidable, Catherine. I can't tell you how much I've enjoyed our game."

He called it a game. She called it a dance. But the concept was the same. "I saved your neck, you son of a bitch."

"And you would have taken it the minute you had me on safe ground. I'd judge you acted on impulse when you decided to pull me back from the brink. I'd probably have done the same." He glanced at the dart gun on the ground beside him. "Or maybe not. Why the darts? Why not a bullet?"

"Eve wants you alive. She thinks you know where Bonnie is buried. Do you?"

He looked down into the fire. "Maybe. I don't know . . ." He didn't speak for a moment. "Then I'm not the only one who tied your hands. Eve did it, too. It could have been fatal for you."

"Eve didn't tie them. I tied them. I make my own choices."

He glanced at the dart gun again. "I can see that." He reached over and picked up the pan of boiling hot water bubbling over the blaze. "Some of them have unhealthy consequences. I don't—" He stopped as he saw her stiffening, as she gazed at the boiling water. "You thought I was going to use this on you? That would be sacrilege. You have the most beautiful skin I've ever seen." He set the pan on the ground while he got a cup from the knapsack, poured instant coffee into it. "I may be a son of a bitch, but it would make me sick to damage it."

"You are sick. Eve says you're insane. She says you admitted it yourself."

"I did." He poured the hot water into the cup. "But it appears to come and go. Isn't that convenient? But all the more dangerous for anyone who might trust me in my saner moments." His voice was bitter with self-mockery. "I'm like a mad dog that should be put out of his misery. I tried to do it myself. But she wouldn't have it."

"Eve?"

"No, Bonnie." He brought the cup to Catherine and knelt

beside her. "Or maybe that was a delusion, too. Self-preservation is a powerful thing."

"I don't care about your delusions. But your sense of self-preservation doesn't appear to be too well developed. You were skipping around on that slope like the madman you claim to be. You must have known I'd have a clear shot."

"But you didn't take it." He smiled. "I was disappointed. But then providence took a hand." He looked down at her. "Are you strong enough yet to take this coffee cup, or should I help you?"

She was still too weak, but she was tempted to take it anyway. She needed the caffeine in her system. But she would probably spill it all over herself, and that would put her at still greater disadvantages with him. "I don't want it."

"And that means you're not strong enough yet." He put his arm under her shoulders and lifted her to a half-sitting position. "You have a choice of spitting it back in my face or drinking it and getting a bit closer to your usual fighting weight. It's up to you." He brought the cup to her lips. "I think I know which you'll choose. You may be pissed off at me for taking you out, but you're too professional not to prepare for our next battle."

She hesitated only for an instant before opening her lips.

"Ah, that's right." He tilted the cup, and the hot liquid poured into her mouth. "You're being totally intelligent." He took the cup away. "Just what I'd expect of you."

She was cradled in his arm, and he was so close she could smell the earthy scent of him and feel the heat of his body against her own. It was . . . disturbing.

His gaze was narrowed on her face. "What are you thinking?"

She met his gaze. "That you stink as much as I do."

Surprise flickered across his face. Then he chuckled. "I like the way you smell. It's . . . basic. I'm sorry the feeling isn't mutual."

It was mutual, she realized. But it shouldn't have been. Or maybe it was because of the almost barbaric interaction between them of the past days. "I prefer a higher plane to basic."

"I know. You would never have chanced taking that bath in the lake if it wasn't important to you."

Her gaze flew to his face. Dammit, she had *known* he was there.

He nodded. "But I had only a glimpse before you took flight like a frightened swan. Your instincts are too damn good." He lifted the cup to her lips again. "Who is Hu Chang?"

"I told you, my friend."

"A very skilled friend. Was he also your lover?"

"No."

He gave another sip of coffee. "A father figure?"

"No. Hu Chang is old enough to be my grandfather. Not that it would make any difference. Age is nothing."

He held the cup steady as he gave her the last of the coffee. "That's right, I remember that when I was reading the dossier on you that you married your CIA partner and he was sixty-two to your seventeen. Not exactly a marriage of equals."

"No, he was a better agent than I was."

"At first."

She was silent, then said grudgingly, "At first."

"You didn't want to admit that, but you were too honest to

lie." He smiled. "But that wasn't the playing field I was talking about."

How had they come to be talking about her private life when it had started with Hu Chang? "You had a dossier on me?"

"You were asking questions about me. You were pushing Eve in a direction I didn't want her to go." His smile faded. "Or maybe I did and wouldn't admit it. She had been out of my life for so long that I didn't think I had the right to have her know I was still alive. But you changed all that, you told her, and there was all hell to pay."

Yes, all hell, she thought. Black's death, Joe's wounding, Eve's agony. "I thought she had a right to know." She added grimly, "Since you were my first choice for Bonnie's killer. But you managed to convince Eve that I was wrong. You must be very persuasive."

"Yeah, that's me." He met her gaze. "Can't you tell? I can persuade the birds not to sing. I can persuade a wonderful little girl to step into my lair so that I can kill her." He carefully put her down and sat back on his heels. "You're blaming yourself for setting all this in motion."

"Don't you?"

"I don't blame anyone but myself. I don't have the right," he said wearily. "I thought I did once, but that's all gone."

There was something about his words that were reaching her, touching her, she realized incredibly. Dear God, what was happening? "You're right, you're the only one to blame." Move away from the terrible intimacy that was obscuring the facts and the way she should be regarding him.

"I'm glad we agree." He moved back to his former position beside the fire. "Are you feeling any better now?"

"Yes." Almost normal, almost ready to act. "Are you going to kill me?"

"I don't think so." His lips curved bitterly. "But we can't be sure, can we? I'm not stable."

"Then are you going to let me go?"

He shook his head. "I'm in something of a quandary. If I let you go, you'll just go back on the hunt. I couldn't be more sure of that. The next time one of us might die. Probably you, since you're more honorable than I am, and you made a promise to Eve. That would upset me." He tilted his head. "Unless you'd promise me not to try to hunt me down?"

She was silent.

"I didn't think so." He looked down at the fire. "So I don't see any solution but keeping you here with me. It probably won't be for too long. I imagine Eve and Joe will come looking for you if you don't communicate with them."

"No!"

"You're thinking I'm setting you up as bait?" He shook his head. "Maybe I am, but not as you think. I'm the prize, not you. Joe Quinn has the same training and instincts I have. Eve may want to keep me alive to pump me, but Quinn won't be able to resist giving me the coup de grace if I set it up right."

"You want him to kill you," she whispered.

"I can't seem to do it myself. I don't think she'll let me. I don't know why. I thought you would do it." He looked back at her. "That would have been the most divine way to go. The journey was probably the most exciting one I've ever taken, and the destination would have been right. But you failed me, Catherine."

He was telling the truth, and those simple words were shaking her to the core. It was too much. She shook her head. "Screw you. I won't be used by you. You want to commit suicide? Get a couple of hara-kiri swords and go to it."

He shook his head. "She won't let me," he said again. "I don't know why. Maybe she's saving me for Joe and Eve. But it's not like her."

"You're nuts," Catherine said curtly. "Now I do believe you're crazy. You're saying that Bonnie has come back from the grave to keep you from killing yourself? Bullshit."

"Is it? Ask Eve if it's bullshit." He held up his hand as she started to speak. "There's no use continuing on this vein. I know it's bizarre and beyond belief." His lips curved in a faint smile. "Chalk it up to another hallucination."

"I will." She paused. "You intend to keep me here all trussed up like this?"

"Yes."

"Then will you loosen these ropes? They're cutting into my wrists."

He studied her expression. Then he slowly nodded and got to his feet. "I don't like the idea of your being uncomfortable. It bothers me." He knelt beside her. "Hold up your wrists."

She lifted them and held them out to him.

"They don't—"

Now!

Her wrists came down whiplike on the bridge of his nose.

She rolled into his body, and her knee lifted and struck upward into his groin.

He grunted and bent double.

She rolled past him, jumped up, and took off for the trees.

She made it five yards before he tackled her and flipped her over.

She brought her tied wrists up and struck him in the side of his neck.

"No!" He was glaring down at her as he straddled her. His nose was bleeding, and he looked as fierce and barbaric as she felt. "Dammit, it's not going to be that way. I told you that I won't have you—" He stopped, staring down at her, the ferocity slowly faded from his expression. "Even bound and drugged, you managed to almost do it. Wonderful . . . Damn, you're wonderful. That's why it should have been you." His one hand was holding her wrists and with the other he loosened her hair, which was tied back in a chignon. His fingers combed through it until it was tumbling around her face and shoulders. He added softly, "And beautiful. This was the way you were when I saw you in the lake. You were all golden silk and shining ebony. I only got a glimpse of you, but it made me so hard I couldn't think of anything else for hours afterward." He was stroking her hair, slowly, sensuously. "And every time I stopped to sleep, I remembered . . ."

He was hard now. She could feel him against her. Feel the heat he was emitting. His eyes were dark and glittering in his taut face. His lips were half-parted and full and sensual. She stared up at him in helpless fascination. Dammit, her anger was abandoning her. She was having trouble breathing. Her breasts felt full, taut . . .

It was impossible. This mustn't happen. She had to get him away from her. She tore her gaze away from his own. "My hands are tied. Is that the way you like it? Are you going to rape me?"

He stiffened. "It was damn close." He got off her. "But it wouldn't be rape, would it? I'd see that it would just be another road of the journey we're on. And you liked that journey as much as I did."

He jerked her to her feet. "These ropes are loose enough. I'm going to tie you to that oak tree so that we can both get some sleep." He was pulling her toward the oak. "Neither one of us has been getting much of that in the past weeks."

"This doesn't make sense. Kill me or let me go."

"We've discussed that, and those aren't options." He shrugged. "And maybe I don't want them to be options. You've cheated me of what I thought was my way out. I think you should keep me entertained until Quinn shows up as a replacement." He shook his head. "And I don't mean that in the sexual sense. I don't believe you'll let me—but that's up to you. Maybe you'll decide that you should use me to distract yourself. I'm at your disposal."

She wouldn't look at him. She was still feeling the heat that had touched and scorched her only minutes before. "Make up your mind. An hour ago you were ready to kill me."

"Was I? But that game is over." He was roping her to the tree. He took her jacket and put it beneath her head to cushion it against the trunk. "I'll let you lie down full length next time

I'm awake enough to watch you. Do you want me to fasten your hair back up?"

"No!" She didn't want his hands on her. That loosening and threading had been unbearably sensual.

"Good. I like it down anyway." He turned and stretched out before the fire. "But I can see how you'd want it out of your way when you were after me. But that's all over now, isn't it?"

"No, this is just an intermission."

"I believe you're wrong. I think we've entered a new phase."

"And I think that you're fooling yourself."

"It's possible." He rested his cheek on his arm, his gaze focused on her. "But it feels different. You look fantastic with the firelight on you. I'm going to enjoy looking at you until I go to sleep." He made a face. "Well, maybe not enjoy. I'm definitely experiencing some discomfort at the moment. But that goes with the territory. It's worth it."

She was silent. "Why are you saying these things?"

"Because we've reached the end of our game. No subterfuge. No tricks. I can be open with you."

"Because you think Joe is going to kill you?"

"I hope he does. I hope I don't fight back." He added soberly, "But I might. You could take care of that if you chose. I'll keep this dart toy of yours and give you your gun back. We could have one final game."

"And let you use me? Screw you."

"I thought that's what you'd say." He smiled. "So I'll just lie here and accept the pleasure of the moment. Tomorrow I'll take you down to the lake and let you take a bath."

"I don't think so."

"We'll work something out that will cheat me, but give you a sense of security." He paused. "How close are we to getting Quinn out here?"

"I'm not sure. Eve said that he's making an amazing recovery."

"That doesn't surprise me. Bonnie is probably helping things along. I'm glad. It was my fault that Quinn was wounded. He was trying to keep me away from Black when the bastard knifed him."

"Bonnie, again? You appear to be as obsessive about Bonnie as Eve." She added deliberately, "I find that very strange when you told Eve that you believed Black when he claimed you killed her."

He flinched. "It doesn't seem strange to me. I love my daughter. I love her more than anything in this world or the next. But isn't there some saying that you always kill the thing you love?" His lips tightened. "That would be particularly applicable if you're mad."

"And not remember it?"

"I used to have blackouts about the time that Bonnie was killed." He tilted his head. "Are you questioning that I killed her? Eve didn't. She believed Black, too."

"I usually question everything. So far the only sign of insanity I've noticed in you is that you're convinced a dead child is controlling your actions. That's pretty weird. Particularly since you never met the kid." She looked at him curiously, "Or did you?"

"I guess you could say I never formally met her. I saw her once when she got off the school bus, and Eve met her. She was very . . . happy. I knew I couldn't show up in their lives and interfere between her and Eve." He shook his head. "But I knew her, Catherine. I knew her, and I loved her. Eve believed me when I first told her that, but she may not anymore."

"Can you blame her?"

"No, I've never blamed her for anything. I'm the one who left her when she was pregnant to fight her way in life with a child."

"She said you didn't know. She said that she didn't want you to know." She grimaced. "And you couldn't help her when you were in that North Korean prison. So it's idiotic to blame yourself for that."

"You're defending me again."

"No, I'm not." But she had been defending him, she realized with frustration. She kept falling into that trap. Why? It didn't make sense when he had bound her to this damn tree, and she was feeling annoyingly helpless. No, not helpless. He had given her choices. None of them acceptable. "I just don't like inaccuracies."

"I can see that would bother you. You're so sharp and clear-thinking that you always want to cut to the bone. I noticed that when I was tracking you." He smiled. "I'm glad I had that time with you, Catherine. You were a constant pleasure."

She went back to the question that he had only waltzed around. "So why are you fixated on those weird ideas about Bonnie?"

He shook his head. "I don't think I'm prepared to discuss that with you now, Catherine. I like the idea of you defending me even if you're mistaken. I want to enjoy it for a while."

She gazed at him in astonishment. "You're enjoying this?"

"Not nearly as much as I'd like, but I've always believed in taking pleasure wherever I could. I learned that in that Korean prison." He stretched like a cat before once more settling his head on his arm, gazing at her. "So yes, I'm enjoying this moment. I'm enjoying *you*, Catherine."

"Why? Are you into bondage?"

He chuckled. "No, I wish I could release you. You can't imagine the excitement you brought me during the past weeks. Every day, there was the anticipation of catching a glimpse of you. Every trail was one that you might have taken."

And she had known that same excitement, that identical anticipation. She looked away from him. "So now you're gloating because you have me?"

"No, this wasn't how I intended it to be." He said softly, "I'm enjoying it because you're beautiful and strong and honest, and I don't believe I'd ever tire of looking at you."

She glanced back at him and wished she hadn't.

Spellbinder. That was what Catherine had thought when she had been going over Gallo's dossier and trying to learn him. Lying there in the firelight, he was completely sensual. Flat stomach, muscular thighs, and broad shoulders, his intent dark eyes and full lips that held the faintest smile. Everything about Gallo was male, sensual . . . sexual.

And she could feel the beginning of her response to that sexuality. The heat that was moving through her veins, that tautness of her breasts, the pounding of her heart.

"Close your eyes." His voice was suddenly hoarse. "Don't look at me."

Her lids snapped shut. He had noticed, dammit. He was aware of her vulnerability and his effect on her. How could he help it? The emotion was vibrating like raw electricity between them. She had to confront it and bring it down. "It doesn't mean anything, Gallo. I won't let it mean anything."

"Then keep your eyes closed." She heard him moving. "And I believe I'll forgo my pleasure in looking at you for a while. I live in the moment, but you don't. I may not be around to experience regrets, but I hope you will."

"All this sob-story stuff you're putting out is getting redundant." She opened her eyes to see him lying with his back to her. "I don't know if I should believe you."

"Maybe you shouldn't. Call Eve and tell her to get Quinn out here. Then you can bow out."

"Shut up. I'll do what I please."

But what would please her right now had nothing to do with her mission. What was happening between them? A good deal of it had to be because of the weeks they'd spent in these woods on the hunt, getting to know each other in the most intimate and dramatic way possible. Life and death and the hunt. It had dominated both of their minds and bodies. Even after the scenario had changed, it was still present, charging every word, ever look with urgency.

But there was suddenly more, and the hunt had taken on the most basic and earthy of meanings.

Eve had said Gallo had killed her child. How could Catherine feel anything for him but horror? Yes, he had been suffering from a mental breakdown. Yes, he was suffering enough now to want to end his life. But that did not stop the horror.

All Catherine's life, she had relied upon her instincts. How could they have failed her in this crucial moment? She could not respect herself if her mind and emotions were being subjugated by Gallo. She was either completely overwhelmed by Gallo and her own desires and unable to separate those instincts from the truth, or there was something terribly wrong.

And at the moment she couldn't sort anything out. Too much had happened. Too much was hovering on the horizon. She closed her eyes and leaned her head back on the makeshift pillow. She would sleep, and tomorrow she would start to deal with it.

Even though her eyes were closed, she still felt as if she could see Gallo, feel him, sense his every movement.

Spellbinder . . .

CHAPTER
12

"I'LL LET YOU GO INTO THE lake without the rope, but I'll be here with the dart gun. Start to swim away, and you'll take another nap," Gallo said. "And I haven't figured any way to save your modesty. I accept suggestions."

"Don't be absurd." She started to take off her shirt. "Do you think I haven't bathed naked with men before? I'm CIA. I spent years in the jungles of South America."

"Pardon me." He settled himself on the bank. "And it never presented problems?"

"I didn't say that." She took off her boots. "But the problems never occurred more than once." She shed the rest of her clothes and waded into the water. "Pitch me that green bottle in my knapsack."

"What is it?" He picked up the small bottle and lifted it to his nose. "It smells like rotten leaves."

"Soap." She looked at him as she reached water deep enough

to cover her breasts. In spite of her words, she had to block the tension that was a product of her awareness of him. "It was created for me by Hu Chang. You know the scent of products is a dead giveaway when you're on the hunt or being hunted." She caught the bottle as he tossed it to her. "You must have something like it. No matter how close I got to you, I couldn't detect your scent."

He nodded. "But yours is very good. I'd like to meet your Hu Chang."

"He'd be interested to meet you. He appreciates competence." She soaped her hair, then dipped her head to rinse it. "You're very good, Gallo."

"How long have you known this Hu Chang?"

"Since I was fourteen."

"Not a CIA man?"

She chuckled. "No, he was very upset when I decided to join them. He was sure they'd corrupt my free will."

"A valid concern."

She shrugged. "I had to make a decision I could live with. I grew up on the streets of Hong Kong, and I survived by dealing information to whoever would pay the highest fee for it. But I could see where I was going. Then a CIA agent, Venable, offered me a job with the CIA, and I took it. The Agency wasn't always clean, but they were trying to protect something besides themselves. That was unique in my world."

"All of this at seventeen."

"I told you, age doesn't mean anything."

"Hu Chang," he prompted.

"He had a shop that sold unique poisons and drugs. It's very profitable on the street, and he was targeted by a couple thieves on his way home. I helped him discourage them. But he was hurt, and I took him home and took care of him until he was well enough to take care of himself. We became . . . close."

"I suppose I don't have to ask how you discouraged them."

"If I hadn't killed them, they would have come back and targeted me, too," she said simply. "In Hong Kong, you don't take chances like that."

"And Hu Chang was grateful." He smiled. "And made you soap that smells like rotten leaves."

"Among other things." She started to wade back to shore. "I'm done. Give me that shirt on top of my knapsack. I managed to wash that one two days ago."

"Use my sweatshirt to dry off." He handed her a dark green shirt. "It's not that clean, but it will absorb the water."

She dabbed her body quickly and reached for her shirt. She had felt more comfortable in the water. She was too close to him. "I feel better now." She swiftly buttoned up the shirt. "In spite of the rotten leaves."

"I never said I didn't like the smell of rotten leaves." He slipped the looped rope around her waist, then took a step back and gazed at her in the shirt, which hit the top of her thighs. "Pity. But I think you'd better put on something else as soon as possible. I'm feeling a problem coming on. I don't want a demonstration on how you deal with this one."

She stared him in the eye. "You have me on a rope. I'm helpless."

"You're never helpless."

"You don't know me well enough to say that." She started

to dress. "I was helpless when you shot that dart into me. Everyone has moments when they're not totally in control."

"You're right. I don't know you. Why do I feel as if I do?"

Because these last weeks had taught them as much about each other as if they had known each other for years. "I have no idea."

"Yes, you do. We may have some gigantic holes in the structure, but the foundation is there."

"Your foundation is with Eve. That's why I'm here."

"Eve . . ." He was tying her to the tree. "Yes, it all goes back to Eve, doesn't it? She holds all of us. You've gone the limit for her in the name of friendship."

"I've gone after a man who has torn her life in pieces."

"I never meant to do it. We came together like a summer storm. We never realized that it would last for the rest of our lives. I tried to stay away."

"But you didn't do it, did you. Why?"

"Bonnie. I would never have interfered with Eve's life. She was right to put even the thought of me out of her mind. We'd both changed out of all recognition, and she had Quinn." His lips twisted. "And I was a man who couldn't even offer her a sound mind."

Her gaze was probing his expression. "You care about her. She told me that what was between you was only sex."

"It was the truth. But Bonnie changed everything. Passion became something else. We both loved Bonnie, and that meant we had to care about each other." He shook his head. "Oh, nothing like what she had with Quinn. There are all kinds of love and caring. I'll always feel that bond with Eve." He smiled faintly. "Even if she did send her favorite ninja after me."

"She didn't send me. I owed her, and I knew she couldn't come here herself." She added, "If you care about what happens to her, why don't you let me go? Do you think that she'll want Joe to come after you? Let it be me."

"But that's changed, too. The dynamics are different now, aren't they? The hunt wouldn't be the same, and neither would the finale." He met her gaze. "No, it has to be Quinn."

She couldn't breathe. "Let me go."

He shook his head. "You'll have to do it yourself." He began to strip off his clothes. "Because I'm going to take this time for myself." He waded into the water. "Something is happening between us. You may not like it, but it's there. I think that we'll have to ride it out."

She watched him as he moved in the water. Magnificent.

Tight muscular butt, flat stomach, totally male.

Totally.

And that maleness was having an effect on her own body.

"We'll have to ride it out."

The sentence brought to mind an image that was causing her body to ready. Stop it. So he was magnificent physically and fascinating mentally. She couldn't be drawn into the web that was hovering. Enemy. She had to think of him as the enemy.

He was coming out of the water. She should close her eyes. Not from any sense of embarrassment. That did not exist for them. But every step he took was causing a jolt of feeling, a surge of heat.

She would not close her eyes.

She met his gaze with boldness as he stopped before her.

"Me, too," he said quietly. "What do we do about it?"

"Ignore it."

"I've never been known for my restraint. I have a tendency to take what I want." There was a glitter of pure recklessness in his eyes. "And I don't believe I've ever wanted anything as much as I do you, Catherine Ling."

She could see the crystal drops of water beading on his shoulders and tangling in the thatch of dark hair on his chest. He was close enough for her to feel the heat of his body. She wanted to reach out and touch him.

Dizzy. The intensity was overpowering. She felt like a damn virgin. She had been married and had a child. She'd had occasional one-night stands in the years since her husband had been killed. But she'd never felt anything of this intensity before.

"Catherine?"

He wasn't forcing, he was asking. She should say yes, and he would cut the ropes. A man was never so vulnerable as when he was engaged in sex. She would be able to go on the attack.

But would she do it?

Dear God, she was afraid that she wouldn't.

She couldn't afford to take a chance of that self-betrayal.

She shook her head. "There's too much baggage. I won't let you complicate my life, Gallo."

He stared at her for a moment in which she saw emotion after emotion flickering in his expression. "You mean the way I've complicated the lives of everyone else around me? Complicated and destroyed." His smile was bitter. "You're right. And I'd do it, too." He turned away. "Just give me the chance." He was dressing quickly. "And you can bet that I'd take advantage of any chance you gave me. So keep me away from you." He grabbed a knife from his knapsack and came back to her and cut the ropes that bound her to the tree. Then he cut the ropes binding her wrists. "Or take off. That would probably be better."

She stared at him in shock. "You're releasing me."

"I'm not stupid enough to let you have any of your weapons back. Though I'm sure that you could be formidable in hand-to-hand." He looked at her. "But you don't want to be that close to me, do you? It might turn into something else."

She shook her head as she rubbed her wrist. "I won't stop, Gallo. Why did you change your mind?"

"Victims. I'm sick to death of victims. I won't make you one, Catherine."

" 'Victim'? You son of a bitch. You can't make me a victim. Who the hell do you think you are?"

"A son of a bitch who seems to have a talent for bringing down even the strongest and most worthwhile." He turned away. "Why don't you get going? There aren't any guarantees that I won't change my mind."

She didn't move. "And you'll wait for Joe. I'm supposed to run the risk that you'll let him kill you? Hell, you tell me that you're unstable. That there aren't any guarantees, that you can change your mind. You have warrior instincts. So does Joe. That creates a scenario that spells big-time trouble. I'm not going to lose him."

He turned to look at her. "And what are you going to do?"

"I'll stay with you until Joe comes and make sure that he survives." She met his gaze. "And if I get the chance, you'll go down. I made a promise to Eve, and nothing has changed that."

"No, I guess that would be your first priority. She's lucky to have you for a friend."

"Lucky? She helped me find my son. There's nothing that I wouldn't do for her." She paused. "But we can end this now. I'll postpone trying to bring Eve your head for the time being. All you have to do is tell me what happened to Bonnie and where she is."

"All?" His lips were tight with bitterness. "That would be fine, wouldn't it? But I can't help you, Catherine. I told you, I don't remember. I don't even remember taking her life."

She glanced away from the unbearable pain in his expression. She mustn't let him affect her like this. "Then we're at an impasse. I stay."

He gazed at her for a moment, then his expression changed. The recklessness was suddenly there again. "Why not? Go with the flow. Step into my parlor, Catherine."

"Bad phrasing. That would indicate that you were in control. You're not, Gallo. This is my choice. You'll never be in control of me."

"A challenge." He smiled, and the recklessness was even more obvious. "Up or down. The compromise would be for us to take turns. What do you think?"

She ignored the inference. "I think if your memory suddenly returns, we'll both be better off."

"But maybe I'm suppressing it. It's possible. It would hurt me, and I'm a selfish bastard. Maybe I don't give a damn about anything or anyone but myself." He grabbed his knapsack and slung it over his shoulders. "I'm going back to camp. Come along if you like. We'll see what comes of it."

"I want my phone back." She picked up her knapsack. "Keep the weapons. But I want my phone."

"A phone can be a weapon."

"I want to call Eve. She may have been trying to reach me. I won't have her worried. What difference does it make? I'm not going to tell her anything that would bring them here. I don't want Joe on your trail until he's entirely well."

He thought about it. "There are all kinds of ways that you could use that phone to bring havoc down on me. You're probably up on every technical advance that could cause me to be traced or destroyed." He shrugged. "What do I care? It should make the game more interesting." He reached into his knapsack and brought out her phone. He disconnected it from its solar battery charger and handed it to her. "By all means, call Eve."

BUT CATHERINE DIDN'T make the call until later that day. Eve had phoned her during the time that Gallo had possession of her phone and Catherine wasn't sure what excuse she wanted to give her for not answering. She could tell her that she was out of tower range. Eve might accept that because she knew Catherine had had problems before when they were trying to track Paul Black through this forest.

But that would be lying, and she hated to lie to Eve. She would just have to play it by ear.

"You're frowning." Gallo looked up from cooking fish over the fire. "You don't like fish? Or you don't trust me? I promise I won't poison you."

"Why should I trust you? For God's sake, you shot me after I saved your life." She made an impatient gesture. "Yes, I know that you didn't regard that as a favor. You said you were trying to get around your ghostly Bonnie's interference in your doing away with yourself." She scowled. "Which is some of the most complete crap I've ever heard in my life."

"My, my, how bad-tempered you are." He tilted his head. "Not that I blame you. It sounds like crap to me, too." He took the fish from the fire. "I don't expect you to believe me."

"It's ridiculous." She glared at him. "And you're not a man who would imagine that kind of nonsense."

"Hallucinations. Talk to the doctors who examined me after I broke out of that prison in North Korea."

"That was a long time ago, and you're not nuts now, dammit."

"How do you know?"

She didn't have any idea why she was so certain. Instinct, again? Lately, she had been thinking long and hard while she had been with him. Carefully sorting out the basic emotion and what her judgment told her was true. But, dammit, she had known him for such a short time that she had to rely on her faith in herself. Yet when had she ever relied on anything else? From the moment she had started the hunt, she had tried to predict his every move, every thought. At times, she had felt as if she could read his mind.

And that mind was clear and sharp and entirely sane.

But this bullshit about Bonnie was a complete contradiction of what she knew was true about him.

"You didn't even know her. You'd never even talked to your daughter. You admitted that yourself."

"I knew her."

"How?"

"Would you like any of this fish?"

"No. How?"

He didn't look at her as he helped himself to the fish. "She came to see me."

"What? You said that you'd never met her."

"Not formally. She never told me her name. But after a while, I knew who she was." He looked up and met her eyes. "You won't let it alone, will you? Okay. It doesn't matter. It will probably convince you that I'm as crazy as I say I am." He poured coffee into a cup and handed it to her. "But that part of Bonnie I didn't imagine. She was *real*. She did come to me."

"What are you talking about? Came where?"

He picked up his coffee and sat down again before the fire. "In that hellhole of a prison. I was being tortured and starved. I was sure I'd either die or go crazy and after months I didn't care. Then I started to dream of a little girl. She had curly red hair and a smile that could light up the world, much less that stinking hole where I was being held. She was very young when she first came to me, but then she seemed to grow older. She would sing me songs and tell me about going to school. She saved my life and my sanity. She kept me from hanging myself in that cell." He took a drink of coffee. "She never told me about her mother, but I knew it was Eve. And I knew her name was Bonnie."

Catherine stared at him, stunned. She hadn't expected this, and she didn't know how to deal with it.

His lips twisted as he looked up and saw her expression. "I told you that you wouldn't believe me. But that was no hallucination. Bonnie was more real to me than the whip or the knife or all the other little toys they used on me. I thought she was a dream in the beginning, but later I knew she was somehow there. How else could I know . . ." He shook his head. "She was real."

He believed it, Catherine realized. Nothing could be more certain than his belief that Bonnie had visited him in that prison. She was silent, then shook her head. "How can I believe you? Have I heard of tales like that? Of course. Astral projection and all kinds of weird stuff. But I've never encountered it in any plausible form. I think perhaps your mind was distorted by what you were going through."

"My distortion gave me a name—Bonnie. At that time, I didn't even know she existed."

"Then it had to be something else." She moistened her lips. "Bonnie was alive when you were having those visions. Did you have them after she died?"

He nodded. "Not often. And then I did think they were dreams. Until recently." He paused. "When Eve told me that she had them, too, and that they weren't dreams."

"What?"

"I thought that would shake you. Your friend, Eve, who is definitely sane and not prone to imaginary visits from a spirit. Yet she was the one who told me that she had gone through years telling herself that her visits from Bonnie were hallucinations or dreams." He lifted his shoulder in a half shrug. "Until she realized that it wasn't true. She wanted to prepare me for the same painful rejection process."

"She told you that Bonnie—"

"Ask her." He took another sip of coffee. "Or not. She might not want to discuss it with you. It's difficult to admit to believing in spirits when the world around you is so pragmatic." He lifted his cup in a half toast. "Like you, Catherine."

"I've had to be pragmatic. I wouldn't have lived to get out of my teens if I hadn't been practical and rejected things that go bump in the night."

"Bonnie doesn't go bump in the night. She smiles. She lifts the heart."

"And won't let you kill yourself." She shook her head. "Can't you see how weird that sounds, dammit? If you killed her, wouldn't she want you to throw yourself headfirst into a volcano? It's what any sensible ghost would want." She lifted her hand and rubbed her forehead. "What am I saying? I'm actually going along with you on this."

"I thought of that," he said quietly. "Maybe Bonnie wants it to be Quinn and Eve who end it. They've been searching for so long . . ." He added wearily, "I don't know. I just want it over. I don't understand any of it. I don't know how I could love her so much and still take her life. If I could do that, I don't deserve to live one more hour, one more minute."

"If you killed Eve's daughter, I couldn't agree more." She finished her coffee and threw the last drops into the flames. "And I'd be glad to help you along if you could tell me where you buried Bonnie. How can you be so sure that you killed her and not know anything else? Because that slimeball said it was true? I don't understand why both you and Eve believed him."

"If you'd been there, you'd understand. Black believed every word he was saying," he said hoarsely. "I'd swear it."

She gazed at him in frustration. So much pain. So much bewilderment. She couldn't imagine the insecurity that the blackouts had given him. How would it feel to come around and not know what violence you'd committed? He had been an Army Ranger and violence had been inherent in the job and the opportunity was always present. In every other way he was such a confident, complete person, and yet this crack was going to widen until it destroyed him.

But both he and Eve believed Black had been telling the truth. As Gallo had said, Catherine hadn't been there. She could not judge.

But why was it bothering her so much?

Because she didn't want it to be true? Because even at this moment, she was feeling drawn to him and was looking for an excuse to take off her clothes and go to him and—

She wouldn't accept that reason. She wasn't a mindless animal in heat.

Though, God knows, she felt like one right now. Hot and aching and ready. Why couldn't she have picked someone with no baggage before she let herself fall into this trap? But there had been no picking and choosing. It had been Gallo since that first moment of the hunt. She didn't know where it was going to take her, but she had to accept that she had to deal with it.

Was this how Eve had felt all those years ago when Gallo had come into her life? Strange that both Eve and Catherine had fallen under Gallo's spell. But Eve had been little more than a child herself, while Catherine was a woman and should have had more control.

Control. Look away from him. Don't ask him any other questions because you want the answers to lead you where you want to go.

He looked back at her and nodded slowly. "It's becoming difficult for you, isn't it? I think you'd like to believe I didn't kill her. It would be easier if I'd tell you that Black was lying. I can't do that." He got to his feet. "You've probably had enough of me. I'll walk over to the creek and give you some space to make your call to Eve."

"Don't you want to know what I say to her?"

He shook his head. "None of it matters any longer. As I said, anything you do will only make the game more interesting."

And he'd already decided what the end of the game had to be, she thought.

She watched him as he strode toward the creek before she reached for her phone.

"I tried to call you," Eve said when she picked up. "I was worried."

"I'm sorry. I wasn't able to receive any calls." And she was being deceptive even though she'd been trying desperately to think of a way to avoid it. "How is Joe?"

"Good." She paused. "How are you? You sound . . . strange."

"I'm fine."

"Gallo?"

"I'm very close to him." She gazed at Gallo across the short distance separating them. "Very close."

"Be careful."

"You think that he'd hurt me? You were defending him for a long time when I was warning you not to trust him. And you were working with him to hunt down Black."

"I think any man who would kill Bonnie would be capable of any atrocity."

"And you're positive he killed her?"

"Gallo as much as admitted that he thought Black had told the truth."

"Thinking isn't knowing. You told me once he loved her. I couldn't figure out how he could do that if he'd never had any contact with her before her death. But you were very sure. How could you be so sure, then change in the blink of an eye? Why were you so sure?"

"He told me something that made me think we had a bond."

"Something about Bonnie? Something you shared about Bonnie? What was it, Eve?"

Eve was silent. "Why are you asking me these questions, Catherine? I feel as if I'm being interrogated."

Catherine drew a deep breath. "I'm sorry." She hadn't known she was going to ask those questions until they'd come tumbling out. She felt as if she'd been driven to verify what Gallo had told her, to find truth in those strange words about Bonnie. Dear God, she wanted them to be true. She wanted to believe the impossible. Gallo had called her pragmatic, but for that moment she wanted to believe. "There's just so much I don't know. But I'm part of this now. I think I deserve to ask about you and Bonnie."

Silence. "Then go ahead and ask, Catherine."

She hesitated, then asked jerkily, "Did you—ever think that you saw your daughter—after her death?"

Another silence. "Catherine?"

Catherine was suddenly panicked. "Never mind. Don't answer. It's a crazy question. I'll call you tomorrow and check on Joe." She hung up.

Why had she done it? That question had been wrong on so many levels. It had not only intruded on Eve's privacy, but intimated that she was not stable. Because sane people didn't see spirits.

Or did they?

Catherine wouldn't have gone forward with that question if Eve hadn't made that cryptic comment about sharing something with Gallo that had formed a bond.

Added to what Gallo had said about Eve telling him that she, too, had an experience with seeing Bonnie, it had been too close to miss. So she had plunged into questioning Eve with no gentleness or tact, and Eve had responded defensively. It was perfectly natural.

But what would she have said if Catherine had not backed off like a cat on hot coals? Why had Catherine panicked? Because she had not wanted to offend a friend or because she had not wanted to hear her answer?

She glanced over at Gallo, standing beside the creek. Damn him. He was the core of all the trouble she had been going through. He had disturbed her physically and emotionally, and now he was causing a rift between her and Eve.

No, that wasn't true. How could she blame him for her

own responses? She had told herself she had to deal with him, and this was no way to start. She had to think clearly and coolly and not let her emotions get in the way.

And not get too close to him until she had come to a few decisions. She had wasted enough time waffling back and forth about Gallo. She would either accept the situation as he and Eve were accepting it, or she would come to her own conclusions and act accordingly.

She looked away from him and started to settle down in her sleeping bag. She would lie there and before she faced him again, she could come to a final decision.

Until then, getting any closer to John Gallo would be the worst thing she could do.

CHAPTER
13

"SHE'S CAUGHT UP WITH GALLO." Eve turned to Jane as she hung up the phone. "I *know* it."

Jane frowned. "But she didn't tell you that?"

Eve shook her head. "Not exactly." She was thinking over exactly what Catherine had said. "It was all very vague and ambiguous. I was uneasy from the moment I picked up the call."

"If she's found him, why wouldn't she tell you?"

"How the hell do I know?" She grimaced. "Or maybe I do know. Gallo is . . . unusual. He managed to convince me that black was white in two separate periods of my life. I warned Catherine that he was capable of dazzling anyone." She added with frustration, "But she's tough as nails. I was hoping that she'd be immune to him."

"Maybe she is," Jane said. "You're only guessing, Eve."

"She was questioning me about— She's been talking to him, Jane."

"About what?" Jane asked.

"She asked if I'd—" She moistened her lips. "She said she wondered if I'd thought that Bonnie visited me after her death. In her wildest dreams, she wouldn't have asked that question if she hadn't talked to Gallo. Why would she? There's no more grounded or realistic person on Earth than Catherine."

"Except me." Jane made a face. "And I've made giant strides in accepting the unacceptable. But, then, I've had a long time to come to terms with Bonnie."

"And you still don't feel comfortable with the idea," Eve said. "Well, neither does Catherine. I could tell that she's upset as hell and trying to fight her way through it. But Gallo has her going around in circles."

"What has Gallo got to do with her asking about Bonnie?"

Eve was silent and then said finally. "He's seen Bonnie, too. At least, he told me he had."

"Oh, shit." Jane gazed at her in shock. "And you believed him?"

"I believed him," she said jerkily. "I believed everything he told me. He said she came to him in that cell in Korea when she was still alive. And that she visited him after her death. I fell for everything he told me. That's why I went with him to hunt down Paul Black when Gallo told me that he'd killed Bonnie."

"Why? How could you believe him?"

"Because I was a fool. It all had to be lies. Why would Bonnie come to him if he'd been the one who killed her?" She shook her head. "And now he has Catherine believing his lies." And that put Catherine in greater danger than Eve had dreamed. An enemy within the gates could be deadly. "It has to stop." She turned toward the elevator. "I can't let it go on."

"Where are you going?" Jane hurried to keep up with her. "As if I couldn't guess. Look, you can't go after Catherine. You don't know what kind of situation you'd uncover up there in the woods. Particularly if you think she's been bamboozled by Gallo."

"You think Catherine would hurt me?" Eve shook her head. "Don't be ridiculous. You don't know her, Jane."

"No, I don't. But you said that she wasn't behaving normally. So how well do you know her, Eve?"

"Very well." Eve punched the elevator button. "I just have to see her face-to-face so that I can set her straight. I need you to do me a favor. Joe won't like this when he hears about it. Stall him as long as you can."

"Stall him? He'll be out of this hospital and on your trail the minute he hears that you're not here."

"He's already had his night sedative. All you have to worry about is when he wakes tomorrow. Find a way to keep him here. One day, Jane. That should be all I need to find Catherine and talk to her."

"That sounds simple, but it would be hard as hell. I'd have to lie. I've never lied to Joe." Jane's lips thinned. "And I won't let you go up there alone. You may trust Catherine Ling, but I don't."

"And leave Joe here in this hospital without either one of us? Joe is the reason you came here, Jane. When you first arrived, you asked me what you could do to help me. Well, now I'm telling you. Dammit, Joe is due to be released in the next couple days, and I was trying to think of a way to delay him going after Gallo. This thing with Catherine is going to blow away any chance of that."

"You bet it is."

"Then give me at least a day to get up there and contact Catherine. I'll try to get her back on track."

Jane shook her head.

"Don't you refuse me." Eve's voice was shaking. "You give me that day. I almost lost Joe. I can't prevent him from going after Gallo, but I can keep Catherine on the job to help him."

"That's not all you're doing," Jane said bluntly. "You're going to go after Gallo yourself."

Eve should have known that Jane would guess her intentions. They were too close not to be able to read each other. "Joe said Bonnie told him that we're reaching the end," she said unevenly. "If that's true, then I should be the one to reach it first." She reached out and grasped Jane's arm. "I'm not afraid of Catherine, and I'm not afraid of Gallo. Give me my day, Jane."

"Damn you." Jane's eyes were glittering with moisture. She reached out and hugged Eve close. "One day, Eve. After that, Joe and I will both be on your trail."

Eve brushed Jane's cheek with her lips and let her go. "Thanks, Jane. This means a lot to me."

"I know. Do you think that if I didn't realize you were on the edge, I'd have given in? It's nearly killing me to let you go." Jane watched her get into the elevator. "I hope Bonnie is right. I hope this nightmare is coming to an end."

"So do I," Eve said, as the elevator door closed, shutting her away from Jane. The search for Bonnie had been a nightmare for Jane also, she knew. Jane's strength and courage had caused her to downplay any pain or loneliness that might have resulted from Eve's obsession with finding Bonnie. But those emotions had been there, and Eve had been aware of them.

It's been too long for all of us, Bonnie. Let me bring you home.

"ARE YOU awake?"

Catherine opened her eyes to see Gallo sitting by the fire a few yards away from her. "I am now," she said dryly. "Since it's obvious you want me to be."

He smiled. "Yes, I do. I was lonely. I held off for a little while, but then I yielded to temptation. I knew I wasn't going to sleep, and I wanted company. I never said I wasn't selfish." He crossed his legs Indian style. "Or that I wasn't curious. About an hour and a half ago, you tucked yourself into that sleeping bag immediately after you talked to Eve. It had all the signs of an escape move. But I'd judge that you're not one to hide your head under a blanket."

"I wasn't trying to escape you. If I had, I would have taken off when you gave me the chance. I had some thinking to do."

"And?"

"I did it." She stared him in the eye. "And I decided you were the most outrageously idiotic individual on the face of the Earth, and Eve wasn't far behind you."

His smile faded. "Indeed? I assume you're referring to what I told you about Bonnie. I told you that I didn't expect you to believe me."

"I don't know whether I believe you or not. It would take a hell of a lot more than a tall tale about a red-haired ghost-child skipping merrily through your life to make me give up reality for that kind of fantasy." Her lips tightened. "But it's clear you and Eve have bought into it and won't be argued out of your Bonnie visions."

"Eve told you?"

"Hell no, she danced around it very warily, but it was clear she was talking about the same bond that you were. She sees Bonnie."

"And that makes us both idiots?"

"I told you, that wasn't what I was talking about. You're both idiots because you believed Paul Black when he told you that he knew that you had killed your daughter."

"He was telling the truth."

"You and Eve kept saying that. Because I trust and admire Eve's judgment, I went along with her when she said she was certain. As for you, why should I doubt anything bad about you when you were the enemy?"

"No reason at all."

"Except your blind belief in what Black said has been bothering me lately. It didn't seem right. And the more I thought about it, the more ridiculous it became to me." She shook her head. "I'm no psychiatrist, but I don't think anyone is capable of murdering a child they love unless they're totally mad. You may have had bouts of instability, but you're not crazy, Gallo."

"How do you know?"

"Because I know you. Just as you know me. After these weeks in the woods, I know you very well. Sometimes I feel as if

I can read your mind. I know your slyness, your cleverness, your recklessness; but you've never shown me any hint of cruelty or insanity." She added flatly, "Which means that both you and Eve have to be wrong when you accepted Black's word." She held up her hand as he opened his mouth to speak. "Don't give me that bullshit. I don't care if Black believed what he was saying. So what if he wasn't lying? That doesn't mean he couldn't be wrong." She glared at him. "You and Eve are both so tormented because of your love and guilt about Bonnie that you can't see straight. She's doubted you from the moment you came back into her life. Part of that was my fault. You were number one on my list as Bonnie's killer. You doubted yourself because of the blackouts you were having and the doctors who told you that you were a little bonkers."

"More than a little."

She shrugged. "Whatever. At any rate, you should have thought instead of reacted. Eve was terribly upset about Joe, so she had some excuse. But you should have known you weren't capable of killing Bonnie."

His lips twisted in a one-sided smile. "According to you, Catherine?"

She was suddenly up and kneeling before him. "Dammit, yes. According to me." Her hands closed on his shoulders, and she shook him. "I'm the only one with any sense around here. You were trying to throw yourself off a cliff, and Eve and Joe were going to hunt you down and kill you. Do you know how that would have made them feel when they found out Black was wrong? Guilt and more guilt. And that damn search for Bonnie would have started again." Her breasts were rising and falling with the force of her breathing. "And I would have been right in the middle of all that angst. No way. I've done enough things in my life that earned me my portion of guilt without you bringing me more. Now stop it, and let's clear this up."

His eyes were narrowed on her expression. "You really don't think I did it, do you?"

"At last, a breakthrough." Her hands dropped from his shoulders. "How many times do I have to say it? Black was *wrong*. He may have believed you killed Bonnie, but that doesn't make it true." She sat back on her heels. "Dammit, you'd think that you wanted it to be true."

"God, no." His voice was hoarse. "I've been living in a nightmare."

The pain in his expression was terrible to see. She wanted to reach out and touch him, comfort him. Don't do it. She was already too close to him.

"You deserved it. All you had to do was take the situation apart and look at the separate pieces."

He started to smile, then shook his head. "You know I still don't believe you. I want to. But I'm afraid that I'll find out that I was right, and you're wrong."

"Then you wouldn't be any worse off, would you?"

This time the smile actually came into being. "Oh, I would be worse off. It's a terrible thing to lose hope." He reached out and gently touched her cheek. "But it would be worth it to have a chance to go down the road you're leading me."

She could feel her skin flush beneath his fingers, and her chest tightened. No, she mustn't feel like this. It got in the way.

She moved her head, and his hand dropped away from her face. "Nice words. Now shouldn't we get down to business? I completely blew it with Eve tonight. I'll be lucky if she doesn't show up here and try to track me down. We need to be gone before that happens."

"And where are we going?"

"If Black didn't kill Bonnie, and you didn't kill Bonnie, then we have to find out who did."

"Logical." He was thinking. She could almost see the wheels turning. "Okay. If Black didn't kill Bonnie and was certain that I did, it was because Queen and Jacobs had told him I had done it. Queen must have even paid Black to shoulder the blame, so that I would search for him all those years. Why?"

"Eve said that she thought that Queen was afraid that if you found out that you'd killed your daughter during one of your blackouts, you'd have a complete breakdown. He wouldn't want you to be put away in a mental institution, where he couldn't control you. Doctors ask too many questions, and you knew too much about his criminal activities." She frowned. "And I accepted that explanation because it all made sense."

"It still makes sense." His lips twisted. "It's difficult to discard it and look in any other direction. Why else would Queen go to all that trouble to make Black a decoy?"

"Unless he killed Bonnie himself."

"And why would he do that? He had no reason. Black might have had revenge as a motive, but Queen was still using me to do his dirty jobs all over the world and had no idea that I was beginning to suspect him."

"I don't know why, dammit." Every question had a road-
block, and her frustration level was climbing. "And we can't
even ask the bastard. Black killed Queen."

"Back to square one," Gallo said. Then suddenly an indefin-
able expression flickered over his face. "Or maybe not. Jacobs."

Her gaze flew to his face. "Queen's assistant?"

He nodded. "You could call him that. Lieutenant Thomas
Jacobs. He'd been joined at the hip with Queen at Army Intelligence for years. And he was partner in Queen's various crooked
enterprises. He was with Queen from the beginning. He was always there in the background, even in that first meeting when
I was sent into North Korea. I never considered him a factor because Queen always dominated."

"But he might know something?"

Gallo nodded. "It's a possibility. Just because he was in the
background doesn't mean that Queen didn't trust him. It was a
long-standing relationship. Maybe Queen even found Jacobs
more valuable because he was the invisible man."

Invisible. Yes, Catherine had not considered Jacobs important when she'd been investigating Nate Queen and trying to
trace Gallo. He'd been completely overshadowed by Queen.
But now he was standing alone and might be the key. "Where
is he? How can we get to him?"

"He was still at INSCOM the last time I talked to Queen
weeks ago. But a lot has happened since then. After Black was
killed, the ledger that held proof of Queen's and Jacobs's smuggling and drug dealing must have been discovered by the local
police. There's no indication in it that it had anything to do with
Army Intelligence, but they would have had Eve's statement

about that. And the book had to be on Black's body at the time I killed him. If the sheriff followed up on it, then Jacobs has to be in big trouble."

Catherine shook her head. "The sheriff didn't mention any ledger to me when I was on the search for you those first few days. But then we weren't concerned about anything but finding you."

"Yes, I felt very important," Gallo said. "I would have felt still more important if I'd known you'd joined them on the hunt. You were much more interesting."

"Don't bullshit me," she said bluntly. "You didn't care a damn about whether I was after you or not. You were too busy trying to get yourself killed."

"And you've already remarked on that particular idiocy."

"It bears repeating. Why didn't you—" She stopped, and added with exasperation, "If you have this intimate relationship with Bonnie, why didn't she just tell you that you hadn't killed her?"

"I don't know. I was in torment. There were moments when I didn't even believe Bonnie was actually there." He shook his head. "I just knew that I couldn't take my own life."

"Then your daughter is the most unsatisfactory spirit in the universe. What good is she?" She turned away. "And it makes me doubt even more that she actually exists. If you and Eve weren't two of the most intelligent and grounded people I've ever met, I'd be sure of it."

"But you're not sure." He smiled faintly. "And it's bothering the hell out of you."

"I'll get over it." And she'd get over the effect Gallo was

having on her. She just had to block those parts of her mind and body that seemed to be acutely and exquisitely attuned to him. "After I find out what happened to Bonnie and I can put you behind me. Then I'll be able to move on with no looking back." She took out her phone. "Put out the fire while I call the sheriff and see what I can find out about that ledger. Then we'll get on the road and try to track down Jacobs."

He nodded and began to extinguish the flames. "As you command."

For the time being, she thought ruefully. Gallo wasn't going to accept any will but his own for long. She absently watched him work about the camp as she talked to Sheriff Rupert. Lord, Gallo was stunning. In black jeans and shirt he looked lean and yet muscular, and the way he moved . . .

She jerked her attention back to what the sheriff was telling her.

As she hung up, Gallo turned to face her. "Well?"

"The day after Black and Queen were taken to the local morgue, Thomas Jacobs showed up with his Army Intelligence credentials and a story about how Nate Queen was undercover and trying to find a way to trap Black. According to him, Paul Black was supposed to be a suspect in the killing of an Army Intelligence officer."

"But they already had a statement from Eve about Queen's involvement with Black."

"Evidently Jacobs was very plausible, and Sheriff Rupert isn't used to dealing with military and government types. He was even impressed with my credentials."

"It was probably not your credentials that impressed him.

He's a typical good old boy, and he appreciates a beautiful woman when he sees her."

"You should know. Evidently, you became buddies with him and the entire sheriff's office."

"It seemed the thing to do at the time. So did Jacobs get his hands on the ledger?"

"No, the sheriff wasn't that gullible. Though Jacobs tried to tell him that it was evidence and was needed to save military lives. It was in Korea, so Jacobs had a good shot at convincing him of his story. It hadn't been translated."

"Has it been translated yet?"

"No, clearly things move slowly up here." She added, "And Sheriff Rupert was a little suspicious when Jacobs didn't mention claiming Queen's body for burial. It didn't seem to be the proper way to behave when Jacobs was giving him this sad story about Queen's giving his life for his country."

"And he had Eve's statement to compare with Jacobs's story."

Catherine nodded. "Anyway, the sheriff refused to turn over anything to Jacobs since he was implicated in the story that Eve told him. He told Jacobs to have his superior contact him, and he'd cooperate. So Jacobs didn't get the ledger, and everything must have seemed to be going downhill for him. His partner was dead, and he was probably going to be revealed as a crook and his Army career would go down the drain." She picked up her knapsack. "Which means we'd better get on the move. Jacobs has had too long to tie up loose ends and destroy any other evidence against him. We'll be lucky if we're able to locate him."

"We'll locate him." Gallo was already moving down the

trail. "Call your chief Venable as soon as we get to the car and see if he can trace him."

Gallo's tone was as grim as his face. He was in battle mode.

Well, so was she, Catherine thought. It was strange that after being enemies these last weeks, they were walking this path together.

Strange and somehow right.

AN HOUR LATER, SHE HUNG UP from the callback she'd received from Venable and turned to Gallo, who was in the driver's seat. "Jacobs took a leave of absence from the office the day after he returned from Milwaukee. His superiors have been trying to get in touch with him since all hell broke loose about Queen's death. The questions began to fly about Queen's and Jacobs's possible criminal involvement. No luck. Jacobs is not answering his phone, and he's just recently moved out of his apartment." She shook her head. "We may be too late. He could have panicked and decided to go on the run. He's probably flown off to someplace in the South Seas from which he can't be extradited."

"Possibly." Gallo was thinking. "But Jacobs wasn't the type to turn into a beachcomber. It would be too savage for his tastes. He was very urban oriented."

"How do you know? I thought you said he was the invisible man."

"That doesn't mean I didn't make the effort to see him for what he was. He worked closely with Queen. There was always a chance that I'd find a use for him. If he did go on the run, it shouldn't be too hard to track him."

"You don't think he'd go undercover?"

Gallo shook his head. "Maybe. But if he did, then I know what to look for."

"What?"

"A casino. Jacobs is a gambler, an addict. It's one of the reasons that he never left Queen no matter how hot the situation got. He was nervous all the time, but he couldn't let go. He needed the money, and he lost more than he won at the tables."

"There are a lot of casinos in the world."

"Then we'll narrow them down."

"How?"

He shrugged. "First, we'll go to Jacobs's apartment and see if we can find a clue as to where we'd have our best shot. Did you get his address?"

She nodded at the number she'd typed into her phone. "His apartment is in Georgetown."

"Then call and see what's the quickest flight we can get to Washington out of either Milwaukee or Chicago."

She hesitated. "Orders, Gallo?"

"I believe in balance. You were giving me enough orders before we got on the road."

And now he was moving, thinking, functioning with lightning efficiency. Why was she complaining? She should be glad she was going to have to fight for dominance. It would make the possibility of finding Jacobs all the more likely. "Have you forgotten that the police are looking for you? We'd do better to hire a private plane. I have a contact with—"

"No time. I have several sets of false ID that Queen and Jacobs supplied me and a couple I purchased from private sources. I could never be sure when Queen or Jacobs would decide to send one of their hired killers after me, and I might have to go undercover for a while."

"Like Jacobs."

"Exactly like Jacobs."

"You're not afraid that security will recognize you?"

"I'll send you through in front of me. No one is going to look at me when you're around. Like Jacobs, I'll be the invisible man."

"Yeah, sure. But if you're willing to take the risk, it's okay with me." She took out her phone. "I'll bet we'll find our flight out of Chicago. The traffic is much heavier . . .

CATHERINE RECEIVED A CALL from Eve two hours later, when they were heading for Gate 23 at Chicago's O'Hare Airport.

Dammit, she didn't want to face Eve now. Should she ignore it?

Of course not. Eve would not forgive her.

Deal with it.

"Where are you, Eve?" she said when she picked up the phone. "And is Joe with you?"

"I'm on my way to Gallo's place in the hills. I wanted to see you." She paused. "And by the noise I'm hearing in the background, you're not there. An airport?"

"Yes, I knew I blew it when I was talking to you before. I had to get out of there before you descended on us. Joe?"

"He's not with me. I needed a little time to persuade you to forget this idiocy. Jane is trying to give me a day before she tells him."

"She won't be able to do it. You know it as well as I do. Joe is too sharp."

Eve ignored her words. "Us. You said us. You're with Gallo."

"You knew I was, or you wouldn't have come running to save me," she said quietly. "I don't need saving, Eve. He's not going to hurt me." She paused. "And he didn't kill Bonnie."

"For God's sake, he has you believing him." Catherine could hear the despair in her voice. "He did it, Catherine. I know how convincing he can be, but you have to think."

"No, you have to think," Catherine said. "You and Gallo are both so twisted and turned around about how you feel about Bonnie that you're willing to jump at any explanation that sounds halfway reasonable. Only this isn't reasonable. Just because Black believed what he was saying is no sign it was the truth."

"You're the one who is jumping at explanations. What did he do to persuade you?"

"Nothing. Except try to get himself killed. I figured that was unusual behavior and deserving of a little thought."

"What?"

"Never mind. There's no way that I have time or enough valid arguments to make you listen. All I can say is that I know you're on the wrong track. I feel it. You're a great one for believing in instinct. You believed in Gallo when I thought you were a gullible fool for doing it. Now the situation is reversed. All I can ask is that you trust me."

Eve was silent. "I do trust you. But I think you're— Where are you going, Catherine?"

"When you can tell me honestly that you'll help instead of try to stop me, I'll talk to you." She drew a deep breath. "Please. I don't want to do this without you, Eve. I've fought my way through this. I'm doing the right thing."

"Then tell me where you're going."

"Start where I did and work it out for yourself. Good-bye, Eve." She hung up.

Gallo was gazing at her expression. "That was painful for you."

"Of course, it was. She's my friend." Her throat was tight. "All I ever wanted to do was help her, and now she thinks I've betrayed her."

"And that I lured you from the straight path." They had reached the gate, and he turned to face her. "Eve should know better than to think I'd have that kind of power over you. She's usually more clearheaded."

But he did have an alluring charisma, and she had been struggling against it for weeks. She only hoped she'd been telling Eve the truth when she'd told her Gallo hadn't unduly influenced her.

Hope? Dammit, of course she'd been honest with Eve. She had to trust in herself as she always had. Otherwise, she had nothing. "You're Bonnie's father. Evidently you were Eve's Achilles' heel when she was a kid of sixteen. It's probably easy for her to imagine that you might be able to sway me to your way of thinking."

"Achilles' heel? That could have all kind of meanings." He looked away from her, and said haltingly, "If it makes any difference to you, it means a good deal to me that you believe so deeply that you're doing the right thing. In a way, that means you believe in me."

"You act as if that's completely unheard of for anyone to have any trust in you."

"Not completely. But I can remember only a couple of people who trusted me to that extent. Maybe my commanding officer, Ron Capshaw, who was in charge of our mission to Korea. I was just a green kid fresh out of Ranger school but he took me under his wing and told everyone he knew I could do the job. I . . . liked him. He made me feel as if I could do anything if I tried hard enough." His lips tightened. "But we had to split up, and he and Lieutenant Silak were killed, and I was taken prisoner." He shrugged. "Other than Ron, I guess the only other person who trusted me to do the right thing was my uncle Ted when I was a kid. He was the only one who gave a damn about me when I was growing up." He grimaced. "Not that I deserved it even then. I was a real hell-raiser. But sometimes you get more than you're entitled to get." He turned toward the gate agent, who was starting to call the flight. "Like now. Like Catherine Ling fighting the friend she loves to save my ass." He took her elbow. "That's our section being called. Come on, let's get this show on the road."

"Gallo, I'm not doing this for any—"

"I know. I'm not assuming anything that you wouldn't want me to assume. Don't worry, I'm not suffering a major character change." The soberness was suddenly gone, and he was smiling recklessly. "You'll still have to watch me and make sure I don't try to manipulate you to get what I want. I'm still the same hell-raiser I was when I was a kid. I just raise it in different ways . . ."

CHAPTER
14

St. Joseph's Hospital
Milwaukee, Wisconsin

JOE WAS WALKING DOWN THE hospital corridor when Eve got off the elevator at his floor the next morning.

She smiled with an effort. "Busy already? Have you had breakfast yet?"

He shook his head. "They'll bring it soon. I thought I'd take a walk to help increase my stamina."

She wasn't sure how to take that. "I expected Jane to be here."

"She was here when I woke. I sent her down to Administration to start the paperwork going to get me out of here." He met her gaze. "When she said you wouldn't be able to see me until later today. But here you are. What happened, Eve?"

"Nothing to make you leap out of that bed and start worrying."

"I'm not leaping. I'm not that far along yet. But I'm getting there." He steadily met her gaze. "And you've been beside me every waking moment since I've been in this place. I've told you to go back to the hotel any number of times, and you wouldn't go. Now suddenly Jane tells me that you have something to do that will keep you away? It doesn't compute, Eve."

Eve made a face. "And I should have known that Jane's too honest to make you believe that everything was just fine."

"She tried, but she's clear as glass around the people she loves." He smiled. "Like you, Eve."

"That's not so bad." She took his hand. "Except when I want to keep you safe, dammit. Did Jane tell you anything?"

"Only that you were going up to Gallo's property. I figured I'd get everything else out of her on our way there. She said she wouldn't let me go alone."

She shook her head. "No, of course she wouldn't. She didn't like it that I made her stay here and try to stall you until I was sure what was happening up there."

"And what is happening?" Joe's hand tightened on hers. "I'm trying to hold on to my patience, but I'm having a tough time of it. Do you know how much I've hated being stuck in this damn hospital while Catherine was going after Gallo?"

Eve had realized that every day lately. She had been surprised that he had not been more impatient. It was not like Joe. "You've been very good about not complaining until it was time for your release."

"What good would it do? I have to be as strong as possible before I go after Gallo. Has Catherine found him?"

"Yes."

"What aren't you telling me?"

"He's convinced her that he didn't kill Bonnie."

"What?"

"You heard me." She shook her head. "Or maybe she's convinced herself. I can't put it all together. All she'd tell me was that she'd fought to believe what I'd told her was true, but that it didn't work for her."

"So why are you here instead of up there in the woods trying to shake some sense into her?"

"Because I called her when I was on the road, and she wasn't at the property. It sounded like an airport. "

"So you came back here." He added, "To save Jane and face the music."

She nodded. "I was expecting you to be angry."

"Not angry. Impatient, frustrated, confused." He shrugged. "It will take some time for me to muster any anger in connection with you. I came too close to losing you. Which puts everything else definitely in perspective." He suddenly chuckled. "Though being human, I'm sure it will come back to me with full force."

"I'm sure, too." Her lips twisted. "And I come in here, and you're walking the halls and building up stamina. Not very reassuring."

"I can't have you taking me for granted." His tone was absent. "Which airport? Did you hear any flight being called?"

"No, just the Homeland Security bag announcement. And a flight arrival from Miami. "

"What time was it?"

"Three forty in the morning. It had to be either Milwaukee or Chicago. They didn't have time to get from Gallo's property to any other airport. When Catherine called me previously, she told me she was still at the property."

"Have you checked with both airports to see if there was a flight at that time?"

"Not yet. I thought I'd let you do it." She smiled faintly. "It will keep you busy for a little while and give you a little more rest before you take the big plunge. I'm going to try to ration your energy."

He tilted his head. "You're not going to try to stop me?"

"I've bought more time than I thought I'd be able to manage—thanks to Catherine." Her lips tightened. "I can't understand how she could—"

"Yes, you can. Catherine and I were wondering the same thing about you a month ago. Gallo is very convincing." He was frowning. "But Catherine didn't have the same history with Gallo as you did, and she's smart as hell. It's a puzzle. What argument did she use?"

"She said that he didn't do it. She told me to start with that and work back."

"That's all?"

"Something about Gallo trying to take his life."

"Killers sometimes do commit suicide."

"That's not what she meant." She bit her lower lip. "I was so sure, Joe. But all I can think of now was how tormented Gallo was in those days when we were together. I could *feel* how much he loved Bonnie. Was I wrong to believe Paul Black?"

"You said Gallo believed him, too."

"And Catherine said just because Black thought he was telling the truth was no sign it was the truth." Eve shook her head. "I wanted to help Gallo. But I may have pushed him over the edge."

"Stop it," Joe said roughly. "Gallo can take care of himself. And now, evidently Catherine is watching out for him, too. And I've never understood why you've always believed he loved Bonnie."

Because she'd never told him. The relationship between Joe and Gallo had been too strained. But she had to tell him now. "Because . . . Bonnie comes . . . to him, too."

"Shit." Joe muttered a curse. "He could be lying to you."

She had tried to tell herself that lately. "He told me things . . . that song about the horses that she loved so much. I don't think he was lying, Joe."

Joe gazed at her for a moment. "Then what the hell is that supposed to mean?"

"I don't know. But would that mean that Bonnie loved him, too?" She shook her head. "And if that was true, how could she love him if he was the one who killed her? None of it makes sense."

"Why didn't you tell me before?" Joe shook his head. "Never mind. I know why. I was jealous as hell, and you didn't want me to think that even Bonnie was against me." He met her eyes. "Maybe the question should be why are you telling me now?"

"Because you told me that you know Bonnie now, that she brought you back. For years, no matter how we tried to overcome it, she's been between us. But something changed." She whispered, "I don't want to close you out of any part of my life. And she's such a big part, Joe."

He was silent, gazing down at their joined hands. "That's damn obvious. And spreading into all kinds of directions and little nooks. I never thought that she'd take me to John Gallo."

She waited, feeling the tension grip her.

"But you have to hand it to the kid. She's always throwing down a challenge." He looked up and met her eyes. "So I think we have to ride with her."

Relief surged through her. "And Catherine."

"And Catherine." He took the pad and pencil from the table beside him. "She may be wrong. Gallo may be the premier con man of the millennium. But I don't want you hurting for the bastard if there's a mistake. We might as well check it out. I'll call Milwaukee airport. You phone O'Hare. It will help if we can figure out where they're going." He reached for his phone. "And then we'll do what Catherine said and start putting together a scenario of 'what if it wasn't Gallo.'"

JOE WATCHED EVE IN THE hall talking to Jane, and he didn't envy her. They had chosen to keep Jane from going with them when they went after Catherine, and Eve had volunteered to break it to her.

Eve had wanted to protect him from the inevitable explosion. She had been protecting him constantly in big ways and small since he had come out of the coma. Ordinarily, it would have frustrated him, but in this instance, he welcomed it. He needed to think, and no one could reason logically when Jane was upset. She would be hurt as well as angry, and it was terribly hard to hurt someone you loved.

He got to his feet and moved across to the window and looked down at the hospital parking lot.

Okay, Catherine had said to assume Gallo wasn't guilty and figure it out from there.

But he didn't want to assume Gallo wasn't guilty. He was still having problems with the antagonism he felt toward him. Jealousy? Maybe. He had always been possessive of Eve, and he didn't like the idea of any other man in her life, past or present. Or maybe it was the fact that Gallo had endangered Eve since the moment he had come back into her life. Either way, the antagonism was present, and he had to deal with it.

So deal with it. Use intelligence, not emotion. He was an investigator. That was his chosen profession and he did it damn well. This could be the most important case he'd ever been given.

Is it Bonnie? This was a strange twist in the path that he'd been on since he'd come back with her from death's door. Strange or not, he could only do what he could, be what he was. Think. Concentrate. Look over the possibilities and see how the puzzle pieces would fit in different scenarios.

Deal with it.

He was still standing at the window forty-five minutes later when Eve came back into the room.

"Jane wants to see you. I couldn't talk her out of it."

"You shouldn't have tried." He turned to face her. "She has a right to vent her emotions on both of us." He smiled. "Don't worry, she'll be easy on me. She'll only try persuasion. She's been almost as protective of me as you."

"And it's been annoying you." She grimaced. "I can't help it, Joe."

"I know. It will take a little time." He paused. "If it will make you feel better, I'm feeling very strong. Sometimes stronger than I've ever felt before. There are moments when I'm not so good, but then I feel a kind of . . . surge. I can get through this, Eve."

She took step closer and laid her head on his chest. "And you won't take stupid chances?"

He chuckled. "Not too stupid." He took a step back. "Now give me fifteen minutes, then I'll face our tigress, Jane. Let's go over those notes about the flights leaving from O'Hare and Milwaukee. I think I know who Gallo and Catherine are going after. I just want to verify by the destination."

Georgetown, Washington, D.C.

"**NOT VERY PREPOSSESSING,**" Catherine said as she looked up at the small two-story apartment building that looked more like a motel. "When I think of Georgetown, I think foreign diplomats and money."

"That's probably why he wanted an address in Georgetown. Even though he was short of cash most of the time, he needed to put up a front." He was climbing the steps to the second level. "Apartment 26?"

"Yes."

He stopped before the door. "Locked. And probably an alarm shared by the other apartment dwellers." He leaned back against the jamb and crossed his arms across his chest. "Take care of it, Catherine."

"How do you know I can?"

"I watched you on camera when you and Quinn were storming my house in Utah. You were obviously an expert. I was impressed. My alarm system was state-of-the-art. This will be a piece of cake for you."

"You're giving me orders again." She was starting back down the stairs. "And I don't think you're an amateur, Gallo."

"I'm not. But you'll be faster. I'll open the lock by the time you get back. Okay?"

She didn't answer as she hurried down the steps and around the back of the apartment units. She would just as soon deactivate the alarm herself. She was accustomed to working alone, and Gallo was a little too domineering for her taste. His attitude was probably natural since he, too, was used to working alone. They would have to learn to keep pace with each other. She remembered that she'd had no real problem with working with Joe Quinn. But Joe had been her friend, and she'd respected him and felt comfortable with him.

There was no comfort about working with Gallo. She might respect his abilities, but there was a constant awareness that aroused an emotion that was close to antagonism whenever she was with him.

An antagonism caused by that physical disturbance that she couldn't suppress or diminish.

She might not be able to suppress it, but she blocked it when she had a job to do.

Take out the alarms.

Piece of cake as Gallo had said. She was climbing the stairs four minutes later. The door was cracked open, and no Gallo.

She glided silently into the apartment and shut the door.

She was instantly assaulted by darkness and the pungent smell of pepperoni.

"No other alarms in here," Gallo said from across the room. He was going through the drawers of a desk, his LED flashlight piercing the darkness. "Very messy. Jacobs was either a complete slob or he was in a big hurry." He took the Rolodex from the desk and stuffed it into his pocket. "No convenient receipts for airline tickets. I don't see any credit-card receipts either."

Catherine went into the kitchen and opened the refrigerator. "German beer. A California wine." She opened the bag on the second shelf. "And some kind of pasta in marinara sauce. He has international tastes as far as food is concerned."

Gallo was heading for the bedroom. "I'll go through the drawers of the bedside table. You check the bathroom."

The heavy scent of a citrus aftershave coming from a bottle on the sink . . . No toothbrush. A half-used lemon soap left in a green soap dish. Catherine picked up the aftershave and held it up to read the name. "Italian. Naples."

"Nothing here but a pack of prophylactics," Gallo said from the bedroom. "It's nice to know the bastard practices safe sex. We're not finding out much more than that. Anything else?"

"No."

"Then let's get out of here and start going through this Rolodex." He was heading for the front door. "If he traveled out of the country frequently, then he probably had a travel agent. When you're uneasy or afraid, then you tend to go to ground in the place that you feel most comfortable."

"And you can't be comfortable unless you visit a place with some degree of frequency." She closed the front door behind her and followed him toward the steps. "So we check and see where—" She suddenly halted on the top step. "Was this too easy, Gallo?" Her gaze was wandering around the parking lot. "I know we're both thinking of Jacobs as a second banana to Nate Queen, but it makes me uneasy that we don't know how he thinks, which way he'll jump. I don't like invisible men."

"I have a general idea how he'll react." Gallo looked soberly up at her from the bottom step. "And I'm not underestimating him, Catherine. He's a cornered rat, and he's not going to like me going after him. He's always resented me. He likes everything neat and able to be managed and manipulated, and I stepped outside the box." He turned and started toward the car. "But I wouldn't worry too much. I became an expert at killing rats in that Korean prison where Queen and Jacobs sent me."

"GALLO AND CATHERINE LING just left your apartment," Nixon said when Jacobs answered the phone. "They weren't in there for more than thirty minutes. They didn't carry out any boxes or anything big."

"But they probably found my Rolodex," Jacobs said through set teeth. Dammit, he should have grabbed it when he'd left yesterday morning. He'd known he'd have to go on the run soon, but he'd been trying to raise a stake to see him through. When he'd gotten word that his superiors had issued orders for him to be picked up for questioning he'd been thrown into a panic. He'd only grabbed his clothes and spare stash of cash and split. "Why the hell didn't you go in after it?"

"That's not what you paid me for," Nixon said. "I don't

know anything about alarms. I'm clean with the local police. I don't want anything on my record. I watched. I reported. If you'd given me the go-ahead, I would have taken care of them." He paused. "I'll still do it. I'm right behind them on the freeway. All you have to do is make an electronic transfer into my bank account."

But I don't have the money to make that transfer, Jacobs thought in frustration. His hand clenched on the phone. He and Queen had used Nixon before, and he was the best man for a job like this. He was almost as good as Paul Black had been with none of the bizarre freakiness Black had always exhibited.

He would rid himself of Gallo once and for all. And then he'd have a chance of being safe. He was not afraid of either Army Intelligence or any other law-enforcement body. He'd be able to survive. The world was crooked, and he knew where all the bodies were buried.

But Gallo was different. He'd seen how crazy the bastard could be. He wouldn't stop. He'd keep on until hell froze over, until he had Jacobs in his sights. Those yokel cops had said Black had killed Queen, but it was probably Gallo's doing. Jacobs had told Queen any number of times that it was dangerous trying to manipulate Gallo. Something about him caused a cold knot to form in Jacobs's stomach. He hated being afraid. He hated the arrogant macho bastards who'd tried to beat him down and crush him all his life.

But he'd shown them that it was brains, not brawn, that mattered. He'd plugged along and kept quiet and let them all show off how smart they thought they were. But it was Queen who had been killed. It was Gallo who was on the run.

Except, now, Jacobs was on the run, too.

"Make up your mind," Nixon said. "Do I get the money?"

"I'm thinking about it. I can't decide without studying all the consequences."

"My time is valuable. I can take care of Gallo and the woman tonight and move on to my next job. Yes or no?"

"I should be able to make a decision within the next two days. Just stay close to them." He hung up.

He mustn't let Nixon know he was weak in any way. But Jacobs knew he'd have to find a way to rid himself of Gallo and the woman. He couldn't dangle Nixon for more than the two days for which he'd bargained. He had to move and move—

His phone dinged to signal an arriving e-mail.

It could be the confirmation on his hotel room at the casino. They'd better confirm his reservations. He'd given them enough of his business.

It wasn't the hotel.

I warned you, Jacobs. I warned you both. Did you think I'd forgotten? Did you think I wouldn't find out what was going on?
You're a dead man.

No signature. Jacobs didn't need a signature.

SHIT. SHIT. Shit.

His heart was beating so hard, he felt dizzy.

You're a dead man.

He had thought that his luck couldn't get any worse when he'd found out that Gallo and the woman were on his trail.

This was worse. This was deadly.

He felt so scared, he was sick to his stomach.

He had to get control of himself. He could get out of this. He'd made up his mind that he had to disappear anyway. It was just reinforced by that damn e-mail. He would tell Nixon to take care of Gallo, and that bitch, and that would rid himself of one threat. Then he would run and hide and not surface until he thought it was safe.

But to do both of those things, he'd have to have money.

Money was always possible, always just around the next bend in the road. He'd pick a place that had always been special for him.

His luck was due to change. It always did.

And this time he was sure he'd score big enough to set him up for life.

Then he'd have the money to give Nixon.

Then he'd be able to squash Gallo and Catherine Ling as if they were vermin. Then he'd be able to keep that bastard from finding and killing him.

Just as soon as his luck changed.

"WE'RE BEING FOLLOWED," Catherine said quietly. "Three cars back, far left lane."

Gallo nodded. "Gray Mercedes."

"And he knows what he's doing. Slow down. I'm going to try to get his plate number."

Gallo slowed, but it took her three attempts to get the number on the front of the Mercedes. The person tailing them was sliding in and out of traffic like an eel. "Very slick. Jacobs?"

"No, Jacobs wouldn't be doing his own dirty work. Not unless he was forced into it." He glanced at the mirror. "But he would have a large number of lethal personnel to call on to do the job. It wouldn't be anyone from Army Intelligence. Jacobs has blown that cover."

"Another killer like Paul Black?"

"That's my guess. Jacobs set up someone to protect his back. He knew that he'd be on the run." He pulled off the freeway. "And this might not be so bad . . ."

She nodded. "Whoever is following us would probably know where Jacobs is hiding."

He smiled. "Two minds with a single thought."

They did think along the same lines, she thought. It was perfectly natural when they had been trained in the same violent schools of engagement. She had discovered that truth when she had been hunting him through the forests. "Then we need to gather him in and squeeze him for information. Pull over to that Holiday Inn, and let's let him find us."

"If he wants to find us," he murmured. "I might have to go find him."

"We'll see." The gray Mercedes was not coming after them, Catherine noticed. Yes, he was as good as she'd thought. It would have been foolish for him to do anything as obvious as driving into the parking lot. He would come back later, check out their room locations, and perhaps position himself for an attack. "In the meantime, while you check in, I'll try to verify his license plate."

"Probably a rental."

"It will be a start." She got out of the car and glanced at the side mirror. A streak of silver-gray Mercedes shot by the motel entrance. Come a little closer. We're waiting for you. "Let's get inside and work on it."

"EDWARD HUMPHREY." Catherine looked up as Gallo came in the adjoining door from his bedroom. "Avis Rental. Residence is in Detroit, Michigan. Venable is contacting the FBI and trying to dig deeper. It's not unusual for a suspect to use the same pseudonym any number of times. There may be a way we can sift it and come up with the right identity."

"Or not." He strolled over to the window and pulled back the drape to look down into the motel parking lot. "It may be better to do a little probing ourselves."

"Is he down there yet?"

"No." He let the drape fall back in place. "But it's still early. He may want to give us time to get settled." He dropped down in the beige easy chair beside the window. "I'll be the one to go for him. Okay?"

"No, it's not okay. How do I know that you'd do a better job than me? We'll discuss it later." She wearily rubbed her temple. "But right now, I'm going to take a shower and change my clothes. I still smell of earth and bark and shrubbery."

"And rotting leaves." He smiled slightly. "What a shame. I've grown to like it."

"Which only proves how weird you are." She got to her feet and moved toward the bathroom. "Call me if you need me."

"Oh, I will. You'll be the first to know."

She inhaled sharply as she looked back over her shoulder. Sensuality. Intense and unexpected. Everything had been pragmatic and commonplace. Yet suddenly there was this searing awareness.

Don't address it. Ignore it.

She quickly closed the bathroom door behind her. Ignore it? Her body was responding the same way it had when she'd watched him wading out of the lake and coming toward her.

She threw off her clothes and stepped into the warm shower. A few minutes later, she was soaping her hair and body. The clean white tile surrounding her was completely different from the primitive lake and forest. No comparison.

Except for the way her breasts were swelling as she thought about Gallo. Except for how her skin felt flushed and silky . . . and ready to touch.

She had thought that she had overcome the sexual magnetism that had so shaken her. She had coolly separated her emotional and physical feelings from logic, instinct, and reasoning. Had she just been fooling herself?

No, she wouldn't accept that she would deceive herself just to get what she wanted. The desire might still be there, but it wasn't what had caused her to embark on this search for Jacobs.

But it could get in the way, dammit.

And Gallo wasn't going to try to tamp it down or walk away from it.

She stepped out of the shower and grabbed a towel from the rack.

That was okay. She'd do whatever she thought was right for her and let Gallo please himself. She was only responsible for her own path. Catherine had never asked anyone for help except Eve. But there had been no question that she would ask Eve to help her find Luke. Her son was Catherine's life, and she'd been willing to sell her soul to find him.

And she hadn't called Luke for the last three days, she realized. It had been toward the end of the hunt, and she'd been completely obsessed with capturing Gallo. Which was another reason why she should distance herself from him. Nothing should keep her concentration from her son. They had not been together for nine years; she owed him all her attention.

She threw on a pair of black pants and white T-shirt and was toweling her hair dry as she opened the door.

Gallo was still lounging in the easy chair, his legs stretched out before him. "Now you smell of lavender. Pleasant, but I miss the—"

"Rotten leaves," she inserted. "I wish I'd never told you about them."

"I'm not. It fascinated me learning about Hu Chang and your Hong Kong connection. I studied your dossier before I met you, but it's the details that create the 3-D image." He added, "I ordered sandwiches and coffee from room service. Would you like anything else?"

She shook her head as she took out her phone. "I'll eat later. I have to call my son."

"It's nearly ten. He won't be asleep?"

"He's a night owl. I don't try to force him into a neat little cubbyhole. He lived a rough life while he was away from me. I'm just grateful he's doing as well as he is." She was dialing as she spoke. "And that he lets me stay in his life."

"Would you like me to give you a little privacy?"

"Why? I'm not ashamed of our relationship. It is what it is. We're working our way through it." She spoke into the phone as Luke picked up. "Hi, how are you doing? Are you reading?"

"No, I was having Kelly teach me about how she does her patterns." He paused. "I don't understand it. I don't think I'm dumb, but she sees things that I don't see."

"You're not alone. Kelly is extraordinary. Her professors say that she's another Einstein. She can start at the beginning of a theory or puzzle and forecast exactly where it's going to go."

"I know all that." Luke's voice was slow, thoughtful. "But she says that if I go back and tell her all about the years that I was away from you, she'll draft a pattern that will help me see things clearly." He added haltingly, "And if I understand it, then I'll be able to forget it."

Catherine had known that Kelly was going to try to help Luke in that way. It was the next best thing to psychological therapy, and Catherine would be eternally grateful if it worked. "Maybe not forget it, but it may help you to let it go. Sometimes, bad things help you to grow, and you wouldn't want to give up the growth. That would mean you'd gone through it for nothing. I don't think Kelly would want you to do that. She's gone through some rough times herself."

"She told me her father was murdered. She saw it."

"And she's trying to learn from it. So maybe she's the right person to talk to you about all of this." She paused. "Unless you want to talk to me. You know I'm here for you, Luke."

"I know."

But he still couldn't talk to her, she thought in pain. No matter how much she loved him, she was part of the problem. She cleared her throat and changed the subject. "How are your studies going?"

"Okay. I finished *Midsummer Night's Dream.* But I didn't care much for it. I've started *Julius Caesar,* and I understand that better."

"Yes, I can see you appreciating *Julius Caesar.*" Ambition and murder and revenge. Luke would comprehend all of those nuances of character from his own experience. "*Midsummer Night's Dream* would have a little too much whimsy for you."

"Maybe I'll go back to it later and read it again if you want me to."

"I don't want you to read it to please me. It doesn't matter."

"I . . . want to . . . please you."

"That's good, I want to please you, too. But let's work on kindness and understanding instead of trying to shape each other's tastes."

"Okay." Another pause. "Are you . . . well?"

"I'm fine. I should be able to get home soon."

"I'd like . . . I know Kelly wants to see you." He added, "Do you want to talk to her, should I go get her?"

"No, don't bother her. Tell her I can't wait to see her and give her my best. I'll let you go now. I just wanted to check in and make sure you were all happy. I love you. Good-bye, Luke."

"Good-bye." He hesitated. "I want you to be happy, too, Catherine." He hung up.

Someday, he would say he loved her. Someday it would happen.

"You said you were working your way through it," Gallo said quietly. "It appears that sometimes it's straight uphill."

"You think that I mind that?" She swallowed hard to rid herself of the tightness of her throat. "We're doing fine. Do you know what he went through? Every day that Luke was held by that son of a bitch, Rakovac, he was told that I was to blame. Every time he was whipped or thrown into a solitary cell, it was all my fault. It's a miracle that he managed to realize that I wasn't to blame. But there have to be residual effects from all that brainwashing. He can't trust me even if he wants to."

"What a bastard," Gallo said grimly. "He's dead, I assume?"

"Yes," she said. "Slow and painful."

"Good, then I won't have to offer to do it for you." He was studying her face. "You had to deal with finding him alone? Your husband?"

"He was murdered the night my son was kidnapped."

"So you had to handle it by yourself. You might have had to do that anyway. He was in his sixties, right?"

"Yes, but I don't know why people keep bringing that up," she said impatiently. "Terry was a good man and great father. That's all that matters."

"If that was all that mattered to you."

"Venable turned me over to him after I was recruited, and Terry taught me everything he knew about being an agent. We were good together."

"As partners or as husband and wife?"

"Both. I wasn't some romantic kid who didn't know what was important. We had a good, solid marriage and had a beautiful child together. I couldn't ask for anything more." She defiantly met his gaze. "So it wasn't anything like what you had with Eve. She said it was crazy and pure sex and nothing else. But in the end, it wasn't about what you were together, it was about the child you had."

"And was that what it was about with you and your husband? Your child, Luke?"

She was silent a moment. "I don't know. We were together for such a short time. Terry wanted a child right away, and that was okay with me. But then, after Luke was born, my son was everything. I guess children change everything."

"Yes."

"You agree with me, but you never knew Bonnie," she said. "I can't believe all that ghost business, you know. You had me going for a little while, but I'm too hardheaded to really think that could happen."

"Hardheaded." He repeated the words reflectively. "What would happen if you'd lost your Luke, and he'd suddenly 'returned' to you? What if he was so real to you that all your doubts were crashing down around you? Would you reject him? Or would you let down the barriers and invite him back into your world?"

She shied away from even thinking about Luke taken from

her in that most final way. Yet she'd had to face that possibility for the entire nine years of Luke's captivity. It was clever of Gallo to bring the comparison with Luke into her rejection of the concept of the spirit Bonnie. "I don't know what I'd do." No, that wasn't honest. "I can't imagine a situation like that, but if it existed, I'd never shut Luke away from me even if it meant being locked up in the booby hatch."

"The defense rests."

"But the situation doesn't exist, and what you and Eve are experiencing could be a hallucinogenic product of the emotional trauma that you've both suffered. Understandable, but with no basis in reality."

"That sounds very slick," Gallo said. "And not at all in keeping with what I've learned about you."

"No, I'm not slick." She wearily shook her head. "The opposite. I'm just trying to fit the pieces of the puzzle together, and I'm coming up short."

"Don't worry about it." He pulled Jacobs's Rolodex out of his jacket pocket. "We'll try to put this puzzle together instead."

She came toward him and watched as he flipped the pages of the Rolodex. "Anything?"

"Nate Queen's address and phone. Several officers' names who probably worked at Army Intelligence." He flipped to the T. "No travel agency. I was hoping to save some time, but no luck. Evidently, he makes his own travel arrangements." He flipped to C. He gave a low whistle. "An entire list of casinos." His finger ran down the list. "Las Vegas, San Juan, Lima, Rio, New Orleans, Mobile, Rome, St. Louis, Monte Carlo . . ." He flipped the page.

"And another entire page. Jacobs evidently traveled the world to satisfy his addiction."

"Too many choices. No indication where he might have gone? No preferences?"

Gallo shook his head, still flipping pages. He reached a list of letters with telephone numbers beside them. "M. S. J. N. It seems that he didn't want to be careless with these particular names." He handed her the Rolodex. "Why don't you give these numbers to Venable and see what he can come up with."

She nodded and started dialing her phone. "No H for Humphrey."

"Surprise. Surprise." There was a knock on the door, and he stood up and moved to answer it. "That should be our food." He checked the security view before opening the door. "I can use that coffee . . ."

Two hours later, Venable called back, and Catherine scribbled down the information.

She hung up and turned to Gallo. "He couldn't trace the S, but they were able to pull up info on the others. Juan Martinez, hit man for the San Juan Mafia, Edward Nixon, no gang association but suspect in three murders in the U.S. and two in London, Randy Jason, former Army Ranger now suspected of two killings for hire in Jacksonville, Florida."

"Martinez is Hispanic?"

She nodded. "And the name Humphrey doesn't sound in the least Hispanic. It would catch attention and be remembered if Martinez didn't look the part. So the gray Mercedes is probably Jason or Nixon."

"Unless Jacobs found another errand boy." Gallo went to

the window again. "Still no Mercedes. Maybe he's not ready to move yet." He turned to face her. "Why don't you try to get some sleep. I'll stand watch."

"We'll take turns. Three hours. Leave the connecting door open." She sat down on the bed. "My internal clock is pretty good. Will you need me to wake you?"

"I believe I can manage." His lips turned up at the corners as he turned out the light and headed toward the door. "I can always use my phone alarm. But if I fall down on the job, by all means shake me."

"And then you'd probably grab me and break my neck." She pulled the sheet over her and closed her eyes. "I'll be careful . . ."

CHAPTER
15

GALLO CROSSED TO THE CONNECTING door and looked at Catherine curled up under the covers like a cat.

She was sleeping hard, having gone to sleep within five minutes of the time that she had pulled the sheet over her two hours ago. Her breathing was light and steady, and her sleep was deep and sound. Yet he'd bet that if she sensed anything that was unexpected, she'd be awake in a heartbeat.

As he would be, Gallo thought. Her CIA training and his years in the Rangers had given them both a military mind-set that would probably remain with them the rest of their lives. Now it was strange thinking of Catherine as a soldier. Her competence was superlative, beyond question; but he could no longer think of her as the hunter who had stalked him through the forest.

He was too aware of her as a woman.

Shit, aware? Understatement.

He had trouble looking at her and not remembering her naked, wet, and shimmering in the sunlight. When she had come out of the water, there had been drops of water on her breasts and nipples, and he had wanted to bend down and lick them, make them taut and ready. Then move between her legs and put his hands—

Hell, he was getting hard just thinking about that moment. And this moment, too.

She was lying there helpless, asleep, and there was a catlike grace about her. But like a cat, he could imagine her moving beneath him, fierce, sensual, springing forward and taking what she wanted.

As she had wanted to do at the lake. Dammit, she had wanted him as much as he had wanted her.

Stop. Block it as he had done since they had started in search of Jacobs. So what if he wanted her more than any woman he'd wanted in years? Screwing her wouldn't be good for either one of them.

Wouldn't be good? What was he thinking? It would be fantastic.

Maybe in the short term, but she didn't deserve any more complications. God knows, he was too scarred to have a decent relationship with any woman. He had come close to almost destroying Eve years ago.

And Bonnie?

But Catherine had said he hadn't destroyed Bonnie.

He closed his eyes as the pain washed over him. God, he hoped Catherine was right, that he hadn't accepted what she had said because he wanted it to be so. But for that reason alone, he should be thinking of Catherine with gratitude and not as a sexual object.

Not likely. He was too damn selfish, and he wanted her too much.

But he could perhaps put off moving to satisfy that selfishness for a little while.

Keep busy. Find Jacobs.

His lids flipped open, and he turned away from the door and moved toward the window in his room.

Let that Mercedes be there.

He pulled back the drape. No Mercedes in the lot, dammit. Where the hell was the—

But he caught a glimpse of silver out of the corner of his eye.

Around the side of the hotel, in the far parking lot. He took his binoculars out of his suitcase. Be sure.

A shadowy figure at the wheel. Light shirt, dark hair, brawny shoulders. No reason for anyone to be sitting in the parking lot at one in the morning.

Jason or Nixon?

It didn't matter.

He let the drapes fall back, turned, and glided silently toward the door to the hall.

Prey.

CATHERINE WOKE with a start.

Darkness. Silence. Something was wrong.

No Gallo.

She swung her feet to the floor and jumped out of bed.

She ran into his bedroom. She hadn't expected him to be there. But his suitcase was open and on the bed. Binoculars on the table by the window.

She grabbed them and thrust the drapes aside.

"Damn you, Gallo." She lifted the glasses and scanned the parking lot. Nothing.

No, to the far side . . .

She threw the binoculars down, ran back to her room, and slipped on her shoes.

Then she was running out of the room. No time for the elevator. She took the steps two at a time as she ran down to the lobby and out onto the parking lot.

She stopped short.

Gallo and a dark-haired man were wrestling on the ground beside the driver's side of the Mercedes.

As she watched, Gallo flipped him over and climbed astride him. His arm encircled the man's neck. Gallo's face was flushed, his lips pulled back and revealing his teeth. Savage, animalistic anger and something close to bloodlust twisted his features. She remembered he had killed Paul Black with that very hold.

"Gallo," she said through her teeth. "Don't you kill him until we find out what we need to know."

He looked up at her, and, for a moment, she thought he would ignore her. Then he drew a deep breath, and his arm loosened from around the man's neck. "I'm not going to kill him . . . yet." He jerked a knife from the man's grasp. "He nicked me and made me a little upset."

She could see the blood on Gallo's forearm. Nick seemed a

good description for the wound. "He didn't hurt you." She came forward and stood over Gallo and the man. "And if he did, you deserved it, you bastard. You left me without a word." Her gaze shifted to the man who was glaring up at her. "Who is he? Nixon or Jason?"

"Why don't we ask him?" Gallo pressed the edge of knife against the man's throat. "Answers. I want answers. Name?"

"Humphrey."

The knife brought blood. "Name?"

"Nixon."

"Very good. Now, where is Thomas Jacobs?"

"I don't know." He gasped with the pain as the knife bit again. "I tell you, I don't know. He hired me to watch his place and report back to him. He was expecting you to go after him when he heard about Queen's death."

"Report back? And that's all?"

"For the time being. There might have been additional work later. He was going to consider it." His lips curled. "I don't think the son of a bitch could afford me. I wouldn't have even taken the job if I hadn't been having a slow month."

"A 'slow month,'" Catherine repeated. "What constitutes a 'slow month' in the assassination game, Nixon?"

"Where is Jacobs?" Gallo asked again. "One minute."

"He was stalling me. He said he'd decide in two days," Nixon went on quickly, his gaze on the knife. "That probably meant he had to find a way to score before he could pay me. He did it once before when he had me take care of one of the bosses at a casino in Atlantic City. The bastard always thought he could beat the tables. Sometimes he did. Sometimes he didn't. But he was always sure he was going to make the big score."

"That's not enough," Gallo said. "More. Jacobs is going to have to disappear for a while, and it's going to take cash. He'd need money to pay you and to find a place to lie low from the police. Where would he go to get the money?"

"How do I know? He didn't—" He cursed as the blood started to run down his neck as Gallo's knife bit deep. "Maybe New Orleans. He told me once he lost his shirt in Atlantic City and the pit bosses were all crooks. He said that next time, he was going back to New Orleans, where he always won big."

"When did he say that?"

"Six months ago."

"Not when he set you up to do this job?"

"No, he didn't mention anything."

Gallo looked at Catherine. "What do you think?"

"I don't know. I think he's telling the truth."

"I'm not sure." His grasp tightened on the knife.

Nixon gasped. "Let me go. I'll find out for sure and set him up for you. What good is it going to do you to slit my throat?"

"Good point," Catherine said. "Let him make a call and see if Jacobs trusts him enough to tell him what we need to know."

"Pity." Gallo took the knife away and got to his feet. "I was beginning to enjoy myself."

Nixon hurriedly sat up. "You'll let me go if I get you what you want?"

"I didn't say that," Gallo said.

"We don't need him. He's not going to call Jacobs back and tip our hand." She stared Nixon in the eye. "Because he knows we'd be after him and never give up. It wouldn't be good business, would it, Nixon?"

"No." He moistened his lips. "I don't care about Jacobs. Why should I?"

"You shouldn't care. As I said, it's not good business." She backed away from him. "Get in your car and turn the speaker on your phone so that Gallo can hear loud and clear." She turned to Gallo. "I'll take a turn around the parking lot and make sure that we haven't disturbed any of the hotel employees or guests while you keep Nixon company."

"Why should they be disturbed? I was very quiet. He didn't even scream." He opened the driver's door and smiled. "But I agree that I should be the one to babysit him. We've grown so close we're almost like family."

"Family? Maybe the Borgias." She moved away from the car and strolled across the parking lot. She doubted if their encounter with Nixon had attracted attention. It had seemed to go on for a long time, but it had actually taken only a few moments. It was the middle of the night, but there was always the chance that someone had glanced out the window. Or that a motel employee had come out for a cigarette. At any rate, she had to check out possible problems before they erupted to become real problems.

They had to move fast to find Jacobs and certainly didn't need trouble with the police.

She was striding back to the Mercedes ten minutes later. Nixon was just hanging up his cell phone. She glanced at Gallo. "Well?"

"New Orleans. Cadalon Casino," Gallo said. "He was on

his way to the airport. Jacobs promised Nixon that he'd have his blood money by day after tomorrow." He added, "Actually, Nixon handled it very well. He displayed a wonderful mixture of greed and venom. Jacobs didn't suspect a thing."

"You said I could go," Nixon said. "You know where Jacobs is heading. I did everything you asked."

"That's true," Gallo said. "But it was really Catherine who said we'd let you go. I really don't approve of—"

"Let him go," Catherine said. "We don't have time to deal with him."

Gallo shrugged. "Whatever you say." He stepped back and gestured to Nixon. "Run along. Frankly, I'd make time to deal with you, but if we experience any backlash, I may still get my way."

Nixon muttered a curse, but he was frantically starting the car and screeching out of the parking space.

Gallo was gazing regretfully after him. "You know that he'll come after us eventually?"

"But it will take time for him to get over the first intimidation," Catherine said. "You frightened him." She turned away as Nixon peeled out of the parking lot. "I can see why Queen thought you were so valuable when you worked for him as a special agent. He said that there were moments when you were like an ancient Viking with the bloodlust on you. He called you a berserker. You can be—" She stopped, searching for the right word.

"Frightening?" He fell into step with her as she moved toward the glass door. "Did I frighten you, Catherine?"

"No." She opened the door. "But I found it interesting to

watch you. I couldn't decide whether you were bluffing or if you really wanted to kill him."

"I don't bluff. Nixon is scum. Would I have cut his throat?" He smiled recklessly. "You seem to think I'm better than I think I am. So I believe I'll let you wonder."

"You're good with a knife. Is that your weapon of choice?"

"I find it effective. Most people have experience with being cut and fear it. Guns are more impersonal. What about you?"

"Sometimes a knife is necessary, but I prefer being impersonal." She added, "Except when I'm dealing with someone I hate."

"Like Rakovac?"

She nodded. "I would have made him suffer as much as a victim of the Spanish Inquisition if I'd had the time. I wanted to take it slow."

"If you run across a similar situation, let me know. I've learned a lot from personal experience about the methods the Inquisition used in that period. I'll be glad to share." He started up the stairs. "I'll call and make our airline reservations to New Orleans."

He stopped before entering his room. "Nixon should really have been eliminated. You know it as well as I do. It goes against your professionalism and my good judgment. Why?"

Because she hadn't wanted to see Gallo do it. Yes, Nixon was scum and would cause them trouble, but she was holding on to her faith in Gallo by a very tentative grip. She had not been shocked by Gallo's savagery, but it had made her wary.

"Never mind." His gaze was on her face. "I think I know." He shrugged. "I couldn't expect anything else."

"No, you couldn't." She went next door to her own room. "I should be ready to go in ten minutes. But I'm going to call Venable and tell him where we're going and see if he can pave the way for us."

"Good idea. Fifteen minutes then."

But there was a missed call on her phone when she picked up her cell to call Venable.

Eve.

She stiffened, then drew a deep breath.

She pressed the return call. "I just got your call. Did I wake you?"

"No. We're not doing much sleeping right now." Eve was silent. "You said to start with the premise that we were wrong about Gallo being guilty and work from there."

"But can you do that, Eve?"

"I'm trying. Joe says that we should trust you. That wasn't easy for him." She paused. "And either way, it's not easy for me. I trusted Gallo, and it hurt me to think that I'd been a fool. Perhaps that's one of the reasons that I was so stubborn about not changing my mind when you were defending him."

"I can understand that," Catherine said. "And I can't tell you I'm 100 percent sure that I'm right. How can I be when Gallo isn't even sure? But I'm 75 percent sure, and before I'm done, I'm going to know."

"You're going after Thomas Jacobs."

"You bet I am. I see you put two and two together."

"Joe and I decided he would be one of the only people who would know for certain why Queen hired Paul Black to take the blame for Bonnie's killing. And we tracked you to the Chicago airport and found out that there was a flight to the East Coast about the time I talked to you on the phone." She added. "Non-stop to Washington, D.C. Have you contacted Jacobs yet?"

"Not yet. We think he's on a flight to New Orleans. We're going to be right behind him." She hesitated, then asked the question. "What are you going to do, Eve?"

"You mean am I going to notify the police that they can pick up Gallo in New Orleans?" she asked. "No, Joe said I should trust you. Dear God, I want to trust you, Catherine. And I want to trust Gallo." She drew a shaky breath. "Joe left the hospital this morning. I'm going to talk to him now, but I think he's going to agree that we're not going to let the police interfere with what's between us. I imagine we'll see you in New Orleans."

"I'm glad, Eve."

"Don't be too happy. When Joe came out of his coma, he said he thought we were heading toward the end, that Bonnie told him that was happening. But I just don't know." Her voice was uneven. "What I'm feeling is too damn tentative. I'm wobbling back and forth like a weather vane."

"What about Jane? Is she coming?"

"No, she's mad as hell, but I won't let her run the risk."

Catherine could see that Jane would be angry as well as worried to death. "She didn't impress me as someone who would take foolish chances. I agree that the situation may—"

"The situation may be pure hell. I've got a gut feeling that it probably will be. Joe almost lost his life. If we're heading for the end of the search, Jane's not going to be caught up in any of it," Eve said fiercely. "I'll call you when we reach New Orleans." She hung up.

Catherine slowly pressed the disconnect.

"We're heading toward the end. Bonnie told him that was happening."

Bonnie, again.

Catherine seemed to be the only one who was not being affected by that small seven-year-old child who had died those many years ago.

Joe, whom Catherine respected as a friend and professional, was evidently accepting the same bizarre concept as Eve and Gallo. Bonnie, returned from the dead. Bonnie, the ghost, the beloved spirit.

"Catherine?" Gallo had opened the connecting door, his gaze searching her expression. "Are you all right?"

"Yes." She glanced at her watch. "Sorry. I haven't called Venable yet. But I can do it on the way to the airport." She threw her suitcase on the bed and started tossing items of clothing into it. "This won't take me long."

He leaned against the doorjamb. "I asked if you were all right."

She nodded jerkily. "That was Eve on the phone. She said she and Joe would see us in New Orleans."

He went still. "You told her?"

"She said she wasn't going to call the police." She looked up from her packing. "She's going to give us a chance. Though she still has her doubts."

"I can imagine."

Because he still had his own doubts and was fighting desperately to put them aside. Catherine had a few doubts herself, dammit, but she wouldn't give up either faith or determination. If she was the only one driving this show, then so be it.

"Joe is on our side." She fastened the suitcase. "Sort of. Maybe. I guess we take what we can get. When are our airline reservations?"

"In another three hours. I could have gotten a connection through Atlanta a little earlier, but it would have only been arriving an hour before the nonstop."

"An hour isn't going to make a difference." She picked up her suitcase. "Let's go."

BUT IT TURNED OUT TO BE nine hours. The entire Gulf Coast was fogged in, and their Delta flight had a six-hour delay. They didn't arrive in New Orleans until close to noon. It was still damp and foggy when the plane landed at Louis Armstrong New Orleans International, and the forecast was for more heavy fog later in the day.

"Where do we go from here?" Catherine asked as she retrieved her bag. "Where's this casino? A high-rise off Bourbon Street or a riverboat on the river?"

"Neither, it's outside the city. The Cadalon is across the Mississippi and has a very exclusive clientele of jet-setters and high rollers. We'll register at the hotel as man and wife. We'll use the Brookman name I used on the airline ticket." He checked his watch. "It's a little early for play, but in a few hours the casino should be humming. We should wait until after midnight to make a play. Though probably Jacobs is at the tables right now. He's going to be very focused."

"You should know a lot about casinos. You made a great deal of money from them, didn't you?"

He nodded. "I taught myself card counting in prison. It's the most valuable lesson I learned in that rathole."

"It's going to be difficult extricating him from a crowded casino. Have you thought about a plan for taking him?"

"A tentative plan." He smiled as he opened the door for her. "But I'm sure that you have one that's not at all tentative. You were very quiet on the plane."

She shrugged. "Simplicity is best. We find out in what room he's playing. I go in and pretend to greet him. He falls unconscious, and we are very upset. He's obviously ill, and we have to get him to a hospital. We take him away from the casino. End of scene."

"Yes, very simple," Gallo said dryly. "Up to the time that he falls unconscious. That might get a little complicated. One of your friend Hu Chang's magic potions? Hypodermic?"

She nodded. "It will keep him out for at least twenty minutes. That should give us time to get him away from the casino."

Gallo opened the passenger door of the rental car for her. "Unless the casino manager wants to handle his transfer to the hospital himself to prevent liability issues."

"That's why I allowed twenty minutes. Otherwise, we could have Jacobs out of there in seven. I've had Venable send me a dossier on the manager of the casino. I'll study it and see how I can get around him." She looked at him as she got into the car. "Or I'll let you handle it. I'd judge you're very good at manipulating people to suit yourself. I'll do everything else. You get us out of that casino before Jacobs wakes up."

"I'll work on it." He got into the driver's seat and started the car. "Anything else?"

"Yes." She took out a slip of paper from her notebook. "Stop at this address on the way out of town. Neither of us has suitable clothes for that kind of casino. It's a boutique that will supply me with a gown that will make me look as if I belong in a casino frequented by the jet set. I told Venable to arrange for a tux for you, too. It won't be designer, but it will be okay. I'm the one who all the attention will be focused on."

"You don't need a designer gown to garner attention. You walk into a room, and every man will do a double take."

"That is true," she said calmly. "Do you expect me to pretend modesty? That would be foolish. Good looks can be a valuable weapon. They can also be a handicap if you want to fade into the background. Either way, you have to accept what you are and make the most of it."

"I gladly accept what you are," he said softly. "I celebrate it."

Sensuality.

She looked away from him, feeling the familiar rush of heat. How many men had hit on her through the years? Why was Gallo different? She didn't know, but she'd better learn to handle his effect on her.

"You'd better not celebrate anything until we get Jacobs," she said flatly. "And I know you like the way I look. I'd have to be blind if I wasn't aware that I turn you on. But it doesn't mean anything. Looks don't matter."

"Looks don't matter. Age doesn't matter. What does matter, Catherine?"

"Kindness. Love. Fighting for what you believe and the

people you believe in." She paused. "And, again, knowing who you are."

"Admirable," he said quietly. "We're alike on many levels. I'm just a bit more shallow and far more attuned to the physical. I'm afraid I can't get over that particular barrier." He paused. "And I believe you may be having a few problems in that area, too. It's been there since the first time we came together, and you've been trying to ignore it. But it keeps coming back, doesn't it, Catherine?"

"Yes." She wouldn't lie to him. That would be a defeat in itself. "But I'll find a way to not let it get in my way. That's not why we're together."

"No, we're together so that you can help Eve and bring me along for the ride." He was looking straight ahead. "And I'm trying to stop being an ungrateful son of a bitch and forget how you looked in all your rotting-leaves glory. I have to warn you— it's not working too well." He gestured to a street up ahead. "I think that's where the address you gave me should be. Do you want me to wait or go inside with you? I have some calls to make to set up my part of our exit plan."

She felt a little of her tension leaving her. His voice was much more crisp, and it was obviously the end of the intimacy that had caused the tension. She was grateful to ignore anything connected to that intimacy at the moment. Honesty and boldness were fine, but she had to regroup and step back from Gallo. "I'll go in alone." When the car pulled to the curb in front of the elegant stone house, she opened the door. "If they need you to be measured for your tux, I'll give you a call. My fitting shouldn't take long. I'm a standard size and Venable knows my measurements."

"Venable must know a lot about you. How long did you say you've been together?"

"He's been my superior since I was seventeen. He recruited me." She slammed the car door and headed for the front entrance. "And by the time I had Luke, he knew more about me than even my husband did. I was an agent and that's all part of the job."

"If I'd been living with you long enough to have a child, I guarantee that no one would have known you better." He smiled and leaned back in the seat. "And to hell with the job."

Cadalon Casino
2:35 A.M.

"I'M READY." CATHERINE CAME OUT of the bedroom into the sitting room and gazed at him critically. "You look very polished."

"I was aiming at being very James Bond." He tilted his head. "I have to keep up with the competition. But 007 never had a Bond girl like you."

She was totally breathtaking, he thought as his gaze moved from the top of her shining dark hair to the silver heels peeping out of the slit in the dark burgundy strapless gown she wore. The golden skin of her shoulders and upper breasts gleamed under the lights, and he wanted to reach out and touch her, stroke her. Exotic, sexy, and so vibrantly alive she lit up the room.

"I've always thought the Bond girls lacked a certain strength of will." She smiled. "But they usually managed to get things done. Did you locate Jacobs?"

"He's playing blackjack and doing very well. He's excited about it. His cheeks are so flushed, you'd think he had a fever." He opened the door to the hall. Don't touch her. Not the time or the place. "I can stay out of Jacobs's way until after you've taken care of him. But both he and Queen must have read the dossier on you that they gave to me. The photo didn't do you justice, but he'll probably recognize you."

"Then I won't give him time for it to register. I can't let him see me until the last minute."

"He'd have to be distracted not to notice you." The hall was decorated in the same elegant nineteenth-century décor as the rest of the hotel casino. Catherine looked like a splendid peacock strolling past the soft pastels of the wall hangings and faded Aubusson rugs, he thought. "But I'm sure that you'll find a way to do it."

"I'm sure I will, too," she said absently. "Eve just phoned me. I tried to call her earlier, but I got her voice mail. They've canceled all the flights out of the Midwest to New Orleans, so they were on a plane to Atlanta. But they ran across the same problem there. They're waiting for a break in the weather. Damn this fog."

"I thought she might be here by now." He gazed out the window at the thick mist that obscured everything beyond two feet. "It's as thick as any London fog."

"Yes, I hoped it might lift before this." She got into the brass-and-beveled-glass-paneled elevator. "I'm glad that they're not here yet. I told them what we planned, but I don't want Joe and her coming into this mess until we have Jacobs secure. If everything blows up in our faces, I don't want them involved."

"But they are involved, Catherine. One might say more than you." He held up his hand to stop her from speaking. "Since we're almost sure that they won't make it before we're done here, I'm not going to worry about it. Though I have plenty of time to devote to worrying since you haven't left me much else to do until after the finale. Where's your hypodermic? You'd have trouble hiding it in that gown."

"It's under the nail of my right index finger." She glanced down at her gleaming scarlet nails. "It was the most practical place." The elevator doors opened, and they were assaulted by voices, music, glittering mirrors, and sparkling chandeliers.

"The blackjack room is beyond the gold arches to the left. Table three," Gallo said.

"Right." She moved out of the elevator. "Give me a few minutes, then follow me."

He nodded. "I'll let you make your entrance. But don't expect me to miss the performance. I've been looking forward to it."

"I don't know why. I told you it's going to be short and simple."

"Whatever you say." He watched her move across the brilliant foyer toward the blackjack room. He was far from the only person staring at Catherine. Who could help it? She was graceful, stunning, completely confident. She was as different as night and day from the fierce huntress who had stalked him in the woods. He wasn't sure which Catherine fascinated him more, and it was too soon to make a choice. He was certain that he'd be seeing other facets of her that would prove equally interesting.

But for the moment, he'd better follow her and be ready to step in and back her up when she needed him. It was a strange role for him. All his life, he had been a loner, and his missions had definitely been solo. Yet he had accepted Catherine's plan, which had not only put him in tandem with her, but in a semi-passive position.

And he had done it with no resentment and even a touch of amusement.

Strange . . .

CHAPTER
16

CATHERINE PAUSED IN THE DOORWAY, her gaze searching the room.

Table three.

Yes, there he was. She'd had Venable send her a picture of Thomas Jacobs on her phone. He was a small, wiry man in his middle or late fifties dressed in a tux that looked a little too big for him. His thin brown hair was receding to such an extent that he was totally bald in the front. But his cheeks were as flushed as Gallo had told her, and his gray eyes were sparkling with excitement as he gazed at the dealer. He had a stack of chips in front of him, and his expression was totally absorbed.

But he might not stay absorbed if he saw someone glance in her direction. She'd better put the play in motion.

She glided forward, moving to the side to approach Jacobs from the rear.

Be anxious.

Let everyone see her concern.

Okay. Stop short as she pretended to see Jacobs.

She inhaled sharply, her eyes widening with panic.

Now clinch it.

She ran toward Jacobs and touched his shoulder. "No, Thomas, you know you can't do this." Her voice was shaking with emotion. "Why don't you listen? You know what the doctor said about your heart. No excitement. This addiction could be the end—" He was turning to face her, his expression wary. As soon as he saw her, he'd recognize her. She had perhaps thirty seconds. "Do you want to kill yourself?" Her tone was agonized. "I won't let you do it. I know I told you I wouldn't stop you if you were this crazy, but I can't let it happen."

He was looking at her face, and she saw his expression change as he recognized her. He jumped to his feet. "Get away from me."

"You have to listen to me, Thomas." Her hands clasped his shoulders near his throat. "I'm only trying to help you."

"The hell you are." He was trying to push her hands away from his throat. "What are—"

"Just leave here and we'll talk." Her grasp tightened, her nails pressing into his skin. "You don't look— Thomas?" His eyes were glazing. "*Thomas!*"

Jacobs's knees were buckling, he was falling.

She instinctively put out her arms to catch him.

No, be weak, be helpless.

She let him fall to the floor as if he were too heavy for her to hold.

She dropped to her knees beside him. "No!"

Tears.

That was always harder, but they came. She could feel the tears flow down her cheeks. "Thomas . . ." She reached out with a shaking hand to check the pulse in his neck. Strong. Steady. He'd be out no more than the twenty minutes she'd told Gallo.

"Pardon me, Mrs. Brookman." A plump man was pushing his way through the crowd surrounding her. "I'm the casino manager, Anthony Solano. May I help you? Your friend is ill?"

"My brother." Her voice broke. "His heart. The doctor told him to stay away from gambling. He had his last heart attack after he lost at Monte Carlo." She gazed pleadingly up at him. "Can you do something for him?"

"Catherine." Gallo was suddenly beside her, his expression mirroring frustration mixed with concern. "I told you not to come, dammit. He doesn't deserve it. Is he dead?"

"No, but his pulse is so weak . . ."

"I saw him fall and called an ambulance. They should be here any minute." He dropped to his knees and was searching through Jacobs's pockets. He pulled out a prescription bottle and opened it. "This has to be his medication. Put two under his tongue."

She took the pills and did as he told her. Then she sat back on her heels, gazing at Gallo in an agony of despair. "Why would he do this? Why wouldn't he listen?"

"You've been asking that for ten years," Gallo said grimly. "Just because he raised you doesn't mean you have to follow him around and pick up the pieces every time he goes off the rails." He turned to the casino manager. "Do you have a defibrillator on the premises in case we need it, or do we have to wait for the ambulance?"

"No, I'm sure we have one in the first-aid room," Solano said. "I'll send someone to check and bring—"

He was interrupted by the shrill whine of a siren.

"Never mind," Gallo said. "The EMT should have one in the ambulance. I'll go meet them." He jumped to his feet and was gone.

"I'm sorry, Mrs. Brookman." Solano was bending over her. "Your brother was a good customer of my casino. I can't tell you how much I regret this happening. Naturally, we'll do everything we can to help."

"There was nothing you could do. You couldn't stop him." Her lips were trembling. "I don't blame you. He is a sick man in more ways than one. Perhaps after this attack, he'll come to his senses." The tears began to fall again. "If he lives . . ."

"He will live," Solano said as he reached out a hand and gently helped her to her feet. "I feel it. I will personally come with you to the hospital and see that he has everything that he needs."

"You're very kind." She leaned against him, her eyes lowered. Ten minutes. Where the hell was Gallo with the ambulance EMTs? "And I'll be very happy to see you tomorrow morning. Tonight it's better if it's only family with him. You understand?"

"Of course. Whatever you wish is—"

"Stand aside." Gallo was pushing through the crowd, leading the EMTs with their stretcher. "How is he? Has he stirred, Catherine?"

"No. He's too quiet."

Gallo bent over him. "Still breathing." He turned to the EMTs. "Get him in the ambulance and get that defibrillator ready. You may need it." He glanced at Catherine. "Do you want to ride in the ambulance or in the car with me?"

"I want to be with Thomas." She turned to Solano as they took Jacobs out to the ambulance. Keep him close. Don't let him have time to think and change his mind before the ambulance pulled away from the casino. "You've been so very kind. Could you walk to the ambulance with me? I don't want to impose, but I feel—"

"No, it is my pleasure and duty." Solano took her arm, and she leaned against him as they walked through the lobby. "I'll give you my card, and if you need anything tonight at the hospital, just call me. I have many friends in New Orleans, and they'll be happy to help you." He opened the front door for her. "And I will be there for you tomorrow."

"Thank you." She let him help her into the ambulance. She gave him one last look from beneath tear-wet lashes. "If God is merciful, Thomas will live, and I'll be able to tell him what a good friend you were to both of us."

Gallo slammed the doors of the ambulance shut.

Fifteen minutes.

The sirens started wailing as they pulled out of the driveway of the casino.

She smiled at the EMT bending over Jacobs before she leaned back and drew a deep breath.

Done.

The ambulance sirens were cut off three minutes later as the driver pulled to the side of the road.

Gallo opened the doors. "Is he awake yet?"

"We're close." She jumped out of the ambulance. "But he has two minutes left."

"Two minutes. You have it down to a science."

"No, Hu Chang does. He gives me a chart with precise measurements." She watched the EMTs quickly bind Jacobs's wrists before putting him into the backseat of the car. "You should give them a bonus. They did very well, and Solano will probably be out looking for them tomorrow."

"I don't doubt it," he said dryly. "Solano's going to be frustrated as hell that he's not going to get his chance to get you into the sack. You had him practically drooling."

She shrugged. "It was just sleight of hand. If he was paying attention to me, he wasn't paying attention to you and the EMTs." She smiled and waved at the EMTs as she slipped into the passenger seat of the car. "Hurry. Solano may start to process what happened."

"You mean your effect isn't as scientifically perfect as Hu Chang's? I beg to differ." He turned away, and she watched him distribute cash, smiles, and a few words to the EMTs before he walked back toward her. "Yes, a bonus big enough to keep them quiet and out of Solano's sight for the foreseeable future. But I'd already arranged it with them before you made the suggestion."

"I just thought that—" She shrugged. "I haven't worked with anyone in a long time. I've gotten used to running things."

"I noticed." He got into the driver's seat. "But I didn't resent it. I found it very interesting watching you work in a civilized venue. You came across as Cleopatra meets Lara Croft."

"I hope only to you." She began to pin her hair back into a

chignon and reached into the backseat for her black pants, shirt, and boots. She couldn't wait to get out of the gown. "Both of them are wily and strong. It was important that I be helpless and pitiful to disarm Solano."

"And sexy enough to keep his mind on his dick and not on what was happening." He started the car. "Personally, I think your magic potion was better than Hu Chang's."

She heard a muffled groan from the backseat. "Jacobs is beginning to stir."

"He's a minute late."

"No, your watch is probably wrong."

He gazed at her with amusement. "I won't argue with you."

"Where are we taking Jacobs? You said you'd rented a house in the bayous somewhere?"

"Yes, it's about eighty miles from here and very deep in the bayous." He was no longer smiling. "And it will give us the privacy we need to have our discussion. I only hope that he can tell us what we need to know."

"You said that he knew everything that Queen knew. That means he would know who killed Bonnie."

He was silent. "And what if he says it's me?"

"Then we decide if we want to believe him or not." Her lips tightened. "Stop borrowing trouble. There had to be a reason why he hired Nixon to kill you."

"Because he knew I'd probably be on his ass for the rest of his life."

"Or maybe there was another reason. We won't know until he talks to us." She glanced back at Jacobs again. "Let's get moving. He's going to be squealing and cursing as soon as he's conscious enough to realize what we've done. I'd rather be off the road and away from the local police."

IT TOOK THEM OVER TWO HOURS to reach the rental house. The fog had returned and was layering a thick blanket that made driving a nightmare.

"I'd swear we've been driving along this bayou for the last hour," Catherine said. "It seems as if the road is going in circles along this swamp."

"No, the land is in the shape of a hook. The house is in the curve of the hook, and the road continues on from there. It should be right around the next bend. Yes, there it is."

"At last."

The large cedar house was no more than thirty years old but, as Gallo had said, it hovered close to one of the bayous. The surrounding trees were over a century old and draped in Spanish moss that added a touch of ancient decadence.

"What is this place? Where are you taking me?" Jacobs screamed from the backseat. It wasn't the first time. Catherine had profoundly regretted the potion hadn't lasted longer. She had given him another injection about an hour ago, but she hadn't wanted to make it too strong. She didn't want to knock him out for too long. "You can't get away with this." Jacobs started cursing again. "The police are looking for you, Gallo. Do you think that you can just walk into my life and kidnap me?"

"It seems that's what we did," Gallo said. "So I guess the answer is yes." He pulled into the driveway of the house. "Quiet down, Jacobs, you're beginning to annoy me. You don't want to do that. You and Queen have told me for years how unstable I am. You used that for your own benefit, but you were careful to make sure that it was never turned on you."

Jacobs was silent a moment, fuming. "It wasn't my fault. Queen was always the one who ran the show. You can't blame me."

"Oh, I think he can," Catherine said. "Did you step forward and tell anyone when they threw Gallo into that North Korean prison? And when he escaped, did you try to stop Queen from sending him out on suicide missions? No, you were sitting fat and happy, pulling in your share of the profits."

"I'm not talking to you, bitch," Jacobs said venomously. "Queen and I knew you were going to be trouble. Everything was going fine until you started digging."

"Be polite." Gallo got out of the car. "I've never told you exactly what those bastards did to me in that prison, but I'm tempted to show you." He opened the rear door and pulled Jacobs out. "I have a number of questions to ask you. If you answer, you may live."

"We can make a deal." Jacobs moistened his lips. "Let me go. What do you care about me? It was Queen who caused all your problems. Look, I have all kinds of contacts. I know every important drug dealer in the Middle East. You may have money, but I can make you richer."

"We'll talk about it." Gallo pushed him toward the front door. "The key is supposed to be in a lockbox under the fourth windowsill, Catherine." He glanced at her and saw that she hadn't moved. "Catherine?"

Her head was lifted as she gazed out at the fog-shrouded bayou.

"Catherine," he repeated.

She shook her head as if to clear it. "It's . . . eerie here. For a minute I thought—" She turned away and moved quickly toward the house. "Fourth window." She retrieved the key and opened the front door. "Pretty obvious. It's a wonder that the place hasn't been burgled or trashed."

"It's fairly isolated." He pushed Jacobs ahead of him. "I'll take him to a bedroom and secure him. Then we'll let him be alone for a while to anticipate." He added softly, "That was one of the techniques I became very familiar with while I was in prison. It always heightened the pain to have to look forward to it first for a time."

"You won't have to hurt me. I'll tell you anything you want to know," Jacobs said. "But you have to remember, Queen was always the one who called the shots."

"That's hard for me to remember." Gallo was pushing him up the stairs. "Isn't a silent partner just as guilty? The only difference is the lack of guts in execution."

Catherine stood at the bottom of the stairs and watched until they disappeared around the landing.

Gallo was furious. She shivered as she remembered his expression as he had taken Jacobs upstairs. His lips had been set, his eyes glittering and reckless. She had been looking upon the capture and questioning of Jacobs as a job, a project. She had forgotten all that Gallo had suffered at Jacobs's hands. Jacobs might be backpedaling and trying to absolve himself, but he was as guilty as his partner. Considering all that Gallo had suffered, it might be hard for her to defuse that rage.

And did she want to do it? She was beginning to be angry as well. Gallo had not deserved the atrocities he had experienced. Someone should pay.

But the reason they were here wasn't so that Gallo could get his revenge.

She turned away and looked around the living room. Flowered wallpaper, an ornate wood fireplace, and furniture draped in sheets. The house had obviously not been rented in a long time. She went over to the window and gazed out at the bayou.

Fog. Moss draped trees. Shadows.

She tensed. Shadows. Of course, there were shadows. It was foggy as hell out there. Nothing was clear or defined.

"I tied him spread-eagled on that big four-poster bed in the master bedroom." Gallo was coming back down the stairs. "Nothing makes you feel more vulnerable than being in that position. Trust me, I've been there."

"And you'd hate to be vulnerable." Her gaze was still fixed on the bayou. "But now you have a chance to get your own back."

"I thought that was bothering you." He was suddenly standing behind her at the window. "You're afraid of what I'm going to do to him."

"Not afraid. I can understand. When I killed the man who kidnapped my son, I wanted the pain to last forever. But how you feel could get in the way."

"I won't let it. But not because I'm getting soft and mushy about the possibility of making him hurt. I'd relish it. But you're in this with me now, and it's disturbing you. He's right about one thing, he was never a prime player in any of this. If I find he has nothing to do with Bonnie's death, I suppose I can tolerate having him tossed into a federal prison for the rest of his life."

She turned to look at him. "I'm surprised."

"So am I." He paused. "Will it be hard? Hell, yes. I could lose control. Keep an eye on me."

"I will."

He chuckled. "Not if you keep staring out at that bayou." His smile faded. "You've been— What's wrong, Catherine?"

"I don't know." She shivered. "I just feel as if someone was watching me. Someone or something. It's probably nothing. Who could be here? We weren't followed?"

He shook his head. "Not unless they were damn good. They would have had to have been tailing us from the casino. It's not likely."

"Imagination?" She tried to smile. "It's a setting that would spark all kinds of fantasies, isn't it? From vampires to alligators crawling up out of the bayou to devour us. I was even remembering that movie about a vampire who lived in the swamps. Shall we go looking for him?" She looked him up and down. "You look like you belong in a vampire movie." She had changed her clothes, but he had only taken off his jacket and tie and rolled up the sleeves of his white dress shirt. The civilized clothes made the huge bowie knife he had sheathed at his waist appear even more barbaric.

He wasn't returning her smile. "I've seen how true your in-stincts can be. You're fairly remarkable." He turned and headed for the front door. "I think I'll take a turn around the property and see if I see anything. Why don't you go locate the kitchen and see if you can find any tea or coffee? Maybe something hot will chase away the vampires."

The door closed behind him.

GALLO RETURNED ABOUT THIRTY minutes later. "Catherine."

"Here. The kitchen is down the hall and to the right," she called.

He appeared at the door a minute later. "I didn't see anything or anyone. No vampires, no alligators."

"But could you even see them in this fog? I believe it's getting worse." She handed him a mug. "No tea, no coffee. Only chicken bouillon. I managed to heat it, but the water from the tap looked rusty. I don't know how it's going to taste."

He took a sip. "Not bad."

She wrinkled her nose after she tasted the bouillon. "Liar."

He smiled. "It's hot. The fog was chilly." His smile faded. "Are you ready? We've given Jacobs time to simmer. I think you'll feel better if we get to it."

"You're being very protective." Her lips twisted. "I'm not accustomed to that kind of treatment, Gallo. It's not as if I'm not used to dealing with this kind of situation."

"I can't help it," he said simply. "I know who and what you are. You probably think I'm insulting you. But I keep wanting to . . ." He searched for the word. "Shelter you. Take it however you like."

She was taking it with a strange melting warmth that was like a river warming her, closing out the chill that had been with her since she had arrived at this house. She'd had friends, she'd had Terry, her husband, she'd had Venable, who had looked out for her as much as he could. But they had all accepted her as totally independent and able to care for herself. They had never intruded on that independence because they'd probably been afraid of how she'd respond. They had certainly never tried to shelter her.

Gallo looked at her quizzically. "You're not saying anything. Do you want to spit in my eye?"

She took another sip of bouillon before she reluctantly put the cup down on the sink. "Not at the moment. But I do agree we'd better go up and start questioning Jacobs."

JACOBS'S EYES WERE WIDE OPEN, and he was trying to make sounds behind the tape Gallo had placed over his mouth.

"Hello, Jacobs. You seem to want to talk." Gallo bent over and ripped the tape off Jacobs's mouth.

He yelled, his eyes bulging with rage. "You son of a bitch."

The vulnerability of Jacobs on that monster of a four-poster bed was as obvious as Gallo had said, Catherine thought. His thin arms and legs were tied to each of the four posts, and his chest was rising and falling with the force of his breathing. She had expected him to be frightened, but he was angry, his expression twisted and ugly.

"You didn't have to do this. I told you that we could make a deal. We could be partners. I need another partner now that Queen is dead."

"But I don't want you for a partner," Gallo said. "All I want is information. Give me what I want, and there's a chance you might survive this. Ms. Ling doesn't want to witness any unnecessary unpleasantness. Now it's your turn to prove it is unnecessary."

"I *can't* tell you anything."

"Let's see if that's true. I hope you're wrong, Jacobs."

Jacobs was struggling and pulling at the ropes. "Let me go."

"That's not going to happen. Now let's go step by step with this scenario. First, you and Queen hired Paul Black to take the blame for killing Bonnie. You set it up so that I'd put the pieces together and come out with Black killing her to avenge what I did to him in Pakistan."

"I told you, it was Queen all the way. I just did what he said."

Gallo ignored Jacobs's words. "Second, you told Black that I had killed Bonnie during one of my blackouts." His muscles were suddenly stiff with tension. "That didn't happen, did it?"

Jacobs gaze slid away from him. "How do I know? That's what Queen said."

"And you only know what Queen told you," Catherine said sarcastically. "Amazing."

Jacobs gave her a venomous glance. "That's right."

"But I didn't do it, Jacobs," Gallo said. "Who did kill her? Queen?" He paused. "You?"

"No." Jacobs's eyes widened in alarm. "I didn't touch her. I swear I didn't know anything about it. Queen handled it."

Gallo tensed. "Handled what? Why would Queen kill my daughter?"

"He didn't. Don't be stupid." He moistened his lips. "You did it. We were just protecting you. Queen was afraid that you'd start raving like you did in that hospital in Tokyo if you ended up in a mental hospital. We were just protecting you."

Gallo turned pale. "You're lying."

"He *is* lying." Catherine stepped closer to the bed, her gaze fixed on Jacobs's face. "Why, Jacobs? Why not just blame it on Queen?"

"It was Queen," he said quickly. "You caught me off guard. That was the reason I went with the story that Queen concocted. Queen killed her. It was all his fault."

"I don't think so," Gallo said. "You're too eager to jump from one story to another. It might be Queen. Hell, I don't know who's to blame, but I'm going to find out." He took out his knife and pressed it against Jacobs's left wrist. "Do you know how quickly you can die of blood loss if I cut your wrist? Shall I do it so that we can see?"

"No!" He was staring in panicked fascination at the blade of the knife. "Don't kill me. It wasn't my fault."

"And it wasn't mine either, was it?" Gallo asked harshly. "I didn't do it, did I? Say it."

"Of course not." Jacobs's tone was almost impatient, his gaze on the knife. "It was only the story Queen made up. He shouldn't have even had to tell Black anything. Queen was always getting complicated when simple would have done as well."

Gallo's eyes closed for an instant as the relief surged through him. He hadn't been sure until that moment, Catherine realized. But the very casualness of Jacobs's answer was more convincing than if he'd sworn it on a Bible.

"Okay, now let's talk about Queen," Gallo said. "You said he killed Bonnie. Why?"

"I don't know. Look, I've told you that he killed her. That should be enough."

"It's not enough," Gallo said. "Talk. Tell me what happened."

"I can't do it. I can't tell anyone." Jacobs's voice was harsh with desperation. "Do you think I don't want to tell you? I *can't* do it."

"Then I'll have to get to work," Gallo shifted the knife in his hand. "And I'm a pretty clumsy surgeon, Jacobs."

Jacobs shook his head. "Don't hurt me. None of it is my fault." Tears were running down his cheeks. "He won't let me tell anyone."

"He?" Catherine asked slowly. "Another hired killer like Paul Black? Did Queen hire someone to kill Gallo's daughter?"

Jacobs's jaw clenched. "Don't hurt me."

Gallo leaned forward, his eyes glittering. "Talk, Jacobs. I'm tired of hearing—" He stopped and a shudder went through him. He took a breath, then slowly straightened. "Listen carefully; you're going to talk, or I will hurt you. I'll give you thirty minutes to think about it. Catherine and I will leave you to consider what's your best option. Then we'll be back, and you'll tell me everything I want to know." He turned toward the door. "Thirty minutes."

"I can't do it," Jacobs whispered. "He'll kill me. You may hurt me, but I have a chance to live. I know he'll do it." His lips were suddenly curled with anger. "This is all your fault, Gallo. You may not have killed her, but it's all your fault. You shouldn't hurt me."

"Thirty minutes." He turned back and taped Jacobs's mouth shut again. Then he strode to the door and opened the door for Catherine. "No more. I don't want to hear anything from you until you tell me what I want to know." He shut the door firmly behind them.

Catherine drew a deep breath as she started down the stairs. "I wasn't sure that you were going to stop."

"Neither was I," he said grimly. "I had to stop now or not at all. It was hard as hell."

"But you said it would be easier after he has time to think about what might happen to him."

"That's the plan. He's not a brave man. It should be easy to break him." He frowned. "But I don't know . . ."

"I don't know either." Catherine was remembering Jacobs's terrified expression. "He was afraid."

"And not of me." His lips tightened. "Which would have meant breaking him would have been twice as hard."

"He should have been afraid of you. You were very intimidating."

"Not enough." He had reached the bottom of the stairs. "But I will be when I go back upstairs. He *has* to talk."

"So what do we do now?"

"We sit in that drafty kitchen and have some more of that less-than-pleasant bouillon." He headed for the kitchen. "And we give Jacobs time to become terrified by his own imaginings."

"Who is he afraid of?" she murmured as she followed him. "Was I right? Queen did employ other killers for hire besides Black."

"But what's the motive?" Gallo shook his head. "I'm not

making any more guesses. I've spent years wondering and guessing and trying to make sense of Bonnie's death. I have to know the truth."

"One truth you do know is that you didn't kill her," she said quietly.

"Thank God." He turned on the pan of hot water. "But that doesn't mean I'm entirely free of blame. Not with Queen and Jacobs involved."

"By all means, reserve a little guilt for yourself. You wouldn't want to let yourself entirely off the hook." She sat down in the chair. "Gallo, just because they were part of your life doesn't mean a damn thing."

"It means that sometimes our lives touch each other, and that has a direct effect." He poured a little of the bouillon into her cup. "And you know that's true from your own experience."

She couldn't argue with him. Her life had touched Rakovac's, and it was Luke who had suffered.

His lips twisted. "And the last thing Jacobs said was that it was all my fault."

"Bullshit. You don't know what he meant by that," Catherine said. "He was blaming everyone but himself." She sipped a little of the bouillon. "I hate this waiting. I hate this whole thing. I wanted Jacobs to break down and sing like a bird."

"I won't hurt him unless he doesn't give me a choice, Catherine."

"I know." And it wasn't as if Jacobs was some innocent victim. He had hired Nixon to kill them. And, in spite of protesting his innocence, he had almost certainly been involved in Bonnie's death. The nightmare had gone on too long, and only

Jacobs could cause it to come to an end. "But I don't have to like it. I hate hurting people."

He suddenly smiled. "You'd rather I cut the bastard's throat and get it over with? You're a strange woman, Catherine."

She shrugged. "I'm what life made me. Just like you, Gallo. And you're not so—" Her phone rang, and she glanced at the ID.

"It's Eve." She pressed the button. "Where are you, Eve?"

"About forty-five minutes from you according to the GPS." She paused. "Is everything all right?"

"Do you mean have we found out anything from Jacobs? Not yet." She paused. "Except that he said that Gallo didn't kill Bonnie."

"And you think he's telling the truth? From what you told me, Jacobs is as much of a sleazebag as Queen was."

"I don't think he's lying." Catherine smiled at Gallo across the table. "Jacobs may be a complete sleazebag, but he was telling the truth about that. And he's scared, Eve. He knows who did kill her, and he's scared shitless." She hurried on before Eve could voice the question. "And, no, we don't know who that is. We're following up as fast as we can. We may have something by the time you get here."

"I hope you do." She was silent a moment. "If it's true, I'm happy for Gallo."

"But you're still skeptical. Oh, well, maybe Jacobs will be able to convince you when you get here. I'm tired of being the only positive voice. I've just had a depressing conversation with Gallo about touching people's lives and changing them for the worse. It works the other way too, dammit."

"Yes, it does. And you're proof of it, Catherine. I'll call you when I'm within a few miles of your place." She hung up.

"She's happy that Jacobs cleared you," Catherine said to Gallo as she hung up.

"But skeptical." He added quietly, "I'm glad you're not skeptical. You've been a beacon in the darkness, Catherine. I know I've been a pain in the ass."

"Yes, you have. In more ways than one." She met his eyes. "And you'll owe me when this is done."

"I'll pay you. Anytime. Any way. I'll invent new ways to pay you."

She tore her gaze away. "How much longer do we have to wait down here?"

"Another ten minutes."

She hesitated. "Maybe we should wait for Eve and Joe."

"And maybe we should have everything settled before they get here. I've never encountered Joe Quinn except for those few minutes before Black stabbed him, but he's never had any warm feelings toward me."

"That's an understatement. You can hardly blame him. Eve is his whole world, and he considered you a threat to her."

"I don't blame him. If I'd been in his position, I would have tried to wipe me off the face of the Earth. I'm just saying that there are giant hurdles to overcome, and this may not be the time to do it." He added, "And do you want to have Eve feeling the same way you do about squeezing the information out of Jacobs? I'm the only one who should have to bear responsibility for dealing with the bastard."

No, she didn't want to saddle Eve with anything more than

she was bearing now. But on the other hand, she didn't want Eve arriving and thinking that Jacobs had cleared Gallo because force was used. She wanted Eve to see the situation and judge for herself. Gallo deserved at least that from Eve and Joe. She said, "I'd like to wait, please. They should be here in another forty minutes."

He opened his lips, and she thought he was going to argue with her. Then he closed them again. "Whatever you like. It's your call." He lifted his shoulders in a half shrug. "Who knows? An extra forty minutes of waiting may be the time it takes to make Jacobs more willing to cooperate."

She wasn't at all sure that call she'd made was the right one. It was a delicate situation, and Eve and Joe were as strong-willed as Catherine and Gallo. It could all blow up when they came together.

"And I know why you made it," Gallo said softly. "I believe you may have a protective gene or two yourself, Catherine."

"I do. I'm protective toward my son." She lifted the bouillon to her lips. "You can take care of yourself, Gallo."

CHAPTER
17

"DO YOU WANT ME TO TAKE a turn driving?" Eve asked Joe as she hung up the phone. "This fog is a hell of a strain on the eyes. We're having to creep along."

"I'm fine."

Yes, he was fine, thank God, she thought as she gazed at him. He was still a little pale, and he'd lost at least ten pounds, but other than those two signs of weakness, he was the Joe she had always known. Since he'd left the hospital, he had been quiet, conserving his strength, but that strength was there. And so was his sharpness and incisive decision making. During their frustrating journey, he had managed multiple flight cancellations, rebookings, and dealing with airport and rental-car personnel with far more patience than Eve had.

He shot her a glance and smiled. "It's not my eyes that kept me in that hospital, Eve. And the rest of me is doing just fine, too." His smile faded. "Jacobs said that Gallo hadn't killed Bonnie?"

She nodded. "But if he didn't kill her, who did? Maybe Jacobs or Queen did it themselves?" She rubbed her temple. "I just don't know. Catherine said Jacobs knew who did it and seemed scared to death to tell anyone."

"He'll be more scared when I get my hands on the bastard," Joe said grimly. His foot unconsciously pressed harder on the accelerator, and the car jumped forward.

"Joe."

"Sorry." He lifted the pressure, and the car slowed. "You're right, we don't want to go off the road into the bayou. Hell, I can't even see the side of road in this muck."

"Then just crawl along. I allowed extra time when I told Catherine we'd be there in forty minutes." She glanced out the thick white nothingness beyond the window. Every now and then, she'd catch a glimpse of the twisted branch of a tree jutting out of the bayou, but almost immediately it was gone. "But I wish this fog would go away. It's really eerie."

"You think so?" Joe shook his head. "I was thinking it was kind of . . . comforting."

"You've got to be kidding. Why?"

"I don't know." He thought about it. "Or maybe I do. Before I came out of that coma, it was like this. It was like a soft blanket of fog that I was traveling through. Only it was dark and glowing, not this white mist. But I knew where I was and where I was going, and I wasn't afraid. The fog around me felt warm and it somehow . . ." He searched for words. ". . . filled my heart. I could occasionally see something jutting out of the fog, but nothing was clear. Except you, Eve. " He added simply, "And Bonnie."

Her throat was suddenly tight. "And there's nothing frightening about either one of us." She reached out, and her hand clasped his on the steering wheel. "Because we love you." She laughed shakily. "But I don't believe that this particular fog is warm and comforting. And I'll definitely disagree if you end up by dumping us in the bayou. I don't care for either swamps or bayous. It makes me remember—" She inhaled sharply, her body stiffening.

His gaze flew to her face. "What's wrong?"

"I don't know. I saw something." She turned in the seat, her gaze on the fog-shrouded bayou. "Someone."

"A fisherman?" Joe asked. "Those would be the only people I'd think might be out in weather like this. Was he in a boat?"

"No. Maybe. I only caught a glimpse—" But that glimpse had startled her. "And it wasn't a man. Or I guess it could have been, but I got the impression— Pull over, Joe!" Her gaze was fixed on the bayou just ahead. "Now."

"Why?" He was frowning as he pulled over to the side of the road. "You think there's someone in trouble?"

"No," she whispered. "Not any longer." She hopped out of the car and ran to the edge of the road, her gaze fixed on the billowing mist hovering over the water. "She's not in trouble. That's all over." Her eyes were straining to catch another glimpse of that small figure moving slowly through the fog. No, she had vanished as quickly as she had come.

"It's Bonnie. But why is she here? And why didn't she come closer? This isn't like her. She's acting as if she's—" A ghost, a spirit, a mystery from the mist. Not like her Bonnie. Her daughter had always been so real when she came to her that Eve had felt as if she could reach out and touch her, hug her.

"Bonnie?" Joe had come to stand beside her, his gaze on Eve's face. "Are you sure? We were just talking about her. You could have been thinking about Bonnie and it translated thought into—"

"Imagining that I saw her?" Eve finished. "No, I did see her. That first glimpse could have been imagination, but then I saw her again as we rounded that curve. She was right there before me. I saw her face." She gestured at the bayou. "She was there, Joe. You didn't see her?"

He shook his head. "Not this time, Eve."

She shook her head in frustration. "I tell you, she was *there.*"

"I'm not questioning you about anything concerning Bonnie," he said gently. "I'm far beyond that, Eve. If you say you saw her, then she was here. I'm only saying that I didn't see her. I've no idea how all this works. It's new to me. Maybe she didn't want me to see her this time. Maybe she only wanted you. You saw her for years and years before she ever deigned to pay me a visit."

"But I never saw her like this before. It . . . scared me."

"Why?"

"She wasn't . . . herself." How to explain it to him when she was bewildered, too. "She was always happy when she came to me. I was the one who was anxious and worried and full of guilt.

She'd laugh at me and tease me and tell me that everything was all right with her. That I shouldn't fret so much about finding her and bringing her home."

"And that's a wonderful thing."

"But she wasn't like that when I saw her a few moments ago." She repeated, "She scared me."

Joe put his hand on her arm and pulled her close. "You said that before. Why? What was different?"

"She was sad. Her face was so sad. Bonnie was never sad." She could feel the tears sting her eyes. "Or if she was, she never let me know. Did she hide it, Joe? Did she hide it so that I wouldn't be unhappy?" She swallowed hard. "And what is she doing here, dammit? First, you're talking about that death fog you went through. Then I see Bonnie, and she's not *my* Bonnie. Is she trying to tell me something?"

"If she was, then she'd come right out and say it, wouldn't she?"

"No, she can be enigmatic as hell."

He smiled. "That sounds very human and very special."

"Yes." Bonnie had always been special, and she had remained special even after that monster had taken everything else from her. Her gaze searched the bayou, but she saw nothing but mist. She could *feel* nothing. She turned away. "She's gone." She moved back toward the car. "And you're probably thinking I'm acting as neurotic as hell."

"No." He got into the car and stared thoughtfully out at the bayou. "It's not neurotic to be upset about a change in someone you love. And you love Bonnie with all your heart. The whole thing is very strange. I've just been trying to piece together the puzzle."

"That's like you," she said as she fastened her seat belt. Joe's mind was always delving and striving to make logic out of chaos. And most of the time, he was able to do it. "When you come up with something, let me know."

He started the car. "I'm working on it. Bonnie appeared to you and wanted you to know she was unhappy about something."

"Maybe she's always been unhappy. She's dead, dammit."

"But you have to balance the experience of years against this one episode. That would mean that there was something unusual happening to change that balance." He paused. "Something to do with Gallo?"

"If he didn't kill her, why would she be sad?" She shook her head and smiled with an effort. "Only you would analyze ectoplasm and try to make it rational."

"Would Bonnie like you referring to her as ectoplasm?"

"Yes, she'd probably giggle."

"You said that without even thinking. So it doesn't seem to me that you have to worry about this one case of melancholy."

She nodded, and this time the smile was genuine. "Not as long as I have you to set me straight."

"No problem." He was gazing straight ahead. "But as you said, this is unusual. We should probably be looking out for 'unusual.'"

"Why?" She tilted her head. "I assume you're not just being cryptic?"

He didn't look at her. "No, I'm just remembering what Bonnie told me, that we were coming to the end. Ends aren't always happy, Eve."

She was silent for a long moment. "You've been telling me that for years in one way or another. Sometimes, I resented it. Sometimes, I was grateful. But you've been preparing me for this, haven't you?"

"I've been preparing both of us for it. I knew the first time I met you that we were going to have to be strong to face what life had dealt us. And the end may be the hardest part of all. It's been a long time coming."

"That's what I thought. I tried and tried again, and nothing came of it. I couldn't find Bonnie. I couldn't find the monster who killed her." She whispered, "And I couldn't see why. I thought if there was a God, then He should help me find my little girl. She was so wonderful. Everyone loved her. God must have loved her, too." She turned her head and gazed out at the thick mist flowing by the window. No Bonnie in that mist. She had come and gone. But she was near . . .

"But lately I've wondered if there's a reason that I had to wait. I don't think I was ready. You're right, whatever I have to face, I'll have to be strong enough to take it. Perhaps I had to learn something about myself before I could bring her home. Perhaps I had to learn about you, Joe. I think I learned a lot about both of us when I was waiting for you to wake in ICU."

"And are you ready now?"

"I think so." Her hand reached for his and clasped it tightly. "We'll have to see, won't we? Lord, I hope I'm ready, Joe."

* * *

"THEY'RE COMING." Catherine turned away from the window. "At least, I think they are. I can barely see the headlights in the fog. They should be here in a couple minutes." She leveled a glance at Gallo. "And, no matter what Joe says or does, you're not to respond with any antagonism, do you understand?"

"I understand that you're expecting a lot from me." He got up from the chair and crossed to the window. "I believe you're talking about diplomacy. We both know that's not my forte."

No, it wasn't, and she could already see that familiar trace of recklessness in his face. "I'm not having it, Gallo. Joe was the victim, and you can be patient if he's pissed at you."

"And if I'm not, then you'll go after me yourself. I believe you're proving that you're protective of more people than your son," Gallo said. "But I admit I like it better when it's me you're protecting." He watched Joe and Eve get out of the car. "Do you want me to go and greet them?"

And watch Eve have to handle the confrontation between the two men who had shaped her life? Catherine was already at the front door and throwing it open. "Come in out of this mess," she called. "I wish I could offer you a cup of coffee, Eve. But we're limited to bouillon." She made a face. "Not even good bouillon." She turned to Joe. "You look wonderful." She gave him an appraising glance. "Maybe you've lost a little weight. But I knew you'd make it."

"That's more than I did." Eve gave her a quick hug. "And you've lost a pound or two yourself since I last saw you."

"I kept her on the run," Gallo said from where he stood by the window. "But no more than she did me." His gaze shifted to Eve's face. "Hello, Eve."

She stiffened. "Hello, John."

Joe stepped quickly forward. "Gallo."

Gallo's expression was wary. "Hello, Quinn. Am I going to have problems with you?"

"I'm not sure," Joe said coolly. "You deserve them. You've been getting in my way since the moment you decided to come back into Eve's life."

The two men were like two lions, arching, frozen in place but ready to attack, Catherine thought. She took a step forward, then stopped. They'd have to work it out for themselves sometime. It might as well be now.

But Gallo had seen that movement from the corner of his eye. "Catherine says I have to be diplomatic since I'm the one who has been causing all the trouble. She's about to step in and take me out."

"I'd be glad to save her the trouble." Then Joe glanced at Eve. "But you may not be important enough for me to be bothered with right now, Gallo."

Oh, shit. Catherine saw that flicker of recklessness appear in Gallo's expression again.

He said, "Perhaps I could up the ante, and that would make you think I'm—"

"Stop it." Eve stepped forward between the two men and faced Gallo. "Catherine said that Jacobs knows who killed Bonnie. That's all I care about. If you love Bonnie as much as you say, then that's all that you should care about, too." She paused. "I thought it was you, John. I'm still not certain it's not. Prove it to me."

"Yes, prove it to her, Gallo," Joe said. "I think we need to talk to Jacobs."

"Fine," Catherine said. "We've been waiting for you." She turned toward the stairs. "If you want to ask Jacobs questions, then come upstairs and do it. Maybe you'll have more luck than we did."

Gallo hesitated and gestured toward the stairs. "By all means, I was looking forward to questioning the bastard myself, but I'll forgo the pleasure. Catherine has already pointed out that I need to be kind and diplomatic to guests."

"And you're doing what she wants." Eve was gazing at him searchingly as she started up the stairs. "I find that curious."

"Do you?" He smiled. "But can't you see I'm terrified of your friend Catherine?"

Catherine made a rude sound. "Shut up, Gallo." She turned to Joe. "Jacobs is going to cause us trouble. I hope he'll be more cooperative now that he's had time to think."

"He'll be cooperative," Joe said grimly as he moved past her up the stairs. "Tell me what he's told you so far. No, on second thought, let me start fresh."

"Lord, it's chilly up here." Eve shuddered as they reached the bedroom door. "What are you doing, Catherine? Are you trying to freeze information out of him?"

Catherine frowned. "It wasn't this chilly before." She opened the door. "I don't know why it would—"

"Dear God!" Eve took a step back, her gaze on the bed. "Catherine?"

Catherine's gaze followed Eve's. She went rigid. "No. Eve, no. We didn't— Gallo!"

There was water on the floor around the bed.

Jacobs was still bound, spread-eagled on the bed.

And there was a knife sticking upright in his chest.

"Shit!" Gallo pushed by them and ran to the bed. Jacobs's mouth was still taped, and his eyes were wide open, staring at the ceiling. Gallo checked the pulse in his throat, but they all knew it wasn't necessary. "Dead. But how the hell—"

"The window." The sheer white drapes were blowing from the open window, and Catherine was there in a heartbeat. "We were downstairs. He had to have come in the window."

Dammit, she could see nothing through the heavy fog.

But she could hear something.

The splash of water being moved, the sound of suction in the mud . . .

"He's in the bayou!"

"Heading south." Gallo had already swung his legs over the sill and was climbing hand over hand down the side of house to the roof of the porch.

Gallo might think he was Spider-Man, but she'd make almost as good time going down to the front door and wouldn't risk falling and breaking her neck, Catherine thought. She turned and was running out the room when Joe grabbed her arm and spun her around.

"One question," he said.

"I don't have *time*, Joe."

"You have time for this one." His glance shifted to Jacobs. "This isn't some con you set up to convince us that Gallo was innocent? He didn't get overenthusiastic and stick that knife in Jacobs?"

Her eyes widened. "I wouldn't do that, Joe."

His expression didn't lose its hardness. "I wouldn't think that you would, but I wouldn't think you'd be so dedicated to exonerating Gallo either. I don't know what's going on with you, Catherine."

She tore herself away from him, her eyes blazing. "And you think because he once managed to convince Eve that he was the sun and the moon, that he'd dazzle me so that I'd lie for him? No way, Joe. He didn't kill Jacobs, and neither did I. We were both downstairs waiting for you. Whoever did this must have followed us from the casino." She turned on her heel. "And now I'm going to go into that bayou and try to catch the son of a bitch."

"Go on," Joe said quietly. "Eve and I will be right behind you as soon as I figure out which—"

But she didn't hear the rest because she was already down the stairs and throwing up the front door.

Swirling fog.

Dampness.

And the sudden splash of movement in the bayou.

"Gallo!"

"Here."

He was already in the water.

She took off her boots and socks, left her gun on the bank, and made sure her knife was firmly in its holster on her thigh. Then she jumped off the mossy bank and moved in the direction in which she'd thought she'd heard his voice.

The water was only up to her waist that close to the bank, but she couldn't be sure what was in the water with her. Everything from water moccasins to alligators frequented the bayous. Just be careful and look sharp. She couldn't see anything at any distance, but she would be able to tell if one of those predators was within striking distance.

Hell, she hated being blind in the dense mist. And Gallo would also be blind. They'd be lucky if they didn't attack each other. But she didn't want to call out again and draw possible fire.

Or another wicked knife like the one in Jacobs's chest.

Move slowly, as silently as possible, in the water.

She listened.

She couldn't hear Gallo moving through the water. Not even a whisper of sound.

Where was—

"Catherine."

She jerked with shock. He was right beside her. His white shirt was plastered to his body, and his sheathed bowie knife was shoved into the waist of his black trousers.

His gaze was fixed on the south. "He's heading in that direction. Every now and then, I can hear him brush against something. Or he'll startle a bird, and I'll hear the wings . . ."

Catherine started forward. "What are we waiting for?"

"He's very good. Damn good. We go too fast and lose his sound, and he could circle and come up behind us. There are times I can't hear him at all. The bayou is deeper once you get a distance from the bank. He's probably swimming." He was silent again. "Do you hear that?"

Birds moving from branch to branch.

"He's going southwest now." He started forward. "You circle and see if you can come at him from the west. I'll track him on the direct route."

"West," she repeated as she started out. "You said Jacobs's killer was so good. Yet we heard him plainly from Jacobs's bedroom."

"He was in a hurry. He'd probably just finished knifing Jacobs when we were coming up the stairs. He needed to get in the water and away from the bank."

"And after those first few minutes, he felt safe and could take his time."

"As I said, he's really good. Be careful, Catherine . . ." He disappeared into the mist.

But that mist wasn't as thick, she realized suddenly. Gallo had gone at least four yards before she had lost him to view. Maybe the fog was dispersing.

She went a few more yards, her hopes rising with every step. They had gotten lucky. Yes, the mist was definitely lifting. They'd soon be able to see the bastard who had killed Jacobs.

And the killer would be able to see them.

"THE FOG'S BEGINNING TO LIFT," Joe said, as he and Eve reached the edge of the bayou. "That will help." He grabbed her arm and pulled her toward the car. "We can't help Catherine much in that swamp. Come on, we'll take the car and go along the road bordering the bayou. We didn't see any sign of a car when we drove up to the house, so he must have parked up ahead and around the curve of the bayou. That's where he'll probably be heading."

Eve nodded as she got into the car. "Then why would he jump into—" She answered herself. "A false trail. So that we wouldn't find his car." A bold move, possibly a deadly move. Catherine and John Gallo had followed him into the bayou and were trying to find him while lumbering blindly in the thick fog. Joe said it was lifting, but not enough.

Please, let us have a break in this damn fog.

"I'll go slow. Hell, I *have* to go slow." Joe had already started the car and hit the lights. "You keep an eye out. He could have come back to the bank anywhere along the road."

She nodded, her eyes straining as they tried to pierce the thick layers of fog hovering on the bank. She rolled down the window so that she could better hear anyone moving in the water. Her heart was pounding, and the muscles of her stomach were clenched with fear.

She had a sudden memory of Bonnie's face as she'd seen it earlier. Sadness. Such sadness.

Why? The death of Jacobs?

Or the death of someone else, someone whose death Bonnie knew would hurt Eve? A chill went through her at the thought. Not Joe. Please God, not Joe. You've just given him a new lease on life. Not Catherine, who had hardly started to know the meaning of joy and had a son who needed her. Not Gallo, who had perhaps suffered more than all of them.

If this is the end, shouldn't it be you and me, baby?

"Eve." His eyes were on the road ahead of him, but Joe's voice was soft but clear. "It's going to be all right. We're going to get through this together."

She nodded jerkily. "I know, Joe."

Together. Yes, they'd be together, but maybe not right away.

Eve could not forget the sadness in her daughter's face.

Let it be me, Bonnie.

CATHERINE STOPPED AND STOOD still in the water as she saw the pale fog-shrouded glow of headlights on the road leaving from the direction of the house.

Joe and Eve.

Smart.

They were betting that the man who had killed Jacobs had a car parked somewhere on that road bordering the bayou. It was reasonable that he'd be heading across the bayou in the direction where he'd left it.

She tried to pull up a mental picture of the curve of the road around the bayou. Gallo had said the terrain was shaped like a hook . . .

And Gallo had told her that they should go southwest.

And sent her west.

But the hook of land surrounding the bayou extended to the east. That would be where that car would be parked. Southeast. And Gallo was heading due south.

And would probably soon veer to the southeast.

Damn him.

Anger was seething through her. The son of a bitch was trying to *protect* her. Who the hell did he think he was? She was every bit as competent a professional as he. She should have slapped that damn macho tendency down as soon as it raised its head. Now it was getting in the way of her job.

And could get them both killed.

But not if she could help it.

She turned and headed southeast.

JACOBS'S KILLER WAS DEFINITELY heading southeast toward the hook of land bordering the bayou, Gallo thought.

He could hear him, and, if he got lucky, soon he might be able to see him.

The fog was lifting for a few seconds, hovering, then closing down again. All he'd need would be those few seconds to draw his knife and hurl it.

If he was close enough.

And he would be close enough.

He could feel the excitement and tension searing through him. Another hunt. But this was nothing like the hunt with Catherine. Even in the darkest hours of those days, he'd known that it was different from anything he'd ever experienced. There might have been lethal danger, but it had been coupled by challenge. This hunt was different. No beautiful, sleek, panther who could turn and rend him in the flash of an eye.

This was only prey.

And the sounds of the prey were approaching closer to that far bank.

The fog lifted . . .

Gallo caught a swift glimpse of the shadowy bank, a gnarled cypress tree dipping its roots in the water, Spanish moss hanging from another tree near—

Near a gleam of metal. A car?

He couldn't be sure. The fog had closed in again, dammit.

But that gleam of metal was a little too opportune. The bank had to be the prey's destination.

He began to carefully, silently, swim toward it.

CATHERINE PULLED HERSELF from the water onto the bank. Now that she had a destination, she could move faster over ground. She should be somewhere near the road, and the car would probably not be parked on the road itself but hidden in the shrubbery.

She moved swiftly through the heavy palmettos and shrubbery that bordered the bank. Her sopping-wet clothes were plastered to her body, and the soles of her bare feet were being scratched and bruised with every step.

Pain.

Ignore it. Block everything out. Concentrate on the job.

She had to find Jacobs's killer before he got away.

Find the car. Wait for him to show.

But she had to be careful. She couldn't kill the bastard even though it would be safer.

Eve still needed him. Eve still had to know about her Bonnie—

EVE STRAIGHTENED IN HER SEAT. "I saw someone."

Joe tensed. "Where?"

"He's gone now. I only got a glimpse. This damn fog. Not close. Around that bend. I saw someone climbing out of the water onto the bank."

"Gallo? Catherine?"

She shook her head. "He was thin, wearing a dark blue or black wet suit."

"Around that bend?" Joe pulled to the side of the road. "Then we go the rest of the way on foot. We still have to use the lights and we don't want to scare him off." He got out of the car. "I can do this alone, Eve."

"No, you can't." She jammed her hand in the pocket of her Windbreaker and gripped her .38 revolver. A weapon to protect Joe as Joe had always protected her. Would it do any good? The more time that passed, the greater the cold dread that was icing through her.

She got out of the car and joined him as he strode into the brush bordering the bayou. "You said together, Joe."

HE *HAD* HIM.

A man in a dark wet suit, tall, thin, moving quickly along the bank toward the gleam of metal that Gallo had identified as a vehicle.

Yes.

Gallo unsheathed his knife as he stood up in the shallow water near the bank.

Dammit.

The prey had disappeared as a fresh billow of fog descended.

No, there he was again. He was moving with a lithe jauntiness as if he had all the time in the world.

You don't have any time at all, bastard.

Bring him down permanently or just wound him? Gallo thought as he raised the knife and lined up the target. It would depend on how long he had before the fog settled once—

Oh, my God.

No!

His hand holding the knife fell nervelessly to his side as he stared in horror at the man in the wet suit.

No. No. No.

Not prey at all.

But the man had sighted prey of his own, Gallo realized. His stance had changed, and now he was in stalking mode. He'd drawn a knife from the holster at his waist.

Stalking whom?

Catherine.

Catherine, standing at the edge of the trees. Catherine, setting her own trap for the man in the wet suit, the man who had killed Jacobs, the man who had killed Bonnie.

Dammit, what is wrong with me, Gallo thought in agony. Throw the knife.

* * *

IT WASN'T A NEW VEHICLE, Catherine noticed as she cautiously approached. It was a beat-up blue Chevy truck, and the tires looked worn, almost bald.

No sign of the driver of the truck.

She'd been listening and hadn't heard anyone come out of the bayou.

But she might not have been able to hear him. She didn't have quite as keen perceptions as Gallo. And he had said this creep was good. She trusted Gallo's judgment.

When it didn't concern his damned chauvinistic attitude toward her.

She stopped. She'd been tempted to check out the license plate and the glove box of the truck. Not smart. Better to wait and do all that later. Now she should wait and watch and listen.

Not much watching with this fog, but she could listen.

No sound.

The fog had come in again, and the truck was only a hazy outline before her. But she'd probably have company soon. Just wait and pounce when he came on the bank.

She stiffened. Something was wrong. She felt it. The hair on the back of her neck was tingling.

"THERE'S SOMEONE OVER THERE in the trees." Joe grabbed Eve's arm and pulled her to a halt. His eyes narrowed. "I think it's Catherine." He froze. "Oh, shit."

She could see why he was cursing as she saw the tall man in the wet suit directly behind Catherine. Nothing could be clearer than that he was on the attack.

"I can't get a clear shot," Joe said with frustration as he put his gun down. "He's right behind her. I'll shoot *her*, dammit." He moved to the side. "I'll see if I can get him from another angle. Don't call out and startle him. I don't want to have him move on her before I can get my shot."

If there was enough time.

It was going to be Catherine, Eve realized in agony. Catherine was the one who was going to die. And Eve had to stand there and watch it happen. She couldn't even cry out and warn her.

But Catherine had been with Gallo in the bayou. Why wasn't he there?

Dammit, where was Gallo?

THANK GOD, THAT BASTARD WAS moving slow, Joe thought as he ran quickly through the brush. He just had to hope that nothing would startle him into leaping forward toward Catherine.

But the angle where he was standing now was still bad for an accurate shot, and he couldn't get closer because the bank curved there.

The cypress tree. He should have a chance of a clear shot from there.

He shoved his gun into the waistband of his pants and started to shinny up to the first branch.

Fast.

Faster.

The man in the wet suit was starting to move more quickly toward Catherine.

Joe was drawing his gun as he pulled himself onto the branch.

Clear shot.

But Jacobs's killer was almost on top of her.

Get the shot off.

Out of the corner of his eye he caught a glimpse of another figure standing in the water several yards from the bank.

Gallo.

What the hell?

Forget it. Level and fire, or he'd be too late to save Catherine.

Hell, it could be too late now.

THROW THE KNIFE.

Take him down.

Gallo's hand was frozen on the hilt as he watched the man who had killed Jacobs glide toward Catherine.

Gallo had to move, but he couldn't do it. Not this time. It was as if everything was going in slow motion for him.

He could see Catherine stiffening, and knew that those wonderful instincts with which he'd become so familiar were in play.

She *knew*.

Even as he watched, he saw her whirl and start to drop to the ground as she saw her attacker.

Too late.

He was already on Catherine, a thin dagger gleaming as he raised it.

It was coming down!

She was going to die.

"No!" The agonized cry tore from Gallo's throat.

He threw the knife.

DEAR GOD, HE'S FAST, Catherine thought as she reached for the knife on her thigh.

Fall. Roll. Then stab the bastard in the gut.

But he was over her, his dagger coming down and—

He screamed as a bowie knife pierced the hand holding the knife and came out the other side!

Gallo's bowie knife. She recognized it. And Gallo standing in the water several yards away from the bank.

It gave her enough time to get her own knife out of the thigh holster.

"Dammit, get out of the way, Catherine."

She glanced toward the trees. Joe. Trying to get his shot.

She rolled to the side.

The man in the wet suit was cursing as he turned and ran toward the bayou, bent low, and zigzagging in the underbrush.

A shot.

Missed.

He jumped into the water, reached out, jerked out the knife piercing his hand, and threw it aside. He dove beneath the surface.

Catherine jumped to her feet and was at the bank of the bayou in seconds.

"Gallo, get him!" she called as she slipped off the bank into the water.

Gallo didn't answer, and she couldn't see him. The fog had come down again.

"Catherine, no!" Joe was suddenly standing on the bank beside the cypress tree. "Come back. Don't take a chance. Don't trust him."

Of course, she wasn't going to trust that murderer. He'd just tried to kill her. "It's okay, Joe. Gallo's somewhere out here, too. We'll get the bastard. He's wounded and losing blood." She was starting to swim away from the bank. "Gallo!"

"Catherine, listen to me." Joe's voice was harsh, his fists clenched at his sides. "It's Gallo I'm talking about. I saw his face. He wasn't going to throw that knife. He wasn't going to save you. Gallo didn't care if you lived or died."

Shock went through her. "No, you're wrong, Joe. He did save me. Look, I can't talk." She began swimming faster. "I'll blow my chance of getting that bastard. You'd better jump in the car and patrol the road. He might try to get out of the water as soon as he can. The blood is going to draw alligators."

"Catherine!"

She couldn't see him any longer. She was surrounded by the thick, heavy mist that felt as if it was going to smother her. She suddenly felt very much alone.

But she wasn't alone. There was a murderer out there who had been within an instant of killing her. Was he close? He could be only yards away from her and she wouldn't know it. It would be smart of him to lie in wait and ambush any pursuers. It was probably what she would have done.

Her heart was beating hard, she could feel her pulse jumping in her throat.

She stopped swimming and listened.

She heard something, a displacement of water . . . Where had it come from? Dammit, where was Gallo? She could have used someone to watch her back.

Gallo doesn't care whether you live or die.

She heard the sound again. Closer.

She tensed, her hand reached down and grabbed her knife.

Come and see what's waiting for you, you son of a bitch. I've been on my own all my life. What was I thinking? I don't need any help from Gallo or anyone else.

Come and get me.

Turn the page for a look at Iris Johansen's new novel

BONNIE

Available October 2011

CHAPTER

1

"WHAT STAR IS THAT, MAMA?" Bonnie lifted her hand to point at a brilliant orb in the night sky. "It's shining so bright."

"That's not a star, it's a planet. It's Venus." She cuddled her daughter closer on her lap. "I've told you about Venus, Bonnie."

"I guess I forgot." She leaned back against Eve's shoulder in the big rattan chair. "Or maybe it's because everything seems so . . . different tonight."

"Different? We sit out here on the porch almost every night, baby." It was a precious time for both of them. After supper, they came out on the front porch and looked at the night sky. Eve had even bought a book on astronomy so that she could point out the constellations to Bonnie. "What's different?"

"I don't know." Bonnie's gaze never left the glittering night sky. "They just seem . . . closer. As if I could reach out and touch them. As if they want me to come and touch them."

Eve chuckled and gave her a hug. "Maybe that's what you

should do when you grow up. Would you like to be an astronaut and go from planet to planet?"

Bonnie giggled. "That might be fun. Like *Star Trek*. But I don't have ears like Mr. Spock."

"It could still work." She smiled as she leaned her head back and gazed up at the sky. "But those stars are very far away, and you don't know what you'll find there. Would you be afraid, baby?"

Bonnie was silent, her eyes fixed on the stars.

"Bonnie?"

"I won't be afraid, Mama." She turned her head and looked Eve directly in the eye. "And don't you be afraid either. I'll be fine."

Eve's smile faded. There was something in Bonnie's expression that was making her uneasy. In that instant, she didn't look like her seven-year-old little girl any longer. Bonnie's expression was serene, oddly adult.

Nonsense. It had to be imagination. "I won't." Eve gave Bonnie a kiss on the tip of her nose. "Because I think we'll keep you here on Earth. No skipping from planet to planet. Your grandma and I would miss you too much." She tugged at Bonnie's ear. "And you're right, your ears don't look at all like Spock's." She hugged her again. "And now it's time for your bath. Didn't you tell me that your school picnic is tomorrow? Run in to Grandma and have her start your bath, and you decide what to wear."

"Just one more minute." Bonnie put her head back on Eve's shoulder. "I don't want to leave you yet."

Eve didn't want to leave Bonnie either. That instant of uneasiness was still with her. Why not stay here until it faded away. "One minute. You're not the only one who has school tomorrow. I have to study for my English Lit test when you go in for your bath."

"But tonight is special, tonight is . . . different," she whispered. "Don't you feel it?"

Every day, every minute, was special with Bonnie. From the moment Eve had given birth to her, she had been the center of her world. But maybe there was something strange and beautiful about their closeness tonight. Something that Eve didn't want to give up until she had to do it. The thought brought an odd sense of panic. "I feel it." Her arms tightened around Bonnie's small body. "Yes, I feel it, baby."

BONNIE CAME RUNNING into Eve's bedroom in her yellow pajamas with the orange clowns all over them. Her wild red curls were bouncing, and her face was lit with her luminous smile.

"Mama, Lindsey says her mother is going to let her wear her Goofy T-shirt to the park tomorrow for the school picnic. Can I wear my Bugs Bunny T-shirt?"

Eve looked up from her English Lit book open on the desk in front of her. "It's not can, it's may, baby. And you may wear Bugs tomorrow." She smiled. "We wouldn't want Lindsey to put you in the shade."

"I wouldn't care. She's my friend. You said we always had to want the best for our friends."

"Yes, we do. Now run along to bed."

Bonnie didn't move. "I know you're studying for your test, but could you read me a story?" She added coaxingly, "I thought maybe a very, very short one?"

"Your grandmother loves to read you stories, baby."

Bonnie came closer, and whispered, "I love Grandma. But it's always special when you read it to me. Just a short one . . ."

Eve glanced at her Lit book. She'd be up until after midnight as it was, studying for that exam. She looked at Bonnie's pleading face. Oh, to hell with it. Bonnie was the reason Eve was working for her degree anyway. She was the reason for every action Eve took in life. Why cheat either one of them? "Run and choose a storybook." She pushed her textbook aside and stood up. "And it doesn't have to be a short one."

Bonnie's expression could have lit up Times Square. "No. I promise. . . ." She ran out of the room. She was back in seconds with a Dr. Seuss book. "This will be quick, and I like the rhymes."

Eve sat down in the blue-padded rocking chair that she'd used since Bonnie was a newborn. "Climb up. I like Dr. Seuss, too."

"I know you do." Bonnie scrambled up in her lap and cuddled close. "But since it's such a short book, can—may I have my song, too?"

"I think that's a reasonable request," Eve said solemnly. The two of them had their little traditions, and every night since she was a toddler, Bonnie had loved to share a song with Eve. Eve would sing the first line, and Bonnie would sing the next. "What's it to be tonight?"

"'All the Pretty Little Horses.'" She turned around on Eve's lap and hugged her with all her might. "I love you, Mama."

Eve's arms closed around her. Bonnie's riot of curls was soft and fragrant against her cheek, and her small body was endearingly vital and sturdy against Eve. Lord, she was lucky. "I love you, too, Bonnie."

Bonnie let her go and flopped back around to cuddle in the curve of her arm. "You start, Mama."

"Hushabye, don't you cry," Eve sang softly.

Bonnie's thin little voice chimed. "Go to sleep, little baby."

The moment was so precious, so dear. Eve's arms held Bonnie closer, and she could feel the tightening of her throat as she sang, "When you wake, you shall have cake."

Bonnie's voice was only a wisp of sound. "And all the pretty little horses . . ."

SHE SHOULD GET BACK to her studies, Eve thought.

Not yet. She couldn't pull herself away yet. Bonnie had been so loving tonight. She had seemed to be reaching out for Eve.

She stood looking down at Bonnie curled up asleep in her bed. She looked so small, she thought with aching tenderness. Bonnie was seven, yet she looked younger.

But sometimes she seemed to have a wisdom far beyond her years. She had always been a special child from the moment Eve had given birth to her. Bonnie was illegitimate, born when Eve was only sixteen. Her passionate affair with John Gallo had lasted only four weeks but had given her Bonnie.

And she had thought that she might give her up for adoption, Eve remembered wonderingly. Gazing down at her daughter it seemed impossible to even contemplate. From the moment she had seen her in the hospital, she had known that they had to be together forever.

Forever.

Those teasing words they'd spoken on the porch had only underscored the fact that Bonnie would be growing up and leaving her someday.

Pain.

She didn't have to think of that yet. Bonnie was still her baby, and she would have her for years to come. Until then, she would cherish every moment as she had done tonight.

She bent down and brushed her lips on Bonnie's silky cheek. "Sleep well, baby," she whispered. "May all your dreams be beautiful."

"Dreams . . ." Bonnie's lids lifted drowsily. "Dreams are so wonderful, Mama. You can reach out and touch . . ." She was asleep again.

Eve turned, and the next moment, she was silently closing the door to Bonnie's room behind her.

"She's asleep?" Eve's mother was standing in the hall. "I would have put her to bed, Eve. You told me you had that test tomorrow."

"I'll be okay, Sandra." She'd called her mother Sandra since she was a child. Sandra had been sensitive about appearing older, and so she had never been Mother to Eve, always Sandra. It was just a sign of how much she loved Bonnie that she accepted her calling her Grandma. "I needed a break anyway." She smiled. "And I don't get a chance to put her to bed every night." She headed back down the hall toward her room. "I wish I did."

"You go to school. You work to support her. You can't do everything."

"I know." She stopped at the doorway and looked back at her mother. "But I was just thinking how lucky I am to have her."

"How lucky *we* are," Sandra said.

Eve nodded. "I know how much you love her." And Eve would have had an even rougher time keeping Bonnie if it hadn't been for her mother. She had been with them since Bonnie had been born. "She has a school picnic at the park tomorrow. I told her she could wear her Bugs Bunny T-shirt. I won't be able to be there in the morning. But I should be able to be there by noon after I take my test. You'll be there until I get there?"

Sandra nodded. "Of course I'll be there. I'm intending to stay all day. I wouldn't miss it. Stop worrying, Eve."

"I just want her to have family there. Other kids have fathers, and I'm always afraid she'll feel . . ." She frowned. "But we're enough for her, aren't we, Sandra?"

"I've never seen a happier child." She shook her head. "And this isn't like you, Eve. You never question a decision once it's made. You're not like me, who wobbles back and forth every time the wind blows. Even if John Gallo hadn't been killed in the Army, you wouldn't have wanted him to have anything to do with Bonnie. You told me yourself that it was only sex, not love, between you."

That was true, and Eve didn't know why she was suddenly worrying about Bonnie's not having a conventional family. It was just that she wanted Bonnie to have everything that other children had, every bit of security, everyone to care about her. No, she wanted more. She wanted her to be surrounded by a golden wall of love all the days of her life.

And she was, Eve thought impatiently. No one could love Bonnie more than she did. More than Sandra did. She was being an idiot to start worrying about something that probably didn't bother Bonnie at all. She had never once asked about her father. She seemed perfectly happy with Eve and Sandra.

"Go study," Sandra said. "Stop worrying about tomorrow. Bonnie is going to have a wonderful time." She turned away. "I'm going to bed. Good night."

"Good night." Eve sat back down at her desk. Don't think about Bonnie. Think about English Lit. Getting her degree was a way to protect Bonnie and give her all the things that she should have. This is what she should be doing.

And ignore this nagging feeling that something was wrong. What could be wrong?

Sandra was right. Bonnie was going to have a wonderful time at the park tomorrow.

NIGHTMARE.

Nightmare.

Nightmare.

"Let's go over it one more time," Detective Slindak said. "You didn't see anyone approach your daughter?"

"I told you." Eve's voice was shaking. "There was a crowd. She went to the refreshment stand to get an ice cream. One minute she was there, the next she wasn't." She stared blindly at the three police cars parked next to the curb, the people standing around in groups, whispering and gazing at her. "She's been gone for three hours. Why are you asking me questions? *Find* her."

"We're trying. Does your daughter often wander away from you?"

"No, never." She stared at her mother sitting on the park bench with another police officer. Tears were running down Sandra's cheeks, and she was leaning against him. "We were at the swings. My mother gave her money for an ice cream, and she ran to buy it. We could see the refreshment stand, so we thought it would be okay. She said she'd be right back. She wouldn't have just wandered away." But if she didn't, then the other explanation was where the nightmares began. "I talked to the man at the refreshment stand. He remembered her." Everyone always remembered Bonnie. Her smile, the way she lit up everything around her. "He sold her the ice cream, then she ran off into the crowd."

"That's what he told us, too."

"Someone else must have seen her." The panic was rising. "Talk to everyone. Find her."

"We're trying," he said gently. "We're questioning everyone. I've sent men to search the entire park."

"They won't find her here. Do you think I didn't do that?" she asked fiercely. "I ran all over the park, calling her name. She didn't answer." The tears were beginning to fall. "I called and called. She didn't answer. Bonnie would answer me. She would answer—"

"We'll try again," the detective said. "We're exploring every possibility."

"There's a lake. I taught her to swim, but what if—"

"It's an ornamental lake, just a man-made token. It's only a drop of four feet in the deepest spot. And we've interviewed a father and son who have been sitting on the bench by the lake all afternoon. They would have seen her if she'd fallen into the water."

"She has to be somewhere. Find her." That's the only thing she could say. That's the only thing that made sense in a world that was suddenly drowning in madness. Bonnie had to be found. All the radiance and love that was Bonnie couldn't be lost. God wouldn't let that happen. They all just had to search harder, and they'd find her.

"We're sending out another search party," Detective Slindak said quietly as he gestured to the officers starting out toward the trees in the distance. "We've put out an all-points bulletin. You can't do anything more here. Let me have an officer drive you and your mother home. We'll call you as soon as we hear something."

"You want me to go home?" she asked in disbelief. "Without my little girl? I can't do that."

"You can't help more than you have already. It's better that you leave it to us."

"Bonnie is *mine*. I won't leave here." She whirled away from Slindak. "I'll go with the search party. I'll call her name. She'll answer me."

"She didn't before," Slindak said gently. "She may not be there to answer."

He hadn't said "or she might be unable to answer," but Eve knew it was in his mind. Cold fear was causing the muscles of her stomach to clench at the thought. Her heart was beating so hard that she could barely catch her breath. "She'll answer me. She'll find a way to let me know where she is. You don't understand. Bonnie is such a special, loving, little girl . . . She'll find a way."

"I'm sure that you're right," the detective said.

"You're not sure of anything," she said fiercely. "But I am." She started at a run after the search team of officers heading for the trees. "This is all a mistake. No one would hurt my Bonnie. We just have to find her."

She could feel the detective's gaze on her back as she caught up with the search team. She knew he wanted to make her stop. He wanted her to behave sensibly and let them do their job. But it was her job, too. She had brought Bonnie into the world. In the end, that made it only her job.

I'll find you, baby. Don't be afraid. I'll fight off anything that could hurt you. Wait for me. I'll always be there for you.

No matter how long it takes or how far I have to go, I'll bring you home, Bonnie.

DEAR AMERICAN AIRLINES

Dear American Airlines

Jonathan Miles

HOUGHTON MIFFLIN COMPANY
Boston • New York
2008

in memoriam

LARRY BROWN

(1951–2004)

bro

DEAR AMERICAN AIRLINES

Dear American Airlines,

My name is benjamin r. ford and I am writing to request a refund in the amount of $392.68. But then, no, scratch that: *Request* is too mincy & polite, I think, too officious & Britishy, a word that walks along the page with the ramrod straightness of someone trying to balance a walnut on his upper ass cheeks. Yet what am I saying? Words don't have ass cheeks! Dear American Airlines, I am rather *demanding* a refund in the amount of $392.68. Demanding demanding demanding. In Italian, *richiedere*. *Verlangen* in German and требовать in the Russki tongue but you doubtless catch my drift. Imagine, for illustrative purposes, that there's a table between us. Hear that sharp sound? That's me slapping the table. Me, Mr. Payable to Benjamin R. Ford, whapping the damn legs off it! Ideally you're also imagining concrete walls and a naked lightbulb dangling above us: Now picture me bursting to my feet and kicking the chair behind me, with my finger in your face and my eyes all red and squinty and frothy bittles of spittle freckling the edges of my mouth as I bellow, roar, yowl, as I blooooow like the almighty mother of all blowholes: *Give me my goddamn money back!* See? Little twee *request* doesn't quite capture it, does it? Nossir. This is a *demand*. This is fucking serious.

Naturally I'm aware that ten zillion cranks per annum make

such demands upon you. I suppose you little piglets are accustomed to being huffed upon and puffed upon. Even now, from
my maldesigned seat in this maldesigned airport, I spy a middle-
aged woman waving her arms at the ticket counter like a sprin-
klerhead gone awry. Perhaps she is serious, too. Maybe, like
me, even *fucking* serious. Yet the briefcase by the woman's feet
and her pleated Talbots suit lead me to conclude that she's
probably missing some terribly important meeting in Atlanta
where she's slated to decide something along the lines of which
carbonated beverage ten zillion galoots aged 18–34 will drink
during a specified half-hour of television viewing in four to
six midwestern markets and I'm sure the ticket agent is being
sweetly sympathetic to the soda lady's problem but screw her
anyway. So a half-zillion galoots drink Pepsi rather than Coke,
so what? My entire being, on the other hand, is now dust on
the carpet, ripe and ready to be vacuumed up by some immi-
grant in a jumpsuit.

Please calm down sir, I can hear you saying. Might we rec-
ommend a healthy snack, perhaps some sudoku? Yes, sudoku:
apparently the analgesic *du jour* of the traveling class. That little
game is what appears to be getting my fellow citizens through
these hours of strandedness, hours that seem to be coagulating,
wound-like, rather than passing. They say a watched pot never
boils but baby it's tough not to watch when you're neck-deep in
the pot. Just how many hours so far, I can't say—not with any
precision anyway. Why are there so few clocks in airports? You
can't turn your head more than ten degrees in a train station
without hitting another clock on the wall, the ceiling, the floor,
etc. You'd think that the smartasses who design airports, taking a hint from their forebears, would think to hang a clock or
two on the walls instead of leaving the time-telling to the digital footnotes at the bottom of the scattered schedule screens.
I take an oversized amount of pride in the fact that I've never
worn a wristwatch since my thirteenth birthday when my fa-

ther gave me a Timex and I smashed it with a nine-iron to see how much licking would stop its ticking (not much, as it turned out). But then airports weren't designed for people like me, a fact becoming more and more obvious as I divide my present between smoking cigarettes on the sidewalk outside and drumming my fingers on the armrests of the chairs inside. But even more odious than the clocklessness, I might add, is replacing the *beep-beep-beep* of those passenger carts with digitized birdsong imitations. Birdsongs! I shouldn't have to tell you that being run down by a twelve-foot sparrow is little improvement over being run down by a militarized golfcart. But then that's a matter for the smartasses, not you, so mea culpa. We must be choosy with our battles, or so I've been told.

It occurs to me that none of this will do me a bit of good unless I state my particulars, to wit: My ticket—purchased for $392.68 as I've relevantly aforementioned and will continue to mention, as frequently as a tapdancer's clicks—is for round-trip passage from New York–LaGuardia to Los Angeles's LAX (with a forty-five-minute layover at Chicago O'Hare; were there a clock nearby, I'd divulge the truer length of my layover, but it's safe to say it's edging toward eight hours, with no end in sight). In that eightish-hour period I've smoked seventeen cigarettes which wouldn't be notable save for the fact that the dandy Hudson News outlets here don't stock my brand so I'll soon be forced to switch to another, and while that shouldn't upset me it does. In fact, it enrages me. Here's my life in dangly tatters and I can't even enjoy this merest of my pleasures. Several hours ago a kid in a Cubs windbreaker bummed one of mine and I swear if I spy him again I'll smash him like a Timex. Cough it up, you turd. But then all this talk of smoking is giving me the familiar itch, so if you'll excuse me for a moment I'm off to the sidewalk, as required by law, to scratch it.

THERE NOW, ALL BETTER. Oops, except that I'm not. Of late I've been suffering weird pains in my lower back and these airport chairs with their gen-u-ine Corinthian Naugahyde upholstery are only aggravating the pain. Throughout my life I vowed I would never be the sort of geezer reduced to conversing about nothing save his health maladies. This was until the day I developed maladies of my own to converse about. Truly, they're endlessly fascinating and impossible to keep to oneself! How can you talk about anything else when your physical being is disintegrating, when you can feel everything below your neck going steadily *kaput?* You certainly wouldn't think of discussing, say, Lacanian theory on a jumbo jet spiraling earthward. Unless of course you were Lacan, but even then: Jeez, Jacques, call the kiddos. Back when I was drinking I tended to ignore my bodily malfunctions—full disclosure: During the later dark years of my drinking, I tended to ignore even my bodily *functions*—but now they've become a kind of hobby for me. I fill my private hours with tender proddings and pokings of my interior organs, in the manner of old women in *babushkas* examining mushy supermarket peaches. Plus there's the time I spend online Googling my various symptoms. Do you know that the first diagnosis the internet will offer you for any symptom is almost always a venereal disease? This must be causing acute distress for those hypochondriacal members of our society allowing their genitals to mingle. In the seventh grade the rumor was that your willy would drop clean off if you tugged on it too much (or put it inside a black girl, an indicia of the cultural clime of mid-'60s New Orleans) which caused me infinite grief and worry. The thought of running to my mother with my unfastened manhood in one hand was enough to put me off onanism for several years. The horror! My mother was a crafty sort who doubtlessly would have tried to reattach the poor thing via the aid of a hot glue gun, some sewing thread, glitter, and cut-out photographs from *National Geographic,*

making my private parts look like an elementary school project about orangutans. "There now," she would've said. "All better."

My mother will be seventy-three next month. I mention this fact since it's not just me, Mr. Payable to Benjamin R. Ford, who is presently out that $392.68 you charged us—due to the current configuration of my life, me and Miss Willa are victims in this together. Mug me, you mug my ma. Ya dirty mugs. Because she suffered a debilitating stroke three years ago, I take care of Miss Willa with the aid of a twenty-seven-year-old dumpling of a girl from the Polish countryside named Aneta who also from time to time assists me with my translations. All this, mind you, within the confines of the 2BR, third-story apt. in the West Village that I've called home since Bush the Elder was president. Back then it provided me elbowroom galore. Now, with my mother shuffling about and Aneta galumphing after her, my waking and sleeping hours are primarily squashed together into one room—a Balzacian garret fitted with a desk, books, and a sofa that folds out into a bed but only if you push the desk against the wall each night. It ain't pretty but we manage.

The stroke may have been the best thing that could have happened to my mother. No doubt this sounds beastly, especially considering that she cannot move the right side of her body and must communicate by scrawling pithy comments on one of the multicolored Post-it pads she keeps piled on her lap, but my mother used to be crazy and now she is not. I don't mean crazy like your old Aunt Edna who's still dancing the tango at eighty and makes uncomfortably blue comments at the Thanksgiving dinner table. I mean manic-depressive schizophrenic crazy, the hard stuff. During a stroke, parts of the brain are starved of oxygen and die, and in the case of my mother, apparently the crazy parts got starved. The stroke cleaved her in two but, hooray and I mean it, left the good half functioning. This isn't to suggest that things are hunky-dory at home but rather to say that things were once worse. To be

honest things were once terrible but then that's another story and you're probably skimming already.

Dear American Airlines, do you even read all these letters you must receive? I imagine them funneling into a giant bin in a sorting room in some warehouse set out in a dancefloor-flat stretch of Texas plain, mounds and mounds of stamped envelopes from all corners of this vast republic, handwritten and typewritten and some scribbled in Crayola crayon, questions and pleas and suggestions and rants and maybe even mash notes from easily sated dinkums who *lurved* the Cincinnati travel tips in the in-flight magazine. Or maybe they're all emails now, unpunctuated, misspelled, flecked with emoticons, sizzling through a grand nest of wires before landing, with a digital ping, inside some doublewide trailer-sized mainframe computer. Back in my very early twenties I actually wrote a thank-you note to the Swisher Cigar Co. of Jacksonville, Fla., to express my gratitude for the sublime if stinky cheer its flagship brand then provided me. I spent an inordinate amount of time crafting that letter and went so far as to cite for particular praise the Swisher Sweet's "cognac-and-campfire aroma." That I'd never caught so much as a whiff of cognac by that time mattered little; it was alliterative, and alliteration bewitched me to such an extent that in my undergraduate years I romanced, in succession, a Mary Mattingly, a Karen Carpenter (not the singer), a Patricia Powell, and a Laura Lockwood, as if culling my dates straight from the pages of a comic book. I remember being bitterly disappointed by the Swisher Cigar Co.'s response to my letter: A coupon for a free box that arrived without even the merest personal acknowledgment of my note. Sure, the coupon came in handy, but really. You have to be careful about trying to make connections in this world, or so I learned.

Aneta helped me pick out the necktie for my trip west.

Why I would trust an Eastern European girl whose wardrobe is founded primarily on Mickey Mouse t-shirts in varying colors including poop brown is beyond me, except that I think I liked having a female opinion on the matter, since the reasons for my trip—the trip you are currently thwarting, fuck you very much—are entirely female. And I do mean entirely. My daughter is getting married tomorrow, though I'm not sure "married" is the correct & legal term since she's quote-unquote marrying another woman. This came as quite the surprise to me though I confess that, at the time I learned of it, any news from my daughter would have been classified as surprising. She's engaged to a woman named Sylvana, meaning my future daughter-in-law is one letter away from being kin to my television set. I don't know if Stella—that's my daughter, named after her mother—will be the bride or the groom and I suspect it's poor form for me to inquire. And how does a father assess his daughter's choice of spouse when it's another girl? I generally know a beer-guzzling, wife-beating, underbathed, unemployable lout when I see one, unless she's wearing a dress in which case it's damnably hard to tell. Sylvana is a lawyer which should be a comfort—oh goody, my daughter's marrying a lawyer!—but that's about as much as I know about her. Of course, I don't know much about Stella, either. Her mother and I split up a long time ago and for complicated or possibly uncomplicated reasons I faded almost completely out of her life: an old story, right, the father as vanishing taillight. The last photograph I have of her is from her high school graduation, and came to me not from either of my Stellas but directly from the Sears Portrait Studio, as if they (the Stellas, maybe Sears) were legally obligated to send me a print. The photograph shook in my hands when I received it because Stella's resemblance to her mother was total and precise, and the venom of that union's crash still lingers in my arteries, still buzzes my

tongue with a chemical aftertaste. Staring at my daughter's portrait was like viewing the evidence of a long-ago crime. Look: I don't deny I was once an ogre. What's harder and more painful for me to gauge is if I'm still one. Yet, humbly, I consider the necktie in my luggage a hopeful sign. That is, if you nitwits haven't gone and lost it.

– – – –

DEAR AMERICAN AIRLINES, permit me to introduce Walenty Mozelewski, who, by dint of dark coincidence, is having transportation snarls of his own. Walenty should be on his way home to Poland (via England, for his discharge) from the war, having fought with the Polish II Corps at the Battle of Monte Cassino (Italy), where he lost his left leg to the combined efforts of a mortar shell and an overworked Swiss combat surgeon. Quite the ordeal, and I'm afraid the shellshock has muddied his brain. He boarded the wrong train and is now on his way to Trieste. This should be a mere inconvenience but Walenty cannot help wondering what would happen if he stepped off the train in Trieste and never in all his life boarded another. It would be like death without the dying, is what he's thinking: the loss of everything—his wife, his two children, his home, his former job as a factory clerk in a factory that makes parts for other factories—the loss of it all, save his breath and his memories. Poor Walenty! He's staring through the window at the winter outside, fogging the glass with his exhalations. Listen:

> Every few minutes or so there appeared a house or houses outside, most at the ends of narrow, lonely, low-walled roads, some of the houses half-ruined and ice-chinked but others with gray tendrils of smoke rising from their stone chimneys and a faint yellow glow visible from inside them. Walenty wondered who lived in those houses, and what

they would do if a one-legged soldier came to their door and asked if he could stay for the night and, if that was fine, then perhaps forever. Or how the soldier would be able to tell which house might be Heaven and which might be Hell, if either they were.

Those last sentences are awkward, I know. But here's the caveat: I haven't actually started translating yet—this is my initial read-through, and since you'll recall that I'm presently stranded in an airport without access to (a) my reference books, and (b) my beloved Lucky Strikes, I hope I'll be excused for flying by the seat of my pants here. (Flying! What a concept. I'd like to do more of it.)

The author's name is Alojzy Wojtkiewicz, and the title is *The Free State of Trieste.* This is the third novel of Alojzy's I've translated, and he's likely to provide me as much help on this one as he has all the others: by which I mean, not squat. He tends to treat me (as he apparently does all his translators) like the new husband of a wife he's ditched: Yes, he'll field a few questions, and perhaps mutter some wan advice, but really: She's your problem now, *kumpel.* Not that I'm bellyaching, mind you. We translators must be realistic. To translate a literary work is to make love to a woman who will always be in love with someone else. You can ravish her, worship her, even ruin her; but she'll never be yours to possess. Less romantically, I've sometimes thought of translation as being akin to cooking. At your disposal is the meat of an animal, and it's up to you to create dishes from it, to make it digestible. But the novelist or poet has the more Godly job. He gets to create the animal.

I met Alojzy twenty years ago when we shared a duplex studio at an artists' colony up in Idaho, back when I was scamming delicious fellowships for the third-rate poems I was writing. (You would be appalled at the amount of state & federal

taxpayer money—i.e. grants, fellowships, other assorted poet subsidies—that went into my pockets over the years, especially if you did a cost-benefit analysis of the poetry it yielded. Though, wait: Aren't you the proud recipient of something like ten kazillion dollars in federal bailout funds? Well then, lookee here at us. Flightless birds of a feather.) Every day at noon the colony's cook would deliver us lunches, and Alojzy and I would sit out on the deck and eat our turkey sandwiches and apples while staring at the Boulder Mountains and then we would chainsmoke and talk about women before retreating back into our studios, where Alojzy finished his second novel and where I took vodka-fueled "naps" between bouts of additional chainsmoking. Back then he was swarthy and thick-muscled, with a square head and torso that made him resemble a piece of Mission furniture; going by his more recent author photos, the last two decades have seen Alojzy progressively swaddling himself in fat, a hard square gone soft and circular. From a distance you might mistake him for a honeybun. This is to be expected, however. When I met him he had just ended a several-year stint as a bricklayer; these days, his primary physical activity seems to be signing his name to leftist petitions with one hand while gripping a half-gnawed sparerib in the other.

But I digress. My aim here was to acquaint you with Walenty, since, for the moment, he seems to be all I have in the world, but I veered into some related humbuggeries and lost track of him. Sigh. Nonetheless, I'm afraid you'll have to permit me my digressions. Digressing, after all, is not so different from rerouting, and let's not pretend, dear ones, that you're innocent of that.

- - - -

DEAR AMERICAN AIRLINES, since when did you start canceling flights in midair? The plane from New York to Chicago was one of those "streamlined" contraptions roughly the size and

shape of an econo-model dildo. We circled O'Hare for an hour before the pilot informed us he was landing in Peoria. Peoria! In my youth I thought Peoria was a fictional place that Sherwood Anderson and Sinclair Lewis had cooked up one night at the tail end of a gin bender. But no, it exists. We sat on the runway for more than an hour before a handsome pilot with exquisitely parted hair emerged to tell us that the flight was "officially canceled." Wha? But he offered us all a bus ride to O'Hare "on the house," kind soul that he was, the revealing of which I hope won't endanger his job. Not that I'd worry too much about him: Go ahead and can him, he has a guaranteed second career as a JCPenney catalog model. The (alleged) cause for this fuckedupedness was (allegedly) foul weather blowing off Lake Michigan but after eight-plus hours in Chicago I can tell you, without a pinch of hesitation, that the weather here is flat-out delightful and you're more than welcome to visit for a round of golf to so verify. Pack some sunscreen.

Yet all around me this nation's stranded folk are badgering ticket agents, muffling their children's whining by stuffing the local variety of hot dogs into their small mouths, checking and rechecking their watches, and, most of all, inexhaustibly bitching into cellphones. Every now and then I walk twenty yards or so to check the schedule screens. I'm not alone in this chore but I do seem to be the only one unequipped with a cellphone. No big shakes there, as I've already made my one call—it didn't go so well—and I'm anyway loyal to payphones. I stand beneath the screens like a child waiting for Santa's sleigh to appear in the night sky, examining each star for the faintest trace of movement, ears overattuned to the jingle of far-off bells. But the screens barely flicker. All flights westward canceled, eastward canceled, everything canceled. The sky above us one giant fermata, an interminable chord lying wounded in the middle of a song, a deadening hollow thrummmmm

- - - -

STELLA IS PROBABLY laughing about this. Stella the elder, I mean. Not a happy, lilting laugh: no, more like an acidic, I-told-you-so laugh, as in *hahaha once an asshole always an asshole haha* . . . ha. The sort of laugh that's sometimes mistaken for a cough or a cancer symptom. Did I mention she was beautiful once? Well, she was. Like the leading lady from a Bogart flick, so I thought back then, with a finely sculpted aristocrat's jaw and eyes as deep, blue, and cold as the North Atlantic glimpsed through a submarine's porthole. The thin lips of a killer and a long narrow ivory neck. A demure chocolate mole on her inner thigh that I blithely befriended. Would it still remember me? Hard to believe that it, at least, wouldn't welcome me home: Hello darlin'. In our lazy postcoital tangles I swear I used to *breathe* Stella, as if inhaling her aerosolized essence, trying to flood my lungs with her. Surely you remember what that's like: lying there in the wet dark, unafraid for the first time in your life, drenched in a balmy peace, content to die. But then, stop, it's useless and mawkish to dwell on such things, right-rightright. Buck up, Bennie. So every tomato has its soft spot, big whoop. You were young like everyone else. Quit making mountains out of moles.

It happened like this: I was twenty-four, she twenty-seven. I'd dropped out of grad school the year before to embark upon a career in romantic dissolution, spending nine- and ten-hour daily stretches in a narrow, gummy cockpit of an Uptown New Orleans bar called Billy Barnes' Turf Exchange. The Exchange, for short, and goddamn what a saloon: ancient coonass bruisers drinking away disability checks, weird old frilly bats from the neighborhood sipping Chambord or Campari, off-duty line cooks and oyster shuckers, displaced hippies, slumming Tulane kids, greasy pool sharks, a cigar-smoking Rottweiler named Punch, Seersucker Bob who never wore anything but, Skee-zacks who used his trumpet as a beer bong, Dead Fred whose ashes were behind the bar, Spud, Pete the Spy, Al the Horny

Wheelchair Homo, Bum's Breath Mike (B. B. Mike for short), Crazy Jane, me too. Our ringmaster was Felix, the owner, a doughy, hairless connoisseur of dirty jokes and fry-batter who would take out his false teeth for a dollar. He called himself Felix the Fat so we did the same. Tuesday was Ladies' Night, the only night Felix would spring for a band, and there'd be so many halter tops a-bouncing on the dancefloor that you felt like you were inside a lottery ball machine. But those nights were the exception. Mostly it was a dim, garrulous joint, filled with neighborhood steadies and worn chatter and smogged with tobacco smoke and cuss words, as comfortable, rank, and beloved as the ratty old pair of house slippers you slide on to fetch the morning news. How I adored it! Back then I was broke, sloshed, undernourished, unwashed, intermittently suicidal, but more generally, and sometimes rhapsodically, happy as hell: what the French call *l'extase langoureuse*, the ecstasy of languishing.

Stella was the cool opposite: sharp, ambitious, level, metrical, severe. An aspiring poet like me, though the style & substance of her poems were the obverse of mine. When we met I was coediting a small doomed lit journal called *Rag and Bone Shop* and she'd just started work on her master's at Tulane. My coeditor's apartment on Magazine Street—his name was Charles Ford; everyone assumed we were brothers—doubled as the *R&BS* offices, and it was there, at one of the parties we always threw after picking the issues up from the printer, that Stella and I met. We'd published two of her poems in that edition of *R&BS*—one about a quilt, sort of, and the other, very literally, about a bottlecap crucifix. It was the former poem that intrigued me, because it ended with a scene of a woman having sex atop her great-grandmother's hand-stitched quilt, "staining it with creation," which struck me as a lovely and vaguely kinky line and made me curious about its author.

Her hair was braided that night and she was wearing a blousy

silk shirt and bluejeans. On the hi-fi: Nick Lowe, the Specials, the Buzzcocks, Ian Dury & the Blockheads. A baroque glass bong circling the kitchen and a local medievalist performing a second line on his way to the potty. We ended up on Charles's balcony overlooking Magazine, Stella and I, sitting on a porch swing with our feet propped on the balcony rail, bubbly drunk. What did we talk about? Who knows. The dis-and-dat of two creatures commencing a mating dance. Crazy mothers (ah, she had one too). James Merrill. Time travel. A shared fondness for neon. My enigmatic coeditor, her downblouse-peering old roach of a thesis advisor. Oh, and yes, I learned she'd never set foot inside the Exchange! Gallantly, I promised to take her. Later, while we were kissing, I opened my eyes to the sight of Charles's naked pale rump pressed flat against the window. From inside I could hear him singing, "When da moon hiz your eye . . . ," and so on and so forth.

We were the last to leave the party. Inside we found Charles passed out openmouthed on his couch, and after carefully sliding down his boxers and finding a marker, we wrote a poem on his ass: *Roses are red / violets are blue / with my buttocks so white / I bid you goodnight.* (Stella would later disavow her participation in this act, citing it as one of the early missed clues of my unsuitability as husband, father, gentleman, etc., but I vividly remember her right thumb curled around the elastic of Charles's boxers, and the brutal glee she seemed to be stifling, because I was surprised [and aroused] by the sexual birr she brought to the task, the way her involvement tipped it, from boozy conception up to the moment we began writing, from frathouse-style prank to dark-edged violation . . . anyway, she denies it.) Downstairs on the sidewalk I kissed Stella some more — those cliffhanger kisses, you know, when you feel as if you'll drop to your doom if your tongues untwine — before she sank into the seat of her car and disappeared. Then I stood there

for a long while, my heart a sparkler spraying light across the sidewalk.

- - - -

YET I'M VEERING off-point once again, aren't I? French-style kisses & whatnot, kerphooey. Dear American Airlines, I apologize. Please understand that these are not the best of times. Outside, by the luggage porters, an elderly woman who was smoking beside me just told me the most dismal of tales: Her husband suffered a "coronary" while driving and plunged his Fiat off a central California cliff but thanks to his seatbelt was saved from dying and was instead reduced to a vegetative state now going on four years. His dear munchkin of a wife sits with him for six hours a day waiting for the random blink of an eyelid that will return him to the mammalian. As she told me this she dug a packet of Kleenex out of her fannypack which I presumed was for her—that story awarded her the right to shed tears—but which she offered to me. I've never been adept at keeping my heart from advertising itself on my sleeve, and I guess I was wearing that wounded, onion-stink expression to which I'm prone. I started to decline the gift but she was rifling through her fannypack for something else. I was hoping it wouldn't be a still-life photo of her ventilated, intubated husband because that risked provoking a fit of blubbering from me. Instead it was a little machine resembling an overweight BlackBerry phone which she explained was a handheld slot machine. This was what kept her sane, she told me, and urged me to take a few spins—in the "virtual" sense, of course—which I did. A cherry, a seven, and what looked like a lemon! Two sevens and a cherry! Loss and more loss. The munchkin said all life requires of us, "by George," is to find one reason a day to go on. Besides playing the little video slot machine, she said, she makes sure to always have something coming in the

mail such as a sweater from L.L.Bean or a new garden trowel from Smith & Hawken. To always be expecting. Before heading back inside—"I hear they're running short on cots for us strandees," she said—she told me the Kleenex was mine and advised me to keep my upper lip stiff. Followed literally this advice tends to make one appear on the brink of a sneeze but nevermind the literal. The old woman gave me her tissues and I'm doing what she says.

– – – –

MIND IF WE CHECK IN with Walenty? For just a minute or two while my lip holds sdiff like dis. Here he is on page 17, having just stepped off the train in Trieste:

> He was unprepared for the raw color of it all. For three years he had seen no color except for the beef-red of wounds and crimson splashes of blood; everything else had been painted in hard, parched shades of gray and brown and black. Mud, gunmetal, rust, smoke, night, char, concertina wire, shovels, ash, corpse-skin, fog, mortar shells, bones, the sharp-ribbed mongrels that cowered growling behind rubble piles. Stepping off the train now, however, was like passing through a rainbow. The station itself, yellow like a daisy, was charged with color: here the gaudy flash of summer silks, there the rose-colored fringe of a woman's drawstring purse, here the phosphorescent gloss of a businessman's navy suit, and strewn across the waxed floors were the salmon-hued confetti of discarded tickets.

("Confetti": a tiny liberty that I'm taking. Alojzy has it as *świąteczne odpadki*, which translated literally means "festive trash." But what trash is more festive than confetti? Ah, the pinprick joys of translating. Anyway, onward . . .)

> Walenty's eyes stung him, and he nearly lost his breath. Save for the few Kiwi soldiers posted in the corners, and the

deadness of his false foot as his shoe scraped the floor, there was nothing to suggest that the war had been anything but a sour nightmare.

He sat down at a table in a café inside the station and, still dizzy and overwhelmed, held the table edge to steady himself. The young girl who came to take his order was dark-haired, with tanned glossy skin, and the pureness of her expression—a mix of boredom, dreaminess, and tender ignorance—made clear to him that she had lost nothing in life, not yet. He noticed a small, fish-shaped scar on her elbow: probably from a childhood fall. No doubt she had cried—the grating, screechy cries he'd associated with children before he went to war, before he'd heard what children are capable of. Deep howls of total vacuumed loss.

"Do you have coffee?" he asked.

"Yes," she said.

"*Surrogato?*"

"No. Coffee."

"Please, then. A cup."

When she returned to deliver his coffee, he noticed her lingering and staring shyly at his prosthetic leg, at his exposed mechanical ankle. His eyes caught hers. "Does it hurt?" she asked finally.

"No," he said. "It doesn't hurt. Not anymore. It just reminds me of hurt. Like a memory that sits right in the front of your brain and can't be budged or extinguished." He did not want to drive her off, to have her think he was a melancholy cripple, the cliché of the wounded soldier, so he smiled. His smile, however, was lopsided and awkward, as if the muscles of his jaw had forgotten their old routine. He hoped it hadn't seemed a leer.

She nodded inscrutably and went off to service other tables. When she returned he ordered another cup, and when she brought it to him he said, "Do you know what's strange?" She waited, so he went on: "In my dreams I always

have two legs. I think that's the worst part. Every morning, after dreaming, I awaken a full man. But then I reach down and feel my false leg and everything that happened to me happens all over again, in that instant, as though every day I am losing my leg and my comrades for the first time. That's the worst part. I dream backwards."

He did not expect the girl to smile at this, but she did. Lightly, she said, "You need new dreams," as if it was self-evident, as if he had said he was hungry and she'd recommended food. She'd made it sound simple.

It's *not* simple, of course, but you certainly can't blame Walenty for hoisting his hopes up. How pleasant to think of the past as something curable, as a benign rather than malignant cancer, no? Almost as pleasant a concept as a world in which tickets costing $392.68 earned you passage to your destination on the date printed on the ticket. But just as goddamn unlikely.

- - - -

SINCE WE'RE SORT OF on the subject of hindsight, dear American Airlines, why don't we discuss how this mess could have been avoided? We won't bother with your official excuse of rotten weather because I've plainly unmasked that one with my frequent measuring of the climate outside, which, at last check, showed a mix of cool and pleasant with a ninety percent chance of continued pleasantness developing through the morning, with winds, like your flight schedules, light and variable. So talk to me. Did banal old greed induce you to overschedule your flights, à la bank robbers unable to stop stuffing their bags despite the wails of nearing sirens? (Peek into that corner office. Do you see fat men eyeing your national route map while twirling handlebar mustaches? Then the answer is probably yes.) Or do you plan so tightly and rigidly that the delay of one plane in, say, Dallas can cause a monumental backup akin to a stalled tractor-trailer on the George Washington Bridge at

8:30 A.M.? Or, similarly, are airlines like yourself susceptible to something like the Butterfly Effect, so that the delay caused by a pickled passenger trying to board an early-morning flight in Ibiza can provoke a chain reaction, with delay piling upon delay, and then cancellation upon cancellation, until poor Chicago O'Hare—the sacrificial goat of air travel—is shut down completely? If that's the case, maybe I'm being too hard on you. Perhaps my beef is actually with Señor Fabio Eurotrash who rolled off a foam-strewn Ibiza dancefloor at six A.M. with sixteen Red-Bull-and-vodkas still fizzing in his gut and whose clumsy pre-takeoff attempt at self-fellatio in Seat 3A forced an interminable delay while his pretzeled ass was removed from the plane. But then why stop there? The beauty of hindsight is that it's infinite. After all, you could reasonably if acidly retort that this entire hash is my fault because twenty years ago I flushed my life down the toilet. Zing! Good one, AA. Or, stepping further back, that it's Willa Desforge's fault for letting a disconsolate-eyed Polack impregnate her one unairconditioned night midcentury in New Orleans. Ouch, sucker-punch! Funny thing is, though, Miss Willa would agree with you on that one. If she could somehow connect the dots, my mother would fix the blame for everything from Pol Pot to global warming to the undarned holes in her socks on that one humid unguarded night that was the end of her and the beginning of me.

And it began, truth to tell, with a possum. Sit tight, I have a story to tell. Apparently we have time.

Miss Willa Desforge met Henryk Gniech at her parents' home on South Tonti Street in 1953 courtesy of, yessir, a possum: a fat, spooked creature with mottled fur that was neither gray nor brown nor white but a splotchy and disheveled mixture of the three, and with a long fleshy tail almost obscene in its nude pinkness. The possum had taken up residence in the attic directly above Miss Willa's bedroom, and, despite weeks of grumbly and intermittent efforts, my grandfather, a trust

and estate attorney for a white-shoe Uptown firm, had been incapable of banishing it from the house. So one Saturday morning he borrowed the neighbor's ladder and patched every hole and rotted edge of the roof soffits and fascias with scrap wood and squares of rumpled aluminum, barring (he thought) any further access by the possum. But possums are nocturnal, so instead of watching my grandfather seal the attic from up in a tree or behind a trashcan, as Gerald Desforge, Esq., imagined, the possum watched from *inside* the dark attic as the specks of infiltrating sunlight steadily disappeared from its lair, like stars fizzling to black in the night sky. That evening, beginning just after twilight and lasting deep into the wee hours, the Desforges were treated to an unusually raucous performance on the ceiling above Miss Willa's bed: scritches, scratches, hyperagitated scurries. "It's trapped and it's frantic," my mother said, but my grandfather was unsympathetic. "It will be over soon enough," he said. "How long can it last up there?"

Longer than one might expect or endure, as it turned out. Every night, for a full week, my mother stared stiffly and sleeplessly at the ceiling while the possum launched escape attempt after escape attempt, clawing at the aluminum and gnawing at the wood, and every night the weight of its suffering seemed to sink heavier and heavier upon her in that bed, like a deadening cloak of blame . . . a guilt quilt.

Of course, to fully understand the situation, you need to know something about my mother at the time. Miss Willa Desforge was an outlandishly beautiful girl, with startling green eyes and hair as black and glistening as a newly waxed hearse, as well as a gifted painter admitted to the John McCrady Art School at the age of twelve and, at fifteen, as a special student to Sophie Newcomb College's art school. But God does not bestow that kind of beauty and talent freely, as you know or should know; His love must be paid. For my mother, the price

"He aims to kill it," she said. "That's a lynching tool."

"A lynching tool? Hush, ain't no such thing. That's a possum grabber. Come on up here, Pest Man," he said, putting a hand to Henryk's back and directing him up the attic stairs. "She's brilliant, like I was saying, but has really fine, fine nerves," Willa heard her father say. She stood at the foot of the stairs and hollered up: "I want to see it. I want to see it . . . moving."

After two or three minutes she heard a scuffling from above —quick scratches and the thump of boots on the attic planks, reverbed footfalls she thought she could almost see dimpling the ceiling—and rat-a-tat shouts from her father ("Get er now, over there, *get er*"). From below Willa screamed—a silly scream, I imagine, like that of the housewife exiled onto a footstool in the old Tom & Jerry cartoons. "What is it?" her father yelled down; he'd learned, as I later would, to take nothing for granted, not even a cartoon matron's wimpy shriek. "What's happening?" she shouted back up. "Don't you come up here," said her father, flooding her with dread. "Don't you dare let him kill it," she responded, her voice caught somewhere between a plea and a screamy demand and crackling in that middle ground. "I'll never forgive you or anyone ever again." (Ah, typical Willa Desforges hyperbole. "If you continue to bite your fingernails," she told me when I was a boy, "you will never be loved. No one will want you and you will die alone.")

Henryk Gniech descended first from the attic. Cradled in his arms was the possum, its wet dark eyes flickering back and forth, random as a flame, but its body still, its claws anchored in the sleeves of Henryk's canvas jacket, its small pink tongue limply extended. Henryk's hands—huge hands, Willa noticed, with the elongated fingers of a French Quarter stride pianist —were around it like a loose net. Brandishing the Ketch-All tool, and panting, Gerald Desforge stood behind him on the stairs. "The boy scooped him up like a pro," he said, obvi-

DEAR AMERICAN AIRLINES

ously exhilarated. Willa was overcome by concurrent desires to
touch and to recoil from the possum, and its carrier, and for a
moment she lost her balance, wobbling toward the wall.

"They ack dead," Henryk said, his first words to her. "Is
sweet."

"Where will he take it?" she asked her father. Then, correcting herself, to Henryk: "Where will you take it?"

With a shrug, he said, "A tree."

"Not one around here, though," said Gerald Desforges.

"Far away," said Henryk.

She didn't think he would kill it, not the way he was holding
it, but she said anyway, almost as a question, "You're not going
to kill it."

"City Park," her father said. "He can take it to the park."

"I'm going with you," she said to Henryk. "I don't trust
you." This was a lie. She did trust him. Though a hired killer,
he had the eyes of an old priest, of a dispenser of daily mer-
cies rather than acrid poison. With fierce and prolonged har-
rumphs, her father objected—but of course he relented, he always did. He'd go to his deathbed fearing entanglement in her
nerves.

Willa waited in the Dixie Pest Control truck—spartan and
filthy, the floorboards swamped with empty Coke bottles—
while Henryk locked the possum in a rusty steel cage in the
truckbed. The Coke bottles clinked together as he drove
through New Orleans, filling the otherwise silent cab with a
glassy random music.

"You must usually kill them," she said after a while.

"No," he said. The bottles chinkled in a pothole crescendo.
"I have . . . secret place. I give gift."

"Where?"

"Is beautiful. Most beautiful place. I show you. You want I
show you?"

As he piloted the truck through New Orleans she tried to

26

guess where he would stop, wondering what beauty might look like to a Polish exterminator, but—down Claiborne Street, then onto Rampart and then St. Claude and into the Bywater —the possibilities kept dwindling. A *gift*, he'd said. With a prick of horror she wondered if he intended to deliver the possum to a down-and-out black family in the Lower Ninth Ward, to cook and eat. Fear of fricassee roiled her insides. But then he turned onto Poland Avenue and kept driving toward the river until there was no more road to drive upon, and he stopped the truck at the wharf. He was grinning as he shut off the motor, as if everything—the beauty, the possum's fate—was gorgeously self-evident.

"I'm confused," she said, and something in her expression— distaste, disappointment—broke his smile. Together, in separate silences, they surveyed the scene: the Mississippi River, so muddy and drab that it barely reflected sunlight; the drydocks across the river in Algiers; the freighters and banana boats with rust stains leaking down their hulls like blood from wounds; old squat warehouses, tin-roofed terminal offices, decomposing boxcars, dry plains of concrete. She inhaled the odors of fishguts, sulfur, and shipsmoke. *Is beautiful*, he'd said. Finally, she might have thought (though she's rarely been prone to self-deprecation): Someone crazier than me.

"Most beautiful place," he said, his tone adding half a question mark to the statement. Gently, she shook her head no: my parents' first disagreement.

This is how he explained it (with tender enthusiasm, but brokenly, asking her constantly to fill the gaps in his story with the words he didn't know): Four years earlier, a ship from Germany had docked at the Poland Avenue Wharf, a fitting place of disembarkation for the ninety-three Polish refugees who came squinting down its gangplank. Most of them were Jews, and most survivors of the Nazi concentration camps, their inner forearms blued with their camp tattoos. A brass band was

there to greet them, along with throngs of volunteers from the Red Cross and the United Service for New Americans, their biceps striped in colorful armbands. Among the arrivals was Henryk Gniech.

I do not know (with certainty, anyway) which labor camp my father survived, or what happened to him there. (Dachau, we believe—that's where the priests ended up.) We know he was a Catholic seminary student who was arrested for wearing a cassock. He told my mother this much. (For several years a member of the Catholic Patron League of New Orleans, which had sponsored his immigration, would visit to gauge his religious temperature; they'd expected him to resume his seminary studies and become a priest, something he'd never intended to do. They stopped coming after my mother entered the picture.) We know, too, that all his family died in the war, and that, along with whatever else he suffered, he was whipped terribly; his back bore a rubbery pink lattice of scars. He never spoke of any of it except, my mother suspected, in his sleep, when he would sometimes sob and utter what sounded to my mother (who never learned Polish) like dark pleas. "Like a child trapped down in a well," my mother put it. No, in rewinding his life, my father never went beyond this one sunlit point: stepping onto the hot concrete of New Orleans, the docks swarming with the soft welcoming chaos of charity workers, the moist air filled with the garish and inappropriate tuba-honks of "When the Saints Go Marching In," which would forever remain his favorite song. (He hummed it as he shaved, showered, scanned the *Times-Picayune*, munched peanuts on the couch.) He considered this his birth, the beginning of Him, as if everything that had come before comprised a lightless womb from which he'd squeezed free.

So this was where Henryk Gniech freed the possum, as he'd freed an ark's worth of pestilent creatures before. The possum sniffed at the air, took several meek steps from the cage,

then skittered across the concrete into a safe crevice between two giant wooden crates, disappearing from sight. This was my father's gift—a second chance on the docks—the greatest gift he knew—the same one he'd himself been given. He smiled, lit a cigarette, hummed the opening bars of "When the Saints . . . ," and returned the empty cage to the truck while Willa stood there staring, watching that dark merciful crevice with the same rapt and emotional attention she might give a Degas in the museum. She had not expected this, no. A new kind of madness. She fell in love that afternoon, and within three weeks she was pregnant.

- - - -

WELL, SHIT. That was a much longer interlude than I'd intended. Are you still there? I am. Still here, I mean. I had to relocate midway through that sepia burst of genealogy because some twiddledee with an acoustic guitar decided to serenade the masses assembled at Gate K9 with an instrumental rendition of "Dust in the Wind." This wouldn't have been so toxic —all we are, after all, is dust in the wind—had he not kept flubbing the changes and, rather than pushing forward with the song, repeating them until he got them right. First time I can recall that I've ever heard a guitar *stutter.* (Revision, like any other grooming procedure, should be kept private.—The Book of B. Ford, 2:13.) I'm now at Gate K12 which seems safe except for this young skinnymarink Asian fellow across from me who keeps chuckling at some apparently textual dialogue he's having with his cellphone. Back in my undergrad days, when the pocket calculator made its first appearance, I kept myself very mildly entertained in math classes by making words out of the squared numerals: 800 for BOO, for example. 5318008, upside down, for BOOBIES. 58008618, likewise, for BIGBOOBS. Ah, what hilarity! I don't suppose that's what my young Asiatic friend is doing though the physical motions are

29

rather precisely reminiscent. It occurs to me just now that if they were to make a mega-sized cellphone—with buttons the size of, say, Lucky Strike packs—my mother could send me text messages instead of so laboriously writing me her shaky-scrawl Post-it notes. Of course, I'd need to be equipped with a cellphone myself for that to work. But still: What a triumph of technology that would be—her Post-it notes finding me any-where, out on the streets or inside a crosstown bus, pinned to the wings of digital homing pigeons.

As to Miss Willa, and the above: These are the facts as I know them, but since the source for them is my mother, pass the salt. Though there's a certain logic to the story. How else could a rawboned & half-mute Polish refugee/extermina-tor have seduced my mother? Frankly if he hadn't been such a gentle man I might speculate I was born of rape. But then of course, dear American Airlines, you don't give a possum's pink ass as to how or why I was conceived. At this point you're doubtless wishing that I'd never *been* conceived, and I'd be ly-ing if I denied being on your side on that one. Add Stella to the bleachers and we could all do a wave. Anyway, I apologize for that sideways waltz into the story of my beginnings. It's clear I should've been a Russian novelist: I can't even write a fucking refund request without detailing my lineage.

Not that this is any fucking refund request, mind you. I'm not sure it's clear just yet but there was a lot more than $392.68 riding on this flight.

MAYBE I SHOULD EXPLAIN.

In the winter of 1978 I became a new father. This wasn't, I should note, by design: As I was an accident of conception, so too was my daughter. An accident begat an accident. In our case, it was a night spent atop a patchwork of blankets on a sec-ond-story porch that led to the startlement of unexpected par-

enthood. I'd just moved in with Stella after a delirious three-month courtship, lugging mostly books—in fact, I don't think I contributed anything *but* books—into her upstairs apartment in a double gallery house in the Irish Channel. A typical grad-student rental place, slummy and peeling but charming in that bohemian way. Since this was the first night in our home we celebrated by cooking something oystery out of my dead grandmother's copy of the *Picayune's Creole Cookbook* and opening a jug of Gallo Rhine wine which at the time we thought was something special. It was a warm spring night, the blooming magnolias infusing the whole Channel with a lemonade smell, so we moved outside to the gallery. Stella lit candles and we smoked a joint and told stories that made us both laugh beyond the brink of tears and, at some point, while we were making love—and however distasteful I find that euphemism, that's precisely what we were doing—with her atop me, I spelled out I LOVE YOU with a fingertip on the wet skin of her back. We stayed out there all night, circled at dawn by bright puddles of melted candlewax.

In those months we were the planet's happiest residents. If I was no longer the *poète maudit*, well, *pbbbbbt*, I didn't give a damn. I stopped drinking alone and suicide was as improbable a concept for me as joining a Kiwanis Club. On the hi-fi, the morose West Coast blues pianists I specialized in listening to were replaced by mindless rock. For silly kicks we put ABBA on the turntable. I wrote nothing but reveled in my giddy muteness. I chopped vegetables and paid bills. I delivered hot tea to Stella when she was studying and read aloud to her while she soaked in our rust-stained tub. The salad days, they're called, though I've no clue why.

It took her a while to tell me she was pregnant. Stella claims she wanted to wring as much happiness out of the unclouded present as she could—and that if perhaps she didn't say it aloud, didn't grant it that oral credence, it might pass like

a fever. That conversation, when it finally came, was pocked with terrible long silences. I told her it was up to her, what to do, though I was hoping she'd abort the pregnancy. We were young, rootless, intent on scouring the ends of the earth. And I doubted—correctly, as it turned out—my potential as a father. The next day she made an appointment at a clinic in Gentilly and for the next two weeks we drifted in slow awful orbit around the unspoken. I had nightmares I didn't reveal to her; or rather, not nightmares, but oblique dreams about losing things. One in which Charles's prized guitar was stolen from my car, another about my share of the rent money disappearing from my desk drawer. On the couch one night we watched a movie, a late-night replaying of *Brian's Song*, and at the end, when James Caan's character died, I noticed she was crying—sobbing. I put my arms around her and said, "I forgot how sad the ending to this movie was," and she replied, quickly, "I'm not crying because James Caan is dead." Just as quickly I said, "I know," but that was a lie. For all I knew she could have been mourning James Caan; the truth was, I didn't know what she was feeling. When we went to bed that night I lay there holding her in my arms, spooning, until the typical sprouting of a hard-on prompted me to shimmy backwards beneath the sheets, to skitter as far away as I could get from her. I didn't want her to feel it. *She'll realize it was me*, I thought dumbly. *Me that did it to her, me that's making her cry.*

She didn't ask me to go with her but I did. The clinic occupied a house on a residential street, with only a vague insignia on the exterior—some archetypal female figure, in a robe, raising her hands to the sky—to distinguish it from its neighbors. There was a guard outside, too, a fat chainsmoking black guy who avoided eye contact. Inside, a waiting room evoked a struggling inner-city dental office, with magazines enfolded in those SUBSCRIPTION EXPIRING! THIS IS YOUR LAST ISSUE! wrappers and Gordon Lightfoot's "Rainy Day People" being

piped from ceiling speakers. I held her hand until her name was called. I hadn't brought anything to read, as that seemed inappropriate, so mostly I stayed outside and smoked cigarettes, uncomfortably sharing an ashtray with the guard. But I had time for only one or two cigarettes, because within fifteen minutes Stella appeared on the porch. Her cheeks were red and blistered with tears and she was clutching her thin sweater-coat to her as if stricken with a paralyzing chill. "I'm sorry," she said. "I can't go through with it. Bennie, I'm sorry but I can't." I moved to embrace her but she stepped back. "No," she said. "No, let's go. Let's please please get out of here."

The best that I can say about the next eight months is that we tried. We cleared out the second bedroom, which had just been transformed into my writing room, and installed a crib and a changing table. We bought *Goodnight Moon* and *Bedtime for Frances* at the Maple Street Book Shop and, from a French Quarter shop, some souvenir voodoo dolls we thought would be kooky/funny to stock in the crib. Because we needed money, I jumped to the other side of the bar at the Exchange, switching from barfly to bartender; Felix the Fat even put a plastic jar with a sign that read BENNIE'S BABY FUND on the bar, though that disappeared as soon as Stella heard about it. At night I put my ear to her belly and tried to listen and feel but always there was nothing. "You don't *feel* that?" she would say. "There. That one. That was a kick." I didn't. Often I was aimlessly angry and sometimes I was thrilled but mostly I was terrified. One night, after closing the bar, I drank myself unconscious, and the next morning Felix called an ambulance because he couldn't rouse me from the floor. He later told me he even tried kicking me in the nuts. As you'd expect, Stella wasn't pleased. A few nights later the sounds of something shattering woke me around three A.M. Stella's side of the bed was empty so I called out her name. More crashes & shatters. I ran to the kitchen and found her standing over the sink, sobbing while throwing our dishes

and glasses in one at a time. Shards were everywhere. I held her and let her cry and then led her back to bed before cleaning up the sharp mess. We never spoke of it again despite the conspicuous barrenness of our cupboards.

Stella Clarinda Ford was born in January: The name Stella was for her mother, of course, and Clarinda we cribbed from Robert Burns ("Fair Empress of the Poet's Soul, and Queen of Poetesses . . ."). It occurs to me that I should also clarify the surname, i.e. Ford and not Gniech. That was my father's doing in the months before I was born. Miss Willa, bound by propriety to marry the Polish exterminator who'd impregnated her, nonetheless refused to become Willa Gniech. ("A Willa Gniech sounds like a troll from Norse mythology," she told Henryk. "Or an epic sneeze.") So without consulting her he went down to the courthouse and changed his name to the most American one he could conjure: Henry Ford. (His ignorance of his chosen namesake's anti-Semitism, considering what he'd been through during the war, added another layer of ridiculousness to it. Yet he was devoutly loyal ever after to Ford vehicles and when he later became a mechanic he would joke that he preferred working on Fords because it was a "family bizz-a-ness.") There was loose talk between Stella and me, prior to Stella Jr.'s birth, about dropping the Ford surname for the authentic Gniech, partly to horrify my mother, but Stella Sr. couldn't help agreeing about the epic sneeze. ("Or an obscene Russian drinking toast," she added. "*Stella Gniech!*")

When I held my daughter in my arms for the first time, naturally I broke down crying. She was so beautiful and small—a gorgeous pink speck of life. But I should also confess that I was drunk almost beyond recognition. I was working when Stella's water broke but she said it was okay, her mother was there, and since the labor would no doubt be long I could join her as soon as my shift was over. But the labor wasn't long and not two hours later her mother called the bar to announce the birth. Of

course everybody bought me shots and there was a grand brou-haha with many more rounds of congratulatory shots and, as sometimes happens when you're drinking, time slipped away. All the regulars stayed past closing and Felix locked the doors and brought out some champagne, and Crazy Jane, slapping the bar, called for cognac which she pronounced "COG-nack." When I finally got to the hospital I was so brazenly sloshed that a policeman tried to stop me from entering but I said my new baby daughter was in there so he accompanied me up to the maternity ward. He was standing right beside me when I lifted Stella Jr. from the hospital crib, tears dribbling from my eyes, along with a nurse who hovered nearby with her hands splayed out to catch the baby if I dropped her. "Go home, Bennie," Stella's mother told me. A London-born professor of British lit at Pepperdine, she had this crisp way of speaking that made her every utterance sound like an arch dismissal; when she was truly dismissing you, it struck like lightning. "For God's sake take yourself home." Stella was asleep the whole time and I lightly kissed her forehead before the policeman escorted me outside. As I staggered off into the dark he advised me to put some sausage-biscuits in my belly, adding a shout of congratu-lations when I was almost too far away to hear.

DEAR AMERICAN AIRLINES, enclosed please find my sciatic nerve. Due to the wear and tear on it from hours upon hours in this miserable fucking O'Hare seating—these patent-pending O'Chairs—I am sending it to you for speedy repair. A return envelope is also enclosed, which you may address to me care of the wheelchair bank across from Gate K8, Chicago, Ill.

I'm not kidding about the wheelchairs. In fact, I'm planted in one right now. They're unattended and apparently free-range and since I saw some young buck lounging in another one, I figured what the hell. Obviously I promise to jump out

at the first sight of a struggling cripple. They're actually the most comfortable spots in the airport save for the "Sleep Number" bed on display in the alleyway between the K and H concourses, which the young buck informs me is currently under siege. "Some dude offered the salesguy, like, two hundred bucks to let him sleep on it tonight," he told me. "Then some other dude anted up five hundred. There's, like, no hotel rooms in the whole freakin' city. They're totally gonna be fighting over that bed by midnight. God, that'd be awesome. The salesguy looks freaked." I suggested that I might wheel myself over there and try to con some Samaritans into lifting me onto the bed, and then wait to see who'd actually try to evict a napping cripple. The kid loved this idea. "Dude," he said respectfully, "you're sick."

I realize that the preceding explained almost nothing about my current predicament—nix that; *our* current predicament —and for that I apologize. "I'm getting there," as I sometimes tell editors inquiring about the pace of my translations. And I hope I'm not laying too much on you but for the first time in my life I'm trying to be honest, trying to set the record straight. You must understand that, at this point, running my life through the spin cycle isn't liable to do me any good. Self-mythologizing, like drinking for fourteen hours a day, will eventually grind you into residue. You look in the mirror one morning and realize: That face, this life, these weren't my intention. Who's that baggy-eyed motherfucker and how'd he get into my mirror? That said, I would've no doubt saved us both a lot of grief had I just claimed up front to be on my way to L.A. to donate my left kidney to a bedridden orphan named Tiny something-or-other. We could have bidden each other hello and farewell in the space of a single heartwarming page. Yeah, well. Yet another opportunity that I've pissed away with words.

From my vantage in this wheelchair I can see the sunset

through the windows. It's a brilliant, operatic one, flame-colored, with the planes cooking on the tarmac luminescent with orange glints. A postcard of hell as seen from purgatory. Or heaven, it's so hard to tell from here.

- - - -

BUT LET'S RETURN TO '79. I'll shoot for brevity, but as should be clear it's not my strong suit.

My Stella was never the reckless sort—a birth-control pill snafu, rather than unguarded passion, had brought us to the present—but I was nonetheless surprised, once we were all home, by the degree of her protectiveness with Stella Jr., whom I called "Speck." Stella claimed I held her wrong, scolded me for tickling her because I might "upset her organs," asked me not to change her diapers anymore because I wasn't thorough enough with the wiping and sometimes forgot to dash her bottom with powder. Once I tried dancing with Speck—a clumsy little father-daughter two-step through the living room—and Stella leapt off the couch as if I'd been winding up my arm to toss Speck out the window. "You're going to *hurt* her," she said, stealing her away with an ironic roughness. She'd get the baby to sleep every night in the crib but after a few hours Speck would cry and Stella would carry her to our bed. At this point I would have to leave because Stella was worried I'd roll over and smother the baby, so after a few weeks I gave up trying and started making myself a bed on the couch on my nights off from the bar. It was lonely out in the living room, so I reverted to old habits by mixing consolatory batches of vodka-tonics. Because I knew Stella would be disturbed by the sight of empty Smirnoff fifths, I hid my empties behind the books in the bookcase and sneaked them out *en masse* when the Stellas were out walking or "making groceries" as we said in New Orleans.

As to those groceries: Stella's parents were helping us finan-

cially and my own mother was intermittently generous (she thought it was poor taste to give money so she peppered the nursery with Steiff teddy bears and pewter rattles from Maison Blanche; all this while our television sat atop salvaged cinder blocks and we shared a single water glass). But money was still tight, so I picked up an extra shift at the Exchange after Bobby, who worked the choice Friday and Ladies' Night shifts, got pissed at Felix in the wee hours and knocked him to the floor with a fifth of Cluny Scotch.

Which brings me to my own issue with violence at the bar. Some lawyers came in one evening—the neighborhood was changing, its fixer-upper houses and vegetarian, drum-circle vibe attracting what would later come to be called yuppies— and were sitting at the corner by the door getting rip-roaring drunk on gin martinis, which were then and there so unfashionable that I actually had to look up how to make one. Bona fide asshole types—the kind of guys still wearing their college ring at forty and telling you what channel they "need" the TV over the bar to be on. One of them was talking about a paralegal he'd recently "knocked up" and chortling about it, which elicited a caustic brag from another that he'd been to the abortion clinic so many times they'd given him a "Buy Ten, Get the Next One Free" card.

I'd been drinking pretty hard—standard protocol behind the bar at the Exchange—and, to boot, a day earlier I'd had a rough row with Charles who'd called me a "washout" who should "stick to breeding" since that's where my true talents seemed to lie. All of which, I'm sure, colored my subsequent actions.

I mixed the Buy-Ten-Get-One-Free guy what's known in the trade as a "cement mixer": a jigger of Bailey's Irish Cream paired with a jigger of lime juice. This combination produces a curdling-type reaction in the mouth, instantly transforming the liquids into a cheesy, semisolid wad. It's a folkloric cocktail

for wreaking vengeance, not for drinking. Because they were all wearing swell neckties I even carefully layered it like a *pousse café*.

"Compliments of the house, and appreciate y'all stopping in," I said, sliding it in front of Buy-Ten then turning my back to him. I heard Buy-Ten say thanks and imagined him puffing up ever so slightly: *Dig this, boys, I'm a hero of the loafing class*. B. B. Mike was sitting down near that end of the bar and had witnessed the making of the drink with the quizzical, head-cocked look of a bewildered but ugly puppy. From his expression alone, as he watched Buy-Ten throw it back, I rightly determined the impact of my cement mixer, but the sound effects were equally suggestive: a gurgling-gargling, a gasping for air, followed by a resounding and spitty *What the fuck?!?* When I turned around, Buy-Ten's tongue was hanging limply from his mouth and his tie was marbled with cum-like streaks of curdled Irish liqueur. I could probably have weaseled my way out of the situation at that point—truth be told, I was feeling almost sorry for the guy—had B. B. Mike, a short, stout cigar-chomper who was a dead ringer for Paulie in the *Rocky* movies, not launched into the largest, longest laugh of his life. His cap tipped backwards off his head and I believe he even held his chest with one hand while pointing with the other. I had no idea that shrieks such as those could emanate from a man such as that. Nor had I any idea that a trio of Uptown lawyers would scramble over a bar to kick the living shit out of an errant bartender. (At the time, I suppose I thought they took priest-like vows.)

They pulped me pretty grimly—I had to get stitches in two places and both my eyes were blackened—but the rest of the bar's occupants, excepting B. B. Mike who was winded from laughing so hard, mounted a riotous counteroffensive that resulted in one of the lawyers (the paralegal-knocker-upper) getting his jaw broken and face lacerated by—you guessed it—a fifth of Cluny's. (Felix the Fat never served Cluny's again, call-

ing it "cursed.") It was an unusual barfight in that it took place almost entirely *behind* the bar, the spatial equivalent of a heavyweight boxing title being fought in a shower stall, which also meant there was lots of damage. Dead Fred's urn got knocked from its sacred upper shelf and his ashes were strewn everywhere. I heard later that Felix made the sign of the cross nonstop while hosing Dead Fred off the floor mats.

I got suspended for two weeks but that wasn't nearly the worst of it. The *Times-Picayune* got wind of the brawl and an overambitious reporter framed it as a repercussion of the neighborhood's tensions—the junkies/hippies/freaks rising up against the suited gentrifiers. The reporter even referenced Hunter S. Thompson's old Freak Power campaign in Aspen and made ironic hay about the bar being named the Turf Exchange. It would have been nice to be a folk hero but the story also noted that the cause of the initial fight was "a conflict over a woman," a not entirely incorrect misconception that must (I've always presumed) have stemmed from B. B. Mike who'd been eavesdropping on the lawyers like me. Probably he said, in classical Mike-speak, that the lawyers had been "talking shit about some broad," and that was enough for the reporter who, ambition notwithstanding, never gave me the courtesy of a call.

Imagine Stella's reaction. Then square it, and square it again, then multiply it by crazy. She'd been suspicious when I came home from the emergency room, all stitched-up and black-eyed, because I couldn't really explain the cause of the quarrel. "Babe, they were jackass *lawyers*," I said, as if that resolved everything. But she knew my conciliatory, hippie-poet ways—not to mention the high tolerance I had, owing to my grandfather, for New Orleans lawyers—well enough to sense missing pieces. But what could I say? We'd never talked about what happened at the clinic—she flatly refused—and there seemed no exculpatory defense, in her eyes, for my reaction to

Buy-Ten's smarmy boast. "What?" I imagined her screaming. "Were you *envious?*" Or perhaps taking the opposite position and accusing me of secretly hating her because she'd chosen, on her own, to abort Speck—nevermind that she didn't follow through with it, and that I was the one who drove her to Gentilly. (By this time I'd been theorizing that her taut overprotectiveness with Stella Jr. might derive from that turnabout.) Frankly I didn't want to reintroduce the word "abortion" into our vocabulary; the psychic wounds still oozed. And what's worse: I *couldn't* honestly explain what had happened—why I'd poured that cement mixer—because to do that would expose the great black hole that I was feeling in my life, the loneliness and constriction and sense of dreams irredeemably deferred, the dankness I felt mixing myself my seventh vodka-tonic on the couch at night, and I didn't see how I could confess all this to Stella without her concluding that I didn't love Speck, her, or the both of them. So I stonewalled.

I kept stonewalling even after the paper arrived two mornings later, which in retrospect was resoundingly stupid. As the old saw counsels: If you're trapped in a hole, stop digging. That morning we had a terrible fight made even more terrible by Speck's relentless bawling. When Stella demanded to know who the "whore" was, I broke into mirthless but uproarious laughter because the word "whore" was so ludicrous and un-Stella-like. The laughter enraged her enough that she ordered me to move out and, to help me start the process, in a frenzy she swept shelves' worth of my books off the bookcase, letting them crash to the floor. Of course it didn't help that a half-dozen empty Smirnoff bottles rolled after them. Clink, clink. Clinkclinkclink.

Overwhelmed, she collapsed to the floor in a puddle of sobs and let me hold her there for a time and even let me fetch her a glass of water which I thought spelled progress. Very calmly she asked again who the "whore" was, and this time I didn't laugh

but told her, with proper gravitas, that there was no whore and never had been. "Oh, Bennie," she said, wagging her head. "Bennie, Bennie, goddamnit Bennie." She studied the water glass for a long silent while, sitting amidst the empty fifths and the splayed books, before smashing it into my face. Yep: surprised me too. Blood and glass exploded everywhere and I was instantly blind in one of my blackened eyes. Dumbfounded, all I could say was "You know that was our only glass." I held a reddening t-shirt to my face while Stella drove me to the hospital with poor Speck wailing in the carseat. When they asked me what had happened, in the emergency room, I proclaimed myself a "revolutionary" and said the nurses needed only to check the day's *Picayune* for proof. That brought the attention of the cop on duty whom I satisfied with a story about colliding with a water glass in my wife's hand when I bent down to pick up the (fictional) cat. "Must be *some* pussy," he said, whether referring to the wife or the cat I wasn't sure.

We lasted another eight months, some of them better than others. Because we were low on cash, Stella removed my stitches rather than paying a doctor to do it. It was a weirdly placid night, almost beautiful in its way, or rather *belle laide* as the French would say: beautiful-ugly. I sat in a ladderback chair beneath the gothic chandelier in our living room, lightly sipping a vodka-tonic, as she pulled out the stitches with tweezers while Speck rolled on the floor giggling and saying *dur-dur-dur.* Maybe it was the vodka but that night as we made love for the first time in weeks I found myself weeping and unable to stop. I was crying so badly that we had to pause midway through. With her head against my rising, falling chest Stella asked, softly, if I was crying from joy or sadness and I responded, "Both." There in the dark she sponged away my tears with her lips. We finished with gorged screams, more than a rarity for us, and Stella fell into a contented-looking sleep, a quarter-smile on her face. Since childbirth she'd developed a snore

—a gentle chordal exhale, like someone sighing through the low holes of a harmonica—and that night I lay awake listening to the music of her breathing and wondering what the hell love was and if this was it. After a while I gingerly lifted her arm off me and made myself a vodka-tonic which I drank sitting on the edge of the bed, watching her sleep. There was no moon but the streetlamp outside the bedroom window cast a white glow upon her that seemed nothing short of sacred. In these moments it was easy to believe that she loved me and I loved her and that everything was as it should be, in an alternate galaxy for which that streetlamp was the sun.

Yet such nights were uncommon and perhaps it's unduly sentimental to dwell upon them. Near the end I was trying to write again and it wasn't going well. Post-Speck, Stella had abandoned poetry and I felt I was expected to do the same. "You're a *father*," she said, as if drawing an impenetrable line between poet and parent. "So was William Carlos Williams," I said. "You're not Williams," came her accurate if deflating rejoinder. Charles and I patched things up and I took to drinking with him on my nights off, first occasionally and then regularly. Charles cultivated a posse of art-minded coeds and there always seemed to be some fresh and earthily alluring girl with an apparent Eeyore fetish telling me I looked "sad," brushing the hair out of my eyes until I'd swat her hand away. One night, in the alley beside the Exchange where I'd led a member of Charles's coterie longing to share a joint, I found myself kissing a twenty-one-year-old from a place called Hot Coffee, Mississippi, whose humid accent was like sorghum to my addled mind. This brief interlude might have tipped further had she not whispered, "I'll do the things she won't." I'm not sure why I was so offended but when Charles tried to stop me from storming out of the bar I pushed his arm away and told him to stay the fuck away from me blah blah fuck you blah. Once at home I lay on the couch, as always, and drank myself

to sleep in front of the salt-colored static on the TV. Maybe I even talked to the static, blah blah fuck you blah, I don't know. That night I hated everyone, particularly myself. This feeling only deepened the next morning when I awoke to the sight of Stella sitting a foot away from me atop the coffee table, crying. It was a mellow, defeated cry. "Look at you," she said to me. I didn't protest, or ask what to look for. Frankly I didn't even try to look.

When the end finally came, we were having—to my mind —another one of those frail good nights. Stella cooked her famous spaghetti & meatballs ("If I shut my eyes almost but not quite all the way, when you're cooking this," I used to tell her, "I see you as an old fat Italian mama with a dark mustache"; she hated this though I meant it with vast affection), and *Fantasy Island* was on the TV set. Stella's adorably snobbish contempt for TV popped like a soap bubble after Speck was born. Sometimes I'd find her and the baby curled on the couch, watching gameshows—hypnotized by Wink Martindale. The downstairs neighbors were out of town so I entertained Speck with some cloddish tapdancing on the old wood floor and even Stella—I think—was laughing. Or maybe I just imagined she was laughing—desire painting perception. In any case, this was the scene: the three of us on the couch, awash in the television's bluesy glow though mostly ignoring *Fantasy Island* because it turned out to be a repeat, Stella and me trading our child back and forth, rubbing our noses against hers, tickling her lips to make her grin. To me the evening looked and felt like peace—not domestic détente, but the real thing. A field of lavender, a northern lake at dawn. Or whatever air-freshener imagery best evokes peace.

Cradling Speck, I said some nonsensical things to her, or rather partly sensical: some sugary riffs about her future. "One day you'll be big, and wear dresses," things like that. I wasn't really paying attention to what I was saying—it was sweet-talk,

lulling blather—until I said, "And one day I'm going to walk you down the aisle and hate every second of it," which caused Stella to abruptly stiffen. "Jesus," she murmured.

I sat there bemused. "What?"

She looked away, pursed her lips, then stood up and walked to the door to the gallery. Finally she called me an asshole.

"Because I said I'd hate every second of it? It was a joke. Just a . . . dumb daddy joke."

She was clenching her eyes shut with the heel of her palm pressed against her forehead. "Stella," I said.

"Because you're *lying* to her," she said finally. She peered up at the ceiling and I could see that she'd been clenching her eyes to stanch the flow of tears. Now they ran loose. "I can take you lying to me but hearing you lie to her . . . Jesus, Bennie, we're not doing this anymore." "We" meant the Stellas. "We can't take you anymore."

Back up, I told her. Whoa. We were having a good night. "No," she said. "*You* were having a good night. There are no fucking good nights for us. There's just us wondering if you're coming home and wondering why we should give a damn. *If* we give a damn." I told her that her saying "us" was a little over the top, that dragging Speck into it was unfai—

"Fuck you! Do you hear me? *Fuck* you!" Screaming, pointing, rage as violent and unexpected as lightning shot down from a cloudless blue sky. "Do you have any fucking idea what you've done to me? You were just a goddamned summer fling, a way to pass the time, and now"—slapping her chest—"look. what. the. fuck. you've done to me."

"Because you got pregnant? Is that what this is about?"

A groaning sound. "You don't *get* it. You piece of shit, you don't get it. This has nothing to do with me getting pregnant and nothing to do with her—"

You just said it *was* about her.

"It's about you, Bennie. You don't care about us—not as

people, anyway, not as your daughter and your daughter's mother, not as human beings, as *flesh*."

That's—

"No, *listen*. All you care about, and barely, is the *idea* of us and the *idea* of you sticking by us—you're here in this room right now because you're loyal to the *idea* of Bennie fucking Ford acting like a man and taking care of his family—no, actually I think it's something worse, sometimes I think we're your excuse for failure—but not because you *want* to be here, not because it matters to you that we're here together. We're just more of your props, Bennie. Just like your Lucky Strikes and your stupid loud Underwood typewriter and that stupid tweed cap that makes you look like an out-of-work caddie. We're all of us, cigarettes and child, just movable props in The Life of Benjamin Ford, little figments of your ego."

—

"Jesus, okay, fine. Let's call it your anti-ego. Every day you wake up and try to, to hew to some delusional idea, the same way your mother does though at least she's got a doctor's note, and by the middle of the day, when life isn't aligning with the idea, you start drinking. Why? Because drinking pushes the life and the idea of it closer together, makes them both so foggy that you can't tell them apart. So you keep drinking until, until they're one and the same but by that time it's all fog, and by that time nothing exists outside of your head at all. And then it's *all* idea, and no life. Have you ever even *thought* how the fuck that makes us feel? No. No. Because we're just employees of, of your imagination, and every day, Bennie, every day"—voice cracking—"we feel that imagination turning more and more away from us, or against us."

—

"That's bullshit. My god, you and your *bullshit*. You couldn't even make it to her *birth*. And do you know why? Because the, the actuality of it didn't matter. It didn't matter to you! It was

already complete in your head, it was finished. You were a father! *You!* It was all about you, your idea of you, the you preening inside your head, the *word* of it—*father*. So what did it matter that me and my mother and your new daughter were at the hospital? Do you have any fucking clue how that *humiliated* me? A cop dragging you off the elevator to see your child? The nurse asked me, asked me the next morning if I wanted to talk to a *counselor*. She wasn't even on duty when you came in —she'd heard about it from the other nurses. With my mother sitting there, twirling her goddamn pearls, she asked me if I needed a *counselor*. That was supposed to be the happiest day of my life and I spent it vomiting *because of you*, not looking my mother in the eye *because of you*—"

—

"Bennie, life is *real*. It's hard and it hurts and it's nothing like the world in our heads and at some point everyone grows up and realizes that and it doesn't mean they've given up or sold out or died inside, it just means they've learned that the ideas are just that, they're smoke rings, vapor, and that people have to live in the world as it is—"

—

"Give her to me. How dare you. Give her to me now."

—

"Coming from you that's meaningless. Maybe you love yourself loving me but I don't think you could feel the distinction —I don't think you're *capable* of feeling it—"

—

"Yes. Maybe. Maybe I did love you, for a time. But does it even matter anymore, Bennie? I mean, so what? And did it ever really matter to you if I did? Did it? How could it have?"

—

"We want you out of our lives. I don't know what else to say."

—

"Look at her. She's screaming. Do you see what you're *doing* to her? Get away from us, Bennie. Get away. I swear to Christ I'll kill you—"

—

Oh fuck this fuck this fuck this. What am I doing? Some twit wearing camper shorts and a WORLDWIDE MINISTRIES, INC. t-shirt just knelt beside my wheelchair and asked gently if I was okay. No, I take that back, he wasn't a twit. *Enough*, goodbye.

- - - -

ON A BENCH BY THE SEA Walenty lifted his left pantleg above his hinged knee and stared at the false limb, running his hand along its length the way a runner might massage away a cramp. The wood—English willow, the weeping tree— was lacquered, but already the lacquer had worn off in spots and it might be possible to get a splinter; he would have to re-lacquer it every so often, he thought, would have to repaint himself as a steam engine gets refinished, an oddly unnatural task. When the shell had hit he'd been scurrying uphill toward the jagged ruins of a stone house where several Nazi infantrymen were making an ill-considered stand. The Nazis were surrounded and the outcome was inevitable. There was no mystery to the ending, no suspense in the proceedings; all of them, the Nazis and Walenty's regiment and the British troops flanking the north side, were numbers and symbols in an algebraic problem that had already been solved.

When the shell hit, it threw him backwards down the hill. He felt his arm break on the loose remnants of a rock wall —even the muffled crack of the bone splitting registered —and when finally he was still he reached first for his arm, hoping to adjust it to somehow lessen the pain. It seemed like several minutes before he realized his leg was gone.

There was no pain, only a sharp dullness like that of frost-
bite. Below his thigh the flesh resembled the dangling ten-
tacles of a squid. His vision kept reddening which puzzled
him until he brought a hand to his eyes and realized that it
was blood, leaking from his head. Even his ears were filling with it. He lay back on the stones and let the blood flow
out of him. He thought he should pray but couldn't bring
himself to make the words. Instead he thought of the *mako-
wiec* his mother used to make for dessert on rare special days
when he was a boy. Expecting the end, he consoled himself
with visions of poppyseed cake. Later, in the field hospital,
his mind creamy with morphine, Walenty had been unsure
what disturbed him more: his lost limb and the shrapnel
holes in his forehead, or that the only crumbs of life that
he found to cling to, when dying on the battlefield, were
cake crumbs.

It's nighttime now, and after a couple of trembly but fortify-
ing cigarettes outside, and yet another joyous pat-down at the
security checkpoint, I've moved to the bar at the Chili's Too
across from G9. I had to wait in a line ten-deep for a barstool,
and I can feel the hot stares from those still waiting, like poison
darts thwacking my backside. Ouch! I suppose it *is* the height
of rudeness to occupy this valuable stool with no set purpose in
mind, other than blasting off page after page of this interminable letter while sipping $1.75 club sodas (no ice) and occasion-
ally checking in on Walenty—all this while my fellow refugees stand in puckered silence, transferring their carry-on bags
from one achy shoulder to the other, wanting only a cold Mi-
chelob and the televised box scores. It crosses my mind to buy
them all a beer but they're mostly devoid of free hands plus
there's probably a Homeland Security rule against that. Sorry,
chumps. No beer Samaritan for you.

I see from the television hanging in the corner that the price
of oil is skyrocketing and that the NASDAQ was down for the

day. Poor NASDAQ. I may send it a get-well card—something cheery, of course, like a Snoopy card. But horrors! The British pound sterling dropped against the almighty U.S. greenback! But wait—what's this? Something called "Light Sweet Crude" was up .31! Dear American Airlines, I haven't the faintest idea what "Light Sweet Crude" is but what an irresistible heading for a personals ad, don't you think? Anyway I'm thrilled that it's up. I might also add that I hope your own stock is through the goddamn roof. Prosperity for all, la-ti-da, la-ti-da. Let's all dance the dollar dance with our fannies in the air.

To be honest, this is the first bar I've set foot inside in five years, and, to be even more honest, I'm not entirely sure why I haven't ordered a drink. At this juncture, fighting the familiar old temptations of the bottle(s) would be like swatting away a wasp while being chewed by an alligator. What's the point?

Eh, resolve. *Resolve*, right: the hayseed cousin of ambition. Doan wanna change the world, jes wanna get the crop in. Mind you, not resolve *against* the booze—I never stopped loving it, even when it was trying to kill me—but, instead, resolve *for* something else, a fixed set of chores yet to be crossed off my list. Look, with the way my brain is wired, it might take me ten years to finish that drink and dammit if I don't have things to do. Still, it's nice to see some old ex-pals. Mr. Galliano there in the back, that tall, lean, goosenecked wallflower. Gentleman Jack out front, that farm-muscled Tennessee bully. Ah, and Smirnoff, Smirnoff, my long-gone true love. We had us a time, didn we? (Cue the barroom piano.) But where the hell did all these other svelte-looking vodkas come from? There's a complete row of them here, out front, preening like pageant contestants in push-up bras. All foreign to me, they must be the new young things, eager and dewy. Anyway, this used to be my crowd. What can I say? I grew up in New Orleans, where cirrhosis of the liver is listed as "Natural Causes" on a death certificate. Was a flailing (flailed?) poet who, corrupted first

by Keats and then by Freud, believed that truth was locked up in the attic of the subconscious, demanding blotto liberation. Developed a profound affinity for intoxicated women, not to mention targeted memory loss. My sweaters had holes. My dog died. I missed the bus, I hated the cold, was allergic to dust, can't dance worth a damn. She left me. I left her. Life went on too long. Or like Berryman wrote: "Man, I been thirsty."

And now my eye catches sight of my face reflected in the mirror behind the bar. A raisin at rest. Hair gray, of course (it went gray at thirty), sprawling out from beneath the tweed driver's cap that I've managed to keep on my head since my teens despite all the things that head has done to itself. Face jowly, wrinkled in all the wrong places, the fishhook scar under my eye—this from where Stella cracked me in the face with that water glass—evident even from this distance. The eyes themselves gone increasingly small and crinkly, as if backpedaling their way into my head. According to my mother, I am overweight—one of my favorite of her Post-it notes: "How did you get so fat?"—but in this room, packed with midwesterners, I seem of median girth. If I suggested to the big-bellied fellow next to me, for instance, that his wiener was purple, he would not be able to dispute me without borrowing a makeup mirror; he has doubtlessly not seen his pecker in years.

Oops, he caught me staring. (At his groin, no less.) Turns out his name is Bob, he's in the radon-removal business, he lives in Oshkosh which is where he's trying to return to after a "bullshit" meeting in Houston, thinks the Yankees don't have a prayer this year, and he opened the conversation, rather perceptively, by saying, "Whoa, you're really scribbling away there. Whaddaya, writing your will?" Hahaha, no, says I, an angry letter to American Airlines. "Well, hell, if you want me to sign it, you can make it a petition." (Dear American Airlines, this is actually not a bad idea. Neither is a full-blown riot. Keep me here past roughly eight tomorrow morning, my

last shot at making the nuptials, and I'll be the one handing out torches and pitchforks.) "But they're all the same, you know," he said. "United, Delta, US Air. Pick your dick flavor." (Note: He could've said "dictator." His mouth was full of pretzels.) During the course of our exchange Bob rarely took his eyes off the televisions—there are four in range—and peppered his talk with screen-induced non sequiturs, e.g. "Geico. That little lizard is funny." Finally we exhausted our conversational topics and Bob said, "Don't let me keep you from your will. Feel free to leave me the bedroom set." I like Bob. A shame about his purple wiener.

I was never a belligerent drunk, you know. Not a *bad* one, in that sense. Never a fighter, if you discount that one incident with the lawyers which doesn't really qualify as a fight since the lawyers effortlessly squashed me. No, I was at first always a happy drunk, giddy and giggly, in love with whatever or whom-ever was near me, and then, at some point, a sad drunk, a quiet snuffler, mulling my dumpy ball of wax. It's all cyclical, is what they said at the meetings (which I mostly stopped attending a year ago, though every now and then, when the going gets iffy, I pop in with some donuts): The booze makes you happy but then it makes you sad but you want to be happy again so you drink more, repeat ad infinitum. Or in my case for about thirty years, give or take a bender. If it wasn't for the alcoholic coma I dropped into five years ago (not fun), and the forced re-hab that ensued (ditto), I've no reason to think I wouldn't still be drunk, and that this letter would have already spiraled into even more blathersome blather. Part of the "recovery process" requires apologizing to all those wounded by your drinking, and, for me, Stella Senior got the inaugural call. "What am I supposed to say, Bennie?" she said. Silence on the line. "What do you want to say?" was what I finally croaked out. "Thanks but no thanks," she said. I felt like a rejected telephone solici-tor. Click.

I'm reminded now, amidst this beery hubbub, watching a web of conversations spin itself through the room (they're all talking about you, dear American Airlines, and I'm afraid your name is mud), from Oshkosh Bob to the babyfat coed in the UMASS t-shirt doing Cuervo shots with her boyfriend (wheee!), on down the bar to the apparent honeymooners who unsuccessfully ordered champagne, to the mustachioed guy telling the unamused bartender, "Know what TSA stands for? Thousands Standing Around, get it?" and then me, here at the corner, nursing my gone-flat club soda while bobbing atop this frothy sea of chatter: The worst part of sobriety is the silence. The lonesome, pressurized silence. Like the way sound falls away when you're choking. Even when I drank alone, the vodka provided me with a kind of soundtrack—a rhythm, channeled voices, a brain crowded with noise and streaming color, the rackety blurred clutter of my decrepitude. At the meetings everyone talks about how much more vivid life is without the booze, but I think, though I never say, that vivid is the wrong word. Life is rather more *clear*. I'm supposed to be thankful for that clarity, I know, for being freed from that dissonant interior music, from all those flatulent trumpets in my brain, and for finally being able to see life as it is, me as I am. Lookit the world and its blinding rays of light, feel the warmth on my new skin. I'm supposed to be thankful, I know, for being finally shucked down to the core of me. But forgive me, I can't help it: Thanks but no thanks.

I've got to get out of here.

– – – –

HOW BANEFULLY PERFECT. I huffed my way back to K8 where I settled myself safely into one of these torturous gray chairs only to discover, upon cracking Alojzy's book, that Walenty is getting sauced with some new friends. Out of the frying pan, into the fire.

The men were drinking German beer and were welcoming to the point of suspicion. They were already drunk, at lunchtime, and many spoke in slurred, Serb-inflected accents which were difficult for Walenty to understand.

(He'd secured a grip on Italian during his long recovery at the Allied hospital in Rome, when the doctors kept operating and reoperating on his brain, but it was a loose grip.)

Others were foreign sailors whose Italian was more halting than his, but the sailors kept to the café's edges, focusing on their drinking with the seriousness of great athletes. Unfamiliar words whirred past Walenty but the warm beer was like nectar and the men were grinning and slapping their legs and falling from their chairs so Walenty nodded and smiled and when the men raised their glasses, which was often, he raised his as well, toasting indecipherable causes. To peace or more slaughter, to beer or death, to what is past or to come, he was never quite certain. *Alla Salute.*

To bring you up to speed, as they say, Walenty has been roaming Trieste since his morning coffee, overwhelmed by sunlit thoughts of the girl from the train station café. (Cartwheels across his heart, that's what she's doing.) He presumes this is owing to the kindness she showed him that morning, something unseen by him for many years. In 1939, when the Soviets invaded, he watched an old man in his village interrupt the beating of a twelve-year-old boy by shooting one of the boy's Russian assailants in the back with an antique hunting rifle. The old man was immediately killed, of course, machine-gunned into two equal pieces, and when the remaining soldier shouted for four men to come out to remove the old man's body, at least forty villagers trickled out from the doorways. That, Walenty thinks, was the last genuine moment of kindness he could recall. On a boxcar headed to a gulag in north-

ern Kazakhstan, he watched a pregnant woman suckle a starving and half-frozen man at her breast but he would not classify this as kind since the man forced himself upon the woman. She was too weary to resist and after a while closed her eyes and absently stroked his hair. In any case, Walenty now finds himself, lightheaded, in this seaside bar across from a wooden pier in Trieste they call the Molo Audace:

> One of the men, bearish and otherwise fierce-looking, with a black mustache draping his mouth almost completely, began to dance, a solitary *Šetnja*

(I haven't the foggiest what a *Šetnja* is; some type of dance, obviously.)

> that took him around and around the room. When he would encounter chairs or tables he would kick them away with comic aggravation, and everyone howled in delight save the pale she-dwarf who ran the café and whose squeaky protests were swiftly shouted down by demands for more beer.

(Ayyy . . . Alojzy is not this clunkish a writer. "She-dwarf"? Jesus. His translator is merely *verklempt*. Possibly incompetent, too. *Traduttore, traditore*, as the Italian pun goes: *translator, traitor*. Or rather, in this case [no pun extended]: *traduttore, minchione: translator, dumbass*.)

> Soon he came to Walenty and offered his arm. His intent seemed anything but insulting yet still Walenty hesitated. This bear had earned stout laughter for kicking away chairs and tables and, overencouraged, might be seeking to sustain the laughter by dropping the crippled newcomer to the floor. The bear would appear generous but clumsy while Walenty thrashed dumbly on the floorboards. Yet the bear was gently insistent and the other men were clapping and nodding yes so Walenty hooked his arm into the bear's and

away they went, dancing grand circles amidst the disheveled barroom. There was no music save the bear's murmury singing, so it was difficult to keep time, but around and around they went until they had exhausted the confines of the little café and they spilled onto the stones outside. All the men and even the blond dwarf followed them out into the sunlight and were soon clapping a rhythm. Startled children ran to watch them and fishermen stared blankly from the pier. The bear was smiling as he sang, closing his eyes as if to recall, with great force of will, something intensely private and peaceful, and Walenty, inspired, did the same. He scoured his mind but it dispensed him only a single image: the girl from the train station café bending to set down his coffee, the cup trembling musically on the saucer. It was not merely the freshest vision in his head, sprung to the forefront by virtue of its newness, or the most beautiful, or the most vivid, but rather the only vision in his head, like a night sky lit by just a single white star. His mind's near-emptiness made him dizzy, and twice he almost fell, but the bear held him tight by the arm and, with his giant head thrown back and his eyes clamped shut still, sang unknown words that filled the hollows of Walenty's mind as food fills a starving man's belly.

Which reminds me, I'm hungry.

IF I'M CALCULATING the time difference correctly, the rehearsal dinner is about to begin in L.A. The table is set with one chair—mine—having been removed, the place settings tightened to conceal an absence going now on twenty-eight years. Though, as Stella Jr. told me, it's technically not a rehearsal dinner: "More like a pre-ceremony get-together" at a "little Alice Waters-y place" on Melrose, is what she said. Well, Stella Jr. always was a good eater. We considered her a

prodigy for never spitting out mashed avocado and I swear to God she once ate an anchovy. My presence there tonight was her idea—a way to reacquaint ourselves, so to speak, before the hoopla of the "wedding." (Those damn quotation marks I keep horseshoeing around that word would probably offend her but I don't know what else to do. Their invitation deemed it a "commitment ceremony" but I can't bring myself to ape that hollowed-out language which smacks of a neutered Spivak pronoun or somesuch.) Tonight was her compromise, her way of sorta-maybe agreeing to allow me to walk her down the aisle. "Why don't you come Friday, Bennie?" she asked me on the phone. "Can you? It's just a little too weird for me to say yes now and then have you show up fifteen minutes before the ceremony. It's been a long time, y'know? I won't be *auditioning* you—nothing like *that*. It's just that I'd prefer to have a real face-to-face conversation with you before you trot me down the aisle. That's fair, right? I mean . . . what if you're a Republican?" We laughed together at that one, which felt good—a squirt of oil in the decayed & rusted joints of our bond.

Dear American Airlines, you should've seen me when the invitation arrived. My original thought was that it was some kind of cruel joke from Stella Sr.—her poisonous & long-simmered response to my attempt to make amends of five years ago. I was so obviously dumbfounded—turning the invitation over in my hands as if it would make more sense upside-down (commitment ceremony), checking and rechecking the envelope's address—that my dumpling Aneta, who delivered the mail to me at my desk, asked if a letter had been misdelivered. There was a bubble of hope in her voice because a misdelivered letter meant that she might have cause to knock at the door of our downstairs neighbor, a heavy-metal guitarist I call Minideth because, when I met him, he was wearing a t-shirt emblazoned with the word Megadeth and because he was then, as now, no more than five feet tall. Aneta is rip-roaringly fond

of Minideth despite the callous heartbreak he delivered her when he failed to acknowledge the plate of pierogies she once left, tremblingly, outside his door. I tried explaining to her that in New York no one trusts gifts and/or unattended food and that anyway she doesn't want to get tangled up with a rock 'n' roller, even a profoundly small one. (They're not like dogs, I explained. The bite of a small dog is the same as the bite of a big one.) A displaced farmgirl, Aneta has yet to develop the hard outer shell of cynicism that urban life demands—she is pure, exposed nougat. When the Times Square handbillers force a flyer into her hands she stops and reads it *in toto* and then hands it back with a sincere "thank you" which sometimes elicits an equally sincere "fuck you" from the handbillers. My mother and I used to bang the floor with the butt end of a broomstick whenever Minideth cranked up the amp volume while practicing—bruisy, barely muffled *ch-ch-chunk-chunk* riffs followed by orgasmically shrieksome solos—until one day Aneta scolded us. *A painter! A poet!* she said. *Complaining about another artist!* We relented without argument—less ashamed than flattered, I think, to be called artists, considering that both our creative spigots went dry years ago. I might add that it's truly difficult not to be heartplucked at seeing Aneta go dreamy & gooey at the sound of Minideth practicing—not to want Minideth to be telegraphing his unspoken, fuzzboxed love from one floor below. In those moments Aneta clicks off the television and, clutching a pillow to her chest, sits in reverent silence on the couch beside my mother, whose sour expression evidences a kind of aural indigestion but who puts up with it anyway. A couple weeks back I asked Miss Willa why. LOVE IS LOVE, she wrote on a Post-it. I scoffed, and told her that was a meaningless tautology. She shrugged.

"No, the letter is for me," I told Aneta, rereading the invitation. Still puzzling over my demeanor, she asked if it was bad news. "No," I said, "the opposite—I think." For the rest of

the day I was unable to work or concentrate on anything, even dinner which I typically prepare for Miss Willa and myself. (I picked up some frozen Salisbury steaks from Gristede's which my mother refused to acknowledge until I transferred her dinner from the compartmentalized plastic tray, but even then she just picked limply at the mushrooms.) My emotions kept seesawing: For a while I would feel anguished and stung, as if an old wound had been reopened, a scab scraped from my flesh, after which I'd feel elated and hope-swollen, as if I'd found the first pale crumb of a trail leading back to my life. Mostly, though, I was terrified. For decades I'd kept the sorrows & joys of that ex-life locked safely away, first by drinking, mixing passive self-pity with ice and vodka, and then later by the daily labor of *not* drinking. I don't mean to suggest, melodramatically, that I ceased to *function* because of it all — over the years I wrote & published & held jobs & maintained a dwindling number of friendships & even tucked into those years a laughably brief and impetuous marriage that isn't worth discussing. But a part of me had been amputated by what transpired between me and my Stellas — if I may continue, haplessly, in my fumbling for metaphors. And now here, courtesy of an embossed envelope, was my severed limb come back to me, the shredded ligaments still curling outward from its raw and oozing red core, the arteries still faintly pulsing.

Three shaky days later, on a Saturday afternoon, I called Stella Jr.; there was an RSVP number on the invitation, which I ran through an internet search engine to ensure it didn't belong to Stella Sr. I didn't know even the first words to say to her: *This is your father?* That struck me as a false title, even more fraudulent than Aneta deeming me a poet. (Ex-father, ex-poet, ex-drunk: Everything I am gets prefaced with an ex.) Therefore, "This is Bennie," I said, when I hooked her on the phone after several hangups on her voicemail. "Bennie who?" she said, and inside I buckled. So it *had*, after all, been a vi-

cious trick of Stella Sr.'s. "Bennie . . . Ford," I said, and then the voice said, "Oh, God. Let me get Stel," and I heard the voice whisper, "I think it's your dad," followed by a lengthy silence. With a prick, it occurred to me that I had no clue what my daughter's voice might sound like. I had only ever heard her coo and cry when she was the small pink creature I called Speck. I, who lived on words, who had eaten them, drunk them, dreamt them, created them, who even now still inhaled and exhaled them, transforming them, in my translations, as a body converts oxygen to carbon dioxide, had vanished from her life before words had entered it. The one thing I might've given her, I didn't.

"Bennie," she said. The voice was lilting, sunny, freewheeling, recognizably Californian. "Wow."

Not knowing what to say, I said, "Maybe you can imagine, but I don't know what to say."

"You got the invitation."

"It was very nice."

"Mom and I went round and round about that," she said. "I won." I had to make a quick little mental leap to connect "Mom" with Stella Sr., as my brain wasn't equipped with that particular equal sign. Mom. The word flipflopped inside my head: Wow. "How *are* you, Bennie?" she said.

"How are *you?*" I replied.

"I'm good, I'm great." We went on like this for a bit. "Hey," she said, "this feels like a weird question to ask—I guess it *is* a weird question, sorry—but is Grandma still alive? I heard she had a stroke or something."

Grandma = Miss Willa, another mental leap across sharp rocks. Mom = Stella. Everyone had a stock role to play but me: The part of the Bennie will be played by Bennie. "She's alive, yes," I told her. "She's in the next room, in fact, watching an *Iron Chef* rerun. The stroke calmed her down a bit. I don't

know how much you know about her. Kind of a yin and yang to it."

An anxious, brittle laugh. "I don't know *what* to say to that."

"Let's just say she used to be more of a handful. Hey, look," I said, sensing in her laughter a wave to surf in on, "I'd like to come to your wedding."

"Seriously? That's fantastic." Genuine-sounding glee.

"And I'm looking forward to meeting the young man." This, of course, was knuckleheaded on two disproportionate counts. One: "*the young man*"? What was that—a flaccid Robert Young impersonation? I winced as the words spilled across my lips. Second:

"Oh, Bennie, yikes. Syl is a woman. I'm gay. I'm sorry, you couldn't have known . . ."

"No, no, hey . . . groovy." *Groovy*, that's what I said. In ransacking my mind for something to say that wouldn't come across as shocked or disapproving or priggish or homophobic, none of which I was, or had any right to be, I burped the word "groovy," which I don't believe I'd uttered since the age of fourteen and even then with a lacquer of irony. Yet as inappropriate and pot-perfumed as *groovy* was, it was far superior to the next batter in my mental dugout: I almost popped out a blithe & sincere "Whatever floats your boat," which was about the worst I could've said outside of citing our mutual love of chicks as evidence of the DNA bond. *Groovy*. Even now, however, with all this time to consider it, I can't tell you what an ideal reaction would have been. Maybe the empty wisdom of Miss Willa's Post-it note: LOVE IS LOVE.

"Mom still hasn't wrapped her head around it but she's trying," she said. "You'll adore Syl, she's totally wonderful." Would I? It hardly mattered. We talked a bit more. Speck did catering for film sets, and had apparently achieved some success because she referenced movie stars by their first names and

lamented her busy schedule with the *dégagé* calm of someone who has everything entirely under control. She'd met Sylvana, an entertainment lawyer, at a "wrap party" two years ago and they were considering having children(!). Adopting *of course*, she said. For their "honeymoon"—does that require quotation marks? Why am I compelled to write about my daughter's nuptials in the manner of a Zagat review?—they were going to Mali and Senegal, where Sylvana had arranged to visit some adoption agencies. Stella Jr. found the prospect of parenting more daunting & fearsome than Syl did, to which I could offer no words of counsel. Syl was a "big fan" of my old poetry and she and Stella Jr. wondered what had happened to my writing, to which I responded, falsely I suppose, that I often wondered that same thing myself. Their bookshelves held a couple of my translations, too, but Stella Jr. apologized for what she gently termed their "neglect" of Eastern European writing. Syl was really big into Third World lit, Stella Jr. said, mentioning a couple of postcolonial writers from the Indian subcontinent with whom I was familiar only as vowelly names on book spines. She and Sylvana loved L.A.—she admitted this was a contrarian viewpoint—and lived downtown which rather extended the contrarian streak. At times our conversation was so light and easy that it disturbed me; with that much water under the bridge, it was hard to believe the bridge could still be standing. Finally I told her I had a request I expected her to deny, and, frankly, I would understand her denying it more easily than I would her granting it. But I wanted to ask.

"Shoot," she said.

I asked if she would let me walk her down the aisle . . . if, of course—here I stammered—there was an aisle.

"Oh, wow, Bennie. That's a jump." What followed was a silence that could be classified as huge. "Mom would flip." Another silence. "We . . . we were planning on walking down to-

gether, I guess. Jesus, Bennie, this has been so . . . so nice but that seems like zero to sixty in an awfully short time." (An automotive analogy—ah, my daughter was L.A. through and through.) "Let me to talk to Syl, okay? After all we're in this together." I told her not to worry, that it was an undeserved longshot, a selfish dream lobbed from a long-lost past. Inviting me was more than enough, I didn't mean to push. Silly me, etc. "I just need to think about it," Speck told me.

I can't say precisely why but after I hung up the phone I put my head in my hands and wept—hoarse, dry sobs I was unable to stifle or control.

An hour later Stella Jr. called back. "Syl thinks it's a gorgeous idea," she said. "That it's beautifully *circular.* Another twist—wait, how did she put this?—of unconventional conventionality. My God, it's going to be a day." That's when she proposed her compromise plan—that we'd meet tonight, at the non-rehearsal dinner, which by my estimate, dear American Airlines, should currently be in the appetizer stage. Insert your own cursewords here. Make sure they're your favorites because they're all for you.

When I went to tell Miss Willa that I'd spoken to her granddaughter, whose mysterious estrangement from us she'd ceased commenting upon twenty years ago, I found her drafting an epic, nine-page Post-it note message with her mother's old copy of the *Picayune's Creole Cookbook* (1901 edition) cracked open before her on the TV tray. "Miss Willa," I said, but she held up a narrow, vein-braided hand to shush me before resuming her labors. When she finally finished she handed me the pile of yellow stickies with a stern nod. I read them one by one. With painstaking care, she'd transcribed, in her wobbly avian scrawl, a passage from the cookbook—a rebuke, I gathered quickly, for the last few nights of me glumly serving her frozen dinners. It went like this:

THE SERVING IS
THE MOST IMPORTANT

AFTER COOKING. NEVER
CROWD A DISH INTENDED

FOR AN INVALID. SPREAD
A DAINTY NAPKIN ON

THE SALVER. ARRANGE
THE FOOD IN A MOST

APPETIZING WAY, LAY
A ROSEBUD OR A

FLOWER FRESH FROM
THE GARDEN ON THE

SALVER, AND BRING
IN THE DAINTY,

TEMPTING MORSEL
WITH A HAPPY, CHEERY

SMILE, THOUGH YOUR
HEART MAY BE SINKING.

"But, Mother," I said. "That's what I'm trying to tell you. My heart isn't sinking."

THAT NIGHT I bought my ticket via www.aa.com, your cluttery but operable website. It was a "Net SAAver" special—for, as I believe I've mentioned, $392.68. It doesn't soften my stance one bit to admit that I liked the nice price. One of your competitors wanted a full hundred dollars more. When I clicked "Purchase and Confirm" I felt a shudder run through my body—somewhere between giddy and forlorn, hopeful and frightened, not an entirely pleasant sensation but not unpleasant either. For a

long while afterward I remained at my desk in the unlit room, smoking cigarette after cigarette while the computer's lava-lamp screensaver threw undulating colors into the thickening & billowing bluish haze. Something terrible must've happened that night—I remember the city filling with sirens.

Drunk, he was unable to walk. The false limb unsteadied him enough while sober; but after glass after glass of beer, Walenty found himself mortally imbalanced, clinging to chairs and tables to stay upright. By now it was very late at night and the black sea out beyond the Molo Audace was calm and moonflecked. The men were saying their good-byes and some were saying ugly things about their wives asleep at home and the work they had to do the next day. Walenty had no place to sleep and he blurted this fact, laughingly, to the bear, who laughed, too—so uproariously that tears ran down his reddened cheeks. Everyone thought it hilarious except the sober dwarf behind the bar who ordered the bear to escort Walenty to a *pensione* on the hill below the cathedral.

With Walenty supported by the bear, they tottered through the streets howling songs in their native tongues, a typhoon of slurred baritone babble. When they awakened the old woman who ran the *pensione* she scolded them harshly and even spat at the bear whose subsequent laughter only enraged her further, provoking another blast of spittle. There was a gray mustache above her lip so slight it could be mistaken for dirt. One of her eyes was blind and milky, and her nubby fingers were sootblacked; one of the fingers, Walenty noticed, was missing a nail. Examining her closer, he realized she was not as old as one might think. She was rather, like the rooms she rented, overused.

The room was small and moldy and the vast stains splashed on the walls suggested a long-receded flood. With the old-looking woman standing in the doorway, the bear

helped Walenty onto the bed, its mattress thin as a cracker, and kissed him and pinched his cheek in the way of Italian men. As the bear left, the woman again spat at him and he ran down the hallway hooting with a laughter that continued even after he was free outside. Lying on the bed, Walenty could hear the laughs spilling down the cobblestoned hill. He slept with his leg attached and was dazzled by placid dreams.

He awoke the next morning just before dawn; even after a buoyant night of drinking, he was still a model soldier. The birdsongs surprised him—the sound was like that of a thousand music boxes being played at once. Lying there, he could not recall the last time he had heard birds. The Germans, went the rumor, had driven them out of Poland, and they'd been wholly absent during the Anzio fighting. Once Walenty had seen a black vulture tearing at the groin of a dead British infantryman. The men had tried to ignore it until they saw a recognizable organ in the vulture's beak and then one of the soldiers, an otherwise calm and stoical Varsovian who had taught music before the war, stood up and shot it. Later they discovered it was called locally *Avvoltoio monaco* and had been thought to be extinct.

When Walenty sat up in bed he was astonished at how good he felt. He had never been a drinker because he was oversensitive to the following day's aftereffects, and he'd expected, darkly, to awaken craving morphine. Now, craving coffee instead, he remembered the girl at the café and ran his fingers through his hair. He had never been so happy in his life.

Dear American Airlines, you miserable fucks, I'm going to keep writing. I'm going to keep writing and writing and writing and writing and you're going to keep reading and reading because for the first time in my life it wasn't me that blew it—it was you. Since you've stranded me here for at best this

day and this night, blaming mute thunder and dry rain and fugitive winds, Acts of God my ass—since you've trapped me here alone, caught between the dregs of one life and the debris of another, then you will sit here beside me, goddamn you, you will sit here beside me and you will listen to me, you will listen for as long as your boot sticks me to the floor, for as long as you hold me here, for as long as my voice holds out, I'm going to keep writing, goddamnit, we have a long night ahead and I'm not going to stop.

- - - -

I MAY, HOWEVER, stop smoking. Fueling my lungs is getting to be an onerous chore. One of the TSA screeners has made it his playful task to discourage me, by unrelentingly pulling me aside for *de trop* inspection whenever I re-pass through the security checkpoint, and while I wouldn't confess this to him, it's working. He's a boisterous senior with a snowy crewcut who probably used to work in industrial sales. "Them things gonna kill ya, tiger," he says to me. (Why "tiger"? An endearing midwesternism, I suppose. Grrr.) "Well," I say, as he runs his wand beneath my armpits, my groin, "I wish they'd hurry up. I've been waiting forty years." It occurs to me that jolly cracks about suicide are taboo at the checkpoints but this one is pretty oblique and anyway my ex-salesman seems to get the joke. Life didn't drop him where he expected to be at his age either. He liked Ike and switched to margarine and opened his hymnal to the page as directed but here he is anyway, still shoveling snow and still polishing a nametag, a thousand miles from Florida. *Hast thou not poured me out as milk,* wailed Job, *and curdled me like cheese?* "You think about what I said," he calls after me. Old friend, you don't know the half of it.

Outside beside the gray Skycap Services hutch is where I smoke. Across the street from me is a train platform and a parking garage where rust has left vertical stains on the con-

crete and steel panels, and, beyond the garage, the giant and completely booked Hilton hotel with its monolithic face of black windows that reminds me, not warmly, of the architecture of Soviet-era Bulgaria. The crowd of smokers keeps growing denser and I wonder if the tension of being stranded at O'Hare is luring some reformed smokers back into the fold; I'm increasingly getting hit on for smokes. The crowd keeps getting surlier, too. I heard one man announce that there were no hotel rooms to be had unless you went south of Gary, Indiana. Another smoker, a postmenopausal woman with a trademark Virginia Slims voice, added that this was partly due to a medical information technologies convention that's being held downtown. Well, whadyaknow. Another fella chimed in that there are no rental cars to be had, either—not a single sedan in all of Chicagoland. "I guess we're snowed in for the night," someone said. "Except there's no snow," someone else retorted (stealing, I suspect, the first guy's punchline), and then the whole gang laughed the most mirthless laugh you've ever heard.

"Hey-ho, here he comes again," my TSA screener said to me on my way back in. "Still kicking."

"Kicking and screaming," I said.

"You get 'em, tiger," he said, this time letting me pass by unhindered.

Along with the smoking, choosing my latest perch is also growing more difficult. It seems mathematically improbable but I feel certain that I've sampled the O'Chairs at every one of the gates here—finding none satisfactory, of course. I'm an airport Goldilocks! Currently I'm at H6, where I'm seated beneath a sign displaying an illustration of an airplane beside an encircled question mark. It seems to signify nothing. (I would know if there were an information booth here because I'm sitting precisely where it would be.) Or, from another angle, to signify everything: immobile planes, meet festering questions.

Anyway, no one seems to notice it. I should note, for the record, that throughout the afternoon I intermittently inquired of the attendant at the American Airlines desk—above which this sign should probably be hanging—just when I might expect to soar away from here but she never could say. (Once it was a he, but same story.) After a while I stopped doing so because it seemed futile plus I was beginning to feel like a stalker. It's never comforting when someone says to you, "You need to try to calm down, sir." But the attendants are facing a lot of heat so I don't hold anything against them. Certainly I wouldn't be able to do their jobs. By now I'd have jabbed my fingers, Stooges-style, into the eyes of a dozen disgruntled passengers, me included. You pinheads ain't flying the friendly skies. Pow! This is America, sit the fuck down.

Stray thought: All day now I've been thinking that O'Hare evokes Purgatory but I've been dismissing this perceived likeness as the product of an addled mind. Yet now I'm not so sure. The figurative sometimes congeals with the literal. Consider the view from my chair at H6: Sprawled 'round me is a crowd of temporary refugees waiting, waiting, yawning, drumming fingers on kneecaps, asking cellphones what they did to deserve this, rereading *The Da Vinci Code* to keep from having to stare at the carpet. Even the million-miler business travelers have run out of steam—the suited laptop jockey beside me is playing a version of solitaire on his computer and the way he's sighing and petulantly flicking his fingerpad leads me to believe that this is his last refuge of mental and/or physical activity. Airports are usually so fluid—people moving like fish in schools. But movement is scarce here tonight: stragglesome wanderers, looking purposeless and disattached, strolling for the sake of motion. Mothers are unduly snapping at children. Middle-aged men are learning to use the unexplored features of their digital wristwatches. A semi-punished lot, all of us: imprisoned within a pause, desperate to ascend.

Not to mention that everything here is colored in varying shades of purgatorial gray: the slate of the ceiling tiles, the wet-concrete hue of the columns, the floor tiles mottled like dusty gravel. The light pale and diffuse, a fluorescent mist. As in Dante's *Purgatorio*, no one casts a shadow. *Time passes on, and we perceive it not.* The escalators move us from one mountainous terrace to another. *What negligence, what standing still is this.* And instead of Dante's angels, with their flaming swords deprived of points, we are guarded by TSA screeners like my new friend advising me to repent from the death-lust of Lucky Strikes, marking my forehead with that bleating electronic wand of his as Alighieri's brow was carved at the gates. Confess thy sins, tiger: *May pity and justice disburden you soon, that ye may have power to move the wing.* Empty your pockets, please. Empty too thy addled mind.

RAY QUENEAU—formerly a minor god of mine, so far as translating goes; this, of course, back when I actually had gods (now I only have you)—once said that true stories are about food and made-up stories are about love. This line flitted into my mind a few minutes ago as I was chewing a "famous" "Baja" Chipotle Chicken Burrito from the Burrito Beach outlet. (I accompanied my six-pound burrito—a steaming hippo turd disguised as cuisine—with an "Arizona Green Tea," in order, I guess, to completely short-circuit my gastrointestinal receptors. Were I, say, a drunk New Orleans attorney, I might leap across the counter to throttle the server for this cement mixer of a dinner, though the homemade gang tattoos sprucing the server's knuckles might give me pause, plus it's not like I didn't have an array of other food-court options. Butter Crust Chicagoland Pizza & McFuggets! Fu Manchu Wok Craaaaziness. Aromatherapy smoothies. But the Burrito Beach had the short-

est line, hence my hippo turd. When I dumped my uneaten leftovers in the trash, the whole can trembled.)

Anyway, Queneau, me chewing: I was idly skimming this dread letter of mine when my eyes happened to stop on the three blank lines that I left between the tale of Bennie and Stella's first encounter and that of my run-in with the sweet old munchkinette outside advocating slot-machine therapy. Three blank lines: a page break, a smoke break, a visual exhalation after that remembrance of Magazine Street. Don't riffle backwards—I can tell you precisely what I wrote: "I stood there for a long while, my heart a sparkler spraying light across the sidewalk." A nice metaphor, isn't it? If maybe a little dainty & saccharine. Naturally I stole it. Sort of stole it, anyway, from a dead Varsovian poet named Blazej Krawczyk whose posthumous collected poems I translated years ago. The verse, so far as I can recall it, went something like this:

On an empty street, past midnight, you lit my heart's fuse.
I watched, amazed, as my chest
heaved white sparks upon the stones.
I laughed because I had never seen it do that.

But when I looked up you were running. You
glanced only once over your shoulder as you fled.
You could not have heard me say your name. *Katarzyna.*
No. All you could have heard was the blast.
For blocks, every windowpane quivered. Dogs
barked, lights appeared as question marks. But
there was nothing to see. You were gone
and so was I.

How brutal! And of course how common. This Katarzyna performing the romantic equivalent of the old Halloween "ring and run" trick. You can almost hear the clicks of her heels on

the rainslicked cobblestones while the poet stands frozen with his poor torso about to explode, the expression on his face collapsing, melting, as the fuse dwindles inward. (Though I doubt Krawczyk would have written those lines had he lived long enough to see suicide bombers dominating the newscrawls ... the modern evocations—wrecked and repressed Arab youths transforming themselves into hand grenades, into fatal pop-up political ads—are just too godawful ugly. Dear American Airlines, you've got far more pressing personal grievances against the jihadists than I do, but still, notwithstanding what they did to my adopted city, and the hot bejesus they scared out of my mother, the fuckers also soiled a great metaphor. If there is any vengeful comfort available to us, though, consider this: A savvy German scholar calling himself Christoph Luxenberg—a shielding pseudonym—recently concluded that the passages in the Koran promising a bevy of dark-eyed virgins to dead Muslim males is a mistranslation. Read in the original Syriac, the Koran instead promises rare and presumably delicious *white raisins*, which, while mildly tempting in the way of dried fruit, hardly approach the moist allure of seventy-two spread-eagled sweeties beckoning with a curled finger in the way of pulp-fiction vixens. Would the jihadists who flew your planes into the twin towers & the Pentagon have licked their lips before impact in the expectation of raisins? Let us not forget that suicide is a profoundly self-interested act. Luxenberg's revelation has lately stiffened my resolve when my translating seems worthless, a chore of lingual accountancy. The right word matters, it says to me. The wrong ones infect, spread disease. Words are everything.)

One thing, however, that I've never been entirely clear about: Did Katarzyna perish in the blast? It's not altogether evident, is it? *Wy byliście nieobecni,* was what Krawczyk wrote: literally, *You were absent.* Krawczyk was three years dead by the time I got to the poem, so I never had the chance to ask. I sup-

pose the answer hinges on whatever emotional luggage you're packing when you encounter the poem. Is the end of love an implosion or an explosion? Was that hussy Katarzyna flattened by shrapnel (metaphorically, of course), hurled face-first to the street, or did the poet's remains float down upon her like flakes of soot, like benign embers hissing in the rivulets of rainwater between the cobblestones?

But then it appears I'm skidding off the runway again. Where was I? Oh yes: the young Me as fizzy sparkler, freckling Magazine Street with my Stellated ecstasy. And then those three blank lines, containing multitudes. That tender, gauzy fade-out. What I'm wondering is why I stopped the story where I did, with that sweet pilfered metaphor that's been jangling about in my pockets for years. (Beyond the obvious reason, I mean: I needed a cigarette.) Unlike Krawczyk's betrayed poet, I didn't go boom that morning. I went back home and mixed a stout nightcap and smoked two or three Luckies before masturbating myself to sleep. Six or seven hours later I helped Charles clean his apartment, bagging beer cans and emptying ashtrays and fielding shit from him for "disappearing all night with that flatchested chick." ("Flatchested?" I said. "You sure? I didn't notice." "You didn't *notice*," he said, with a roll of the eyes. Well, I didn't notice.) Then we went to the Exchange where I got luminously hammered and considered calling Stella—I still had her number in the back pocket of my jeans—but didn't, mostly owing to the presence there of an art student named Valerie who, when she drank gin, tended to get nearsightedly horny, and who happened that night to be drinking gin. Normally I hated talking to her—she was from upstate New York and thought she was doing aesthetic missionary work down South, irrigating the Sahara of the Bozarts—but the saucy things she said under the influence of gin were terribly hard to ignore, e.g. "Gosh, I'm feeling so edible right now." Gulp. So why not finish my story there? Me, the walk-

73

ing, talking sparkler—drunk with new love, but drunker with vodka and erotic *bons mots?* Or for that matter, why not wrap it up a few dark hours later when I stumbled home from Valerie's barefooted because I'd been too drunk to find my shoes? (The next night, when I did finally call Stella, and we talked for three hours, it emerged that I'd been shoe shopping that afternoon. The joke, for weeks after, was that I'd bought new shoes to impress her. Her joke, not mine.)

But then Krawczyk wasn't writing about the beginning of love, let's remember, Bennie. He was writing about the end.

After my and Stella's final argument, kindled by my conjuring of Speck's far-off wedding, naturally I retreated to the Exchange. The typical male drinks heavily in such situations, so I suppose I was typical though toward the far end of the bell curve. To put it mildly I drank my fool head off. I toppled off my barstool and vomited in the bathroom trough and spent much of the evening collapsed against the shoulder of B. B. Mike who goodnaturedly obliged me though not without calling me a drooling homo. Some Uptown cuties slumming it for a bachelorette party sneaked a plastic tiara onto my head—without ever speaking to me, I mean; that's what kind of spectacle I was—which I didn't even know was there until long after I'd left the bar. That must've been four or five hours after my entrance; all I know is that I departed, on foot (Felix the Fat confiscated my keys), and in a light rain, well before last call.

The key was gone. We kept the spare housekey hidden beneath a struggling potted cotton plant in the hallway; the key was for me because I was always forgetting my own keys, or, on rarer occasions like this one, having them taken away from me. I rapped on the door for several minutes—a frantic rat-a-tat—at first as quietly as I could (for Speck's sake), and then with mounting urgency and volume. When that didn't work I pounded the door with the side of my fist. Inside me was a

shotgun-patterned anger that even today I can't precisely explain: I was angry at Stella for no longer being in love with me and angry at myself for deserving that unlove. I was boiling in guilt for the . . . for the shambles I was, and with rage for the shambles I thought she'd made of me. I hated her for wanting to leave me even though a part of me wanted to watch her go. I hated her because I loved my daughter and my Stellas could not be wrenched apart. I hated her because the sight of myself reflected in her eyes made me recoil. I hated her because all I'd wanted in life was to fuck and drink and make poems and die young and in the saddle singing yahoo. I hated her because I could abide neither her presence nor her absence. And I hated myself because I was a shitheel father who didn't even *get* the joy of parenthood until six or seven months in when Speck was old enough to react to me, to *reflect* me — which meant Stella was right, that down deep I considered myself the sun, the center of all orbits, my mother's child after all. And I hated myself too because when I drank I became someone else and I loved that someone else while I was him and despised him when I wasn't. And finally I hated everyone/everything because ultimately there was no escape, I was trapped within myself and my life, there was no ending or outcome that wasn't going to hurt me or them or us all. Yet at the same time I didn't or couldn't believe all that. There were words that could fix this, there had to be. We could bandage or bury this night & all the others like it with the right words, by saying them, believing them, crawling inside them together, inhabiting their worn confines, lighting a candle, and growing old within them. And while I punched that door harder and harder — I remember this — I thought of walking my daughter down the aisle on her wedding day. My mind fastened upon that frilly, cast-off vision that had so weirdly, inexplicably led me here, that daydream — no, that sweetened-condensed nightmare — that I'd never actually *had* before stating it aloud (why *would* I have? What man dreams

of giving away what he loves to someone else, slicing off and serving a piece of his heart? That's almost like aspiring to be Abraham on Mount Moriah, rearing back with the knife over beloved Isaac. If anything I dreamt of my daughter traveling the world solo, absorbing its Technicolor marvels, writing me lavishly detailed letters from Borneo and Budapest, footloose and earth-soaked and wholly unbothered by the anklebites of marriage, the drowsy bleakness of domesticity)—there in that hallway I fixed upon that sweet, poisonous anti-dream that, in its revealing, had ignited all this, had triggered this end, and as I pounded and kicked the door I said to it: *I'm not a liar Stella I'm not.*

Nothing. I dropped to my knees and punched the door more weakly then put my ear to it to see if I could maybe hear her breathing on the opposite side. That's when I realized I was wearing the plastic tiara. Discovering that reignited my rage and I went outside and around the corner of the house to a spot beneath our bedroom window. A narrow, grassy channel separated our house from the neighboring one—too wide to pass an egg from window to window but slim enough to confidently toss one across. There was no light in our bedroom window above me but of course she was in there, I knew it. Where else could she be? By now the rain had strengthened and I was soaked through. Enraged and intoxicated, and above all else wounded, I stood below our window and with all that was in me I bellowed out her name.

Almost instantly, however, I went silent—struck mute by the interior echo. "Oh shit," I finally said aloud. Had Stella been named anything else, and/or had we lived in any other city besides New Orleans, my desperate call would have been just my desperate call. In that alternate universe the neighbors might have peeked from behind the curtains but they wouldn't have laughed or, worse, joined in. But you simply cannot shout the name Stella while standing under a window in New Or-

leans and hope for anything like an authentic or even mildly earnest moment. Literature had beaten me to this moment, had staked its flag here first, and there was nothing I could do outside in that soupy, rain-drenched alleyway that could rise above sad parody. Perhaps if she'd been named Beatrice, or Katarzyna—maybe then my life would have turned out differently. Maybe then my voice would have roused her to the window, maybe then I could have told her that I was sorry, that I could be a better man, that I couldn't promise I knew everything it meant but I loved her. Instead I stared up at that black window, shutmouthed and impotent, blinking and reblinking my eyes to flush out the rainwater. "Stella," I whispered. The French have an expression: "Without literature life is hell." Yeah, well. Life with it bears its own set of flames.

————

WHEW. ME AGAIN. As to the three blank lines immediately preceding this: Dear American Airlines, you don't want to know what they contain. Suffice it to say that I no longer possess that six-pound "famous" chipotle chicken burrito, physiologically speaking, and the evidence suggests that I may have been stricken with an O'Hare strain of *E. coli* that may soon annihilate me in a way the vodka never could. I know why the trash can trembles.

But help me out here. For the past ten minutes or so, among other activities, I've been pondering why airport bathrooms hardly ever feature graffiti. Truckstop bathrooms serve much the same purpose—as pitstops for travelers on the go—yet their walls are almost always festooned with rich commentary. *Jesus saves!* (The rejoinder: *But Satan invests.*) *Don't look for a joke here, it's in your hand. Please don't toss cigarette butts in the toilet, it makes them hard to light. John 3:16.* (Rejoinder: *Matthew 3:20—just missed you.*) Etc. And my personal favorite, which I saw scrawled on a condom machine in an Allentown, PA,

truckstop: *Insert baby for refund.* In high school, a friend and I actually dialed a "For a Good Time, Call" number spied on the bathroom wall of an Uptown New Orleans po' boy joint. When a female voice answered we threw the receiver back and forth like a fiery ember until her plaintive, patient hellos got the best of me. "Yes," I said, appropriating, for whatever reason, the voice of TV's Maxwell Smart, "I'm calling in reference to a good time." "Oh, God," she said. "My ex-husband Bobby wrote that where he used to work. I thought he'd scratched it out—he said he did." At this point the conversation should have ended with an apology from me and the buzz of a dial tone from her, but without so much as an awkward pause she asked if I'd had the roast beef and gravy (the restaurant's claim to glory) and I said no, I'd had a peacemaker (fried oysters & shrimp), which she said was okay but not nearly as good as the roast beef and gravy so long as you got it "dressed" but not with pickles because pickles were gross. The conversation continued like this, lazily, while my buddy lay on the couch asphyxiating himself with pillows—he was certain I was en route to high-speed carnal glory the moment he heard me venture that "sometimes dressed is good." After a while I abandoned the Maxwell Smart voice, which must have clued her in to my age because swiftly thereafter she begged off the phone. I learned several lessons from that call: (1) that the world was a much more lonesome & wicked place than I'd realized (her *ex-husband?*); and (2) that my native New Orleans, where dialing a number found on a bathroom wall yielded you a discussion about po' boys, was a truly weird city. (Allow me now to make the sign of the cross to bless its drowned soul. I remember watching the news after Katrina hit and thinking—outside of the hot grief I felt for all those homegrown refugees and old ladies being plucked from rooftops and, Jesus, that poor kid being stripped of his snowpuff dog—thinking: There it goes, my past. Washing away in the flood, godspeed.)

Really, though: It doesn't make a lick of sense, this lack of wordage in the restroom stalls. Airports are petri dishes for boredom, rage, nicotine withdrawal, and gastrointestinal discomfort—the presumed nuclei of anonymous bathroom verse—and yet the walls here are as blank as a dead man's eyeball. The only marks at all are random scratches that I'm at a loss to explain, unless jetsetting circus tigers use these loos. You would think that some enterprising and disaffected soul would be inspired to write something along, say, these lines: *I fucked in Florida, I fucked in Maine. / I fucked for three days on the coast of Spain. / But I'll never be happy, never be free / until I fuck this airline, like it fucked me.* But no, nothing. Not a sign of life in these restrooms save the sounds and smells of businessmen voiding the fruits of their expense accounts. Perhaps it's true what they say. Maybe poetry really is dead.

Mine certainly is. The last poem I published was in 1995; the last poem I wrote, not counting the ditty above, came maybe a year later. It would be false modesty to say no one noticed though just barely. Mostly, it was an amicable split. That great old line of Larkin's—"I haven't given up poetry; poetry has given me up"—doesn't apply here. No, exhausted from decades of quarreling, we each gave up on the other. My mother still hopes for a reunion, goading me with a stick rather than a carrot: NO ONE, said one Post-it, REMEMBERS THE TRANSLATOR. "Oh, Miss Willa," I whined back, "no one remembers the poets anymore either." Officially (by which I mean, when familiar bartenders asked), my reason for quitting was that poetry had finally struck me as a futile weapon against the world. Iambic pentameter is no sword with which to slay evil or even ennui. That sort of thing. And though I sometimes believe that, usually I don't. All I have to do is remember the streaming red blood that poems—other writers' poems—drew from me over the years. The way certain poems guided me through life like blue runway lights. Or more accurately like pinball bumpers.

My mother awards herself credit for what she terms my "artistic bent"—at this point, a nice way to describe my toolbox of personality disorders. For letting me, as a toddler, wallow in piles of books while she sat before her easel in City Park. For being moral and sophisticated enough to ban "Little Black Sambo" from my bedtime reading. For subscribing to *Highlights* and helping me write my first published work, a letter to the creators of the "Doctor Fate and Hourman" comic books (which, now that I think about it, was a letter of complaint—one might say I've been working toward this moment all my life). The "artist" in me, she's always claimed, descends from my Desforge roots—is derived exclusively from the sap from her family tree. All I inherited from the Ford *né* Gniech side, according to Miss Willa, was my nappy hair and my inexplicable love of consonants.

As with most matters, she's wrong. My father didn't read for pleasure—nothing about English provided him pleasure, and Polish lit was nearly impossible to come by in New Orleans—but in his mind was a storehouse of remembered Polish verse: Mickiewicz, Witwicki, Slowacki, all the nineteenth-century Romantics. On nights when my mother was "away" (hospitalized, primarily, or taking night-school classes in Japanese pen-and-ink drawing or Advanced Bridge, or communing with her revolving cast of "best" friends who would invariably "turn" on her), he would lie next to me at bedtime and recite reams of lilting, beautifully incomprehensible poems: *Gdybym ja była słonecykiem na niebie, Nie świeciłabzm, jak tzlko dla ciebie.* For me, it was lingual white noise, those Polish consonant endings like evanescent static, whispers of *shhh*, the rise and fall of octosyllabic verses rocking me to sleep as pitching seas lull a sailor. Perhaps he felt he had nothing else to give me—he could no more decipher a volume of Uncle Remus than he could a Greek bible—or perhaps (my preference) he relished those sparse and covert moments when he could speak

his mother tongue freely, and could share it with me. Miss Willa, convinced he was lamenting his life with her whenever he spoke Polish, and piercingly ashamed of his Polack origins, forbade his speaking it in the house. By this time he had quit his exterminator job and was working at an automotive shop on Poydras Street—because it specialized in imports, my mother tended to refer to him as a "Rolls-Royce specialist"—and beside me at night he smelled of motor sludge and cigarettes and whatever acidic solvents he scrubbed his hands with so that my mother wouldn't fuss about his oil-encrusted fingers. My fond memories of him are few: He worked, he ate, he enjoyed the *Lawrence Welk Show* for the polkas though any moving images sufficed, he fixed the sink when it was leaking and tended to the fireplace on Christmas morning while my mother buzzed about the living room demanding to be told the day was *perfect*. But in those dark, poem-strewn moments he was nothing short of magical—a wizard conjuring forth my dreams with his clandestine and incantatory language.

Without stretching the matter too far, you could say that poetry raised me. By the time I hit adolescence, my father was a gray shadow passing soundlessly through the house, the ghost of a martyred handyman, and my mother remained, as before, a case for a psychological bomb squad. They were less parents than cellmates and we all privately marked off the days of our confinement. My father won this grim contest by dying when I was fifteen—the victim of an unexpected heart attack that struck him in his sleep. For so sudden a death, and at such a pregnable age for me, it was a strangely unemotional passing. He was only forty-eight but his death felt like that of a nursing-home patient who'd been bedridden and cancer-racked for years: an act of mercy, a gift rather than a theft. I don't remember even crying at his funeral. I felt as if I was waving goodbye as he embarked upon a new and better adventure. Send me a postcard, *Tata*. Be brave.

In any case, I found myself nearing manhood with scant instruction on living, so for lessons I turned to books, and in books of poetry—particularly those of Baudelaire, Keats, Neruda, Lorca, Yeats, the Beats—I discovered the life I thought I wanted: heart-fueled, reckless, close to the bone, earthly existence set to a rolling, overspilling boil. Let me say upfront that this is no way to read poetry. When Neruda writes about how great it would be "to go through the streets with a green knife letting out yells" until you die of the cold, he does not intend for you to take him literally. The dearth of green knives in your neighborhood cutlery emporium ought to be clue number one, but just you try explaining that to a vulnerable seventeen-year-old. Because I loved the way words & images bounced through my head when I read poetry, the way it *impelled* my life as nothing else did, revved it like a floored gas pedal, I began writing it.

I won't afflict you with the subsequent details of my C.V., which are boring even to me. Suffice it to say that I experienced some degree of "success" in my thirties, almost all of it due to poems I'd written in my twenties, and while those years did feature a fun and dizzying burst of acclaim & minor awards & tweedy/boozy hoopla—I remember thinking *This is it, the Byronic jackpot* when a pair of lithe & giggly female grad students showed up unannounced at my door one night, bearing a fifth of vodka and a book of poems they wanted me to sign—it all quickly fizzled out. One of the girls awarded me an unsolicited handjob but her manner was so clinically lackluster—I felt as if I was having a pimple squeezed—that I stopped her partway through, complaining of a stomachache. When she inquired if it might be gas the night sunk that much further. I milked my brief limelight for what I could—fellowships, grants, community-college readings—but, as I was unable to sustain the momentum (i.e., having bankrupted my cache of youthful poems), my sell-by date soon passed. "I have seen the

moment of my greatness flicker," Eliot wrote, and, oh Tom, I know the sight. I don't want to draw the line too rigidly here, or assign sentimental blame, but the fact remains: All the "success" that I had stemmed from the fevered work of my twenties, from the poems I wrote pre-Stellas. By the time anyone noticed the fire, it had already burned down to ashes. Despite my sweaty efforts, I was never again able to match the tone & quality of those early, fumbling, greasy, howl-at-the-moon poems. I was a confessional poet who no longer wanted to confess. Sometimes, when I read my work in public, I felt like a stand-in—an acquaintance presenting the works of a deceased poet, like Kenneth Koch at Frank O'Hara's memorial service reading O'Hara's grand, sweet poem about talking to the sun. "This was the work of a great poet," Koch told the crowd. Immodest words to that effect would run through my head as I read: *This is the work of a great poet. Such a shame that he's gone.* A few hours later would find me plastered at some professorial cocktail party, saying *pbbbbt* when anyone would ask what I was currently working on. After a while only the misfit male grad students fell for my drunk poet routine but they're easy marks anyway. They'd feed me vodka till five A.M., hoping for a tragic Dylan Thomas moment—a pickling they could eulogize.

I went to Poland in 1989, in those heady months when the Iron Curtain was being drawn back from Europe. It was a poet's exchange program for which Alojzy nominated me, and, typifying their history, the Poles got the short end of the stick: me. On second thought, though—scratch that. I've been far too glib already. My time in Poland deserves better. I was supposed to stay for five months but squeezed out more than a year, and even now my memories of it blend and blur: blissfully late late nights in Krakow's candlelit cellar barrooms, drinking bison-grass vodka and chainsmoking those awful Mocne cigarettes and talking capital-A Art with students and poets and on-the-brink novelists and with my omnipresent friend Grzegorz,

a crazed, Santa-bearded Crakovian sculptor who disturbingly worked in the nude—all of them contagiously fizzing, crackling, bursting with newly unleashed ambitions—in short, late nights of talking ideas with people for whom words & ideas *mattered*, who had been held captive for so many long years by a single well-intentioned but awful idea, who believed in ideas because their every waking moment thus far in life had been shackled to a bad one and who were now casting about, freely & deliriously, for a new idea, for one that would lift them from the ruck of their history. Down in those cellars I witnessed warmhearted fistfights and boozy, table-pounding declarations and long-private daydreams being traded like baseball cards. For Jan, a poet jaded by what he called the "incompetence" of art in Poland, the dream was to write like a swarm of wasps: finally, that is, to sting. A young philosophy student—Pawel, I think was his name—wanted to open a French restaurant, though he had never tasted French cuisine outside Proust. Grzegorz, on the other hand, longed to someday leave a yellow rose at the Dakota apartment where John Lennon was murdered, and, while he was in New York, to "fuck a powerful Negress."

And then, also, the long sweet quietudes: the hours of those gray-drizzled or snow-muffled mornings that I devoted to learning my father's language, speaking aloud to myself in my seedy little apartment on the lovably foul Ulica Czysta (which translates, inappropriately, to Clean Street) and with my elderly, pince-nez-wearing tutor, Albert; and to rummaging through Poland's literature like a mad pirate sinking his arms elbows-deep into treasure, ransacking the Jagiellonian library so thoroughly that even the night watchmen knew me by name. Polish lit is often derided as hermetic, too history-steeped and insular, but I suspect being raised in the South immunized me to this. It seemed natural to me for literature to obsess over defeats and the long fingers of the past. (I was partial to lost causes even be-

fore I became one.) As for my *ex officio* duties, I wrote madly, like the tousle-headed writers depicted in movies tossing pages over their shoulders, and while the poems seemed gorgeous and muse-kissed at the time, it was all, I saw later, well-intentioned dreck—the moment & themes were too big for me. I wrote one poem about some children I saw applauding the arrival of housepainters at an unidentified building; at that hinge of history, in this paint-peeling city, even housepainters bore a messianic glow. Yet the poem, like an unfocused photograph, failed to capture the true pith of it all. Maybe all poems fail in that way. An ode to Venus can hardly rival the sensations of Venus's skin against yours, the press of her naked thigh on yours. It's all secondhand. Black dots on paper that are so intrinsically uninteresting that even a bored dog can't be cajoled into sniffing them.

I'd be remiss, though, if in presenting this slideshow of Poland I neglected to mention poor Margaret. ("Poor Margaret": This is how she's titled in my mental Rolodex, saddled with that adjectival goiter.) She was technically my first wife since Stella and I never officially tied the knot. (We were too cool for that.) I married Margaret on the basis of a single one-night stand and a subsequent torrent of letters: an inadvisable courtship, to be sure. We met at a cocktail reception for foreign art-types at the residence of some communist bureaucrat—a subminister of *kultury* or somesuch. A fat man with the pinched red face of an infant and such a stink to his breath that you could smell his laughter from across a crowded room. He was also unbearably pompous which was why, aside from the limitless vodka that kept floating my way, I found myself wandering his house secretly tucking meatball canapés into various drawers and cabinets. A decidedly undiplomatic gesture, I know, but the image of that overripe baby sniffing sourly through his house, a few days hence, amused me to no end.

It was Margaret who caught me. She was an art historian

visiting from Connecticut, ten years my senior, a bit thick in the haunches but attractive in a wallflower way. I found her round little eyeglasses fetching, and too her easy, salty laughter. Also that she thought my meatball-sabotaging charming. She said she had a soft spot for "rogues" which made me wince because I'd never heard anyone say that word sincerely aloud. "Well shiver me timbers," I responded, insincerely. Except that she did, in fact, sincerely shiver my timbers a few hours later, when we ended up back at my apartment shredding one another's clothes. I was about to write "like teens in a basement" but then it occurred to me that, despite their hormones, teens rarely do that. It's middle-aged people, desperate to crank up the volume on their fading lives, who do that. In any case she actually ripped my shirt open, the airborne buttons going *ping* against the walls. Once we were in bed she paused to confess, meekly but not primly, that it had been "a long time" since she'd been with a man. I brought her face close to mine and told her, "It's okay. I've never even *been* with a man." Most likely I cadged that from a movie but so what? She laughed that salty laugh and thereafter things went wonderfully, sleeplessly haywire. She was so vocal that when my landlord, an elderly widower, encountered me in the street the next morning, after I'd taken Margaret to the station to catch a train to Warsaw, he dropped his loaf of bread to applaud. Grounds for a marriage? Survey says: X. I'll skip the rest of the story, an epistolary tale for the most part. The marriage was so brief that I think I used the same bath towel for its entire duration.

All of which is a long and perhaps overrevealing roadmap of how I went from poet to translator. My first translations were favors for the pals I'd made in Krakow: exercises in friendship, more or less. It was sweetly satisfying, however, to place their poems in American journals—and in a way that I'd never felt when publishing my own work, I felt *generous* to the audience, as if I was bequeathing something of value to them, rather than,

as I felt with my poems, coughing something on them. What's more, I felt freed from the minefields of my own authorial persona; in my translating I aspired to invisibility, and invisibility felt like emancipation. I also found, somewhat to my surprise, that I actually savored the work, was tickled by the process: I *enjoyed* untying all the Gordian knots, piecing together the lingual puzzles, dressing and redressing the words & phrases in my own native garb. And, too, there was something liberating about the imperfection built into the craft. The act of translation is one of approximation. A translation can approach the art in its source language but never quite touch it; close proximity is all, the nearness of its hot breath. As a translator, I could never hope to clone, say, the rose that is a poem—my work could only yield, to paraphrase Nabokov, a thorny cousin to the rose. "What a translator tries for," the great John Ciardi wrote back in the '60s, "is no more than the best possible failure." For someone who'd made a life's habit of failing, this sentiment held a balmy appeal. *The best possible failure.* By the time I started translating, it was all the epitaph for which I could hope. Fail, fail again. Fail better. Am I failing now? Yeah, silly question. Go ahead, you bastards, laugh all you want.

– – – –

ON THAT NOTE, dear American Airlines, let's check in with Walenty. But let me warn you: My friend Alojzy has engineered a plot twist that I'm not sure I can fully swallow. The *pensione* to which the Bear—now a capitalized bear, for whatever reason, a full-blown *Niedźwiedź*—delivered Walenty turns out to have been the family home of the waitress from the train station café. Small world, no? And the beastly, old-looking, loogie-lobbing woman who runs the joint? Alas, that's her mama. This strikes me as too facile a coincidence—I mean, why have Walenty encounter the girl (whose name is Francesca, FYI, though nicknamed Franca) at the train station at all? Why not

have introduced her the following morning, at breakfast—with the same cup of coffee and the same dreamy exchange? My vague guess is that Alojzy might be trying to suggest a kind of lining up of the stars (in Walenty's head, that is), invoking a sense of fatedness. Seems like a misstep to me, however. If at first the plot evoked—albeit faintly, and with much more somber intent—the early parts of Nabokov's *Pnin* (although, on second thought, the louder echo is of Antal Szerb's *Journey by Moonlight*), now it's channeling Spanish-language soap operas. *¿Es su mama?! ¡Ay dos mio!* But then again I abandoned my belief in fate or anything invisible years ago. It wasn't fate, after all, that caused a businessman in Long Island, driving home from the train station (this was in the news a few weeks back), to crash head-on into a car being driven by his teenaged son. It was the two fishbowl-sized martinis he drank after work plus the tall-boy Budweiser he downed on the train.

Regardless, it's Alojzy's damn book. I just untangle the consonants. Here goes:

> She was worried that he would tire but he insisted he was fine; he wanted to walk, he told her, to walk and to walk and to walk. And so they did, into the old *città vecchia* and up the steep ascending lanes, past fish markets and confectionaries and cramped, airless little bookshops and shops selling lampshades and linens and others selling sausages and dried mushrooms and the roasted coffee beans that perfumed the narrow streets. The pockmarks of sniper bullets freckled some of the buildings and there were rows of empty, shuttered shops that must have been owned by Trieste's Jews before the Germans had vanished them; Walenty turned away from these sights, however, refusing to admit them, locking them out. In these moments his pace quickened and Franca confusedly struggled to follow. They did not speak of the past, and often, like elderly couples, they didn't speak at all. They finished at the waterfront where, sitting on the quay,

they shared a local variety of cake that Franca called *pres-nitz* and watched the Adriatic in its implacable blue stillness. Across the bay were terraced vineyards and a white castle and nearby an old man in a cotton suit was transferring the scene onto the canvas propped upon his easel. His lips were moving constantly and it appeared he was conversing with his colors. Walenty noticed the absence of flags on the flag-poles which momentarily swelled his heart. He asked aloud, "Where am I?" Taking his hand in hers, Franca smiled and called him foolish. "You are in Trieste," she said.

A perfect ending, you might think. Cue an accordion *serenata* and the closing credits ("The text in this book was set in Livingstone, the only typeface designed by . . ."). Except, of course, that it's not the end. It never is.

‒ ‒ ‒ ‒

OKAY, QUENEAU. Here's a true story and it's not about food. It's about Willa Desforge and Henryk Gniech, the Fords of Annunciation Street, and their befuddled, reclusive little son Benjamin, and maybe it's about love and maybe it's not but then who am I to say? I'm just a mordantly sober guy in an airport trying to avoid staring at his broken shoelace.

The year was 1963. I was nine years old and mere days away from being ten, and was preoccupied that week, as I had been for months, with two issues: the horse I desperately wanted for my birthday, and the threat of nuclear annihilation. The horse was any black-and-white paint horse similar to the kind ridden by Michael Landon's Little Joe on *Bonanza*. That particular horse was named Cochise though Little Joe more commonly called it "Cooch." ("Cooch," I might note, was Stella's code-word for her genitalia, which, while nicely circular, obviously made dirty talk an impossible exercise in nostalgia for me.) Cochise drank water out of Little Joe's hat and Little Joe also once shared his coffee with Cochise which I thought splen-

did. A coffee-drinking horse! Perfect for New Orleans—I presumed my horse would fancy our local chicory blend. Naturally I was too young to understand zoning laws and the spatial requirements of livestock but I felt certain my own Cooch would like our backyard just fine and would enjoy being ridden to and from school where I could tie him to the bike rack so long as I left him a bucket of water or a tall *café au lait*. My father barely acknowledged the idea—"Ah . . . no"—while Miss Willa seemed vulnerably noncommittal. "Horses attract flies," she said, but that struck me as a manageable objection. I would blitz the backyard with a thousand sticky flystrips that would twist in the breeze like Tibetan prayer flags. I would keep a flyswatter holstered at all times, and my friend Harry Becker, who lived down the street, promised to do the same for little or no charge. Together, we would make sure the flies weren't a problem.

There was nothing I could do, however, about nuclear death, which I felt certain was close at hand. Its looming shadow, in fact, was my unspoken rejoinder to my mother's other demurral—that perhaps I wasn't old enough for the responsibilities of a horse. *But I'm as old as I'm ever going to be*, went my thinking, what with nuclear winter blowing in soon. I felt its irradiant imminence every time we crawled under our schooldesks when the air-raid siren blew, my eyelids pressed against my left forearm, my other forearm shielding the back of my head, my jutting rump nevertheless fully exposed to the blast wave (that's how America's children would perish, ass-first)—and me wondering all the while whether I would see the fatal flash of light through the shield of my eyelids plus arm & if I would actually feel my hair burning which frightened me slightly more than death (on count two, the nuns said no). I felt that imminence, too, whenever *Bonanza* was interrupted by that dread test of the Emergency Broadcast System and the room temperature seemed to instantly drop by ten degrees. Is that how

it would end? From Lorne Greene to a long chilly beep to the thundering Armageddon? "Had this been an actual emergency, you would have been instructed to tune in to your local radio station." I pictured myself running to the cabinet-sized radio/record player in the dining room and furiously dialing in WTIX-AM ("Fun-lovin' WTIX, the Mighty 690!") and listening to the end of the world surfing in on a commercial for Rex Root Beer or that Ponchartrain Beach jingle: *At the beach, at the beach, at Ponchartrain Beach; you'll have fun, you'll have fun, every day of the week.* "Come ride the Scrambler and the Flying Coaster and see the sixteen lively French poodles on the Poodle Expre—" Ka-boom! Come see the giant orange mushroom cloud! The end of everything, you, me, & sixteen lively poodles included! Because of its status as a port city ("a *crucial* port city," the nuns said), New Orleans would be obliterated in the first wave of attacks; this, we were told, was the price we had to pay for living in such an important town. Also it was rumored that the Russians hated Mardi Gras and/or for that matter all parades of a festive nature.

Owing to this fear of mine, which caused even innocuous events like the sighting of a falling star to mutate into moments of fear & trembling (was that a missile?), my father and I tended to divvy up sections of the morning paper in an unorthodox way. The front page went to me and the comics went to him. (Neither of us ever had much use for the sports pages.) I would comb the headlines for clues of our impending doom—the Cuba problem was still sizzling that spring—while my father read the comics wearing *precisely* the same studious expression as me. If the state of the world confounded me, the state of American humor confounded him even more. Perhaps Lucy stealing the football away from Charlie Brown too closely mirrored Polish history to be funny, I don't know. Surely he found Andy Capp's dialect indecipherable (I did too). But then you need to understand that reading the comics wasn't leisure for

him: My mother was constantly bemoaning his humorlessness, and he wanted to please her. For him, this was study — a concerted effort to break the code of funny, and perhaps make her laugh. Dagwood Bumstead was his Cyrano, his tutor in romance.

After a while we would trade sections and there would be no sound save the clinking of our spoons and the slurping of mushy cornflakes. I always started with the *Family Circus* which, however corny, tended to soothe & console me. I felt a kind of voyeuristic delight in viewing, through the keyhole that its round border evoked, the quiescent hijinks of a "normal" family — Jeffy's cute-isms, the dopey antics of Barfy the Dog, the dad's frazzled cheeriness. I read somewhere once that scholars had concluded that the cave paintings at Lascaux etc. do not, as previously thought, depict actual events, or animals that the painters had actually seen — what they portray, instead, are animals the painters *wanted* to see, events they *wished* had happened. Is it overreaching to suggest an aesthetic link between prehistoric cave drawings and Bil Keane's *Family Circus?* The kid munching cornflakes says no. The *Family Circus* was my fatty mammoth, my glimpse of the idyll.

Anyway, 1963. It was a Friday, I remember. My birthday was coming on Monday. Finished with the comics & cornflakes, I asked my father about my horse. The backyard had not been properly prepared and I was worried about the work still needing to be done. Transforming a garage into a stable seemed like no minor feat. Would there be time?

"You cannot have no horse in New Orleans," he said.

"There are horses at the fairgrounds," I said.

"Those are racing horses."

"My horse can race. He'll be fast."

"You cannot have no horse in New Orleans," he repeated.

On most mornings Miss Willa tended to sleep in, leaving my father and me to outfit ourselves for work & school, so

I was mildly surprised that morning when she breezed sing-songy into the kitchen. Not entirely surprised, though, since she'd been on one of her blissful streaks lately—what I would later come to understand as "manic episodes." She'd returned to her painting and she'd enrolled in a flower-arranging class; the result was a house overgrown with dried cattails, golden-rod, celosia, purple flax, pepperberries, statice, baby's breath. Every corner was spiked with parched flora. Three magnolia wreaths overlooked the upstairs toilet alone and even my bed-room had been invaded—by bushels of French lavender that perfumed the room so strongly that I reversed the box fan in my room to blow *out* the window.

My father always left for work fifteen minutes before I left for school, which was when I'd sneak in some television. On this day, however, after he left, my mother sat down at the ta-ble with me.

"Benjamin," she said. "Would you like to skip school to-day?"

Even then I was savvy enough to be suspicious. "Why?"

"*Why?* What kind of answer is that?" She sounded a mock harrumph. "Well, I was thinking we might should look at some horses."

You can imagine the detonation of my glee, the way it blew apart my reservations—and, too, my volley of sputtered yes-yes-yesses. My own Cooch! Hot diggety it was happening. The horsemen of the apocalypse would not find me without a steed. I made for the door but she stopped me.

"We'll need to pack you some clothes," she said. "And go pick out some books and toys you'll want to take along."

Naturally I was thrown off by these comments but the last thing I wanted to do was to splash the opportunity with cold questions. I should note that she'd skipped off with me be-fore: twice to Florida, once to New York (we got as far as At-lanta). But children are inherently optimistic, and, of course,

brimming with greed. To employ a horsy metaphor: I purpose-fully donned blinders as I packed up random belongings and hauled my suitcase to the garage and into the backseat of our three-year-old Ford Fairlane. I knew enough to fear my mother's plans and potential delusions but if they yielded me a horse like Cochise, so be it. Eyes on the prize, baby. Hi-ho Silver. I must have waited in the front seat for more than an hour—fiddling with the glove compartment, rolling the window up and down, chewing the corners off my fingernails. Every so often my mother would load something else into the trunk and happily promise "one more minute." While I tried to stay sanguine about it all I'll admit my heart dropped an inch or so when I saw her stuffing all those dried flowers into the trunk along with her easel and her collected works on canvas. Clearly we were doing something more than driving to Jefferson Parish to scout horses. The trunk wouldn't close so she tied it with kitchen twine.

"There," she said, sliding behind the wheel. "Are you ready?"

"Where are we going?"

The car was rolling out of the garage when she said, "New Mexico."

For the most part I processed this in silence, until we were well outside New Orleans and following Highway 61 on its straight-arrow course toward Baton Rouge. Miss Willa had the peculiar and discomfiting habit of speaking to me as if I were a contemporary, and she chatted and chattered as we passed through those little swamptowns: about Mrs. Marge next door whose husband was in debt to some gangsters; about Charlotte Deviney who was in the hospital for reasons relating to her "uterus" which for all I knew was the technical term for a unicorn's horn; but mostly about the painter Georgia O'Keeffe who I soon gathered was the inspiration for our journey. According to my mother, O'Keeffe had carved herself the per-

fect artist's existence in New Mexico, a place she (and thus my mother) called "the Faraway." New Mexico was stark and haunting and blessed "with the most amazing light," as opposed to Louisiana where, she claimed, there was "no sky." This was baffling to me: What was all that blue in the windshield? Our native landscapes, she told me, were visually impenetrable—nebulous monochromes of moss and muck, devoid of angles and color and light. "Look at it out there," she said. "It's mud. We live in mud. How can you paint mud? How can you live in mud?" In "the Faraway," she said, it was different. Dawn's light dousing the desert was a miracle that would squeeze tears of awestruck joy from our eyes. The sun there was close enough to touch with a fingertip.

I spied a roadside fortuneteller—Highway 61 used to be rife with those—and begged her to stop. "That's ridiculous, Benjamin," she said. (I've never been Bennie to her, always Benjamin—and, I should note, to her alone.) "Those people are charlatans and anyway darling we don't need our fortunes told. We know exactly what lies ahead for us. Things are going to be different for you and me. They're going to be better."

"What about Dad?" I finally asked.

She sighed: Oh, him. There was a silence while her arms tensed against the steering wheel. "Do you love your father, Benjamin?" she asked.

Did I? The question had never occurred to me before. Of course I did. Was it possible not to? He was my father. He poured my cornflakes and shared the paper with me and at night spoke crazywords to me that I clung to like bobbing liferafts. "Yes," I told her.

She sighed again and fetched a Salem from her purse. Publicly, Miss Willa was always quitting smoking, or about to be quitting. She'd announce to us that she was done with cigarettes but then immediately retreat to the bathroom to sneak one. We were always finding filters floating in the toilet bowl,

trailed by a tea-colored stain. "Willa!" my father would say. "Someone's cigarette has floated up from the sewers again! We must call plumber."

"Your father is a good man," she said, cracking the window to draft off her smoke. "He is. He's a gentle man. I'll give him that—he wouldn't harm a fly. But he doesn't understand people like you and me. He doesn't want the same things we want. He wants food on the table and a job to go to and he doesn't care what the food tastes like or what the job is. Do you know he's never asked for a raise from Mr. Prejean? Never. He's just too different from you and me. Maybe it's what he went through during the war—that was a hard time, you know."

She took a contemplative drag on the Salem. "He just wouldn't understand the Faraway," she said. "You can have horses there and I can paint. As many horses as you like. That's the life we were meant for, Benjamin. That's what we're headed for."

It was brutally cunning, I realized later: By weaving my desires into hers, by brushing my horses onto her chimeric landscape, she made me an accomplice. Why were we abandoning my father? Because he refused me a horse. Because he was different from us. For one hundred miles she belabored the point: A boy needed wide-open spaces; a woman needed freedom and romance and *life*; the two of us were sun-craving flowers planted in the damp shade; "your father" wouldn't miss us, would barely notice our absence; she'd left him dinner in the icebox plus there were leftover porkchops; God bless the Faraway, Benjamin; the Faraway is our destiny. A thousand LIVE CRAWFISH signs whizzed past. Tourist courts with algae-scummed swimming pools. Spring cotton fields fuzzed with tender green growth that you could only see from certain angles. Crushed, buzzard-picked armadillos that went *unk* beneath our tires. Skinny black kids playing too close to the road,

stilled by our passing; for a few inscrutable seconds their hard stares would meet mine as my mother gassed us westward.

Outside Opelousas we stopped for gas and lunch. I remember I ordered *boudin* sausage which repulsed her. "I think there's pig's blood in those," she warned. "Anyway it's not a good idea to trust the food outside New Orleans." She let me buy bubblegum cigarettes and I chainsmoked them into Texas, my window cracked to exhaust the powdered-sugar smoke. I thought twice about ditching the gum out the window, wondering if such discarded sweets were what lured doomed armadillos onto the highway. So instead I gobbed the spent pieces together with my hands and wrapped them in newspaper. By Huntsville I had a baseball-sized wad.

"Is New Mexico important?" I asked her.

"Important?" she said. "To us? I think it's terribly important."

"No," I said. "To the Russians. Do they think it's important?"

"I don't know what you mean."

"Well, New Orleans is important because it's a port city and that's why the Russians are going to bomb it. Are they going to bomb New Mexico, too?"

"Oh, honey, no. Where do you get all this? You don't need to be afraid. The Russians wouldn't bomb New Mexico. It's too beautiful and there's no one there anyway. You won't need to worry anymore."

I found this information hard to digest—and weirdly disappointing, too. For all my nightsweats about nuclear attack, there was something mesmerizing and exciting about it as well, something that felt the way a dangerous bout of lust would strike me later in life—an amalgam of dread and desire that made my heart race, that injected my veins with the sizzle of doom. I *wanted* to worry about it.

We ate dinner at an Old West–themed restaurant where the waiter wore a cowboy hat and a string tie and called me padnah. "You see, honey?" my mother said. "We're in the West now. It's different." She suggested I order sarsaparilla which she claimed was the soda of choice for cowboys but it tasted just like root beer to me. When the jukebox played Marty Robbins's "El Paso" my mother sang along until I begged her to stop. Her church-pew soprano on "wild as the west Texas *wi-ihhhhh-nnnnn-d*" was drawing stares. "Oh, don't be so serious," she said. "For heaven's sake, you're just like your father sometimes." To keep myself occupied I drew a sloppy crayon portrait of the waiter on the back of the kids' menu. "Oh, how wonderful," my mother said. "Let me show him." I protested, lividly, but she showed him anyway. "Ain't that some'n, padnah," he said with an unmistakable air of bullshit. "My son is very talented," my mother said, clasping my hand. When the waiter was out of earshot she asked me if I didn't think he was handsome. I shrugged.

"Oh, you don't know, you're a *boy*," she said. After glancing at the nearby tables, she leaned in toward me, speaking as softly as a wartime confidante. "Benjamin," she said. "Let me ask you something. Would it bother you if there was a new man around?"

"What kind of man?"

"Not so loud. Just someone to take your mother dancing once in a while. And maybe to play with you. Throw a ball, that sort of thing. Why, maybe a man who knows something about horses."

"I don't know."

"But it wouldn't bother you?"

We spent the night in a cabin-court room at a motel my mother chose because of the huge white steer horns that crowned its roadside sign. "How fun," she said. The blankets on the beds were decorated with the same horns. There was a

black-and-white TV in the room but the antenna was broken
and it didn't get any channels, so I dipped into the Gideon Bible I discovered in the drawer of the nightstand between our
beds. Midway through the Book of Revelation—I've always
started books at the end—my mother ordered me to turn off
the light. After that I lay awake listening to the purr of highway
traffic and watching the glow from passing headlights roam the
walls of our room. "This is nice, isn't it?" my mother said to the
dark. It wasn't obvious she was talking to me. "Goodnight," is
what I said back. "Yes," she went on. "It's good that it's nice."

– – – –

PARDON THE INTERRUPTION but guess who was just here?
The Munchkin! (Cribbing from Alojzy, and his upgrade from
niedźwiedź to *Niedźwiedź*, I have promoted her from munchkin
to Munchkin.) Surely you remember: the one with the handheld slot machine and the comatose husband and that packet
of Kleenex currently tucked in my satchel. I was "scribbling
away" (to use Oshkosh Bob's phrase) at the above, adrift in my
own mental Texas, when I felt a finger jabbing me in the chest.
Rather hard, too: a barfight-quality poke. "Hey, buster," she
said to me, flashing a bridgeworked smile. "I was heading out
for some air and saw you sitting here."

"I could use some air myself," I told her.

As we walked through the terminal she asked me, "Have
they told you when you're getting out of here?"

"By April, guaranteed," I said.

"Holy moly," she said. "You're joking."

"I am."

"Well," said she, "anything is possible."

Out on the sidewalk I lit her cigarette for her. "Oh goody,
a gentleman," she said. Then, holding the lit cigarette away
from her, examining it with distaste, the way Stella used to
sometimes appraise me in the mornings, she said, "These darn

things. I went twenty-two years without. And then I got the call from the state police, saying Ralph had been in the crash. I didn't even make it to the hospital before stopping to buy a pack. I had to pick my jaw up off the floor when they told me the price. I think they were sixty-five cents back when I quit the first time. Darn things."

"They keep my hands occupied," I said. "Otherwise I might strangle myself."

"Now I know you're joking," she said.

I was. But anything is possible.

She'd been to Vermont to visit her daughter and grandchild. Her daughter was married to a high-strung political aide who, while smart, worked "for a Socialist." Her granddaughter was two, she told me, and while otherwise angelic, had "sleep problems." ("Sleep *issues*, I mean," she corrected herself, having obviously been corrected herself.) The parents thought it best to let the girl "cry it out" so after putting her down in her crib they inserted earplugs and pretended to read magazines downstairs while grinding their teeth between spurts of bickering. From the first night, Granny Munchkin found the little girl's shrieking unendurable, and so planted herself cribside, humming lullabies to her. It didn't work, she told me, but it was *something*. A psychiatrist might have noted the parallels between this and her longrunning vigil at her husband's bedside, but I am not a psychiatrist. I am a smoker. I noted that it must have been nice to see her daughter.

"Oh of course," she said, shrugging lightly as if to conceal a dinge of sadness. "We go back and forth sometimes, about Ralph. She thinks it's time for us to let him go. I don't think that's up to us. Who am I to say what's hopeless and what's not? Leave it to the angels."

She asked if I had children. "A daughter," I said, shrugging lightly myself. I gave her the skinniest skinny about that: Speck getting married tomorrow, me trying to get there. The single-

sentence summary to which this letter and maybe my life is one long blazing footnote. The conversation moved on, nostalgically, smokily, to the good old days of air travel—the regulation era, with its red-eye flights and goopy-but-satiating meals and dapperly dressed travelers and (here comes my two cents) svelte and allegedly immoral stewardesses and rear-of-the-aircraft smoking sections—and then the Munchkin said *What the heck* and slid another cigarette from her pack. After I'd lit it she extended a hand to me and said, "Margaret."

"Bennie," I said, pumping her plump hand. "Margaret? I was married to a Margaret once." Ha ha, me. Always playing the rogue. Cue a jellybowl laugh from Ed McMahon.

"Well, I hope you were good to her," she said, with what looked like a wink but might also have been a stigmatic tic.

Whoops. How to respond to that one? I stared for a moment, blinking, watching a baggage porter gnaw a fingernail while leaning against his empty cart. I thought I was good. Tried to be. Damn we were lonely people, the two of us. The day after our berserk tryst in my apartment I received a telegram from Margaret in Warsaw: MORE, SHE SAYS, MORE. Who could fail to grin wolfishly after opening that one? Later that night I composed a slapdash poem for her about our night together, as seen from the perspective of one of my sacrificial shirt-buttons. To be honest I didn't remember all that much of the evening—my blackouts were never fully black, more like burning charcoal: some parts black, some parts gray, some parts orange and blistering—but I recalled enough fleshy details for the purposes of light verse.

The letter she wrote back was so deliciously smutty (as opposed to my cutesy Donne-ish ditty) that I felt I should be charged by the minute for reading it. And then rereading it, whew. Before I had time to respond I received another letter from her, this one winsome and chatty and more but not exclusively concerned with matters above-the-waist. Much of it

was about the nineteenth-century painter whose work she was in Poland studying (Henryk Rodakowski) and how I resembled one of his subjects—minus, that is, his rabbinical beard, pear-shaped physique, bulbous copper nose, and obvious blighted penury. The eyes, she said. Something about those starving-hound eyes. (Woof, I said to the letter.) She'd made a rubbing of Rodakowski's tombstone while in Krakow, and enclosed a copy of it for me—an adolescent gesture, to be sure, like your college girlfriend sending you a rubbing of Jim Morrison's grave from Paris, but then perhaps it was an adolescent affair all around. An end-of-summer-camp romance. Or no, scratch that: rather two middle-aged sadsacks fumbling loosely in the dark, pretending they could start fresh. Pretending that springy bed with the parchment-colored sheets was the backseat of an Oldsmobile parked by the lake, pretending the steamy odor of vodka on my rottening skin was the smell of 75¢/gallon gasoline or a horny teenaged boy's drugstore cologne.

Forgive me: I've ladled too many memories into your bowl already. But allow me one more spoonful. (Your better alternative is to put me on a plane but I can see that's too much to ask.) I haven't thought about poor Margaret in more than a decade, meaning never sober. And now comes Margaret the Munchkin, High Commandant of the Margarets Brigade, wanting to ascertain that I was good to her sister-in-Margarethood. Well, define good. I've been trying for years, lady, without success or even noticeable progress, like some pinhead into his third decade of trying to outwit a Rubik's Cube.

We continued our correspondence even after she returned to the states, Margaret and I. If we weren't writing daily, then almost daily. How I loved those letters! With each one she became something new in my mind, transformed and retransformed in my squiffed imagination. When I was feeling shallow & thick-witted, I would read her letters about Rodakowski and her work, as well as her responses to my old poems (which

she poignantly tracked down via an out-of-print-book search),
marveling at her incisiveness and feeling somehow wiser by my
association, by the fact that I had made her shriek those voluptuous arias in my bed and then telegram me their echoes
the next day. In my lonesome unloved hours I would read her
saucier letters, lowering myself into the hot bath of her affection, blood rushing to the center of my body. In the funhouse
of my mind my images of her—scarce and scattered to begin
with—grew bent and warped. Who was this woman? Did the
trail of freckles between her breasts that I remembered, those
caramel droplets of sunlight that I kept following in daydreams,
truly belong to her? Or were they some other woman's, or no
other woman's? I had only her continuous stream of letters
and my dim memories of that night which seemed ever less
trustworthy as the weeks passed. Admittedly, I draped her in
hopes. Here might be a woman who could save me, I thought,
who could rescue me from myself. The old drunk's fantasy. Or
maybe: Here was a woman I could love. Raptly, I began envisioning our life together: me writing beside a fire in some log-
chinked, Frostian Connecticut farmhouse (she'd written to me
about the farmhouse, though the chinked logs were my imagined detail), sipping but not guzzling brandy (my naive ambition was never to quit drinking, only to moderate it), some An-
glo-Saxon breed of dog snoring at my feet, big marshmallow
snowdrifts visible through an ice-latticed window; her drinking
muted blends of tea in another room, studying Rodakowski's
fat-nosed portraits until that lush desire—which was primarily
what I knew of her, firsthand anyway—overcame her, with the
force of a popped champagne cork, at which point she would
sashay into my room and straddle my chair and et cetera et cetera until even the fire would be blushing. Rinse and repeat. I
cherished the thought, as they say. Maybe being in Poland at
the time contributed something to my imaginative fervor: Everyone around me was dreaming big. Everything seemed pos-

sible. Moreover, I wasn't me over there, or at least didn't feel the soggy old weight of being me. Perhaps, courtesy of Margaret, I could prolong not being me—especially since my Polish visa was set to expire. My letters grew increasingly fictional, in spirit rather than statement; I wanted, desperately, to enact this delusive life I'd cooked up, and needed to sell her on it.

After two and a half months I proposed marriage. By letter, of course. This was after an especially rotten night of drinking during which I'd been roughed up by some students, after Grzegorz abandoned me at a party to which he'd earlier dragged me. I was the only one there over twenty-five and apparently my benign two A.M. flirtation with a sweet little number in counterfeit Levi's irked the boys. I suppose, not without empathy, that they were tired of rich old foreigners trying to bed their women. The Russians had been bad enough; now they had to contend with this tanked American poet, slurring lines from Keats. One of them put me in a full Nelson, hoisting me by my underarms, while another led us out the doorway to the stairs. They hauled me halfway down the stairs before chucking me the rest of the way down. Something—the banister, the vodka, or a combination of both—knocked me unconscious for an hour, maybe two. Suffice it to say that it wasn't a pleasant awakening. We drunks always talk about "hitting bottom" but usually without this much precision. If my soul could have quit my body at that moment, could have stood up and brushed itself off and walked away, leaving that corporeal husk crumpled at the foot of the stairs . . . well, unfortunately I didn't know how to pull off that particular magic trick, so the point is moot. Just before dawn I staggered home, chanting *enough* in every language I knew. As the dawn crept across Krakow I wrote Margaret to ask her to marry me, sealed the envelope, and sucked down some ibuprofen. Then I slept, vampirically, until nightfall.

She called me to respond. This was maybe a week and a

half later. I hadn't remembered the odd squeak in her voice; it sounded as if it stemmed from a mechanical issue, as if some glottal hinge was rusty and perhaps she needed to gargle some WD-40. I asked if she had a cold which she denied. "Must be a bad connection," I said. She accepted my proposal ("yes, she says, yes"), as you already know, and we set about planning a wedding. Or rather she did: She knew an "interfaith minister" who performed weddings in her study. I said it sounded peachy. I was nearly forty years old and I'd never called anything in my life peachy before, not even a peach. This was either a very peachy sign, or a decidedly bad omen.

She picked me up at JFK. Thankfully she was holding a sign —MORE, SHE GETS, MORE; very charming, though the trope was beginning to wear—because I didn't recognize her. In my defense she was wearing a different dress and had gotten her hair severely chopped. Also I'd never noticed she was flat-footed. My fiancée was 4F. She wanted to make out in the airport but, as sweetly as I could, I suggested we move along, and not only because airports strike me as woefully inappropriate venues for passion. Her Connecticut farmhouse was indeed a farmhouse, somewhere underneath its vinyl siding, but the farm had disappeared decades ago. Split-level homes from the '70s surrounded it like architectural weeds. There was a lake nearby, as she'd written, covered with a rind of antifreeze-colored duckweed; an open meadow had formerly separated her house from the lake, but now two houses were under construction there, gagging the neighborhood's last breathable space. She had a paddleboat tied up at the lake, she said. The blue one. She suggested I take a spin.

That's mostly what I did, to be honest: spin. I'd head out to the lake in the mornings, sometimes with the newspaper but usually not, and paddle the blue boat out to the middle of the verdigris lake where I would sit drinking for hours. In no time at all the duckweed would reclaim the glossy black trail

of my wake and I would drink myself to a floating stillness. Even the day after our wedding—a short, crisply secular exchange of vows witnessed by Margaret's younger sister and her department chair—found me on the lake, rather than on my new bride. To be frank I was having problems in the bedroom; for whatever reason, my body wasn't much interested in being there. Reaching under the sheets inevitably yielded a defeated sigh from Margaret. She'd pull the covers up over her unfreckled breasts and together, in silence, we'd watch the cracks on the ceiling. Their entertainment value was nil. Every night the same rerun.

Sometimes, when I was out on the paddleboat, I'd see kids fishing from a footbridge at one end of the lake, but I never saw them catch anything. I admired their faith. I watched burgers get grilled, lawns get mowed. One time I saw a guy in denim shorts, having exhausted himself yanking the starter cord of a recalcitrant push-mower, pick the damn thing up and heave it down the lawn toward the lake, then kick it for added measure. Not romantically, this reminded me of the night I'd proposed; why, I'd been that mower. When the guy glanced up and saw me staring, he pointed at the machine as if to assign blame. I gave no response. Sometimes, too, I'd spy Margaret, my new wife, at the edge of the lake, leveling the same stare at me as I'd leveled at the mower thug. Sometimes she'd wave. Sometimes I'd wave back. On occasion she'd leave a picnic lunch, cold lemon chicken or something, the knife and fork tied together with ribbon. The ribbon broke my heart. Oh what the fuck had I done this time.

Margaret ended it. Or rather it was Margaret who spoke the ending aloud. I didn't have the guts. "This is silly," she said matter-of-factly one evening. "You don't love me."

"I want to," I said.

"It doesn't work that way," she said. "It's not a matter of willpower."

We were remarkably sanguine about it. That is to say, she was. I was just me. More than anything else she felt foolish, she said. It had just felt so good to *connect*, she said. The *connecting* felt so good, so strong. Part of her, she admitted, had felt swindled in these final few days, as if she'd fallen for some swarthy con artist's ruse. Yet she'd decided she wasn't the one who'd been duped—I was. I'd conned myself. Weakly, I argued, but it was all for show. After a while she brewed us some coffee and when she delivered me a mug she was unhappily laughing and saying, "Never in a million years did I think I'd end up in a fly-by-night marriage. My oh my. Well, Lorna"—that was her sister—"had you pegged from the get-go. Said you can't base a marriage on a one-night stand. I told her to loosen up. I said you don't turn away love because it doesn't ring the doorbell wearing a suit and carrying roses. Sometimes it comes, I don't know—in through the window."

"Like a mosquito," I said.

"I hate it when she's right."

"We could try counseling," I offered.

"Oh Bennie," she said. "Shut up."

Cut now to the present, or rather to the nearer past.

"No," I answered the Munchkin. "I wasn't so good to her."

She arched her eyebrows. "There's always tomorrow," she said.

"Oh Jesus, I haven't seen her since—"

"To be good," she said. "There's always tomorrow to be good. Now, here," she went on, rummaging through her fanny-pack until that handheld slot machine appeared in her hand. "I've got a cot in there someone's going to steal, so you've got to be quick. But take a spin. Go ahead."

Why not? I depressed the fat oval button at the base. Two bars and a cherry. Close but no cigar, or no cigarette to be more accurate. "One more try," I said.

"That's the only way to win," she said.

Rightly, as it turned out. Three sevens! "Jackpot!" I bellowed. Count 'em, baby! I flashed the machine at the Munchkin and did a giddy little shuffle on the sidewalk. The baggage porter paused from molesting his fingernail to watch me for a moment, and had he not swiftly resumed his chewing I might've tried high-fiving him. Some skin for my win, my brutha! Read 'em and weep. There must be thousands of human beings stranded at this airport but at that odd moment I was the only one dancing. Go figure.

"See?" said the Munchkin. "Nice going, buster."

"What do I get?" I asked her.

"'Get'?" she said, and considered it for a moment. "Well, not money, if that's what you're hoping. You get points."

"Oh," I said, deflating. "What do I get with the points?"

She looked at me as if I was an idiot. "Happiness," is what she said, softly prying the machine from my hand.

- - - -

DEAR AMERICAN AIRLINES, it occurs to me that those whizbang handheld slot machines might be a good investment for you. Here's how it would work: Passengers would be handed one of the machines with their boarding pass. At the gate, thirty minutes prior to the scheduled departure, everyone would have to take a spin at the very same time. If everyone hits jackpot simultaneously, a massive cheer goes up and the plane departs on time. If not, they wait one hour and try again. The upside for you is that we passengers would bemoan our bad luck rather than castigate you. Fate would get the blame, not the poor gate attendants who in this scenario will just shrug and smile and bid us better luck next time. Your planes would take off at about their normal rate but the populist heat would be diverted. See? I offer this idea to you *gratis* though you should feel encouraged to cite me in the press release. It would make my mother so proud to see me in the business pages. In fact,

here's my quote: "'Americans love gambling, but their main form of gambling—heading to the airport—has been flagrantly rigged for years,' said Benjamin Ford, a transportation consultant who devised the system for the Texas-based airline. 'The Jackpot Take-Off® from American Airlines is a game of pure chance, and takes the flying game out of corporate hands and delivers it into the hands of the people.'" Tweak as needed, and you're welcome.

Speaking of Texas: I believe that's where I left off with my tale of mother-son adventure, my childhood roadtrip with Sally Paradise. So as they used to say in the western pulps: *Meanwhile, back at the ranch.* I remember Texas lasting forever —my mother asked me to draw a picture of it, so I drew a straight horizontal line and called it quits—but we made it to New Mexico by the second evening. I don't believe my mother had a clear destination in mind, other than New Mexico, i.e. "the Faraway." We drifted north toward Santa Fe, which was near to where O'Keeffe's Ghost Ranch was located, but Miss Willa was jumpy and anxious once we crossed the state line, as if she expected the Faraway to be rapturously self-evident—as if she thought she would recognize one of the abstract landscapes from O'Keeffe's *oeuvre* and then need only to park the car. Suddenly invalidated, the Texaco roadmap we'd been unfolding and folding since New Orleans sank beneath a pile of candy wrappers and other travel-debris on the floorboards. "We're close, Benjamin," she said. "I can feel it." That evening's sunset was characteristically crimson but insufficiently magnificent for her. "It must be too dry," she said. "The air needs a little moisture for a *really* fiery sunset. You'll see."

We were on an ominous desert sideroad after dark, without a single distant lightbulb in sight, when I shrieked. I felt a sudden hot pain on the skin of my ankle—a sharp, scalding stab—and instantly, because we were out west, presumed I'd been bitten by a rattlesnake that had somehow taken up

residence in our car. "What?" my mother screamed, flinging an arm over my chest as the Fairlane swerved across the road throwing sideways bursts of gravel. "Snake!" I screamed back, which only increased the swerving; it felt like we were spinning 360s down the road. I skittered up onto the seat and grabbed my stinging ankle which to my befuddled surprise I found wet and hot, as if I'd been attacked by . . . soup. "I'm covered in poison!" I announced, holding up my dripping hand, and as my mother said *Wait wait* and braked the car there was a tremendous explosion from under the hood followed by billows of steam or smoke (we weren't sure which) that came rolling across the windshield. The car spluttered and startled and I was thrown forward onto the floorboards where a blistering liquid rained all over me. When the car came to a standstill at the roadside we leapt out of it in tandem and ran panicked circles around it, in opposite directions, meeting at the front of the car where my mother gathered me into her arms to examine my wound and to issue a cc'd prayer to Jesus, Mary, and Joseph. "Oh, Benjamin, no," she said, which convinced me I was a goner even though the pain was dissipating. "I don't see any bite," my mother said, and brought a wet fingertip to her nose to smell it. She frowned. "I think it's car stuff."

"What kind of car stuff?"

"I don't know. Not gasoline. It smells . . ."

"Like what?"

"Like pee-pee — a little bit. Though sweeter . . ."

"The car peed on me?" I asked.

"Tinkled," she said. "We say 'tinkled.'"

Together, we turned our gaze to the Ford Fairlane. Steam was cascading from beneath the hood, and typhoons of it, smelling weirdly like corn syrup, were engulfing us. My mother stood up and gingerly approached the hood, ready to leap backwards, the way a pup appraises some unfamiliar thing that may or may not be alive and befanged. Meanwhile I walked be-

yond the rear of the car to assess our location. We were on the side of a two-lane road smack dab in the parched New Mexican nowhere. One of those "blue highways" Americans have taken to romanticizing now that our cars don't break down every four hundred miles. There were no road signs, and not a single car or truck had passed us or was showing distant, glimmering hints of approaching. The silence was downright stunning, if you got far enough away from the engine's hissing demise. No light, no sound, no humidity: the absence of everything. I remember thinking this must be what space was like—the night sky was breathtakingly overfreckled with stars—or the aftermath of Armageddon. Or the Faraway, I thought.

"Your damn father," my mother was muttering when I returned. "He spends all damn day tinkering with foreign cars but doesn't take care of his own cars, excuse my language. But isn't that just like him. Well, I guess he gets the last laugh."

"You said he doesn't laugh."

"It's a figure of speech, Benjamin," she said. "Now what do we do?"

I went to fetch the roadmap but it was soaking in a pool of antifreeze, the source of my scalding. I remembered that the map had cautioned drivers navigating the desert to always carry water in case of emergencies but we'd neglected that advice. For the first time I noticed how cold it was, which surprised me—I'd thought the desert would be hotter than New Orleans. Shivers overwhelmed me.

"I think we should lift the hood," I told my mother.

"You do it," she said.

A hot blast of steam clobbered me, not unpleasantly, as I unlatched and raised the car's hood. We stood for a while watching the roiling steamclouds and listening to the stalled engine rattle and ping until my mother suggested we climb back into the car to stay warm. "You should turn off the lights," I said. "That runs the battery down."

"So you're a mechanic now?" she snapped back. "Did your father teach you that?"

"Everyone knows that."

"Don't you 'everyone' me, Benjamin," she said.

"Well, it's true."

"I suppose you want to grow up to fix cars, is that right?"

"I don't know."

"Maybe you should have stayed back with your father then. The two of you could be greasemonkeys together. Just imagine! You could tinker with jalopies and never wash your hands and fall asleep in front of the damn television set, excuse my language, and eat those miserable pirogues every night for dinner. There's a life."

"Pierogies," I said. "*Pirogues* are boats."

"I know what a *pirogue* is! I misspoke! And you have some nerve correcting me, young man. Honestly. *Pirogues*, pierogies. Your father wouldn't know the difference so long as he had ketchup." She lit a cigarette, smoking it with the ravenous inhalations of a junkie. "Oh for God's sake look where we are. Blast your father anyway."

When a car passed, without stopping or even slowing, my mother said, "There went our chance. There it went. Our last chance."

"I'm cold," I said.

This frail admission seemed to calm or steady her—to pluck some maternal string within her, however untuned. Gently, she said, "I know, honey. I'm cold too. It's our New Orleans blood. We weren't designed for this." She reached over and ran a hand through my hair. "Everything will be okay, I promise."

Roughly a half-hour later the interior of the car filled with a dazzle of white light; a pickup truck had pulled in behind us. We listened to the sputtery growl of its engine, filtered through an injured muffler, and the creak-clank of its doors closing, with our eyes fixed on the car's side-view mirrors for a glimpse

of our rescuers. We each had a view: There were two men, approaching our car on both sides. The man on my side was young, somewhere in his twenties, and wearing a straw cowboy hat, bluejeans, and a woolen vest festooned with stripes of blue, purple, and black. The moment his face appeared in the window I could see he was an Indian or what are nowadays called Native Americans—glossy black braids dangled at the sides of his coppery face. When our eyes met he grinned, displaying wet purple gums where his two front teeth ought to have been, and with a knuckle he rapped on the glass.

"Oh my God!" my mother screamed. "*Indians!* Lock the doors, Benjamin, lock them *now!*"

I looked at the man on the other side of my window. "Need help?" he mouthed.

"For the love of dear almighty God I will not be scalped," my mother was saying.

"I think they want to help us," I said.

"They want our *scalps*, Benjamin! They're going to rip our foreheads off!"

The man outside my window—sweetly frowning, hands on his knees—appeared very puzzled. He stood up, looking at his companion across the roof of our car, and shrugged. I raised my index finger to him, to say please wait. He frowned and shrugged again but didn't walk away.

"They want to help us," I told my mother.

Miss Willa's hands were on the steering wheel, tight like a race-car driver's, and I could see her chest heaving. She seemed on the verge of vomiting but in an instant I saw that it was sobs coming, not vomit. Her grip on the wheel tightened even more as tears ran down her face. Her head bobbed up and down as if the tears were too heavy for her neck to support. A croaking sound echoed up from her lungs.

"They aim to kill us," she sputtered. "I saw it in a movie. Oh, Benjamin, what have I done?"

"No, Mother," I said. "Our car needs fixing. I think they want to help."

"Why?" she screamed, and then screamed it again, and then again, banging the steering wheel with the flat of her hands so violently I felt sure the wheel would snap off. "Why does this happen to me? Why can't it ever be the way it should be? Tell me that, why?" In a frenzy she searched the car for something else to hit and for a moment I feared she would slap me. Instead she punched the window with the side of her fist, six or seven times, and each time with an escalating shriek; I saw the Indian on her side jump back.

"Tell them to kill me," she said. "Do it."

"They're not going to kill you."

"What do you know?" She was hissing at me. "You don't know anything. Do you have any idea what it's like to be an animal in a cage? Why in God's name do I even try anymore? You tell me that, Mr. Know-Everything. Tell me! All I wanted was to give you a better life. You! You've ruined me, you and your father. Y'all have sucked the life right out of me. I can't even sleep at night. What's the point of dreaming? There is no point with you two. It's cruel, is all it is. All I wanted was to give you a horse. A stupid damn horse. That's why we're here, Benjamin," she said, and at this she started sobbing again, barely able to make the words, "for your stupid damn horse."

"I don't want a horse anymore," I said. My voice was cracking. "I'm hungry. I just want a cheeseburger."

Maybe it was the word *cheeseburger* that did it: How truly dire can your situation be if the word *cheeseburger* is involved? For what felt like a long time she wept, with her eyes clamped shut, and then she wiped her eyes and inhaled deeply to compose herself and wiped her hands on the pleats of her dress. When she said it was okay I got out of the car and spoke to the Indians who didn't ask about the woman sitting alone inside. Was I thus aware, at that single-digit age, of just how to fetch

my mother from her mental Faraway? Did I know, consciously, that appealing to whatever splinter of maternal dutifulness was embedded within her—by lamenting that I was cold, or hungry, or hurt—would sometimes reel her back in? Children are instinctual creatures, wholly capable of strategy. I must have looked pathetic there, a skinny-legged child all but swallowed by the dark passenger seat, begging his mother to put aside her wild, discordant visions—the purple fantasies of idyllic independence and artistic freedom and sexual license clashing with her provincial fears of the unknown, with her numskulled nightmares of cinematic savages carving off her forehead—so that he could fill his small belly with a *cheeseburger*. Acting pitiable was a tack that would serve me well with my mother, as a child, but decidedly not so well with others, as an adult. I remember when Stella smashed me with that glass: I merely sat there, dazed but not entirely so, letting the blood pour down my cheeks and onto my shirt, contorting my face in the noble way of the punchdrunk & bloodsmeared Rocky Balboa when Mickey was begging him, in the ring-corner, to let him stop the fight, and invoking, furthermore, that most poignant detail: that Stella had hit me with our only water glass. As if my sole concern was for our domestic infrastructure—my eyesight be damned. I didn't curse and run to the mirror to flush my wound and pick the shards from my eye. I didn't push her away. I just sat there passively, using the gush of blood to appeal to her sense of pity, which was not so dissimilar to the pose I adopted in my "confessional" poems: that of a child, wounded and confused by life's fangs, pleading for a cheeseburger when all I really wanted was to scream *Stop stop I want out.*

We rode back to town in the Indians' truck. The driver had a kind, jowly face and his round belly was capped with a silver belt buckle the size of a 45-rpm record. The other Indian, the one whose face had appeared in my window, was his nephew, and he was drunk. His eyes resembled the famously red pop-

pies that O'Keeffe was so fond of painting. The uncle had looked at our engine, while my mother sat in the car, and said a lot of automotive gobbledygook that even today I would probably have a difficult time following, though I vaguely remember his diagnosis: a hole in the radiator, a torn-up belt, some grim et ceteras. I asked him if he could fix it and he said no but told me he had a cousin who could—farther down the road, in town. He'd tow it in the morning. There was a "nice motel" in town too; the uncle pointed to his truck and said for us to load up. My mother never said a word to them; every now and then, on the ride to town, a little sob would escape from her and she would cover her mouth as if she'd burped. A preacher on the radio filled the silence for us with the story of a man who lost a finger to a grain thresher but whose prayers caused a new finger to grow from the nub of the old one. When the radio preacher shouted *Hallelujah* the Indians repeated it, even the drunk nephew who blazed through four cans of Coors on the way to town while staring out the black window.

They dropped us off at a motel with an unpaved parking lot and told us where we could find our car the next day. In a more humid and genteel version of her New Orleans accent, my mother called them "saints" and "Samaritans" and pressed into the uncle's hand a dollar bill, which was examined and accepted without comment. I felt I should follow them and say something more, but didn't. My mother's hand was planted on my shoulder while she blithely waved goodbye with her other hand.

I never got my cheeseburger though to be honest I was never that hungry. My mother went into the room, which smelled of antique cooking grease, and resumed weeping while I sat in an aluminum chair outside the door, bundled in a thin wool blanket, minding the activity at the town's single intersection. Those semis sounded like thunder. After a while I went to the front desk and asked the old woman there how to make a

long-distance call and she guided me through the protocol of calling collect. It was two A.M. in New Orleans but my father answered on the first ring.

We celebrated my birthday at a diner across the highway from the motel. My mother was in no mood to sing—she didn't have enough money to pay for the motel plus the car repair and was stricken with worry; she didn't know my father was on his way—but the fat waitress and a coffee-slurping trucker beside me serenaded the delivery of a bowl of ice cream in which a forest of ten candles had been planted. "You're a man now," the trucker said to me. "A big ol' man." He pulled a quarter from my ear and let me keep it and also gave me an American Legion baseball cap way too big for my head. My mother made me ask for his address so I could write him a thank-you note. The trucker laughed and said the diner was as close to home as anywhere and the fat waitress confirmed that with a caustic chuckle as she refilled his coffee mug. To me it seemed like a condition to admire.

My father arrived early the next morning—it was still dark. When we opened the door he was standing there holding a present for me, wrapped in the *Times-Picayune*'s Sunday comics pages, a handsome toy horse with moveable legs. At first my mother was angry and accused him of hunting her down like a lost dog. They fought and she locked herself in the bathroom while my father sat on the edge of the bed with his head in his hands. She softened when he paid the motel bill and got the Fairlane out of hock at the repair shop. The plan was for us to follow him back to New Orleans. Outside the diner, after breakfast, my father sat in the Fairlane and revved its engine to assess its durability for the long drive home. "Okay, okay," he kept saying. We stood together beside the car door, my mother & I, me holding my toy horse and her stroking my hair. The air was dusty and filled with the screech-hiss sound of truck brakes and drifting gray puffs of diesel exhaust. The mesas to

the west looked nothing like O'Keeffe's landscapes: They were muted and dunnish, bleached by the high late-morning sun, all traces of life burned from their flanks save for a stubble of metallic-looking plantlife. It was what I imagined the world would look like in the aftermath of nuclear war: the tops blown off the mountains, the land stripped of color, the air tinged with a toxic haze. Yet the evocation didn't frighten me. Let the world melt in flames, let it rip my forehead off. Let anything come. "It's good," my father said of the car. "If this needle start to go high, you pull over."

I remember my mother's smile: a half-smile, really, but affectionate, in her way. We'd been through this before: those two times to Florida, when I was too young to remember it all, and that time in Atlanta when my mother's cousin Sylvia placed the call to my father while her husband secretly disabled our car (I learned later) by stealing the distributor cap. She would flee, and my father would inevitably fetch her home. Maybe that was always the point: marriage as an awful game of hide-and-go-seek. Maybe my mother never expected, or even intended, to actually escape. After all she was terrible about not finishing her paintings and her suicide attempts were almost always dramatic half-measures. Standing beside the car in that hot cloud of road dust and tailpipe vapors, her hair tossed by the wind, she smiled at my father and said to him, "I don't know why you always do this."

"I did not know," he replied, with neither tenderness nor bitterness, "that I had choice."

TWO A.M. AT O'HARE. The airport resembles refugee camps I've seen on the evening news except for the more upscale luggage and the Starbucks cups strewn willy-nilly amongst the refugees. People are even curled up atop cardboard boxes. Cardboard boxes! Where did they find appliance-sized boxes

in an *airport?* This world never fails to withhold its juicier secrets from me. An hour or so ago they issued a stern last-call for cots which were being distributed at Gate K2. Oh screw it, I figured: The Munchkin deserves cushioning, not me. Let the children sleep while this old coot goes spelunking back through his life, swinging this lamp in a dumb search for truth. So I've staked out a place up here by the ticket counters where it's not quite so crowded and where there's easy access to the nifty sidewalk smoking lounge. I found a seat with a broken chair arm and though I tried to snap the arm off, to widen the seat for the relief of my aggrieved spine, it wouldn't budge. Boy howdy this place is well-armed against comfort.

I should note that your giant neon logo, with its nuzzling A's and that art deco eagle betwixt them, currently looms above me, showering me with a buzzy blue light. How acidly appropriate (to crib the aa-alliteration). And now that I think about it, how ironic too: AA. If you ever ditch the sign for a newer one, I know a rehab clinic that would love it. That jumbo sign hanging in the "group room" would make for the flashiest AA meetings ever.

They've closed the gate terminal—my TSA angel, alas, has abandoned me, has escaped to his mattress at home—so it looks as if this will have to be it for me tonight. My final resting place, hahahahaha

- - - -

TWO A.M., YES. Not quite so lonesome as three A.M., the bittersweet hour that inspired so many blues songs, but near enough. Even in this overlit airport, beneath your radiant blue A's, dear American Airlines, one can't fully escape the seeping darkness. It's like black oil, flowing in slowly beneath the automatic doors. When the doors slide open the blue glow recoils . . . oh for chrissakes dear American Airlines, are you still reading this? Well of course you're still reading this if you're read-

ing *this*—this sentence, I mean. It's just confounding and some-how heartening, at this point, to imagine *why*. Who are you? You there, alone, dutifully turning these pages of mine, some-where . . . yes, you. I presume you're in Fort Worth—that's where this letter is addressed—and, the more I think about it, probably tucked into a cubicle inside a sleek, low building on the outer edges of the corporate compound. One of those anonymous office-park buildings in which the sole splash of color is provided by the lobby Coke machine. Reading this is your job; for the moment, then, *I* am your job. How odd. I have my own caseworker in Texas! Howdy padnah.

I suspect you're young, or youngish; sifting through the cor-porate slushpile is the stuff of an entry-level gig, of the ladder's lower rungs. I imagine you think of your life that way, too: as a ladder which you've just begun to climb. Allow me to take a wild stab, with apologies up front for any errant shots. You're a native Texan, or at most an Oklahoman, Fort Worth's radius of allure being somewhat limited. As a corporate citizen, I suspect you're a traditionalist, a casual God-fearer, perhaps the recent graduate of one of Texas's fine universities. Maybe the Uni-versity of Dallas (I did a reading there once), or perhaps Mid-western State—a no-nonsense school, a sensible campus, one of those hatcheries for the big corporate pools. Yet you like the concrete virtues of working for a large corporation. The transparency of your future, the way it can be quantified, is a comfort to you. To be frank I envy you: You aren't victimized by your daydreams. I don't mean this condescendingly, mind you. Your bootstraps are sturdy, you've got a plan. Your feet are planted firmly on the ground. You've got the world tight by its tail, etc.

And yet here you are—what time is it there, what day?— reading this. When you tore open the envelope and slid out this crazyass sheaf of paper your jaw must have dropped and you must have wheeled your office chair to the edge of your cubicle

divider, holding these pages in one hand as if weighing them and saying to your neighbor in the adjacent cubicle, "We've got a record-breaker." Maybe you said a "nutcase"—it's okay. Maybe even a reference to Jack Nicholson in *The Shining*, with his hundreds of pages of the same droning sentence. That one's out of line but, awright, I get the impulse. There was probably much astonished laughter traded between the two of you, and maybe you even showed this letter to your manager who wagged his head with grim amusement. Yet still you're reading. You could've stopped a long time ago. Maybe your manager even ordered you to stop. "Hey, (your name here)," he might've said. "Enough with the nutcase already." It's not as if you require further argument to fulfill my refund request. In your mind you long ago awarded me that check, solely on the basis of my Bunyanesque efforts. (Or is it only a voucher for a free trip that you're permitted to grant? In that case, friend, I urge you not to bother.) Let's not forget there are other, more crisp letters for you to read, to sort through, to respond to. *Dear* _____, goes your daily mantra, *Thank you for your recent letter to American Airlines. Thank you for your recent letter to American Airlines.* So many letters, so many judgments, so many names instantly forgotten if indeed they ever penetrated your brain. Plus so much else to do in life, oh the hours can't contain it! Your mother is calling. Your oil needs changing. Your aunt's birthday is Saturday. The folks at work want to meet up at T.G.I. Friday's again—hey, why not, they're a great crew. Your college pals are emailing—forwarded jokes and inspirational messages, you can't keep up. Yet still you're with me—for reasons known only to you, you're listening.

What a weird & warm feeling that suddenly swells me with! Like finally putting a face to God—or at least God's secretary. I can't help thinking of that scene in Karol Szczepanski's novel *The Drummer of Gnojno*—alas, never translated into English—in which the hero is out on the street hurling

mad, foamy-mouthed curses at the stained-glass window of the church (which is not so unlike, come to think of it, your giant blue logo above me) when the elderly pastor emerges and, after hobbling down the steps of the entrance with his cane, asks the hero to please direct his curses at him instead. The hero begins, haltingly, but when he looks into the priest's eyes he collapses weeping into his arms and says over and over again that he's sorry. It is so much easier, after all, to love or hate an idea. Perhaps, then, I should apologize for my prior hectoring & harangues—for my own mad, foamy-mouthed curses. When I called you a miserable fuck, understand that I meant it collectively, not personally. Obviously it wasn't you who threw the track-switch on my life or even on my current itinerary. No, young friend, I owe you better. You've heard me out this far so it's time for me to start coming clean. I'm afraid I've been dressing the corpse as always. There's much I haven't told you.

- - - -

NOT SO FAST. A fella needs to smoke, okay? My doctor says otherwise but he's paid to say that. During my last visit he had me blow into a plastic tube fitted with a Ping-Pong ball I was supposed to raise by exhaling into the tube. I suspect it was rigged. That Ping-Pong ball struck me as curiously heavy. Perhaps a golfball in clever disguise? "You have the lungs of a 150-year-old man," he said, har-de-har. (I was tempted, in response, to quote a line from Bukowski—"It's so easy to die long before the / fact of it"—but reconsidered. Quoting poetry is the quickest route to a blank stare, unless you're in the sack with a lady in which case it's a dangerous toss-up. For example, I once heavy-breathed these lines of Lorca's (per Merwin's excellent translation) to Stella: "Your belly is a battle of roots / your lips a blurred dawn. / Beneath the tepid roses of the bed / the dead moan, waiting their turn." Her unexpected reaction was to shove me off of her and accuse me of conjuring her gang-rape

by skeletons. And she was a poet! Or had been anyway. To assure her of the lines' proper romantic context I had to scurry off to locate the poem in its entirety. "To see you naked is to remember the earth," I read aloud to her, "the smooth earth, swept clean of horses." Because Stella was a horse-lover, these lines tanked as well.) Instead of quoting Buk to the doctor, I cheerily said thank you though he obviously hadn't meant the 150-year-old-man crack as a compliment. Sawbones scowled at me which I found unsavory since, really, I'd only matched him jest for jest. Apparently it's fair to make funny only about bodies you don't inhabit.

When I got home I bragged to Miss Willa and Aneta that the doctor had pronounced my lungs "antebellum" which went straight over Aneta's head but sparked a crispy Post-it note from my mother: NOT FUNNY. Of course we shouldn't discount the possibility that my impious reference to days in Dixie "not forgotten" was what caused her to bristle, rather than my sinking physical state. Her emotional allegiance to the Old South is infinite. If she takes any pleasure from living in New York, it is in having her prejudices about Yankees certified with every fair-weather outing. Once she saw two tattooed lesbians—hardcore dyke-types, from Aneta's description—passionately making out outside a Bleecker Street barroom at noon. It so disgusted and disturbed her—the in-public element of it, I mean, the lack of decorum; Miss Willa is not entirely a ninny—that she went on about it for days, weeks. So I've naturally kept the livelier details of Speck's wedding from her. WHAT KIND OF NAME IS SYLVANA? she Post-it-asked. "Polish," I replied, and she gasped and rolled her eyes before remembering our dear Aneta's national extraction. Poor Miss Willa. Hounded by Poles all her life.

Speaking of Poles: I wrote earlier that my father's death was oddly unemotional for me, a statement that might benefit from clarification. To be frank it seemed like such a relief for him.

I sometimes wonder—less now than I used to—how he ever reconciled the arc of his life, how he ever sketched out that self-narrative in his head. The there-to-here story you mull while lying awake in bed at three A.M. watching a spider traverse the ceiling. Or while immobilized at some godforsaken airport. Just imagine, though, working as an exterminator after surviving Dachau, making & disposing of corpses from nine to five. Flipping the switch on the gas, that sort of thing. What an unholy struggle it must have been to keep from connecting the dots—little wonder he sneaked his victims away to the docks. And after losing everything, let's not forget: his country, his family, his faith, more or less in that order. How high his hopes must have been—must have *needed* to have been—for America. Imagine that brass band welcoming him to shore: *I want to beeeee in dat numbaaah*. What did he think he would find there—here? What must his dreams have looked like? But then it's possible, isn't it, that he had none. Merely blank hope, an empty canister to be filled with the secondhand dreams of a new and scarless country. The dream we call American: a house, a wife, children, an immaculate green lawn, those legions of darker-skinned people whose worse-off situation exists to comfort us about our own. (One of my father's ironies was his adopted racial attitudes—he tossed the word *NEE-gar* around like doubloons from a parade float and was a party-line seg voter. History, even scalding personal history, doesn't always transmit the expected lessons. Memory and meaning, I've found, often book separate rooms in the brain.)

But let's not fool ourselves that the American Dream sufficed. No, you didn't see him at night, not watching the television but rather looking *through* it. I'd try to play catch with him and in his distraction the ball would bean him in the chest. Sometimes in the early morning—like a farmer he always woke at five A.M.—I would find him alone at the breakfast table engaged in what looked like deep prayer but wasn't.

Back when I was an altar boy, and weighing a future as a priest as ten-year-old Catholic boys in New Orleans often did, my mother disclosed to me that my church-shirking father, "of all people," had been studying for the priesthood when "the war started." What a shocker, since my father's favorite English word was *goddamnit*. When I quizzed him about this he waved me away, offering only this: "I had a date with God but He never showed up." ("Henry!" my mother seethed, pushing me from the room. "Don't you dare say things like that to him.") That line whirled back to me five years later, after his death—specifically, when my mother and I were sitting in the funeral director's office, them trying to decide what to inscribe on the tombstone. It seemed like a fitting epitaph but I kept this opinion to myself. That my first reaction upon seeing him in the coffin that day—dressed in a suit he'd never worn, a rosary curled around fingers so begrimed the makeup couldn't mask it—was a proud, tender smile, rather than tears, caused me hot grief & guilt for years thereafter. But I couldn't help myself—all I could think was that he'd gotten *out*. Go, Dad, go. At the wake one of my father's coworkers from the import shop, a beefy Cajun guy with forearms like Popeye the cartoon sailorman, put a hand on my shoulder and said, "Your dad's in a better place, kid." The standard rap. With a nod I replied that yes, I knew it, thank you. But I doubt we had the same place in mind. He was thinking entrance, I was thinking exit. It's the same door but the sign makes all the difference.

But back to the smoking: For the first time since my absurd arrival here, I found myself alone on the sidewalk. Just me and the pavement and my little orange-nubbed cigarette and a red trash barrel onto which a happy sign is pasted: "We're glad you're here," signed by Mayor Richard Daley and endorsed by the Walgreens corporation. I was standing by the trash barrel, half-drowning in old thoughts *à la* those above, when the automatic doors behind me hissed open, startling the hell out of

me. I turned to see who it was—hoping for company, I suppose; hoping for something—but no one was there. A glitch. When the doors closed, I turned back to resume smoking until the doors slid open and closed anew. After that I watched for a while but, observed, the doors wouldn't open. Not until I turned my back to them again. Hearing that sizz of their motor, I spun around and lunged at the doors and shouted *A-ha!* But nothing; no one. Such an odd & lonesome sensation. For a moment I thought how wonderful it must be to live in that angel-patrolled world of the faithful, the world of Cajun mechanics with bulbous forearms, of the Munchkin with her patient, hope-fueled vigilance, of the hobbled old priest from *The Drummer of Gnojno* and the not-twit in the WORLDWIDE MINISTRIES, INC. t-shirt who knelt beside me several hours ago and laid his moist hand on my own spindly, Olive Oyl–ish forearm. To see the opening and closing of the doors as evidence of angels' invisible guard duty, of their soft comings and goings.

How much simpler to lay one's head against an angel's chest and whisper, "Now."

– – – –

NEVERMIND. Let's check in with our correspondent Walenty Mozelewski, who is standing by in Trieste. Walenty, can you hear me? Will you please give the airline an update on recent developments there?

> The Bear was obviously weary of Walenty's shrugs and averted eyes. "I am asking you as my friend," he said, "and as my fellow fighter." Noting Walenty's wince, he said, "But I am not asking you to fight! Only to march alongside us, for a show of strength—not any use of strength, I assure you. Only your voice! Surely you can lend me your voice for a day? Surely you feel a sense of responsibility to justice —to mankind? We did not earn these wounds, me and you, for mere sport."

Though, forgive me—some background is in order, isn't it? I forget that you're not reading along with me here. It's hard not to think of those towering blue A's above me as akin to the Eye of Providence, that divine, all-seeing eyeball that adorns, among other things, our precious dollar bill—tracking my every movement, my every grousing seat adjustment—or more darkly Tolkien's evil Eye of Sauron, but then, strike that, I'm trying to be nicer. Here we are at page 192 of Alojzy's novel, and this is what has recently unfolded: Walenty and Franca, no surprise, have become covert lovers. She steals away to his room at her mother's *pensione* in the predawn hours where they tenderly couple under the musical conduction of Trieste's birds which have become, for Walenty, his primary interest outside of Franca. He leaves his window open and scatters bits & ends of bread throughout his room to lure in the birds, much to the angry dismay of Franca's mother who, ignorant of his motives (and even more ignorant of her daughter's daybreak trysts with him), chides him for his slobbishness. Sometimes in the afternoons he lies on the bed and watches the birds flit through his room. His life is like a misted dream of warm skin, the sugar-dusted trills of birdsongs, the cool seaside air, his postcoital coffee, and his afternoon beers with the Bear—the unattainable attained. Or something like that. It's all a bit Hemingwayesque but that's hard to avoid when you've got a wounded ex-soldier drinking away the afternoons by the shore. For what it's worth, Hemingway would've had Walenty shoot & roast the birds.

True, Walenty's money is running out, and occasionally he's visited by thoughts of the old life—of his two sons, particularly. He's had no word from his family in years but feels confident about their fates since he left them in the care of a cousin, a powerful black-marketeer in Warsaw. Or is it less confidence than indifference? Franca's two brothers are classic ruffians—one of them tripped Walenty at breakfast one morning, and though both brothers laughed and neglected to help him

up Walenty convinced himself it was an accident and laughed along with them. Yet he can't help but wonder if this sort of thugdom is what life holds for his sons, having been tucked away with a band of criminals while the war ravaged on. Franca warned him about her brothers—if they find out about us, she told him, they'll . . . but he pressed a finger to her lips.

And now there is the Bear, who has revealed himself to be a communist rabble-rouser and a Tito partisan. Tito, the Yugoslavian bully, wants to claim Trieste as his own; the Italians, of course, have their own title staked. Tito's followers are massing for a demonstration, to be held two nights hence, and the Bear wants Walenty's support. Walenty, on the other hand:

"You don't understand," he told the Bear. He'd promised to walk Franca home from work today, and already he was late; thus he spoke swiftly. "I don't ever want to hear words like justice or peace or unity or victory again—not ever. I've heard them enough. They've been exhausted within me."

"You don't want justice?" said the Bear, less shocked than confused.

"Of course, but I want it to be invisible," he said. "I don't want to be forced to hear it or think about it or say it or, worst of all, to act upon it. I just want it to be, and for it to leave me alone."

"My God," said the Bear. "What did you fight for?"

"For *this*, don't you understand?" With a wave of his hand he encompassed the sea, the sky, the beer glasses on the table, the route he would walk to meet Franca. "For the skin of a woman and coffee in the morning. For birds. I fought to stop fighting."

"For sex and birds? You're mad. You're describing an animal's life!"

"Yes!" Walenty said. "That's precisely what I want. The life of an animal—a small, unbothered one, something humble like a mouse or even a rat. I want to eat and drink

and sleep beside a woman and not think about yesterday or tomorrow—in fact I don't want even to think. I am owed this. I want only to be alive."

The Bear was quiet for a moment, drumming his fingers on the table. Then he suddenly leaned in, and spoke gravely. "Do you know how I spent much of the last few years?"

Walenty raised his palms. "I don't want to talk about the—"

The Bear's voice became serrated with a low anger: "You listen to me."

(The Bear has never explained his wartime service, if indeed it was service—only vague references to combat in mountains.)

"I spent it eating *rats*. We caught them in traps we made with sticks and large stones, deadfall traps that crushed them, and sometimes because it was too dangerous to light a fire we ate them raw. Once we found a nest of newborn rats and we were so happy because even though there was much less meat, the meat was sweeter. We pinched off their heads with our fingers and ate them whole. So do not tell me you desire the life of a rat. I have pulled their bones from my teeth and wiped their blood from my lips and I have stopped myself from vomiting so that I would not lose their precious sustenance. You know nothing of rats."

Now it was Walenty's voice that simmered. "You do not need to explain starvation to me," he said.

"But apparently I do!"

"You're not understanding what I'm saying," he said.

"I understand that you are a man and are tired of being a man," the Bear said. "But look at you. You are still a man."

That Walenty relents is only partly due to the Bear's badgering. (Yikes, pardon the furred word choice: The badger couldn't bear the bear's badgering.) Back at the *pensione* Walenty has been tutoring himself in Italian with the aid of Franca's school-

books, most notably a translation of Tolstoy's little parable "Three Questions," about a king whose fretting over a trio of questions—When is the right time to do things? Who is the most important person? What is the right thing to do?—gets answered by a hermit and a fellow with a belly-wound. The hermit and the wounded fellow aren't important to us, but this is:

Remember, then,

wrote Tolstoy (via Alojzy),

there is only one time that is important: now. The present is the only time over which we have power. The most important person is the one beside you, for no man knows if he will ever have dealings with another. And the most important thing to do is to make the one beside you happy. For that purpose alone was man sent into this life.

Which is really just a slightly more profound rendition of Stephen Stills's "Love the One You're With," but it's enough to convince Walenty he should grant the Bear this favor: that he should march with the communists to the Piazza Unità, that he should at least hoist a fist in the air for his new friend.

When they assemble in the late afternoon Walenty is startled to see a homemade coffin at the head of the parade. "We are reburying one of our comrades," the Bear explains. The crowd is much smaller than the Bear had promised—fewer than a hundred—which makes Walenty feel uneasily exposed, more like a soloist than a back-row choir member, though he gleans some small comfort from his lack of the red scarf that all the other partisans are wearing. One end of a banner—*Zivio Tito!*—is forced into his hands, and though he tries to protest, he's quickly stifled by the movement of the crowd: They start down a hill, solemnly chanting at first but growing more raucous and unruly with every white-helmeted Allied MP they

pass. If not for the banner in his hand, Walenty thinks, he would steal away; but the banner would collapse, and his absence would be noted. He tries to ignore the Triestines lining the streets to watch their passage—old men and women sizing them up in hostile silence, their arms folded stiffly against their chests. Children by their sides with hard bullets for eyes. For the first time since arriving in the city Walenty feels noticed, *tangible*, a player in the city's history rather than an unseen & unfelt observer, no longer an imperceptible fugitive from another life. His escape, it occurs to him, has been discovered; and a coffin is leading him home.

At the Piazza Unità, where blinding glints of sunlight zigzag off the Palazzo del Governo's gold mosaics, the parade is intercepted by an opposing crowd of Italians, also chanting and carrying banners: a counterdemonstration of demonstrably larger size & heart. There is much shouting and fist-waving which soon deranges, up at the head of the lines, into spitting and shoving. As soon as the first punch is thrown (at or by the Bear, as it happens), an American Jeep loaded with baton-wielding New Zealand soldiers speeds toward the crowds—in reverse, for whatever reason. As the partisans scramble to avoid its path, the coffin dropping to the ground with a splintery crack and a thud, Walenty notices the man hoisting the other end of his banner fetching a long-bladed knife from a scabbard hidden beneath his coat. Taking this as his signal to flee, Walenty tosses down his end of the banner and tries to cut through the rigid line of Italian spectators massed on the perimeter. But he is tripped, then held firmly to the ground. For a moment his face is mashed into the stones until he is flipped onto his back, revealing his attacker. It is Franca's eldest brother, grinning. "*Shiava*," he says (*Slav*), and aims a loose glob of spit at Walenty's mouth. The spit smells of *grappa*, and it coats Walenty's nostrils and upper lip. Legs flailing, he hears his own wooden

foot hammering the stones, the sound identical to the crack of the dropped coffin meeting the earth.

- - - -

ON THAT FINAL NIGHT of my life with the Stellas, after I'd staggered back home from the Exchange and been struck mute in the rain beneath our bedroom window, I hiked to an all-night diner on St. Charles Avenue that I'm certain no longer exists. The city health department was always on the verge of shuttering it—the famous story was that a ceiling tile broke open one night and an extended family of rats came raining biblically down upon the tables—and surely some Javert of an inspector was finally able to padlock it. The other rumor was that the overtattooed line cooks regularly slipped LSD into the eggs, but this was more of a hypothesis to explain the squeamish, loopy sensations you felt after a late-night meal there than a bona fide allegation, though anything was possible. The jukebox was stuffed with a comprehensive selection of Ernie K-Doe tunes and the waitstaff was almost entirely composed of young Russian women who in retrospect might have been imported sex slaves. They had a carnal but melancholy air about them as if sex was available but no one was going to enjoy it. I ordered some coffee but my hands were trembling so badly that I subsequently ordered some vodka with which to spike my joe. Per my usual tack when drinking, I ordered a plate of food but barely touched it. Throughout my life waiters were always asking me if something was wrong.

At the next booth, I remember, was a skinny kid in a black t-shirt sitting with a girl who was too obviously infatuated with him. I eavesdropped. The kid was a drummer and was trying to impress upon the girl the importance and sublimity of New Orleans rhythm. She was nodding, and saying *Mkay, mkay,* but the kid was on a roll, his Adam's apple bouncing like a backwoods preacher's, and at one point, painfully bored with the

topic but not with him, she said to him, with a fluttering of eyelashes, "You're crazy, do you know that?"

I turned around to face them. "No, he's not crazy," I said to the girl. "He just can't love two things at once."

I was just trying to help. Or something. In New York I would've been told to mind my own fuggin bidness or worse the kid might've awarded me a cool shiner. But this was genteel New Orleans where even the strung-out drummer-boys were gracious. "Thank you," he said, with just enough sarcasm to gild the lily. After turning back to my uneaten eggs, which looked up at me with poignant yellow eyes, I heard the girl call me a "creep" and convince the kid who was "crazy" to relocate to another booth. I waved my fingers at her and said, "Toodleloo."

The creep stayed there until dawn but never stopped shaking. The morning might have felt cleansing had I ever ceased drinking, but I hadn't, and when the sunlight hit me on the sidewalk it felt like falling glass shards. I ended up at Felix's apartment. He was annoyed to be awakened but was otherwise hospitable, though not enough to put his teeth back in. He was wearing the kind of oversized t-shirts that coeds sleep in and I couldn't help wondering where a shopper might locate such an oversized-oversized t-shirt and what sort of mythically large *sasquatch* the Filipino textile-factory worker who sewed the shirt must have imagined she was dressing. It was a white t-shirt that was only a half-shade lighter than Felix's pasty skin; he resembled a snowman in mid-melt. Felix didn't ask any questions and immediately fixed me an Orange Blossom—what these days in New York is called a "gin-and-juice"—because he didn't stock vodka. His apartment was legendarily revolting (a former barkeep at the Exchange had anonymously telephoned the aforementioned health department to report it), with a rusted and trash-filled oil drum in the center of the kitchen over which three or four ugly tomcats fought for access, and porn strewn

everywhere. There was nowhere you could sit without a glossy vagina or breast staring you vacantly in the face. These did not strike me as happy vaginas but then I was never any expert.

Always on the cutting edge of technology, Felix the Fat was eager to exhibit his new prize, a "videocassette recorder," and to demonstrate the pinnacle of its utility he popped in a video he'd just scored via mail-order from California. It was a compilation of scenes of men ejaculating on women's faces. "One hundred percent cumshots," said Felix, pulling a chair close to the television set in order, in those pre–remote control days, to control the action. Proudly noting the Fast Forward feature, he said, "Watch this one. In her hair! Oh, man. Genius." I noticed his teeth resting on the coffee table; they were aimed at the television, as if watching alongside us, and I feared they might come chattering to life to provide the play-by-play to Felix's color commentary. Some of the cumshots made Felix laugh and others struck him as tragic ("What a dribble. Lookit that. She's disappointed"). Others angered him and others filled him with awe and admiration. "You know," I finally said to him, in an inappropriately reflective tone, "it's never even *occurred* to me to do that to a woman." Felix guffawed and said, "That's why you got a baby and I don't," which struck me as the loosest possible interpretation of that difference between us.

Strangely, I found some solace in the video. Compared with the men on the tape, I was almost Lancelot. Even after Felix left in the afternoon, to open the Exchange, I watched the video —over and over again, actually. Not in the rub-a-dub way Felix watched it, the way it was intended to be watched—a *Captain Kangaroo* rerun would have been more arousing to me. Rather, it said to me: Yes, I was a lout, a ne'er-do-well lush, a narcissistic chaser of vainglory (What did I hope for, mailing my poems out to the world? Just who did I envision reading them? A crusty committee of award judges debating whether to hang a medal around my neck? No, I imagined a woman in

full swoon, a brunette for whatever reason, clutching my poems to her chest and overcome with the sweltry desire to rescue me from myself), a man forever on the hunt for the easy way out, with an eye perennially cocked toward the exit. But I wasn't a beast, I told myself, I wasn't evil. Look at those bastards on that tape, I thought, just *look* at them. There wasn't hope for them but there was for me.

Later that afternoon I went back to our house. I'd showered and shaved though was unfortunately still dressed in the same clothes as the night prior, and I was more or less sober or perhaps to be accurate not drunk. I had a single slug of gin before I left, to steady my nerve. Or maybe it was two slugs, to reflect that my body was threaded with more than one nerve. The key was still missing so demurely I knocked on our door. I'd considered flowers but that struck me as such a wormy Andy Capp maneuver. Nevertheless I had everything in mind to say—the outlines of a Marshall Plan for my own reconstruction. I'd go light on the drinking, stick only to beer. I'd quit the Exchange, and get a better, *real* job—maybe at a bookstore, that sounded nice. I'd write only on the weekends, like a hobbyist. Stella had once suggested I "see somebody," as in a psychiatrist—what in those days we called a "shrink." Sure, why not. I'd need to reserve a few demons for my poems, I thought, but certainly I had enough that I wouldn't miss those a shrink might slice away. I'd even take up jogging if that's what it required: me with a sweatband on my head, huff-puffing down Magazine Street. Anything, I could do it.

No answer. "Stella?" I said. "Stella?"

From the bottom of the stairs I heard my name called. It was Robbie, our downstairs neighbor. He was a chef at a French Quarter restaurant, a turtle-soup joint favored by midwestern tourists. Wide-eyed folks wearing Mardi Gras beads in August, that crowd. Robbie was married to a painter named Sally, a languid, too-gentle woman who was difficult to con-

verse with because negativity seemed to mentally bruise her. If you complained about, say, the rain, she'd note how it was all part of the wonderful ecological cycle. Nevermind that you'd left the windows down on the Caprice—blessed Gaia was having a bath. She actually enjoyed reading Thoreau—yeah, exactly—though I'm certain she never caught his jokes. Stella adored the two of them, however, and pointed to them as a model couple, as a condition to aspire to. "You should talk to Robbie sometime," she'd once suggested. "He's such a great husband, you could learn something." I noted to her that when I passed their doorway I almost always heard Kenny Rogers on the hi-fi. Case closed, so far as I was concerned.

"I've got the key for you," Robbie said.

"Oh," I said, jaunty-like, and padded down the stairs.

He disappeared into his apartment, leaving the door cracked enough for me to catch a couple of verses of an Anne Murray song. This was not a moment to be rolling my eyes but I rolled them anyway. When he handed me the key he said, "I'm really sorry about everything."

About what everything?

"Stella going out to California," he said. "She was pretty, um, distraught and, you know, I'll bet this is really hard for you. I mean, of course it is. Women, jeez-us"—slight cognitive dissonance, him saying "Women, jeez-us" with Anne Murray's voice backing him. "But look," he said, "these things happen. I'm sure you'll work it out."

I climbed the stairs in a hot muddled daze. At first glance the apartment looked the same. Robbie was off his fucking rocker! Or a sick joker. There were my books, here was our TV on its cinderblock throne, there were the framed photos scattered throughout the living room. Almost all of them showing Stella and Speck—as the photographer, I was always excluded from the recorded memories. For a moment I was relieved; I half-expected to encounter the symbolic whoomph of

an empty apartment, stripped of even its meager furniture. But then I looked closer. Stella had emptied the bedroom closet of most of her clothes, save the despised maternity wear. Speck's drawers were vacant except for the onesies she'd outgrown. Her storybooks were still there, and her toys littered the floor (there was that voodoo doll, lying facedown like a shooting victim), but her very precious, must-have Baby Bear was absent from the crib. That absence was like the period at the end of an awful sentence congealing slowly into view: *They're gone*. Stella must have packed them up that night, after we'd fought, while I was at the Exchange slumped against B. B. Mike with a tiara on my head, and caught a redeye out to L.A., to camp with her parents. Maybe it was even an American Airlines flight she booked—a chancy stab at grim coincidence. For a while I wandered the apartment, conducting a stupefied inventory of what she'd taken and what she'd left, as if to ascertain the degree of her seriousness, the quantifiable finality of it all. Could she truly desert her copy of Sylvia Plath's *Ariel?* She adored Plath. Her scribbled little annotations flowered the book's every other page. Was life with me so terrible that she would abandon all her shoes? I put one to my nose, as if to capture a last fading trace of her, but it smelled only of ripe new leather. Plus I couldn't help wondering what I was doing: Feet repulsed me, even hers. Then in the nursery I noticed a little poop stain on Speck's changing-table cover, a narrow little butterscotch skid mark, and for whatever reason the sight of that snapped me, twig-like, in two. Clutching the edges of the changing pad, I shook with sobs—weeping over my daughter's crusted shit.

"Bennie?" It was Robbie.

"Yeah," I called back to him. I wiped away my tears with my shirtsleeve which smelled alarmingly of vomit. I searched for stains but saw nothing and all I could figure was that I'd drunk so hard the night before that even my pores had puked. For God's sake, was all this really happening? "Coming," I called.

He was standing in the open doorway with Sally beside him. He looked concerned; her expression, on the other hand, was decidedly prosecutorial. Owing to Sally's earth-mother garb —a blocky dress of batiked and embroidered cotton; a mutant variety of footwear falling somewhere between house slippers and garden clogs; and a rainbow-striped hairband—I was reminded of that old tagline from the Chiffon margarine commercials: "It's not nice to fool Mother Nature." Mother Nature looked pissed. I don't think she'd ever forgiven me for passing out in the bushes once and crushing some of her pansies. The broil of her current visage made me wonder if she'd helped Stella pack. "We just wanted to make sure—we just wanted to see if you were okay," Robbie said.

"Sure," I said.

"These things happen," he repeated. "Things will work out."

"Of course," I said.

Things didn't work out.

⸰ ━ ━ ━ ━

NOT A CHANCE. I placed a call to California forthwith. Stella's father, Frank, who was some sort of midlevel state judge and taught political science on the side, fielded the call. "Ben," he told me, full of sighs, "my daughter has been through a great deal and can't speak to you right now. To be realistic, I think it's going to be a while. I understand that there's a child at stake so this is not a simple matter, but I can assure you that Little Stella is getting the best of care. You're going to have to accept the responsibility for this and give Stella the time she needs to sort out her life. I happen to *love* my daughter"—the compare/ contrast implication made vivid by his emphasis—"and I don't intend to see her suffer one bit more."

What I wanted to say, in response, went like this: You *love* your daughter? Well, how about this, Frank—she *hates* you,

she fucking *abhors* you. Here, you want proof? Look, right here, Plath's *Ariel*. (Christ, how could she have left that book? And me with it.) Right here, page 42, "Daddy." Plath's best poem, so far as I'm concerned. See how the page is marked up? With three shades of ink, *three*. And here, take a look at what's underlined: *There's a stake in your fat black heart.* (Did you say a child was "at stake," Frank? Tragic word choice.) *Oh Daddy you old bastard you.* Come on, Frank, let's talk about your oh-so-tender affair with your graduate assistant. Who caught you, Frank? That's right, Stella, and she was eleven, and the grad student was *blowing you*, Frank, sucking you off in the family sedan. Here come da judge, how cute. Stella was just looking for her bike in the garage, that dainty pink Schwinn with the pompoms on the handlebars, you remember it. She was supposed to be at a friend's house, of course. I know everything you said that day, Frank, everything you promised her and all the spidery ways you begged her not to squeal to Mommy after you'd zipped up your trousers and told the grad student—what, to "stay put," to "hold on," to give you "a min-ute"? Yeah, she told me the whole story, Frank, and you prob-ably don't want to hear why & how but it was one night in bed early on when her reluctance to perform oral sex had reached the point of noteworthy awkwardness and we lit up a joint with our backs to the headboard and it all came streaming out, a sad tale but one so coldly, coldly related. I liked the detail of the grad assistant reapplying her lipstick in the rearview mir-ror while you were pleading with your own little Stella. Niiiice, Frank. A classy bitch. What was that line of Plath's? Something about where Daddy put his "root." Well we know where you put your fucking root, Frank, right into that polluted, lipsticked inlet, into that cheap mouth that *bit my pretty red heart in two.*

That's what I wanted to say. But I didn't. Instead I said, "I happen to love your daughter, too."

Frank said, "Well . . . ," and hung up.

As it happens, that was the day I switched from buying fifths of vodka to quarts, which is really just a matter of efficiency but let's not pretend it wasn't symbolic. My AA sponsor, Dirk (his actual given name, believe it or not), characterized this as the day that I *justified* my alcoholism. Dirk was a high-flying wine journalist before crash-landing into the program, and claimed to know something about justification—drinking was his job, & a man's got to do his job, etc. Lucky for him he switched from the wine business to the saint business: Nowadays he runs a Chelsea soup kitchen and wanders the city draping blankets on homeless folks.

Naturally my whole Marshall Plan disintegrated when Stella left. Two days later I was behind the bar at the Exchange, pouring my famous "two for one" shots: one for you, two for me. I tried calling Stella again a few days later, hoping the cooling-off period might be finished. This time I got her mother and you can just imagine how *that* went. I had to put down the phone midway through the conversation due to me bursting into flames. I wrote Stella a few long letters—not quite *this* long—which went unanswered. Then one night at about three A.M.—that dread hour again; Christ, the blood & despair that comes spilling forth when that cuckoo sings thrice—I dialed California and in an exceedingly ugly & weepy stupor told her father that I had *rights*, I could see my daughter, Stella had *kidnapped* Speck, *stolen* her, that I was going to huff and puff and blow the fucking house down. "Ben," he said calmly, "you are your own worst enemy. You should go to bed."

"I know all about you, Frank," I said. Menacing-like, grrr.

He didn't seem to catch my drift. Or else he was a cooler tomcat than I'd expected. (I suppose I figured he'd instantly break down, cupping the phone and whispering in falsetto, "What? *What?* Oh God what do you *know?*") "Rest assured," is what he shot back, "that the pleasure is reciprocal."

In my pickled mental state all I managed to say was *"Vice*

versa," which didn't make a lick of sense, not even as a pun. Frank sighed and hung up so I yelled at the dial tone until that escalating chime sounded and that nasally female phone-voice advised me that if I'd like to make a call please hang up etc. That call was enough to get a rise out of Stella, since about a week later I got a letter from her. Handwritten, dated, distressingly formal. The Cliffs Notes go like this: It was over. There was no use trying to fix it and the only thing I was feeling right now was guilt, which suggested that I wasn't completely inhuman but guilt was still, in the end, a selfish sentiment and thus more of the damn same. I could see Speck only after I'd completed care at an alcohol treatment facility and made other assorted penances, and Frank—"my father," she called him, not "Daddy"—had a team of lawyers prepared to enforce all that. Graciously, I suppose, she did admit that I wasn't solely to blame for everything, but said that, "quite simply," she needed to get on with her life and I needed to get on with mine. Signed it: Sadly, Stella.

- - - -

SO THAT'S WHAT WE DID. Sort of. Stella got on with her life, anyway. She finished her Ph.D. at Pepperdine and scored a teaching post at UCLA which she kept for several years before she met & married Jon, a public-schools administrator with two sons from a prior marriage, and then she opened a boutique nursery in Pasadena which is apparently quite successful. (Snazzy website, anyway. A hundred different varieties of camellia in stock.) I know all this because for a few years in the '90s I was on their Christmas-letter list—an error, I felt sure. Due to those letters, I know that Jon—the last name is Kale, like the spinach; hence, I've always envisioned him as a cross between John Cale of Velvet Underground fame and the Jolly Green Giant—is fond of flyfishing and mountaineering though a knee injury in '96 or '97 put the kibosh on the latter. He's

also an amateur wine collector, so their family vacations tended to follow the route blazed by my AA sponsor Dirk when he was sipping himself silly around the globe: Chile, France, Portugal, New Zealand. One Christmas letter mentioned—ostentatiously, I thought—that "the enclosed wine cork" was a happy memento of that year's travels, but my letter didn't come with a cork. I even fetched the envelope out of the trash to make sure. Where was my goddamn cork? So perhaps my presence on the list wasn't an error after all. I imagined the two of them debating whether or not to tuck the cork in with my letter. "No," I could hear Stella saying, "he'll probably eat it."

And me? By now you know the bones of that story. The hardest part was what to do with Speck's disposable diapers, the ones Stella had left. There must have been fifty of them, stacked neatly in a wicker bin under the changing table. Charity Hospital couldn't be bothered with such a puny donation. I was sure that orphanages still existed but because they were no longer called orphanages I didn't know how to look them up in the phonebook. The local battered women's shelter seemed suspicious of my offer, as if my fifty Pampers were a Trojan horse that would grant me entry to the shelter so that I could knock around some broads. It was a year before I mustered the cold strength to put them out with the trash.

Just as Stella demanded, I did enter an alcohol treatment facility: a shabby but sweetly bucolic place upstate where vast herds of deer grazed on the lawns and where I once saw a bear though no one believed me. By that time, however, Speck was already out of college. In the long interim I made a somewhat harrowing mess of myself and decided, without really deciding, to act like the monster I presumed down-deep I was. Or that Stella thought I was, same difference. Shortly before I left New Orleans, I was fooling around with an equally alky divorcée named Sandra ("*Sahn*-dra"). She claimed to have been a model once but that seemed dubious from a visual point of view. She

also claimed, repeatedly, to have blown Mick Jagger during the Rolling Stones' "Tour of the Americas" in '75, but, you know, same doubts. We'd float from bar to bar fighting and losing our shoes, like in one of those love stories from Bukowski. One night, while she was doing to me what she claimed to have done for Mick, I withdrew at the last second to do precisely what I'd seen those chuckling neanderthals do in that video of Felix the Fat's. I had to hold Sandra by the hair for a moment. "You . . . FUCKING . . . PIG!" she screamed, wiping her cheek with a shirt of mine she'd plucked from the floor. I suppose I thought it was going to make me feel better, to seal my fate like that. Instead I felt worse. To boot, it wasn't much of a performance—Felix would've given me a thumbs-down. Even as a monster I was hopeless. I apologized to Sandra and knocked back a few vodkas while, to make herself feel better, she told me the Mick Jagger story again. Sounds like a charming fellow, that Mick. Does a little leprechaun laugh when you tickle his balls.

LOOKEE HERE, dear American Airlines. Morning is breaking. As an old saxophonist pal in New Orleans used to say, when dawn would find him with a beverage in hand: The sun done caught my ass again. His name was Charley and he died of a heroin overdose ten years ago. I threw a surprise birthday party for Stella once that featured Charley, hidden in the bathroom, launching into a rendition of "Happy Birthday" on his sax. A lovely moment that made me feel like a king though Stella didn't feel like quite the queen I'd hoped she would. She ended up crying by the end because she claimed the guests were mostly my friends, not hers. I could have pointed out that she didn't have many friends but I wasn't that kind of dummy. Stella was a harsh judge of character and few people passed muster. The handful of friends she had were always under caustic scru-

tiny, mostly for moral trespasses. Whereas I've always been an indiscriminate collector of people who tend to float in and out of my life without much passport control. Years of bartending inure you to human foibles or so I've always suspected. A regular at the Exchange, a sixtyish fellow who'd once been a successful financier before some mysterious disgrace toppled him, used to say, "I'll talk to anybody, on three conditions. You gotta make me laugh, or make me think, or make my dick hard." After hearing this spoken the fifth or sixth time I asked him what happened when he encountered that rare human specimen who could achieve all three. "I propose," he said. Well, we never could keep track of his wives. The last one was Filipino; the unkind rumor around the bar was that she was mail-order.

Most everyone around me is still asleep, but miserably so—curled up on skinny white cots or cardboard mattresses or on the hard blue carpet, contorted in chairs, propped up against the walls & windows with their dry mouths open, like corpses after a shooting rampage. Corny pink light is streaming through the windows, transforming the dust motes into floating glitter. Like little sea creatures suspended in the water or whatever the stale analogy might be. The window-washers have already arrived—what a rough early schedule they've got, though some of them must be grateful to avoid rush-hour traffic. The sanguine ones, anyway. This one near me seems blithe enough. He's a short Mexican dude with a flat Mayan face, shining up the windows via a mop-head attached to a six-foot pole. I've always heard that interior housepainters suffer sky-high rates of alcoholism, the theory being that staring at varying shades of off-white for daily eight-hour stretches drives them to drink. I wonder how it is with window-washers, always looking in or out—at glassed-off worlds immune from their touch. Eight-hour blinks of ivory-taupe-oyster-eggshell-alabaster-argent-pearl, the hermetic seal of glass, the guilt of abandoning one's

child to write laughably mortal lines of poetry: I suppose we all have our excuses, our *justifications* as Dirk would say—our reasons for wanting to escape life for a while, sometimes longer. Some just better than others. Ah, the window-washer's cellphone just rang. Someone must have called to tell him a joke because he's laughing like mad, damn close to tears. I can't quite make it out; I used to have a fair grasp of Spanish but along the way I lost that too. He's doubled over with rabid joy, & hooting so loudly that a few of the sleepy refugees nearby are grimly yawning to life, casting annoyed glances down Mexico way. Rise and shine. Ees morning in America.

Early in this letter I mentioned that I'd placed my one call yesterday, & that it didn't go so well. Let's just say it didn't go as well as the window-washer's call. I'd just been bussed in from Peoria. No one would tell me a cottonpickin thing, as Miss Willa would say. From the payphone across from Gate K7 I dialed Speck's cellphone. "It's Bennie," I said. ("Bennie!" she sang back.) "I'm stuck in Chicago," I explained. "Total nightmare scenario—my flight didn't even make it here. We landed in Peoria and they made us walk to O'Hare. Well not really, but close. Anyway, everything is canceled. It's a complete effing mess." (Did you catch that? Me tidying up my language for my daughter.) "They won't say when I'll be en route but it's not looking promising for tonight—"

"*Shit*, Bennie," she said. Her voice was different: pricked, strained, impatient. I hoped it was just prenuptial jitters, or some knotty tangle of a wedding detail she was dealing with, or that maybe my ears were overattuned, my antennae too sensitive.

Nope. "We had a deal," she said.

"Which I'm doing everything short of hijacking a plane to keep my end of," I said. "And if you need me to do that, I will." How? I thought of Woody Allen, in *Take the Money and Run*, trying to escape from jail by carving a gun from a bar of

soap. A decent tactic save for the rain that reduced the gun to bubbles.

"I'm sorry, Mom is being a total nightmare about *everything*" — "total nightmare scenario," meet "total nightmare." "One of Syl's law-school friends is stuck at O'Hare, too," she went on. "The two of you should get together to commiserate or something. Jesus, Bennie, I don't know . . . this is all getting a little weird and uncomfortable. Maybe we should just skip the whole walking-down-the-aisle thing and play everything by ear tomorrow, okay? Just say hello and start from there? Maybe not rev the engine so high at the get-go?" Another automotive metaphor, I noted: Perhaps a daub of the sludge that used to crust my greasemonkey father's hands had found its way onto the DNA. "Just get here as soon as you can, okay? Oh wow, I think Syl's brother just walked in. (Is that Wyatt? Ohmigod, just a sec.) Bennie I gotta go. Get those planes moving, 'kay? Chop chop."

Transcribed like that, it doesn't sound too bad, does it? Honest but genial, even a little hippy-dippy: That's my girl. No, you had to hear the clenched tone of her voice, the way her words groaned to a stop—I was just one more wedding headache (a wed-ache?), another abrasion in her life. But then what did I expect? A long time ago I'd recused myself from that life, confident that she was better off without me—or was I just, as I suspected of Walenty, *indifferent* to her existence? Over the years, in rare semisober moments, I wrote her letters that tried to explain my absence but inevitably I got soused and scrunched them into the trashcan. But, Christ, listen to me—how I hate it, that droning & hollow refrain: *I wuhzzz drunnnnnnk.* It's too easy to stuff the story of my life into a bottle like some rinkydink toy ship. One of those things you see at the souvenir shop and say, gee, how'd they fit that *in* there? It's a gimmick, an old trick, don't buy it. I think it was Seneca

who said that alcohol doesn't create vice—it merely brings it into view. One of those dainty pearls of wisdom I found in the rehab-clinic library. I've got enough for an elegant necklace.

After she hung up I banged the receiver against the payphone three or four times—slowly, and with mounting force, my eyes shut so tightly that I wouldn't have sensed the flash of a nuclear blast rocking Chicagoland. *We had a deal.* No doubt I would've bashed the phone further, would've smashed it down to its wiry guts, had a retiree at the payphone beside me, wearing a t-shirt reading SNOWBIRD AND PROUD, not exclaimed, "Whoa, buddy, whoa there, what the hell?" At that point I wanted so desperately to kick something that I hopped around on one leg with the other leg cocked and loaded for bear. But the only things to kick were the wall and the Proud Snowbird and since both seemed innocent, down went my leg. That's when I felt the collective gawks of my fellow passengers at K7, bemused and slightly alarmed, zeroing in on me. "You got a problem there, buddy?" said the Snowbird Who Was Proud. An excellent question that I could have answered at length but chose not to.

Instead I fell into the closest O'Chair I could find, frightening off a woman and her toddler son in the seats across from me. Fine, go—that's right, I'm infectious. Or I'm the bogeyman. Not a terrorist though. Oh, for chrissakes all of you stop looking at me. Lou Dobbs of CNN is up on the TV screen accusing Mexican immigrants of spreading leprosy—you people want crazy, watch him. Hands trembling, I fetched a white legal pad from my satchel and began writing: *Dear American Airlines,* and so on & so forth etc.

JESUS FUCKING CHRIST, you want to see trembling hands? Look at this, it's like my mother's shaky stroke-scrawl, I can't

even make the damn words—dear American Airlines, you pigs, you *pigs*, you grabby fucking pigs! Just a few minutes ago—for fuck's sake, the *sun* is barely up—officers of the Chicago Police Department commenced to roaming the airport shouting for everyone to wake up and give back their cots because, as they thunderously explained, "the airline needs its gates." Screw your gates! To think of that poor old Munchkinette with the vegetative husband being rousted from her sleep by the fuzz! How dare you?

That's the exact question I asked one of the cops but it didn't go over well at all. He was a young crewcut guy, with a severely acned face suggesting that his muscle-lumpy physique was derived from chemical supplements, with shallow blue eyes spread too far from one another on his face, skin like a raw bratwurst. "Hey, have some manners here," I said to him. "These people are just sleeping. They've had a rough night. You don't need to shout at them." Spoken without a touch of menace or hysteria, I can assure you. I know I haven't slept in the last thirty-some hours or so but I'm not entirely cracked.

"Back up, sir," the cop growled at me. I was a full yard from him. Any farther back, I would've needed to email him.

"How dare you treat these people this way?" I said. "This isn't their fault. It's the airline's fault. If the airline wants its gates, it can put us on planes." The cop muttered something into the miniature radio-mike on his shoulder and then said to me, booming, "Sir, I am *ordering* you to back up, and get out of my face." "I'm not in your face," I said. "And you don't need to shout at me either." Okay, to be accurate I probably should've pinned an exclamation point onto the end of that last sentence; by this time I was admittedly flustered. "Back off, *NOW!*" he roared, and in my peripheral vision I saw two or three other cops moving sharply our way.

I looked down at his gun. It was a chunky, square-handled

pistol of what type or caliber I can't say. The holster was made of smooth black leather, resembling more an oversized cell-phone case than the elongated, pantsleg-shaped cowboy holsters that I strapped onto my belt as a child, the kind embossed with horsey scenes that I would've sported while riding my own Cooch through New Orleans. It didn't appear to have the expected strap over the gun's handle; I looked for a telltale snap or somesuch, but the gun seemed wantonly unsecured, like a hand inside a loose mitten. So it wouldn't be hard, I thought. Just grab it. Distract the beefheaded cop by actually getting in his face and just—grab it. He'd go flailing backwards once the pistol was mine, whooping into his shoulder microphone, while the other cops would stream forward with their guns drawn, snapping commands; in a moment they'd have me surrounded in a semicircle. *Put it down NOW put it DOWN.* And then all I would have to do—how simple it would be, how ludicrously simple—is raise the gun in the air—not straight up, not aimed directly at the ceiling; at more like a forty-five-degree angle, high enough for the bullet to whiz over everyone's head but low enough to make everyone duck—and fire. Bang. Once, twice at the most. That's all it would take to bring a hail of bullets upon me. It was so easy to imagine: micro-mists of bloodspray popping across my shirtfront as my body filled with holes, that pretty pink morning light streaming like bright lasers through my perforated torso, me slowly swaying, swaying like a drunk maudlin dancer on an otherwise abandoned dancefloor, that same skewed light catching the bursts of smoke from all that gunfire, each little cloud curling out of the barrel and drifting into the next cloud as they spiraled upwards toward the ceiling. Nothing could be simpler. And all it would take is one quick movement, hardly a gymnastic one. I bit my lip and stared.

For too long, though. By the time I finished picturing it, I

had cops close on all sides of me. One of them was a short La-
tina, damn close to midget size, who put a gentle hand on my
biceps and said, "You need to sit down, sir."

"These people didn't do anything wrong," I said, startled to
hear my voice breaking.

"Just go sit down," she said. I did.

WELL. LOOKS LIKE I'VE spilled the beans with that episode.
Or "come clean," as I believe I phrased it earlier. Maybe you
already deduced it, I don't know. Despite myself, I seem to be
scattering hints the way my father used to sow grass seed on our
little parched lawn. The truth is that I've been mulling it for a
long time—for the last couple of years, at least. Making my
exit, I mean: Bennie's great escape. Back in my twenties I used
to toy with the idea of suicide, but in retrospect never too seriously. Those were just hormonal doldrums, I suspect—swel-
ters of misguided Romanticism, overdoses of Hart Crane *et al.*
The dipshit insouciance of youth. I imagine we've all experienced those moments when we're in our cars and approaching a curve at fifty-five mph and the thought occurs: If I just
neglect to turn the wheel, fail to follow the curve—whoops,
the end. Yet there's a vast difference between wanting to die
and not caring if you do or don't. I've done both now—the latter for much of my life—and to be frank I prefer the former.
The desire for action—even final, irrevocable action—feels
so much better than no desire at all. The tingle of ambition
is still a tingle, even if the ambition is merely to quit. Funny: I
was surprised, once I'd made up my mind, how *comforting* the
idea seemed to me, the way it brushed the cobwebs from my
head. Once I'd decided it—this was about four or five months
ago, give or take—I found myself *whistling* as I moseyed down
the street, the picture of dopey contentment. I slept less, I
worked more efficiently. At times I played air-guitar along with

Minideth's floor-muffled solos. I even engaged in that clinical-textbook practice of giving away my belongings. To Aneta, mostly: rows and rows of Polish books, and a bunch of cool linden-wood boxes from the Tatra mountains that I'd brought back with me from Poland.

I'd never really figured out what to put inside the boxes, besides cigarettes and spare change, so this wasn't a dramatic liquidation. But Miss Willa noticed anyway. We are not generous people, my mother and I, and we're packratty to boot. Spurts of gift-giving raise an eyebrow. Of course you have to bear in mind my mother's own bitter flirtations with suicide; if anyone knew the routine, she did. I recall my father going haywire upon discovering that my mother had given her brand-new set of Tupperware to Mrs. Marge next door. She claimed to have developed a distaste for the color but my father, unconvinced, launched an inquisition. Ignorant of the subtext, I thought my father was being quite the miser. But he knew the terrain. Back in those days she would lie in the bathtub slicing at her wrists with a paring knife, but never quite deeply enough to crash through to the other side. I remember my father carrying her out to the car one summer night, wrapped in a blood-stained sheet. This predated the Tupperware incident by a few years—I must have been six or seven. It was dusk, I remember; she'd sent me to bed early for no valid reason I could discern. This upset me, because an early bedtime was usually punishment for some misdemeanor or other, and to my knowledge I hadn't done anything wrong. I'd even eaten the fried soft-shell crabs she'd served for dinner which was noteworthy since I was convinced they were actually battered spiders.

My bed abutted the wall with a window overlooking the front yard, and I was sitting at the open window watching some boys playing baseball in the street beneath the old green oaks. The neighborhood mothers kept chipping away at the game by calling their sons home, and when the third-base runner

got beckoned—"Willie!" his mama yelled. "Red beans!"—the other boys catcalled him for a while ("Red beans," they chided after him, "rehhhhhhhd beans!," Willie waving them off with his baseball glove, shuddup) then turned their attention back to the game. "Okay," one said. "Ghostman on third." And I remember thinking how magical that seemed to me, a *ghostman* on base, and then, as more mothers called, more ghostmen entered the game, until finally the boy with the bat was called in and then it was only ghostmen beneath the firefly-specked oaks—ghostmen that no one could see but me, watching them round the asphalt bases from my skybox above, my face pressed lightly to the windowscreen.

I heard the frantic clump-clump of my father on the stairs but, charmed by the vapors of the baseball game, I didn't stir. And then I heard the front door slam and saw my father below me, carrying my mother the way new brides get carried across the threshold in old movies, and I heard my mother's weak sobs as he dumped her into the backseat of the car and then peeled out of the driveway. Ripped in two by fear and dread, I screamed after them—I *wailed* out the window, clawed at the screen. I don't know if I understood she might die, though by that time my grandfather had already passed so I was familiar with the mechanics of it—what I knew was that she'd suffered another "accident," and it took a long terrible time for her to recover from those accidents. Long chaotic stretches when my grandmother would move in and my father would drive me to the hospital every Saturday to visit my mother who would ask questions about the toy trucks or plastic army-men I'd brought with me but who would break into unexplained sobs when I'd try to answer. I remember removing my pillow from its case that night, after my shrieks had subsided, and putting the pillowcase over my head. It wasn't an attempt to suffocate myself, but rather an effort to shut out the world as completely as I could—to ensure that when I opened my eyes, I would

see nothing, not even a ghostman. This was my analgesic: pure blackness.

My mother's too, I suppose. Back when I was hospitalized, she flew up from New Orleans and sat by my bedside letting all the stories spill out, her long and melancholy rap sheet. I'm not sure what her precise intention was—I had enough on my mind, thank you—but I think she blamed herself for my demise, at least partly, and figured it was time to fess up. She even told me—and this caught my attention—that she'd tried to take me out with her once. I was just shy of two years old the day she sat us down on the St. Charles streetcar tracks—"We were dressed to go shopping," she said, recalling even what shoes I was wearing (Buster Browns)—and rocked me gently in her arms while waiting for the streetcar to obliterate us. Dumbly, of course, because the streetcars have brakes, but then she wasn't thinking rationally. After just a few minutes a cop spotted her, which led to a year in an institution but no criminal charges. I have no memory of it, and it seemed to me then impossible to imagine: a toddler pointing down the tracks saying, "Train? Train?" and his mother—*my* mother—whispering, "Yes, darling, train," with mascara streaked across her wet cheeks. "Yes, dear, the train is coming." For a very brief moment, after she'd finished, I was incensed by this story—after all those years of warped bullshit, carting me off to Florida and Atlanta and New Mexico and then finally, when I was fourteen, to Saskatchewan (which really teed off my father, because he could never pronounce Saskatchewan; he gave up and called it Alaska), poisoning me against my poor damn father, poisoning me against everything, really, save some tweedledee vision of artistic/Romantic fulfillment cribbed from a flagrant misreading of *Madame Bovary*—now I learn she'd once tried *killing* me. But when I looked at her from my hospital bed, sitting on the edge of that aluminum folding chair, her rings clacking together as she wrung her hands inside out, I felt only a ter-

rible, crushing pity. I extended my arm to her, which she used to wordlessly sponge her tears for at least half an hour. "It's a disease," she said then, "and I don't know why we have it. Why couldn't I have cancer instead?" I remember looking around the hospital room, as blue-gray and sterile as this airport, and saying quietly, "Yes, cancer would be nice." The pair of us, two whales unable to find a shore on which to beach ourselves.

So I should know better, right? Maybe. As I said about my father's weird strain of racism: History isn't always the best teacher. And as cockeyed as I'm sure this sounds, I can't help feeling that my mother's long sorrow stems from her *failures:* her inability to push through to the end, to reach the pure blackness of that farthest Faraway. Like that feeling I had when after three days in the coma I woke up with a tube down my throat: Oh, shit. *Now* what? Thanks but no thanks, as Stella would say. I closed my eyes but I was still there. I'm doing my best not to wax maudlin here, but really, what's the point? Please. You there, in Texas, with your future bright & shiny as a gleaming new nickel, you with the 401(k). Tell me what to do & why. Focus on my work? On unscrambling second-tier Polish lit for the two hundred or so readers halfheartedly clamoring for it? (Hunkering down on my job was what one counselor advised. I asked if he ever read poetry. "Well, not for enjoyment," was his answer. That helped.) So then, what—take up a hobby, get a puppy, instigate pinochle games with my half-collapsed mother? In *Darkness Visible* William Styron wrote that hearing Brahms's Alto Rhapsody (Op. 53) was what stayed his own shaking hand, fomented his own key change from minor to major. Naturally I went out and bought it. Halfway through I got bored and retired to the kitchen for a glass of skim milk, yum. Hearing the music bleeding from my open office door, Aneta ventured that it was "bool-tiful." I sent the CD home with her and Styron died anyway.

The thing is: My plans were all in place—vaguely, anyway;

I hadn't yet decided the means of my exit—until Speck's in-vitation arrived, providing an unexpected wrench. The more I thought about it, though, the more I liked the way it fit into my scheme—my "exit strategy," as pundits say about wars. At first I thought I would merely attend the ceremony. I figured this might somehow seal it for me, to see the evidence of my squandering—to confirm my own meaninglessness with it, owing to my footnote of a presence, A, and B, to afflict my-self with the sight of the path not taken. Like when a contes-tant on the old *Let's Make a Deal* show picked Door #1 behind which was a worthless zonk and then Monty Hall revealed the jawdropping prize behind Door #3 inspiring said contestant to want to gouge out her eyes with a hotel icepick. Less selfishly, however, I thought this might afford me the opportunity to tell Speck I was sorry, and to say farewell. And for what it was worth, to say the same to Stella. Part of me feared that this was cruel—how dare I reenter Speck's life in the last days of my own?—but another part of me rejoindered: At least you'll have made your peace with her. Better she remember a human than a sour mystery—a ghostman on third. But then I remembered that old promise I'd made to her, when she was really just a speck, that riff about walking her down the aisle one day, and I thought: Bingo. Wouldn't it be grand to fulfill *one* pledge in life, to reach at least one destination in this snarled journey? To go out on a high note, as it were. To do *something*—however small, and maybe, to everyone but me, however hollow—be-fore quitting the game. Envisioning it, I felt this sweet warm peace washing through me, an unfamiliar sense of composure. Nothing quite like happiness, mind you—more like the sat-isfaction you get when you tidy up your desk and clear a path for the day. In the weeks that followed I gave more and more of my belongings away, even the fancy stereo in my office that had failed, despite its crystalline transmission of Brahms's Alto Rhapsody, to toss me a life-ring. I left it in the downstairs hall-

way affixed with a sign reading FREE TO GOOD HOME. (Almost instantly I regretted that, however, because I find it damnably hard to work without music playing. Creature of habit, I suppose. I moved my clock radio into my office but that sounded like hell unless I stood there holding the wire antenna out the window.)

To be honest, I'm considering doing it out there. Not actually *in* California, mind you; on top of everything else, that strikes me as just plain rude. No, I've got Nevada in my head. There's no waiting period for buying handguns, & no license/permit restrictions either, plus there's all that gorgeous desert. Can you imagine? You follow a gravel road out to where it ends, miles and miles and miles from nowhere—beyond the beyond, as they say, the real Faraway. Leave the keys in the car and start walking. Just pick a direction and walk. The place to stop will be obvious. I've got the top of a cliff in my head, someplace with a vast and soulshaking view of the desert, all that beige nothingness splayed out before me. I'm thinking a drink might be nice, too—one last vodka-tonic to accompany the sunset. No wagging your finger. I'll pick up one of those medicine-dropper-sized airline bottles—maybe I can score one on the plane. But nothing bigger, no: You want a clear head at a moment like that. And then once the sun goes down, I'll lie back on the rocks and check out the stars for a while. I imagine they're something out there, like in New Mexico. I won't spook you with the rest. Just picture the stars—that's what I'm doing.

The "easy way out," people always sneer. What a crock. My mother had just gotten up when I was readying myself to leave for the airport yesterday morning. She was sitting in her wheelchair while Aneta combed her hair. Aneta sings to her, lightly, when she does this—sweetened, slow-mo renditions of classic rock songs, usually. She can make Foghat's "Slow Ride"

sound like a nineteenth-century Polish lullaby. I asked Aneta to give us a minute, which puzzled them both.

"So I'm on my way to the wedding," I said, and Miss Willa nodded. Her eyes were on Aneta, straightening the photos on the wall to occupy herself as she waited outside in the hallway. I'd never sought privacy from Aneta; my mother sensed something was amiss. "The car should be here any minute," I said.

Miss Willa looks so old and fragile with her hair down like that—so raw with age, with all those coarse, bone-colored strands hemming her face. So damn helpless, is what I mean. But she'll be okay: We made a decent bundle from selling the ancestral home, pre-Katrina. I've done the math. I added her name to the lease. I even added her to my bank account so that she could cash any checks payable to me post-you-know-what (note: this means my refund check from you). And she'll understand—peas in a pod, all that. "Okay, then," I said, and then, somewhat to my surprise, my eyes began welling with tears. Well, shit. I didn't want her to see this, so I took her head in my hands, aiming her gaze downward, and bent down to kiss her forehead. I said, "I love you, no matter what," then I planted my lips on her forehead for much longer than I'd intended because I couldn't seem to detach myself. We're not prone to soft moments like this and I can't deny that a small part of me wanted to bite her—not to wound her, necessarily, but to suck out that poisoned brain the way frontiersmen used to suck the venom out of a rattlesnake bite, pa-tooey. Or maybe to wound her, let's be honest. For a moment, the scent of her freshly washed hair reminded me of the wisteria bush that sprawled beside our garage in New Orleans and sugared the springtime air, but this was just an olfactory illusion, a doleful trick of the mind. It was only old-lady shampoo from the Duane Reade sale rack. It had nothing to do with my life.

When finally I stood back up I could tell my bluff had failed

—I saw confusion and fear pooling in her eyes. She fetched her
Post-it pad and pen from the side pocket of the wheelchair and
wrote me a short frantic note which I folded and slipped into
the inside pocket of my coat. "The car service is here," I said,
though it wasn't, and with her bony hand in mine I kissed her
forehead again, this time crisply, with the softness and brevity of an alighting housefly, before walking down to the street
where I sat atop my suitcase with my head in my hands. My
driver was from Bangladesh, said he had relatives in California.
Midway up the FDR Drive I unfolded my mother's note. No,
it said. That was all. I stared at it for a long while, watching
it darken as the car dipped into tunnels below buildings then
watching the sunlight flame it in my hand when we emerged
from the gloom. No. At first the driver didn't mind me smoking but finally on the Triborough Bridge he said enough was
enough. "Please, sir," he begged. "Please no more."

THIS JUST IN:

"The earliest we can get you out is on the 11:15," said the
ticket agent, name of Keisha.

"Arriving when?"

"Let's see"—click, tap, click of her keyboard—"1:35."

"No, no, that's too late," I said. "I have a wedding at two.
There's no way for me to make it in time."

"Sir, I'm sorry but that's the best we can do."

"No, no, it's not. Look, I've been here since yesterday morning. I didn't even *fly* here—I was bussed from Peoria on your
top-secret bus line. I haven't slept since Thursday. My sciatic
nerve is so frayed from sitting in these chairs that I'm going to
need my entire midsection replaced. I ate a hippopotamus turd
for dinner. I was almost tear-gassed by the Chicago Police Department. All because my daughter is getting married this af-

ternoon and I have to be there—I am *going* to be there. Quite frankly it's a matter of life and death."

"The first flight is at 9:50 and it's"—click, tap, click—"already overbooked. I'm happy to put you on standby for that one but your chances are pretty much nil. I'm just being honest. As you know we had a weather situation yesterday and we're doing our best to catch back up. Everyone here is in the same boat."

"A boat!" I said. "Like a rowboat—that'd be faster. Can you put me on a rowboat? I'll row."

"I apologize again, sir. I've got you on the standby list for the 9:50 and here's your boarding pass for the 11:15. Gate H4, boarding will begin at 10:45."

"I don't think you understand—"

"Sir, there's a very long line behind you and if I could get you out any earlier, I promise you I would. Gate H4, and thank you for flying American."

Slinking back to my seat I spied an American Airlines "Premium Services" cart heading toward me. Figuring what the hell, I flagged it down. If anyone deserved Premium Services, I thought, I did. I might note, however, that this sense of entitlement is atypical for me. Several years back I was hosting a visiting Polish poet of limited international repute who had a taste for American strip clubs. For "pole-dancing," said this Pole. We were ensconced in an "upscale" Midtown joint where bluejeans were prohibited—I happened to be wearing such, but, undaunted, my charge had dragged me four blocks east until he found a little cockpit of a store where he bought me a flamboyant pair of polyester slacks of the type worn by marchers in the Puerto Rican Day parade—and where you were expected to order Dom Perignon by the bottle while you ogled the strippers. It wasn't long before said poet was cuddling a girl named Cookie who asked if we wanted to visit the "VIP

room." Now, I understand that access to the VIP room is available to any schlub with a hundred-dollar bill, but I still couldn't follow them there. I'm just not V.I. so why pretend? I waved them on. After a while my poet returned looking glum. Cookie had munched a Slim Jim while straddling his lap—struggling with his English, which he was adamant about practicing when stateside, he called it a "meat wand" which I thought wonderfully poetic & precise—and to boot he had lost a contact lens between her bosoms. As a man of the people, I felt vindicated. I wasn't Very Important but I still had my eyesight.

Anyway. Premium Services. A plump woman roughly my age was behind the wheel. She looked kind enough, I thought, with the sweet face of a cookie-baker. Not Cookie. A cookie-baker. V.I. Difference.

"Mind giving me a lift?" I asked.

"That depends, handsome," she said. "Where ya goin?"

"Los Angeles," I said. Noting her expression, I offered to share the driving.

"Sorry, hon," she said, with what appeared to be sincere reflection & regret. I got the feeling that had I said Cleveland she might've gone for it. She beeped the horn to get through the crowd, but it wasn't a horn sound—rather that digitized birdsong again. Her motorized sparrow flitted down the concourse and out of sight. My friend Walenty, I thought, would get a kick out of that. His dream car. The thought of him tooling up and down Trieste's hills in that little buggy, one arm on the wheel and the other around Franca, carving his way through the crowds by tweeting that avian horn—now there was rare cause for a smile.

- - - -

SHORT-LIVED, I'M AFRAID. Franca's brother is dead. Walenty's banner-carrying partner, the fellow with the long-bladed knife, saw Walenty being pinned down and spat upon and

made a banshee charge. He grabbed the brother's hair and, after hoisting him upward, plunged the knife between his shoulder blades. Walenty's gaze darted between the two men atop him: Franca's brother, woozy and painstruck, flexing his arms sideways the way one mimics a chicken, as if to squeeze out the blade, then a ribbon of blood unfurling from his mouth as he toppled forward; and behind him his killer, Walenty's defender, for a moment looking as stolid and content as a butcher carving a ham, not even breathing very hard, until he was yanked upward into the raving crowd. To Walenty it appeared that he ascended, in the manner of saints, an impression borne out by the man's expression: His pupils went suddenly round, as if the abrupt loss of gravity was beyond comprehending, and then he was gone, chewed & swallowed by the crowd. Trapped on the ground beneath Franca's brother, Walenty viewed the subsequent riot as a torrent of boots and legs—kicking him, squashing him, leaping over him. For so long he had dreamt that bittersweet dream of his lost leg returning to him, and here now was its nightmarish obverse: a rain of useless legs.

If it hadn't been for Franca's brother's corpse, shielding him, he would have been smothered in the stampede. The New Zealand troops squelched the riot with a bit of tear gas and a great deal of whacking people on the heads with batons; then the medics moved in. Owing to his bloodsoaked torso, the medics presumed Walenty a riot casualty and delivered him to an Allied field hospital by a river. That's where we find him now. He's caught the attention of the man overseeing the local police force, a Kiwi colonel puzzled by this one-legged Pole discovered hiding beneath a corpse.

"Your name again?"

"Walenty Mozelewski. *Starszy kapral, Drugi Korpus Wojska Polskiego.*"

"In Italian please. Or English? Eh? Little bit?"

161

"I was a corporal. In the Polish II Corps. You remember Monte Cassino?"

"I was there."

"Me too." Walenty patted his leg. "Some of me still is."

"And now you are here."

"It was an accident."

"Losing your leg, you mean?"

"No, coming here. To Trieste."

"Please," the colonel said. "Explain."

So Walenty does. When he comes to the detail of Franca, the colonel throws his hands in the air and says, "Of course! A girl. It's always a girl. Dig down deep enough and I'll bet you'll find a girl was the cause of this whole goddamn war. Some German bird who wouldn't spread her legs for little Adolf, right? Brassed him off good. Go on." When Walenty finishes, the colonel offers him a cigarette and then lights one for himself.

"A case of *hamartia*, then," the colonel finally said. "Do you know it? It's a word from the Greek playwrights. An innocent act that results in criminal consequences, that's what it means. Like Oedipus bedding his mother and all that. Really a sad story, yours. You boarded the wrong train and now a young man is dead because of it. And now I have to deal with the mess of this young man being dead. Hot blood around here. The people, I mean. They're hotblooded. The damn Jugs are just the half of it. In the meantime, of course, you've got to go home."

"I don't have a home," said Walenty. "The Germans slaughtered it and then they divvied up the meat at Yalta. Now Russia is gnawing the bones."

"How poetic. Well then, you don't have to go home," the colonel said. "You just have to go someplace else. Up the boohai for all I care. But I fear I do have to insist. Considering the trouble and all."

162

"This is someplace else."

"Not anymore," said the colonel.

This is someplace else. Not anymore. Jesus. After smacking head-on into those lines of the novel, I closed the book and tucked it back into my satchel and went outside for a smoke. Probably for the last time, however, because the line through security to get back into the terminal area is coiled from here to Sheboygan. It looks so daunting to me, in fact, that I've reoccupied my former seat here beneath your towering blue A's, outside the secured terminal by the ticket counters—my old graveyard-shift perch. I need just a minute before inserting myself back into that snaked misery. I'm not quite prepared, yet again, to place my floppy shoes onto that stuttering conveyor belt; my shoes have been X-rayed so many times in the last twenty-four hours that I feel sure they've developed malignancies. By the time I reach L.A. they'll be three-eyed and glowing. And the indignity of sockfeet! Don't get me started.

It must be nine or so. I suppose I could ask to be sure. "Nine-oh-seven," the attractive young lady next to me just answered me after conferring with her cellphone. Though the sheerness of her attire might lead one to question her quote-unquote ladyhood. She's wearing a loose black tanktop of the kind worn by professional basketball players and it hasn't escaped my attention that she's braless under there. Earlier when she bent down to retrieve an *Us Weekly* from her carry-on I glimpsed her entire left boob in profile, a soft, inverted cone the same color as fresh buttermilk, with a delicious pink tic-tac of a nipple. The doodle on the left side of this page is the result of me pretending to write while cutting my eyes sideways. It's stunning the way a sight like that can completely derail whatever thoughts are chugging through your noggin. Even presumably focused thoughts about life, death, etc. To be or not to be. Should I stay or should I go. That age-old question ring-

a-dinging through history. But then you spy a wink of creamy boob and everything falls apart. You're reminded that, familiarity with Slavic languages and theories of poetic closure aside, at your core you're just another mammal, hungry and horny, who'd be a fool to want to abandon all this. Part of you screams *More* while another part whimpers *Enough*.

The young lady's companion is a lanky, sour-faced delinquent in baggy, wounded-denim shorts and a black t-shirt that reads RAGE AGAINST something or other (I can only make out the top half). I hate to don my geezer goggles but why does this young generation talk endlessly of rage but never succumb to it? I haven't heard a bona fide howl in years. It's all spitballs from the back of the room. Not long ago I saw notice, in a full-page Food Emporium ad in the *Times*'s food section, of a sale on "Raspberry Rage Muffins" (four-pack for $3.99). So this is what it's come to, I thought. They're mixing rage into muffin batter. This particular young rager near me is preoccupied with his cellphone display (of course) despite his license to gawk at or even stealthily fondle the free-range breasts that have me in such a lather. I want to slap the backwards baseball cap off his head and shout, "Dammit, boy! Look at her! She won't be yours forever and there is no forever anyway so pay attention! Take her to the bathroom and fuck her until you're both squealing and laughing and so drenched with one another that everything else ceases to exist! Now! Now, dammit, now!" Like some carnal-minded Old Testament prophet in rags: Fuck now or forever hold your peace. Rage rage against the dying of the coot to your left. On the outside chance that he's her brother, however, I'll refrain.

I need to call Speck but it's too early there. Seven-something A.M., by my calculations. You have to assume she had a big night: hoisted champagne flutes, ebullient toasts, etc. Can you imagine if I'd been cajoled into giving a toast? Hardly a thing I could have said that a random busboy couldn't have said

just as well. "Nice to meet you," would have been the gist of it. Then a glass held high and: "*Stella Gniech!*" No, it was probably for the best I wasn't there. I wasn't missed and let's face it I never was. Oh fuck it, maybe this whole trip was a mistake. Only now am I foreseeing the difficulties I've set for myself. What if she asks if & when we can get together again? Maybe she & Syl love New York. Everyone loves New York (except me). How the hell do I field that one? In my mind I've always envisaged her like her mother: as a well-bricked wall of resentment and earned apathy. *Thanks but no thanks.* Naturally I've rehearsed saying sorry & goodbye but always to inanimate objects. My desk lamp must be tired of hearing me apologize. Is it owing to Stella Sr.'s frozen rebuttals that I've assumed Speck will respond in a manner similar to that lamp? Notwithstanding the "we had a deal" exchange, she's offered me nothing but warmth. When I look at Speck's high-school photo, tucked incongruously into my picture album amidst flashbulb-bleached shots of me, boozed-up and drowsy-eyed, posing beside various Polish *littérateurs*, I can see Stella Sr. so vividly—even the wry angle of Speck's smile is hers. But I sure haven't discerned Stella in Speck's sunlit voice. A quandary, shit. Seems I've readied myself for rejection but not for forgiveness.

But enough about me. I fear my self-indulgent streak is more exposed than even my neighbor lady's teat. The fate I meant to address after smoking was Walenty's, not mine. What the hell does he do now? Franca is surely lost to him. He thought he could start over, could slide from one life to another as one flits from train to train in the subway—the poor fool thought he could escape. Imagine him now, roaming that New Zealand army encampment by the riverside. Wandering numbly through that too-familiar drab maze of canvas tents and marquees, guy ropes, latrines, ambulances, notice boards, gasoline heaters, stacks of empty ammo boxes. A black bicycle propped against an oil drum. A lone Kiwi lance corporal lazing in a chair

tossing paper airplanes into the dirt. It must be getting dark by this time, with a fat pearl of a moon starting to dominate the sky. Walenty strays down to the riverbank—the sentry lets him pass; bugger it, the war's over—and sits awhile there, listening for any birds calling from the scraggly woods on the opposite bank; he hears only a few distant twitters that sound like a lost child, mewing in the pines. Alone, he watches the river blacken, a few moon-colored ripples fretting its surface. He tries likening his situation to the river's—"Perhaps the river," Alojzy writes, "knew things he didn't"—but he comes up empty. How many metaphors have we poets scooped from rivers? We steal them by the cupful, endlessly ballyhooing rivers' ebbs and flows, analogizing their fluid & imperturbable routes. Wordsworth on the Thames, etc. But in the end it's all dreck, or if not dreck then some form of bathetic aspiration: for our lives to course as smoothly, shifted but never stopped, draining into some glorious & storied sea. I'm reminded here of some lines from a young Grodków poet, name of Jacek Gutorow, about *the wind maneuvering in tree-tops / like a relatively poor metaphor, or maybe the metaphor / was accurate but life didn't live up to it?* Now there's a fucking question. Walenty flings a stick into the water and tracks its downstream float until it disappears into the gurgling dark. *This is someplace else*, he'd told the colonel. Please, he thinks now. Please, it has to be.

AT TEN-THIRTY, eight-thirty Pacific time, I dialed Speck's cellphone from a payphone nearabouts Gate H4. I got her voicemail and hung up. Dispatching the news in a voicemail message seemed crude but then again I had only fifteen minutes until boarding. Though more like thirty because, let's be accurate, boarding never starts on time. I wondered about those in-seat phones on the planes. I've never seen anyone actually use one, so perhaps they're merely decorative, like the orange

trees with inedible fruit you see planted all over Sunbelt subdivisions. Them oranges look swell but try just to eat one, blech. Fearing I'd be the butt of some technological joke (the whole planeful laughing at me for trying to place a call, much the way a professorial chaperone in Tempe, Arizona, once cackled at me for peeling an ornamental orange), I re-retrieved my calling card from my wallet and was about to dial Speck again, to leave her my glum message, when the payphone rang. I leapt back as from a hot wire. After a moment I concluded it might be Speck—calling back the number that had appeared on her cellphone—but couldn't be sure, so when I answered I said, politely, "American Airlines."

"Bennie?" It was Speck.

"It's me," I said.

"Why'd you say 'American Airlines'?"

"Well, it's their phone," I said.

"Are you coming?"

"I am, but I'm going to be late," I said. "Too late for the ceremony—I'm sorry." Until that moment, when I spoke it, I believe I'd been harboring delusions that I might still make it—that the plane would have a secret turbo function, that the scheduled landing time was really just a worst-case scenario. That somehow this was all still going to go as designed. That I would walk my daughter down the aisle as I'd once imagined, make my amends, and get outta Dodge. Saying it aloud, however, I felt my entire plan break into a thousand crumbs—*cake crumbs*, I thought, courtesy of that line from Alojzy's novel shooting across my mind, quick as a falling star.

"That *sucks*, Bennie," said Speck. "What time do you arrive?"

"They say one thirty-five," I answered glumly.

"Then you'll make the reception, no prob," she said, as chipper as I was forlorn. "That's the fun part anyway. You have the address, right? The band we've got is amazing. The End of

the End of Love. They're clients of Syl's. They were on *Letter-man* on Wednesday! Did you see it?"

"No, I missed that," I said.

"You'll *love* them," she said. "I can't wait to see you, Ben-nie. God, to *meet* you! Isn't that weird? There's a ton I need to know. Everything, right? Are you around on Sunday? The reception will be totally nuts so maybe you and I can have brunch on Sunday."

"Sure," I said. "Yeah."

"Okay, cool," she said. "See you soon. Oh wait, don't hang up, Mom wants to talk to you."

I didn't see that one coming at all.

- - - -

"BENNIE," SHE SAID.

"Stella," I said back.

She asked where I was and I explained. Of course not everything: just the landing at Peoria and the jangly bus ride and the canceled flights as depicted on the empty, blinking schedule screens and the thwarted American citizenry sleeping on cardboard boxes with wadded-up clothing for pillows . . . and, in passing, and partly (I suspect) because my situation felt suddenly smaller, as if cast in a withering new light, the pernicious effect of the chairs on my back. The O'Hare Factor, I entitled it. "Seriously," I said. "I'm hurting here." She asked if I'd slept and I answered no though I worried this would make me sound off my rocker—which technically I am but why the hell broadcast it? Striking a sympathetic note, she said she hoped I had a good book along at least. I said I did. "A great one, as a matter of fact." I asked her how things were and she said "crazy"—but thoughtfully, as if things really were crazy. And then I said, "I hope I'm not adding to the craziness."

This made her laugh, or rather pretend to: *ta-HA*. I believe I've told you about that vinegary laugh. "Rest assured, you are,"

she said. Then she asked me to hold on while she ducked into another room. "That's what I wanted to talk to you about," she said. She paused for about the same amount of time it takes to load a pistol. "Okay, look. Here's my speech. Don't screw this up."

"Hold on—"

"I said it was a speech. Just listen. She's thrilled about you coming. In some bizarre way she's always idolized you, or at least some vision of you that I never had the heart to puncture. Or to be more honest the ability to puncture. You've always been like some kind of astronaut who was too busy circling the damn moon to come down to see her. She's pigheaded—you'll see. I'm sorry you're missing the ceremony or whatever they're calling it but I've got to confess I'm *extremely* relieved you're not going to be walking Stel down the aisle. Jon wasn't thrilled about that and neither was I. Mind me asking where that impulse came from?"

She didn't remember. The spark that set off the blast, & she didn't remember. Had I made it up? For a scant moment I panicked, fearful that some scene from, say, a nineteenth-century Polish novel, in which some numskulled fellow pledges to walk his infant daughter down the aisle one day, had lodged itself, shrapnel-like, in my soft and pickled brain. But no, I remembered. This was my life, I was there. This was where the road had forked. Had I perhaps overinflated the significance of the exchange? The lacuna in Stella's memory said yes but one must consider perspective. A piece of driftwood floating atop the blue ocean is hardly worth noting unless you happen to be clinging to it.

"Just something I got in my head," I said, close to a whisper.

Too close: "What?" she said. "Bennie, you're mumbling."

"You know how it is when I get something in my head," I said.

"Yeah, you always did put the pig in pigheaded," she said, following it with what sounded like a genuine laugh—a soft trill. Whether she was laughing about me or at her own wit was unclear. "It was a little *weird*, though, didn't you think? It's been a long time, Bennie. And not to be too literal about things but she certainly isn't yours to give away."

"Giving her away—wasn't the motive," I said.

"Well, moot point, right? Looks like the weather in Chicago saved us from that awkwardness."

"The weather here is *fine*," I said. "It's not the weather! What it is, the goddamn airline overscheduled itself into a corner and—"

"Whatever. Are you sure you're up to this, Bennie? Because she's not going to let you drop in and then disappear. That's not fair to her. You only get to run once."

"*You* ran."

"Oh, please," she said. "Don't even start. Please, *please*. And you followed? A handful of drunk phonecalls doesn't qualify you for martyrhood. But there's no use rehashing all of that. What happened, happened. And everyone's better off for it."

"That's one interpretation," I said.

"What's the other one? Come on, Bennie, we made our choices. Everyone does. You chose your barstool—the great saloon poet, right? While I raised our daughter. La la la. Life goes on."

"I ditched that barstool, you know. I tried to tell you that—"

"Jesus, you did, and I've owed you an apology ever since. That call couldn't have come at a worse time for me." She paused, as if deciding whether to explain any further. "I really *am* sorry," she went on. "I started a letter to you after that but for whatever reason it never got finished. When you called we were neck-deep in a terrible situation with Phil"—Phil was her stepson, Jon's younger son—"with alcohol plus drugs

plus more than I want or can bear to remember and your call caught me smack-dab in the middle of it all. We'd just shipped him off to his *second* stint at a clinic up in Orange County, Jon was in the midst of selling his wine collection to get all the alcohol out of the house, and, no offense, Bennie, but you were about the *last* thing I needed at the moment. All I could think was: Great, maybe I'll get a call from Phil in thirty years saying sorry, Mom, had a rough go of it for a while, sorry for all that. I swear, what is it with you guys?"

"How is he?"

"Phil? He's fine, he's great actually. He's back in school with a respectable GPA. Has a sweetheart of a girlfriend he met in the program."

"That's good," I said. "That's good."

"How about you?"

"Oh, about the same."

"As Phil? Or . . . you don't mean . . . as before?"

"As Phil. Except for the parts about the GPA and girlfriend. But that's fine, you know. Miss Willa makes a decent prom date so long as the music isn't too loud and they play a rumba or two."

"That's funny," she said. "God, your mother . . . that's actually funny. I am sorry, Bennie. For a lot of things. I *did* start writing you that letter, once things had calmed down with Phil, but . . . I don't know, I'd put it all *away*, you know? It was all crazy back then, and it's so hard for me to recognize myself in those memories that I just—just filed it all away and locked it and tossed the damn key. You know, it's funny, one therapist said that was the right approach while another said it was dead wrong. So who knows?"

"They both cashed their checks, right?"

"Exactly, yes. Sheesh. We were just stupid kids. We made a giant mess of things but we survived, okay? And for all the op-

eratic crap, Bennie, we made a beautiful girl. If she doesn't take your breath away then . . ."

"I'd give my life to take it all back, you know," I said suddenly, and hearing the faint, fleet echo of my words coursing through the wires, I asked myself—no, *demanded* of myself —if they were true. Because if they weren't true then there was no point to any of this, no point to me. But they were—all of them. A long silence swamped the line until Stella exhaled and:

"Yeah, fine, but you *can't*," she said. "God, Bennie, that's so like you. Offering up the impossible. The stupid ideal. It used to tear me in two. I never understood why life was never *enough* for you."

"I don't . . ."

A gate-change announcement drowned me out. Omaha, Gate H7. From down the terminal I heard spurts of applause breaking out, someone whooping.

"What? I can't hear you," Stella said.

"Nothing," I said.

"You know, a few years back—this was right after 9/11, and I guess you were on my mind, being in New York and all— anyway, I saw this science article in *Time* or *Newsweek* or one of those. This article about butterflies."

"Wait—"

"No, just listen. This biologist did an experiment and he found that if you put a male butterfly in a cage with a live female butterfly alongside a *photo* of female butterfly, the male almost always went to the photo first. And I remember reading that and thinking, my God, that's *Bennie*. Always drawn to that . . . what, that frozen image, rather than the real thing. Always stalking the dumb illusion."

Perhaps this was incisive—transcribing it now, I see her point—but what I gathered at that moment was that she considered me the kind of man who'd hump a paper butterfly.

"Sounds to me," I said, "like a biological explanation for the porn industry."

"Jesus, why did I think you'd take me seriously? You never change. Look, I have to go. Stel's calling me. Just come see your daughter, will you? Don't expect too much but don't do too little. She's enough."

I took a deep breath, filling my lungs with that stale airport oxygen. "I know she's enough," I said. "I mean I think I do." They were boarding my flight. The First Class passengers and Admirals' Club members had already vanished into the gangplank, none of them looking particularly classy and certainly not like admirals. Midshipmen at best. The gate agent announced that boarding would be done according to the "group number" printed on the boarding passes. Where was my boarding pass? Oh fuck me had I lost it? I tapped my shirtfront pocket. There it was, I had it, I was fine. Through the terminal windows I saw a plane rolling by outside like some great lumbering beast, some prehistoric meateater. "Bennie?" Stella said. I watched the passengers forking over their boarding passes to the gate agent. The permanence of the agent's smile seemed unnatural, painstaking. I refilled my lungs. Damn but I wanted a cigarette. A drink. Another chance. A soul scrubbed clean. A world made better not worse by my footprints upon it.

"I'm not sure the word *sorry* does anything justice," I said. "It's such a loose fucking word, isn't it?"

"Bennie, what are you saying?"

"I mean, how can one puny word like that encompass all the shit you did—I don't mean *you*, I mean us, everyone, me—but also all the, all the things you *didn't* do? It's the inactions that keep you up at night. The actions, they're done. They're done. The inactions, they never go away. They just hang there. They rot. How is *sorry* supposed to stretch across all that?"

"It's life, Bennie, not linguistics," she said.

"Is it? In Poland they say *przykro mi.*"

"Which means . . . ?"

"It doesn't really have an English equivalent, not culturally anyway . . . somewhere between 'I'm sorry' and 'I'm in pain.'"

"Say it again?"

"What?"

"The Polish thing. Say it again."

"*Przykro mi.*" Uttering the last syllable I heard my voice falter and I had to scrunch up my face to hold back a sudden torrent inside my head. I felt myself slacken and slump against the Plexiglas divider. "*Przykro mi,*" I said again. "*Przykro mi.* My God you don't know."

I heard Stella sigh. "You broke my damn heart, you know," she said.

"I broke my own, too," I said.

"Well that was stupid," she said, and when we laughed together my eyes brimmed with tears that were neither happy nor sad but merely wet.

I SHOULD NOTE that the preceding few pages were written at a cruising altitude of thirty-five thousand feet. In Seat 31D, to be precise. Dear American Airlines, I'm on my way. The seat assigned to me was 31F, the one beside the window, but I offered it to the pretty young Chinese girl who was occupying this aisle seat when I boarded. She doesn't speak English so I had to pantomime my offer of the window seat and for a moment the poor girl got all flustered, thinking she'd made an error. *Sah-lee, sah-lee,* she apologized. Since pointing to the window with a generous smile didn't yield me any communicative success, I sliced my hand above my eyes while turning my head to and fro in wan imitation, I suppose, of an Apache scout searching the horizon for invading honkies. This was my way of suggesting that she might enjoy the view. When she finally got my drift she thanked me profusely and after settling into

her window seat cracked open a notebook that my wandering eye noticed was filled with English phrases written alongside their Chinese counterparts. "Where is Gate 5?" "Excuse me, can you help me with my baggage?" "Where are the taxis?" Etc.

It reminded me of the failed system I devised for my mother back when she first moved in, pre-Post-its. Into a spiral-bound notebook I entered every sentence I could imagine her needing to say, the idea being that when she wanted to express something she could page through the notebook until she hit the sentence she wanted, then point. I tried to be as comprehensive as I could—in addition to humdrum requests for food, water, medicine, and whatnot, which I arranged by category, I also listed generically critical opinions about television shows, a wide array of weather commentaries, and her own trademark expressions (e.g. "My hair looks like something the cat dragged in"). Under the "Miscellaneous" rubric I even included me-directed unpleasantries like "Watch your language" and "How is your work coming?" This phrasebook took me hours to compile—the plural isn't an exaggeration—so I was stunned and not a little infuriated when after a middling skim she hurled it, with obvious disgust, into the trash. Taking a ballpoint pen to one of my Post-it pads, she wrote on three consecutive sheets: I HAVE MUCH MORE LEFT TO SAY THAN THAT. I hadn't considered that it might be disturbing for her, to see the entirety of her remaining life—and what is life if not the words that we speak?—reduced to fifteen or so looseleaf notebook pages, sharp convenience notwithstanding. Thus began our Post-it note epoch. The era of LOVE IS LOVE and other uncollected tersenesses.

I shouldn't pretend not to notice the connection between reducing one's life to a handwritten phrasebook and reducing it to a complaint letter to a corporation that doesn't give a flying, delayed, or canceled fuck. Or stuffing one's autobiography into

a bottle as I believe I said earlier. We all hope to be more than we are which is often the problem. What I neglected to include in my mother's phrasebook was something like hope—not the sentences she needed, but the sentences she *wanted* to need. *My recovery has been remarkable, hasn't it. I met a handsome gentleman today. Are those flowers for me? I would like two tickets to Paris, please. It has been so wonderful to paint again. We danced all night. I won't need this silly notebook any longer.* Take away Miss Willa's delusions and she has nothing. Banish the Faraway and she's lost. As the sole surviving representative of the life she's spent decades trying to escape, I could defensibly resent it all, but then what's the point? To varying degrees we're all victims of our pregnant imaginations, of incurable dreams of transcendence. Thorns hoping to become the rose. The religious among us, counting on seventy-two lustsoaked virgins and/or plump white raisins in the afterlife, or more locally reunions with childhood pets and predeceased spouses or the all-you-can-eat king-crab-leg buffet in heaven's cafeteria, are just the mildest examples. Think of Henryk Gniech, believing he could outrun the nightmares of Dachau by fleeing to New Orleans, or believing he was granting a merciful reprieve to those legions of varmints he abandoned on the docks. Imagine the terror of that possum, the one that resulted in my birth, as it navigated the hot maze of crates and forklifts and shirtless longshoremen on the docks, starving and thirsty, skittering up Poland Avenue in desperate search of food and water, or the comforts of a tree or a fellow possum, unstrung by the honking, swerving cars and the nasty schoolchildren hurling rocks at this rarely seen creature. See it cowering behind some greasy spoon's trash dumpster as night falls, motherless or childless, tremblingly alone. Which was the better fate? Maybe the answer is that there are no better fates. You can't escape what you are be it possum or poet. Maybe you get what you get. Or as the old saw goes: You

buy your ticket, you take your chance. Which by the way you might consider for a motto.

On occasion—after the Stellas had left me and, stripped of Speck's physical presence, I was able to think of her more as an abstraction—I used to wonder how things might've turned out had Stella gone through with it. The abortion, I mean. I admit this sounds wicked but the devil's advocate is by nature devilish and anyway I'm not expressing regret—only probing the divide between what was and what wasn't, what is and what isn't. We would have driven home in silence from that clinic in Gentilly with a somber pitstop at a K&B drugstore to get some feminine pads to stanch any bleeding. We would've watched something on television that night, something silly and irrelevant like a Bob Hope special, me faking a cringe when Charo bounded onstage. Maybe I would've fixed myself a drink. ("Is that okay?" I would've asked, Stella waving her defeated permission with all the brio of an invalid shooing a mosquito.) And then Stella would have cried herself to sleep—I know her; everything unspooled in the dark—and I would have held her, stiffly, sadly, hurting in unlocatable places. And sooner or later the unspoken guilt would have wedged a divide between us, a gulf of sour air. We would have become, to one another, constant reminders of a loss, the salt to the other's wound. And then, maybe slowly but probably rapidly, we would have slipped apart. A fluttering eyelash in the Exchange, and the woman to whom it belonged, would have dislodged my stance like tectonic plates shifting beneath my feet; or a better man, named Jon, with tales of alpine glory, would have whisked her from me. What I mean is that maybe there never was a happy ending for us. Or rather, we had the happy ending—Speck—but it wasn't enough for us. Or rather for me. What I mean is that maybe it never could have been different.

Which is more powerful: that realization or a gun? It's all

so clear up here. At thirty-five thousand feet you can see the curve of infinity. It's all so possible.

As I write this the girl near me is scrutinizing her notebook. Every now and then she leans back into her seat and lifting her gaze to the ceiling she silently mouths one of the English phrases, to seed it in her memory. *Excuse me. Excuse me. Where is Gate 5?* Whenever she does this I catch a glimpse of the sky outside, and for whatever reason I find myself losing my breath, as if I am a child aloft for the very first time. Christ, my friend, do you understand how fucking *beautiful* it is up here? The clouds look like glaciers, cold whiteness extending as far as the eye can see and then farther and farther and farther into dreams. Imagine the first pilot to crack the cloud barrier—what a blind rush that must have been, to break down the door of heaven.

Dear American Airlines, I'm not leaving. I apologize for all your time but I've changed my mind. You can keep your money after all.

- - - -

BUT THEN I almost forgot: Walenty. No offense to Alojzy, but I've taken the liberty of rewriting his ending. I won't reveal Alojzy's actual conclusion except to note that it's violent and unjust—you can guess the reaction of Franca's surviving brother when Walenty reappears at the *pensione;* Franca's reaction is less predictable but no less brutal—which is how Alojzy has always viewed the world. Please don't feel cheated. *Nothing's lost,* to crib from James Merrill. *Or else: All is translation / And every bit of us lost in it.* With apologies to Alojzy, then:

> At the train station he ordered a cup of coffee. The girl who delivered it to him was hardfaced and curt and demanded he pay immediately. She tapped her thigh while he fished the change from his pockets. Soon afterward he saw her ar-

guing behind the counter with a young man in an apron who rolled his eyes at her with such frequency and exertion that he appeared to be suffering from vertigo. A small boy of three or four was merrily roaming the café and cocking his thumb and forefinger at customers as if to shoot them dead. Pow! he exclaimed to little or no response. When the boy's gun was aimed at Walenty he put his hand to his heart and tossed his head back which caused the boy to grin and jump and burst into a cheer. This caught the attention of the boy's mother who stood up from her breakfast and heaved the boy away by his collar. She dragged him beside her chair where she swatted him on the rump with enough force to make Walenty wince, spitting fierce words at the boy that Walenty was unable to understand save one: *father*. Stricken, the boy lay on the floor crying while the mother, eating small bites from a bread roll, ignored him.

Because the coffee tasted burned and oily and the boy's sad shrieking was soon intolerable, Walenty strayed outside to the platform. The train was late by half an hour and when it arrived the stationmaster charged out of his office toward the engine angrily brandishing a sheaf of papers. Among the passengers disembarking was a man in a heavy woolen suit and a fedora. He was carrying flowers and scanning the platform.

Boarding ahead of Walenty was a slender young woman in a lace dress, traveling solo. The hem of her dress snagged on a piece of metal as she was climbing into the car, causing her to slip backwards into Walenty. He caught her by the waist and holding her there, like dancers in a *pas de deux*, he reached down to unsnag the dress. It had torn just a little and behind him Walenty heard two women say *awww*, noting between them that the dress was real lace. When the woman in the dress turned to thank Walenty he could see that she'd been crying; her gray, longlashed eyes were rimmed with a pinkness like that of raw meat. She disap-

peared to the rear of the car but if he listened closely he could hear her choked-back sobs, random but persistent, at least until the train started moving and his ears were overwhelmed by the clatter.

The last thing Walenty saw, as the train left the station, was the boy. The man with the flowers had his arms around the boy's mother, the flowers, in his left hand, pressed hard against her back. Far below them the boy was clawing at his father's legs, trying to climb his way into the embrace, and as the train rocked forward Walenty saw the father raise his right arm as if to—but that was all. The stationmaster's office blocked the view and in an instant there was nothing left to see. Walenty sank down into his seat and closed his eyes. There was no Free State of Trieste and there never could be.

Yours sincerely,
Benjamin R. Ford

Burg

		DATE DUE